Jam on the Vine

JAM ON THE VINE

LaShonda Katrice Barnett

THORNDIKE PRESS

A part of Gale, Cengage Learning

GALE
CENGAGE Learning·

Farmington Hills, Mich • San Francisco • New York • Waterville, Maine
Meriden, Conn • Mason, Ohio • Chicago

GALE
CENGAGE Learning®

Thorndike Press® Large Print African-American.
The text of this Large Print edition is unabridged.
Other aspects of the book may vary from the original edition.
Set in 16 pt. Plantin.

LIBRARY OF CONGRESS CATALOGING-IN-PUBLICATION DATA

Barnett, LaShonda K. (LaShonda Katrice), 1974–
    Jam on the vine / by LaShonda Katrice Barnett. — Large print edition.
      pages cm. — (Thorndike Press large print African-American)
    ISBN 978-1-4104-7844-3 (hardcover) — ISBN 1-4104-7844-0 (hardcover)
    1. African American women—Fiction. 2. African American
journalists—Fiction. 3. Segregation—Fiction. 4. United States—Race
relations—20th century—Fiction. 5. Large type books. I. Title.
PS3602.A77585J36 2015
813'.6—dc23   2014048769

Published in 2015 by arrangement with Grove/Atlantic, Inc.

Printed in Mexico
1 2 3 4 5 6 7 19 18 17 16 15

*In loving memory of
Big Mama
–for roots*

&

*To
Ruth
–for wings*

CONTENTS

PART II

I'm learning how to listen
to the rhythm of the night.
How to keep it simple,
How to make it sweet and light.
Smooth and free and easy
or slammin' in a jam
and know for just a moment
the music that I am.
— Abbey Lincoln, "Learning How to Listen"

If I were able I'd say it.
Say make me, remake me.
You are free to do it
and I am free to let you . . .
— Toni Morrison, *Jazz*

PART I

1
JUBA
SEPTEMBER 1897

Ivoe liked to carry on about all she could do. Still, how to mend a broken promise had her beat. She had given her word not to go beyond the pantry, passing many dull hours there while Momma finished her duties in the kitchen. At six, seven, eight, obedience was easy. The trouble with nine came when Miss Susan entered the kitchen to tell Momma the dinner menu. With her low, husky voice and tall, boyish frame, Miss Susan made a handsome woman. She had a moon face full of light freckles and cheeks that called to mind two perfect peaches. Her eyes, and the creases that framed them, crinkled up to slits whenever she smiled. Miss Susan laid the *Starkville Enterprise* on the table. "I bet you can't read these headlines for me." Ivoe hitched up her legs on the lower rung of the stool and cleared her throat: " 'Germans No Longer Love Us: Their Sympathies Are All on the Side of

13

Spain' and 'The Senate Will Have to Yield on Sugar and Wool . . .' " A relieved smile drew across Momma's face as Miss Susan nodded contentedly. "I suppose this means you're almost grown. Grown folks always read while they wait." Ivoe wanted to tell Miss Susan the terrible job of waiting belonged mostly to children and none of the children she knew owned anything to read.

On a good day Miss Susan left the paper behind while Momma cooked but not today. Ivoe sucked in her breath, ducked past her mother, and crept down the hall to the library, grateful for the crimson carpet between her broken shoes and the fine wood floors. The Starks had money. Something to do with cattle, corn, and cotton. It was all around her in the books — more numerous than the schoolhouse's stash and better looking. After May-Belle, Papa, and them, Ivoe loved books best. Books were a friend to anyone who opened them. Blowing a whirligig to make the sails go 'round or talking up a storm to a corn-husk doll was all right for passing the time, but you never went anywhere new or met anyone special like you did in the pages of a book. In Golden-Haired Gertrude and Old Mother Hubbard she found steady companions and had traveled as far as Arabia without ever leaving Little Tunis.

How to get a book home was something Ivoe thought about a lot. Books were hard to steal; books had to be carried; books could not go missing in a house for too long a time. Newspapers were easy. She could slide one under her clothes and walk the half mile home while its reader would think it mislaid. The scheme had worked plenty times before, but that day the newspaper was not in its usual place or on any shelf she could reach. She darted across the foyer and up the back staircase to Miss Susan's bedroom, where everything was dressed in some shade of yellow and smelled like honeysuckle. Swallowing was a chore with such a dry mouth, and the drum in her chest thumped extra hard. How would it look? Tiptoeing around where she had no business being. Crouching on the floor, she raised the bed skirt. Dust. She shimmied open the top dresser drawer — nothing but fancy brooches and pearls. In the far corner, the marble-topped stand beside the chair caught her eye. Eureka! (Or, as Momma would've said, "Had it been a snake, it would've bit you.") She slipped the newspaper under her shirt, half of it cool against her chest, the other half snug between her

15

britches and her underpants.

She threw a kiss to Momma and flew through the kitchen door quicker than grass through a goose. Just the thought of reading made her run fast as her legs could carry her. Beyond the gazebo, past the outbuildings at the edge of the yard, she trotted past the plantation bell to the narrow dirt road bounded on both sides by downy fields. Some of the flowers were still learning to be themselves; three-leaved stems like poison ivy held blossoms soon to burst open pink, pink like the flesh of a watermelon. They would follow the sun just like morning glories till the field looked like a snowstorm hit it, all white and full of fluff. She waved to the white children from the Baptist orphanage and to the Negro children she wouldn't see at school until early November when cotton-picking season was done. She skirted the corncribs, the millhouse, minding her step along the steep slope of watermelons ripening on the vine.

At the bottom of the hill in the valley subject to floods and the felling of trees, Ivoe's home was jammed together with four dozen cabins on the worst land in Central East Texas. Nobody in Little Tunis lived like the Starks, who had too much of everything. Their homes, fronted by a yard of rocks, or a cluttered chicken pen, sometimes both, held only the essentials: a table, chairs, a resting place. You could tell by a cabin's kitchen who lived there. Down the road Ivoe knew she would find a banjo and tools for dyeing since the new couple made pretty music and indigo fabric; across the way where Mister James and his wife lived — a saw and a heaping laundry basket. The story of Ivoe's family was found in the beads Momma held while praying, Papa's sledge and file and the black dust his shoes carried in at the end of the day.

Ivoe ran through the yard, stopped to pluck a fig, bounded up the porch steps, and threw open the door. Quiet enough to hear a mouse pee on cotton. She had beat Timbo home. She yearned to spread the paper over the floor and draw her finger along every line of print under the amber sun, molten and gorgeous, pouring through the door like sorghum molasses, but instead slammed the door and dashed to her room. Whenever she rushed Momma liked to say, "Hurry now makes worry later." Sometimes, though, it meant you could hide your treasure without anyone finding out. Her chest heaved the way it did when Papa pushed her high on the tree swing in the churchyard. Some parts of the paper remained the same — advertisements from banks, insurance companies, a travel ad — TAKE A SEA TRIP HOME! Occasionally, a funny drawing made her laugh, but she was more taken with the articles — like stories only better because they were true. Of the three headlines she'd read to Miss Susan, one excited the most: "Spain's Possessions in America Few — Little Cuba the Last to Go!" At school, Miss Stokes had miles of smiles when Ivoe rattled off how Spain had lost Florida, California, and, in 1845, Texas, when Congress bought it for $7 million — higher than anybody could count. Ivoe felt it was only right to report exactly when Spain lost Little Cuba.

The sky looked like a field of bluebonnets when she helped Momma with supper that evening, marking time until the heavy staleness from the corncribs rode the wind down the hill to huddle around their cabin till dawn.

After her brother fell asleep, Ivoe drew the curtain down the middle of their room and felt around inside her mattress stuffed with straw and corn leaves and old newspapers. She lit the lantern to a low flame. Holding the paper at arm's length like the well-dressed men did on the oak benches along Main Street, she gave the paper one quick snap open, drawing it close to her face to breathe in ink, rag linen, a promised adventure. She commenced reading — faster than Miss Stokes said they should — because oil was expensive, burned at night only to prevent injury like the time she got caught in the bramble, fell over a pile of logs, and hurt her arm on the way to the outhouse. Reading about grown-ups playacting in a Houston theater was worth the accident.

Someone was shaking her.

For as long as Ivoe could remember, Papa chided that she could sleep through a carnival, while Momma said in a tone meant to shame, "Nothing comes to a sleeper but a dream." Ivoe sank deeper into her hiding place as the knot in her throat tied and tightened. The theft was bound to catch up to her. You could get away with one ugly deed but two was like herding hens through a waterfall. Burning up oil to read stolen newspapers would lead to the worst whipping 'cause Momma would never understand why reading was worth lying and stealing for. Under the quilt she rubbed her hands against the mattress cover to get rid of any traces of smudged ink.

"Turn this bed loose and put some clothes on. Be quick about it now."

"Where's Timbo?"

"I ain't never liked to chew my cabbage twice. What did I say?"

It surprised Ivoe to find her father asleep on a pallet in the kitchen. She tiptoed around him, half filled the kettle, and lit the stove. She picked the lint from her braids and bathed. Returning the kettle to its proper place inside the hearth, she saw the *misbaha* on the mantel. There was trouble; Momma's prayer beads were never left out, and in the eastern corner her mat remained flat against the floor, as if the morning prayer had been interrupted. Ivoe took a pear from the table and recalled a scene from the night before: Timbo drenched in sweat, pushing aside his plate after a few bites. Now in the next room she heard Momma's voice, soft and tender, different from the one that had yanked her from a dream.

"You won't be going to the mill today," Lemon said, blotting her son's warm face with the back of her hand. Didn't make no sense. Summer peas, chicken, cornbread — they didn't have no business putting the boy in such a bad way. She scratched beneath her headscarf, between the braids, her eyes falling on a few pennies scattered on the little table next to the bed. She thought of

Monday's shopping and frowned. Wasn't the first time she had saved two cents buying unsterilized milk. (The only folks she knew to pay five cents for the sterilized were the Starks.) She shook her head. What was it about that nickel that made her think she had to break it? Ennis wasn't keen on milk and Ivoe didn't drink it, but Timbo turned up two or three bowls at every meal. "You know you got to boil milk good before you drink it," she muttered softly.

"I drank milk straight from the cow plenty times," Timbo said, wincing.

"Shhh. Open your mouth." She tilted Timbo's chin to count the brown speckles on his tongue. In a short time the boy would be racked with fever. "Ivoe, look in the spice drawer and bring me the ginger." Lemon tried not to think the worst. When cows fed on hay with devilish white snakeroot mixed in they passed bad milk and anybody who drank it was liable to — She shook her head at the nub of ginger floating in the center of Ivoe's small brown hand and thought, Just once I'd like to go for a thing and find there's plenty of it. "Here, Timbo. Suck on this. Be sure to get lots of water in you. Papa be up soon. Come on, Ivoe. Let's go."

Timbo was in a bad way for Momma to

21

move so quickly and so quietly, Ivoe thought. Usually by midmorning her mother had already laid out the day's chores twice and talked about what was going on in her garden, saying things like the okra and lettuce were getting along fine; the tomatoes weren't acting right or the beets were meddling with her runner beans. Today, they hurried in silence down the road alongside Riley's cornfields. As they rushed along the fringes of the orchard, the trees taunted Ivoe with their fragrant bounty. She wanted to stop and climb for a nectarine but knew better than to ask. A mile past their cabin, past the schoolhouse and Old Elam Baptist Church, they arrived at the Arms of God, the Brazos de Dios River, where the one-room adobe house of their only relative stood tucked away in a thicket.

Ivoe was excited to join her great-aunt May-Belle in the cellar lined with shelves taller than her father, which held jars of remedies that had cured her horrible itching last spring and stopped Momma's arm from swelling after a snake bite. There had to be something to heal her brother. She wondered who among the children at school would like the mysterious cellar. It seemed May-Belle had been pointing and talking about its holdings all of Ivoe's life, and there were still objects Ivoe had no stories for. At five or six, she thought the *juanchiro* was a table until May-Belle told her the Tiwa Indians called the tall drum "one that speaks with thunder" and let her bang it all afternoon. Eagle feathers from the warbonnet of a man her great-aunt once loved now lay atop the drum. The copper mask of a long-nosed god and feathered serpent was payment from a Caddo woman, after May-Belle delivered her daughter, to ensure a long life and peaceful afterlife. In the pile of colorful scraps on the table Ivoe recognized material from her favorite skirt and a blue smock May-Belle had worn. The green skirt was missed but the quilt her great-aunt was about to make would be all the better for it.

Momma called out to May-Belle twice, eyeing the hutch for a clue. In the place of the missing medicine bag, she wrote a message: *Come quick. Timbo got milk sickness.*

On the return home Ivoe's best effort to make haste was no match for the heat galling her mother.

"You got molasses in your tail this morning?"

"No, ma'am."

"Ain't you got a sick brother?"

"Yes, ma'am."

"Then get a move on."

"Momma, it's so hot the cows not mooing and the chickens not clucking," Ivoe said, wanting to melt the worry that made her mother hard as tack candy.

"But somebody's running her mouth instead of her legs now, ain't she?"

They lumbered over the dry ridges of the river bottoms and past the granary. When Ivoe fell behind, she broke into a gallop to catch her mother's stride. Lemon glimpsed a thirsty trough and shook her head as if to say her garden wouldn't make it through September.

By the time they arrived at the Starks' house, where Lemon had cooked for twenty years, the news of Alfred Stark's passing had already come from three people. Now Lemon paused before more signs of death: a Confederate flag waved from the gabled roof; a plain chassis stood before the front door, black draperies at its glassless windows. You weren't liable to find flags or chassis in Little Tunis, where Negro families spoke of loss through trees whose limbs held colorful bottles placed upside down with the necks facing the trunk, to trap any evil spirits. What bottles would they use to protect Timothy? Lemon shivered as she swept the Salat al-Janazah, funeral prayer, from her mind.

Inside the three-story manse, Earl Stark directed two carpenters to set up his father's coffin in the parlor.

"You mind your manners and don't touch nothing," Lemon whispered to Ivoe as they passed him to climb the staircase.

Posed like the letter *T,* Susan Stark stood on a stool in her underclothes while a seamstress measured for her mourning wardrobe.

"Was anybody with him?" Lemon asked.

"No. Minnie found him early this morning — slumped over his coffee in the kitchen," Miss Susan said.

"Seem like he was feeling fine yesterday."

"Most of the time you couldn't tell what Alfred was feeling . . . Moses on the mountain, Ivoe! I don't believe I've ever seen feet like those on a girl child. How old you getting to be?"

"I just turned nine."

"That must make your brother —"

"Fourteen. Timbo's fourteen — and he's rightly sick, Miss Susan." As soon as the words left her mouth, Ivoe regretted them. In telling private family business she had broken an important rule.

Lemon eyed Ivoe coolly. "Ain't her place to say it, but yes, my boy is sick. I came to tell you I can't work today. I got to get back

25

to him."

"Fine, soon as you see to the kitchen. I imagine plenty folks'll come by. You'll have to do some shopping. You talk to Earl? You ask him what to prepare?"

Lemon shook her head. It had not occurred to her to talk to Earl. She had offered him no sympathy on the passing of his father and, now as she thought of it, she had not even greeted him properly. "Look to me like you and Earl handling things. I ain't never seen my boy like this."

"It's fine, Lemon. You and Minnie decide between you who's going to do the flowers. Alfred left explicit directions for his death: twenty-eight white lilies in all the vases and twenty-eight in the casket with him. He didn't want to be embalmed so put candles everywhere before unpleasant odors bar everyone from the funeral. I started to turn facedown all the photographs but had to stop. Go through the house and don't leave one unturned."

"Now, Miss Susan, I don't plan on staying —"

Susan waved at the seamstress to stop and stepped down from the stool. "Lemon, my husband has died. I'm sure God created more loving spouses, but surely you're not supposing —"

"Now, Miss Susan, we go back years and I been a good worker for every one of them. Even on my worst day, sick and all, I been more than decent. I ain't never asked —"

Ivoe watched her mother, who always preached about obedience, move her hand from her pocketbook along the side of her leg. It was a habit she knew well because she often did things that made her mother pat her thigh for patience. Until that moment, she had not doubted that Timbo would be fixed by one of May-Belle's remedies and a little rest.

"— and I ain't asking now, Miss Susan. You gonna have to get on without me. Ivoe, let's go."

Later that evening, Ivoe watched her mother at the stove. The long day and its trouble had her beat. After their return from the Starks Momma had prayed extra long before starting the wash. As she pulled the steaming bedclothes from the big cast-iron pot to hang on the line, Ivoe saw her crying. She told Momma Timbo would be all right as soon as Aunt May-Belle showed up and not to cry.

"Who said anything about crying? Aren't you hot out here? If you don't want to see me sweat, help me." Ivoe reached into her mother's apron pocket for clothespins, which she held three at a time between her lips as she clipped one and then the other on opposite ends of Timbo's sheet, placing one in the middle. People often asked Ivoe why her mother dried clothes at night. Momma hated when the wash took on the scent of the air around it, especially after the beef was cooked over hickory wood every morning behind the smokehouse, where they sold it by the pound. Night drying also prevented their special things — like her favorite indigo dress — from bleaching in the sun. Standing next to Momma at the line, she thought to grab her around the waist, squeeze her tight, but finishing the chore seemed more important.

"Momma, I'll get up with the sun and take the clothes down."

"Appreciate that."

She reached for something else nice to say when a moan followed by a foul smell filled the kitchen, calling Momma to Timbo's side and leaving Papa and Ivoe to eat in the stench of her brother's shit.

Ivoe stood outside the wire fence wishing she could stay among them. Too many flies swarmed around the cattle and there was no place to hide from the sun. Still, she was better off. School made her sick, and Timbo needed her more. He hadn't eaten in three days, not even when Momma made his favorite, cracker pudding. Ivoe did her part, soaking the cloth in the pail by his bed, mopping his head whenever she got up to use the outhouse. She had even said a little prayer, doubtful that Papa's God or Momma's Allah was listening since no copy of *Gulliver's Travels* had made it to her last Christmas. Maybe her prayer for May-Belle to hurry up and deliver that baby and return to Little Tunis was easier to handle. It couldn't hurt to ask twice. She was standing on one foot, shaking loose the rocks and dirt from her shoe, when she saw the Indian children through a veil of rippled heat. She curled her fingers around the hot wire fence and took a deep breath.

"Alligator, Alligator," they said cloyingly.

The first time the Caddo Indians teased her Ivoe knew that they were right. When she walked, the worn welt separated from the sole of her shoe, calling to mind the open jaws of an alligator. Still, for the "Sharing Hour," a custom in their class every Friday, she determined to win their favor. Five children had told five stories about Negro life in the Brazos Bottoms. Ivoe told a different tale about the people who had lived there a century before. Since she was an iddy-biddy girl, Aunt May-Belle had spoken of the Caddo Indians. Every day when Ivoe took lunch she recalled one story in particular, as she watched the Caddo children eat corn mush from an orange clay pot so beautiful it shamed the rough casks in her own kitchen. Smooth with age and sized like a small pumpkin, lines and curved impressions gave life to two identical faces. "I know all about the twin brothers on this pot," Ivoe began, confident her story could best Scheherazade's finest. "My great-aunt said many years ago Father Sky gave special gifts to his sons. To this one" — she pointed to the openmouthed figure — "he gave a tongue that flashed like lightning. And to the other one, a voice like thunder." Curiosity cut through the class like a breeze through the hackberry grove in spring. A girl younger than Ivoe asked what the brothers did with their gifts of thunder and lightning. "Mostly they play with them. You know how sometimes a dark sky turns bright then starts to crack up?" The girl nodded, her eyes equal parts trepidation and wonder. "Well, that's just one brother trying to outdo the other one. Aunt May-Belle says there's no harm in it. Sometimes they just get out of hand."

"Out of hand" was what Momma said whenever Ivoe followed her own mind and she was glad for the chance to use it. "Know how you can tell when the brothers get out of hand? Lightning runs out of the sky. Sometimes it splits a tree in half or pulls the roof off somebody's cabin." Satisfied that the twins lived in the sky, a little boy wanted to know where all the other Indians had gone. Ivoe drew their attention to the map hanging in the front of the class and pointed to the state above Texas. "They're mostly in Oklahoma now." The twelve-year-old Caddo girl, who knew all about Oklahoma but could not read the letters to spell it, let out a nervous laugh.

It had crossed Ivoe's mind that sharing her story might encourage the Caddos to speak to her and give her the chance to ask them about the fine beaded moccasins they wore. Maybe they would even become friends. But in the days that followed, as the Caddos let everyone else feel the pot, they ignored her. And now, the consummate proof of their dislike was heard in her new nickname.

"Alligator, Alligator, don't be late."

Ivoe dreaded the day ahead — her shoes smacking the wood floor all the way from her desk to the chalkboard, the Caddos' snickering. She hated not hearing Miss Stokes's reading from *One Thousand and One Nights* but turned away from the schoolhouse anyway. If genies really did exist she wished one would make Timbo feel better so he could smile at the Caddo girl (that's all it ever took for him to win the girls at church), or make the Caddo boy jealous of how fast he could run, since everybody knew the only way to friend a boy was to best him at something. If the genie couldn't see clear on fixing Timbo right away, maybe he could arrange for the new pair of shoes she knew better than to ask of her parents. At the end of the day, Papa was put off by his children; you could hear it in his voice when he said to Timbo: "Now how come a man what works all day gotta come home to children what begs instead of giving they pa a kind hello?" Momma was no better. If Ivoe reminded her of the promised shoes, she was liable to hear, "Didn't I just make you a dress?," or "What about that new lunch pail Papa done give you?" There was no telling when she might get a new pair, so she wiped her eyes and headed for Deadman's Creek, her favorite retreat for sulking. At the creek, she hunted for a long time in search of a branch neither too short nor too brittle. She stood on a boulder jutting out of the cool water and poked the belly of a sunfish with all the force she could muster.

That evening Ivoe heard worry and anger in the rattling of every kitchen drawer, the slamming of every cupboard. Even the plate her mother set down spun to its final resting place, prompting Ivoe's eyes to well.

Lemon took her time tidying an already neat kitchen, then filled a glass for her daughter, sucking her teeth when a little water spilled. A child's cry sure can remind you just how ugly life can be, she thought. Wasn't enough to have a sick boy in the next room. What in the world had the girl so wounded? Ivoe still needed to learn how to not pay any mind to every little wrong some fool fixed on her. It was a young Earl Stark, Lemon recalled, who had taught her neither to bend nor break at hateful words. Listening to his parents' foolishness about the people who lived in the Bottoms, Earl did what children sometimes do with information they don't understand. Lemon was about Ivoe's age when she heard him patting juba with a friend the way she had taught them, while they sang:

Chicken when they hungry
Whiskey when they dry

Cotton when they hard up
Cotton when they die
A nought's a nought
A figger's a figger
All for the white man
None for the nigger.

It was all Lemon could do to stand there
and not reach for the child, to rock away
some of the hurt. She looked out the window, figuring the time left before the red
sun disappeared and her man came home.
"Nothing dries quicker than a tear, girl.
Don't you mind them that talk bad about
you. That's what folks do when they living
low to the ground. And them that's close to
the ground don't deserve your tears, your
sweat, your nothing. Look over they heads.
It ain't hard to do. Look over they heads.
Less you learn how, you won't make it past
my garden. Now, excuse yourself. Go get
your lessons." She listened for the flip-flop
shuffle out of her kitchen before going to
the cupboards, where she scanned the items
two or three times, as if her gaze might
multiply them. Four jars of tomato jam, a
couple of pints of dilled okra, a two-pound
bag of beans, and a cup of salt. She went
over in her mind the number of chickens in
the pen while removing the *misbaha* from

around her neck. Timbo had filled three pails of vomit that day and fever still gripped him. Ivoe needed shoes, but without the little money her brother brought in . . . and she had already missed four days of work tending to him.

Lemon lifted the pail of water she kept stowed under the table, splashed her face and washed her hands up to the elbows and her feet to the ankles. She knelt and bowed her head to the floor three times. She prayed the obligatory Maghrib, then raised her hands to her shoulders, the tips of her fingers just below her ears, to begin the Sunnah. Her right palm over the back of her left hand, the wrist of the left gripped by the right, she recited Du'aaul Istiftaah and the Ta'awwdhu, seeking refuge with Allah. She counted tasbih, glorifying Allah one bead at a time: *"Subhan'Allah, Alhamdulillah, Allahu Akbar."*

The clink of the glass beads at her great-aunt's waist sent Ivoe flying off the porch to the edge of their yard to greet the old woman. Aunt May-Belle dressed like Momma: a wraparound skirt down to her ankles, a blouse buttoned to the top, and a long ivory scarf thrown overhead like a veil that hung loose past her shoulders. Ivoe stood on tippy-toe to kiss her great-aunt's cheek and took her hand, leading her through the swept dirt yard bordered on both sides by tin tubs of altheas and wild honeysuckle.

"Good thing you came to see about Timbo. He ain't in no kind of shape at all."

Flowers potted in clay casks along their course gave May-Belle a feeling of contentment shown in her storied face. A musky scent drew her eyes to the fig tree shading red spinach ready to bolt, but it was the tomatoes glimmering like rubies on emerald vines that made her gasp in delight.

"You know, Ivoe, May-Belle's getting old. My eyes pretty good but I need for you to do the reaching and the bending. You be my arms?"

Ivoe nodded.

"You be my knees?"

"Yes."

"A bluebird danced a jig on the branch outside my window this morning. I said to it, 'Bluebird, what good word you got for me today? That Ivoe dependable?' Bluebird say, 'Yes'm.' Guess he knew what he was talking about."

Ivoe grinned. "Then no schooling for me today?"

"Not in the schoolhouse. Plenty schooling

all around you in nature." To prove her point, May-Belle opened her hand and showed what looked to Ivoe like a rock made of ice. "You see this? This here what we call horn quicksilver. Gonna add a little cherry bark and some dandelion greens to boil with it to make a tea what fix Timbo up proper."

Ivoe took the porch steps confidently. It was only a matter of time before she and Timbo would be swimming in the creek again.

"My stars! Them tomatoes is fit to be ate," May-Belle said, closing the door behind her. "Them and that fig tree smelling up the whole yard. Looking pretty too. You got something special in mind for them?"

"Special nothing, honey. We fixing to eat them — some now, some later. Reckon I'll can a few like always," Lemon said.

"Well, 'cause you ain't got nothing special in mind don't mean nature ain't got no designs on them. Mark my words, they fix-ing to do something."

"Right now, May-Belle, them tomatoes not on my littlest mind. That tree neither. Timbo can't sleep for fever and too weak to chew."

"He be all right. Maybe not on your watch

or mine. But on Allah's watch he be all right."

"I been praying the Fard and Sunnah every day, hoping Allah's watch will tick faster. Now listen, May-Belle, don't you pay no mind to the sweet face that girl's gonna put on you." Lemon fixed her eyes on Ivoe. "Don't you let her go to the creek. Last time she come running home hollering and carrying on so till I thought something terrible happened. Legs and feets was all covered with them devilish bloodsuckers." She handed Ivoe a jar of water for the journey, eyeing her for some recognition. "I don't care nothing about you standing there with your mouth all poked out. You know I'm telling the truth. Now take this and get on."

May-Belle rested a hand on Ivoe's shoulder as they entered the hackberry grove. "Won't be too long before I have to learn you all the remedies," she said.

"I rather learn with you than go to school, Auntie."

"When you start to put the bad mouth on school?"

"Me and school don't fit."

"You needs book learning, you hear me? Schooling put notions in the head what was never in mind before and we mean for you to get all you can get." May-Belle raised a hand above her eyes. "Now you see that red tree out yonder? Go get me some of that trunk." Watching the girl climb the tree (to Ivoe, who loved tree climbing, the bark had to come from the top), May-Belle wondered why a child as curious as this one was put off school.

"You know, Ivoe, when I was about your age I sure hated to come to the woods," she said, taking two handfuls of bark from the child.

"How come?"

"Scared of trees."

Ivoe's eyes widened. "How you stopped being afraid?"

"I acted like they was peoples — friends of mine. Even give them names." May-Belle chuckled. "Anybody what saw me talking to those trees probably thought my dough wasn't all the way done but that's how I figured to use my little bit. See, Ivoe, when we children the Creator gives each and every one of us a little bit of courage. And when that little bit is gone we get some more. You can't get no more less you use up what the Creator done already give. Now, less you want to grow up a big and strong woman with iddy-biddy courage what's only fit for a child, you better use up what you got." She pointed down to a patch of tiny yellow flowers. "Now, grab me some of that."

Ivoe plucked the calico dress sticking to her damp chest as the sun drummed hot fingers against her neck, making her long for the creek. "Leeches don't scare me no more, Auntie. All you got to do is peel them off. Timbo say you got to be quick about it. And I'm quick. Momma just don't know how quick I am. She —" There was no chance to hope that they would spare her this time. The voices calling to her from the distance were already too close.

"Look who finally learned alligators don't belong in a schoolhouse."

Ivoe recalled her mother's advice, but her own little bit of courage was as fresh on her mind as the dandelions she crushed.

"Alligator, you hear us talking to you?"

"I hear you," Ivoe grumbled, releasing mashed flowers to grab the shoes she had tossed aside. When the boy recovered from the smack, like hot steel against his face, he ran off just as Ivoe knocked his sister to the ground, striking her all over with her broken shoes.

Upland a mile from the grove where May-Belle watched Ivoe scramble, neither encouraging nor discouraging the scuffle, Lemon left the Stark house. Miss Susan had fixed her wagon all right, relieving her of all duties because she had done what any decent mother would do, looked after her son instead of kowtowing when Mr. Stark died. She ain't put it that way, exactly. Never knowed any Stark to hit a thing directly. They had to go all the way around the mulberry bush, up one side and down the other, before they even thought about striking center.

No need for double kitchen help now that Mr. Stark was dead, Susan had said. "Minnie can handle it." *Ssth.* Minnie always was the favored one, even though she had to be told things twice and couldn't plan a meal. Tell her to scramble an egg and Minnie would leave most of it stuck to the skillet. How did Susan expect to get along in a house that size with help that took a day and a half just to dust? Lemon thought. Give them Starks my best cooking for years. Cooked meals I be too tired to fix for my own. Now Mr. Stark gone and what I got to show for it? What I got but a head full of worry and a heart fixing to break?

Over the years, to make up the difference between all that she gave the Starks and what she could give to her family, Lemon lined her shoes with folded scraps of paper filled with sugar and spices from the Starks' pantry. On the journey home, she delighted in what special foods she would prepare for Ennis and the children on her day off. At times when there was barely enough money for chicken feed, it awed the family when a cake appeared. "Timothy, Ivoe, what I tell you?" Ennis liked to say. "Momma is some magician. And a good-looking one at that." Now in the deep apricot haze of Texas twilight, Lemon looked around her garden for some evidence of her magic. As she took the porch steps, worry sank its teeth in and gnawed away at the things she thought she knew for sure, like her ability to provide for her children and the fact that one day they would bury her and not the other way around. She opened the door so pre-occupied she did not notice her husband sitting at the kitchen table.

"Well howdy-do to you too," Ennis said. "Fever broke. And he's keeping the tea down. May-Belle say he be wanting to eat something soon."

Lemon sat her bag aside and kissed Ennis on the crown of his head. "She gone?"

"Yeah, she gone." Ennis cleared his throat. "Ivoe, come on in here. What with deliver-ing two babies, seeing about Timbo, and all that fighting, I reckon May-Belle was good and tired. Ain't that right, Ivoe?"

Ivoe felt her father's eyes all over her as she handed her mother a bunch of wilted buttercups picked on the way home.

"Fighting? Who been fighting?" Lemon said.

During her father's retelling of that afternoon, Ivoe set a place at the table and served her mother the supper she and Ennis had fixed together.

"Well, maybe that'll do it," Lemon said.

Ennis eyed his wife curiously. "Do what?"

"Liff da curse —" Lemon mumbled through a mouthful of cornbread. "Lift the curse that got this one here thinking she ain't no better than her shoes. I just hate lifting her own curse meant bringing a curse downside the heads of those other fool children." Lemon's deep laugh made Ennis chuckle at Ivoe, who commenced a little jig around the table, waving her fists in the air like a champion pugilist.

"Now ain't that just the fairy from the Christmas tree?" Ennis chided. "Fighting and dancing in the same day. Go on and get in that bed you hate to cut loose when morning come."

The stinging worry about how they were

43

going to make ends meet kept Lemon awake. After the children had gone to sleep, she emptied her bag of belongings once kept at the Starks'. The news of her firing didn't upset Ennis but she knew he missed the money already. He went over a list of white folks who came to his workshop. "You think you wanna work for any of them?" She didn't want to work for anybody ever again but she told him she would think about it. Presently, the quiet of the cabin brought to mind forgotten advice from her mother: "Sometimes you got to go to the water — be with it a while — to quiet the waters in you." When was the last time she'd taken a late-night swim in the creek? It was too dark out for a trip alone. Where had Ennis slipped off to?

Lemon got out of bed and dragged the long washtub in from the back porch. While the water boiled, she pulled her braids apart, freeing the coarse hair that framed her face like a crinkly mane. She added the last drops of rose geranium oil to her bath and leaned back, raking her fingers against her scalp. An image of Timbo flashed in her mind, sweat popping out on his forehead while he hunkered over his food. Let him keep on eating like that, she thought, sliding deeper into the tub just as Ennis touched

44

her head.

"Your sweetness come to greet me out in the yard," the raspy voice whispered. "Thought I was gonna have to fight wild dogs off the porch to get to you. Or get Ivoe up to fight them for me."

Lemon leaned her head against her husband's thigh. "Where you run off to?"

"Had to tend to some business. I'm back now. What you want with me?"

They moved against each other, tilting three of the bed's legs an inch above the ground so that the shorter fourth leg collided with the earth. During their lovemaking Lemon often talked to Allah, a feverish, rapid talk that marked the ardent thrust of her hips. Ennis met the sweat that rained on him, craning his neck to suck the salt off her breast or lower lip, even in the middle of a sentence like now: "— this man." Bump. "Thank you." His rough hands fastened on her hips reminded her that she was not the only strong one in their family. "— so good to me." Bump. His breath quickened in his chest and he held it until the moment her eyes emptied of worry and duty and filled with a light that nearly broke his heart. "This here —" Bump. "— is —" Her mind filled with green tomatoes in profusion on all her vines. He saw a shower

45

of golden embers against a blanket of bright white heat. Then they both gave up the world.

Every day except Sunday Ennis walked a mile to the small shack where he had learned to smith alongside Booker Kebby, Lemon's father. He hauled in bushels of coal and buckets of water for the slack tub; picked up the tools and scraps of iron left on the floor; and cleaned out the forge. Covered in fine black dust and itching from it, he sat down at the bellows and waited for the iron to turn hot. Usually, he thought of Lemon. How he found her crouched among a tangle of vines and looked past the glow of her sun-kissed skin, the fullness of her breasts, to her way with the fruit. He thought that anyone who handled tomatoes like you'd handle a baby must know how to love. And love is what he desperately wanted.

Day one he wanted to tell Booker that without touching her he had already climbed so far deep inside his daughter's love wasn't no way no kind of light would ever reach him unless she made it so. He bided his time. The day Booker grabbed his arm and pointed to the two numbers bubbled on the skin of his shoulder, he knew he had a chance.

"When you was a boy, why Stark bring you down here, have me put this on you? What you do?" Booker said. Ennis explained that after delivering something to Iraj in the kitchen, he had come upon a glass of water on a table on the porch. Thinking of the two-mile walk ahead of him, he tried to resist but he couldn't. "Stark must've seen me from somewhere in the house," he told Booker, truthfully. "He said any man what drink from another man's glass couldn't be trusted and deserved punishment."

The story of the first woman who should have loved Ennis was a mystery. No one knew who his mother was or where she had gone. Each of the stories passed on to him could have been true: his mother was suspected of well poisoning and drowned herself in the creek to avoid being hanged or worse; after being caught in the cotton fields with a box of matches she was sold; she had run away to Mississippi. Ennis claimed the latter because he liked the idea of a mother deciding her own fate, but in reality all he could remember of his life began in the last cabin on the road with all of Little Tunis's male orphans. Old Man Williams lived there, tending to boys from the five-year-old Ennis to the sixteen-year-old Joseph. Sometimes babies were given to Paw Paw until stable young parents came forward looking to grow their families. Older boys, who shucked corn at Riley's, had simply shown up and put themselves in his charge. Though he was blind, Paw Paw knew all of his boys by touch. At night, after his tales of ghostdogs and haints, he called each boy before him. Mindful of the things a child requires, he was sure to touch them, to ask what good they had given the day and if they had eaten enough. A boy's absence from one of Paw Paw's accountings brought trouble to everyone. Once, Ennis, always big for his age, approached Paw Paw as himself, then again later, when Timothy's name was called. Before Ennis could turn away Paw Paw gripped his head. He ran his fingers over Ennis's face a second and third time, as if reading a garbled message. He sensed the boys looking to each other for who should tell the truth and drove his walking stick into the ground with a fierce clap. Ennis watched the oak staff shimmy and wondered if Paw Paw could drive him into the ground like that. Timothy had run off, Ennis said. When Paw Paw returned with the boy two days later he gave Ennis the only whipping he ever got — for pretending to be somebody else.

Recalling his son's namesake brought Ennis a worry list as long as the Brazos and just as crooked. He shifted on his work stool and raised the anvil to the forge. Who could he talk to about a little extra work? He needed to go see Riley, let the man know Timbo would be right back on the job soon as he could. Anybody who missed too much work during harvest was bound to be let go. Another leather string, a little sewing, might hold Ivoe's shoes together one more month. But the way she was growing up so tall, come winter she would need a new coat. In the race between what he could give his family and what they needed, need always won. Truth like that stared you down. More than hurt you, it numbed you — even to a hungry flame. Ennis cussed and stumbled backward to the slack tub, his right arm bubbling with blisters.

Lemon stepped down from her porch to the garden. She lifted a listless vine, cast an anxious eye over her parched vegetables, and sighed. Two weeks and not a drop of rain. This autumn bore no resemblance to other harvests she'd known. Ivoe spent more time at the creek than at school; the slightest motion of Ennis's hand made him wince; and the little money Timbo made

49

barely kept them in soap and flour. She wearied at the thought of hiring herself out. After a day tending house and caring for Ennis, leftover energy was given to her garden, the place she always worried a wrong thing into rightness. She was on her hands and knees, smoothing a milky-brown mass over the earth, when a pair of fancy shoes appeared near her trowel. She raised her head and squinted up at the visitor.

"Miss Susan, this here ground's real sensitive. Now it know what to make of feet but it don't know nothing about shoes. You keep standing there, we fixing to go without okra this fall."

Susan lifted her skirt and took a few quick dancelike steps sideways, landing her on the narrow gravel path that separated the large patch of greens from the runner beans.

"Lemon, what do you have in that bucket?"

"Manure and a little soda water. May-Belle puts it on her vegetables and they come out looking right pretty, tasting good too." Lemon stood and wiped her hands on her apron. "Now. What can I do for you?"

"My Earl sent me here after some of your tomato jam. The other morning Minnie served it and he plum had a fit. Didn't have to tell him where it came from. He remembered your momma Iraj's jam from child-hood. Used to be the day just couldn't start unless he had some slathered on his biscuits. No doubt about it, he said, this came from Lemon. He's got a real hankering — sent me here to get all I could from you."

White folks sure had some funny ways. And no shame at all. "Well, I got some in the house," Lemon said, tugging on the sides of her floppy straw hat as she walked cautiously down a row intended for radishes.

Susan followed Lemon past the leafy red sage that surrounded the small cabin. She glanced admiringly on the yard, a pleasing jungle of hues, and thought, Colored people sure are at home in nature.

Lemon reached for the jars, taking care to put her words right: "Now, Miss Susan, much as I wish I could — well, I can't just *give* these to you."

Susan extended a closed, gloved fist. "Lemon, you know better than to think I wouldn't offer you something."

Lemon looked at the gold coin. "That's mighty generous. Mighty generous indeed." Two and a half dollars would cover new shoes for Ivoe and leave a little extra for seeds. When the carriage drove off, she counted the tomatoes on her vines.

"Plenty. Just need some more jars and a wagon."

2
LOVE, A CURIOUS THING
OCTOBER 1897

The Sunday Ivoe returned from Old Elam
Baptist Church with three orders, Lemon
knew her family would be all right. Folding
eggs into cornmeal, she leaned her head a
little to the side and listened, trying not to
smile. Above the noise of the whisk she
could hear jubilation in the child's voice.

"Beulah Brown wants three jars of
chowchow. And Mamie Johnson say with
your tree looking like it do she know you
must have some mighty fine fig jam. Reverend Greenwood told me to tell you just
'cause you don't show your face at church,
he won't hold it against you. He said put
him down for two jars of tomato jam. He
even gave me the money."

The whisk stopped. "How he know how
much to give you?"

Ivoe's eyes flashed the way a child's does
when she is about to reveal a long-kept,
happy secret.

"First he gave me a dime. He said you probably wouldn't charge no more than a nickel for each jar. But I told him a dime would only get him one jar not two."

"A dime, Ivoe?" She would never have thought to ask for so much.

Ivoe hesitated. Her mother always said — in the voice she used when she wasn't keen on something — that the folks at Old Elam were more hat than saddle. "But he gave me a quarter and told me he'll be looking for his jams next Sunday. Momma, just think of all the customers you could get if you came to church."

Ssth. And get carried away with that foolishness? Lemon thought as her whisk started up again. Clapping and stomping and praying to the blue-eyed savior on the wall? Booker and Iraj taught her better than that. Years ago in the Bottoms — before the incident at the river with the twenty-eight — for practicing Arabic and passing on the Qur'an's lessons sometimes your tongue was cut out. Booker Kebby had been determined she would pray in the tongue of her ancestors. Her father taught her the same salats learned by his father at the madrasa. In Alabama, before they were sold to Mr. Stark, word on a raid of the women's quarters for contraband made her mother and May-Belle hide their Fula mothers' *misbaha* in the only place a woman could hide anything. After all of that she should give up Islam? Give it up — for the gospel according to whom?

Lemon handed Ivoe a basket. "I seen rivers run less than that mouth of yours. You fixing to stand there all day or help with some of this work?" Soon it would be time to teach her how to bring a crop from a seed. "Let me get started on Beulah's chowchow. Fetch me some peppers. Might as well bring in some tomatoes too. Miss Susan be back around here before you know it."

Ivoe had half a mind to leave the best tomatoes on the vine. She was put out with Miss Susan for firing Momma. Now newspapers were impossible to come by. She missed how the paper gave her new words to learn. Recently, her teacher had brought a great book that required the effort of the biggest boys in class to carry. On a walnut stand in the back of the schoolhouse the *American Dictionary* lay open to the middle. Ivoe's hand was the first to shoot up whenever Miss Stokes read from *One Thousand and One Nights* and came upon a word they didn't know. Flip-flopping in broken shoes was worth the chance to look a new word up. She was excited and comforted by the feel of the dictionary's thin pages, soft and cool to the touch. Often reprimanded for sulkiness when another pupil interrupted her searches, today her irascibility had been rewarded. Miss Stokes said if granted permission from her parents she could remain after school to have extra time with the dictionary.

Time with the dictionary was on Ivoe's mind as she crouched by the crawling vine, gently twisting, heeding Momma's clue: ripeness was found in color not softness. When she saw a tomato whose redness at the bottom matched the red around the stem, she gave the fruit a gentle tug. She chose the peppers with equal care because a task well done was sure to put her in Momma's good grace, where she needed to be.

Lemon emptied a cup on the kitchen table, stacking coins in neat piles as she counted. In a month she had paid off the wagon and bought new boots for the four of them. Sometimes she treated herself to rose water or picked up something special for Ennis. Still, it would never be enough. She returned the cup to its secret place and left the cabin.

Bright orange and light yellow leaves barreling down from the sweet gum trees and the trace of corn dust, where a combine had just harvested the field, often soothed Lemon, but during troubled times it was her habit to think of her mother and father. Before their deaths, she and May-Belle had joined her parents and a Starkville merchant family for Friday prayers. Her new ritual, when May-Belle was called away, was to pray alone in her garden — Surah 2:115: "Wherever you turn, there is Allah's face." The invitation to attend *jumu'ah* in the back of Mr. Al-Halif's seed store, where a small room was devoted as a makeshift mosque, had come early that week when the shop-keeper stopped her on a jam delivery.

"You and May-Belle are the only Muslims in the Bottoms but we are all Arabized coloreds in a country of Christians . . . We must worship together."

Abbud Al-Halif landed on the Texas coast just before the Civil War with other Syrian and Turkish Muslims and a shipload of camels to tend for the army. "Camel transportation between Texas and the western frontier failed . . . And no Reconstruction for the masses of Syrians out of work after the war," he had explained to Lemon. He had been lucky, striking out for Central East Texas with his wife in 1875 when a man decided to build a bridge across the Brazos, connecting Burleson and Bryan Counties. He built Pitt's Bridge with other immigrants, mostly Italian, living in a tent on a peat bog. He tended cattle for the Starks. Doing "godless work," until he eked out enough savings to open a store on Main Street.

The red-and-white cover of *Joseph Breck & Sons Garden, Field, and Flower Seeds* caught Lemon's eye. She lingered the longest in its pages, which promised everything from perfect petunias to giant goosefoot. Pages and pages of seeds from as far away as Asia, a gardener and truck farmer's dream. She studied the photographs, enticed by potherbs from the Balkans, and wished she could send away for some. It soothed her mind a little to thumb through the nursery catalogs while waiting for Mr. Al-Halif to conclude his business. As he locked the door behind the last customer, Lemon spoke in a tremulous voice.

"Allah has saw fit to grow my family and I ain't glad about it."

"Have you prayed?" Mr. Al-Halif asked.

"Too much guilt. I made *duas.*"

She was in no state to pray and had repented for her other considerations. Long as Ennis had love, she couldn't puzzle out how not to bring another of his babies even though they grow and need all the while. Ennis had the kind of love that saw to needs. How many times had he made something from nothing? Now that money was coming in they would be all right. If the baby didn't cause sickness she could work till delivery. But what if folks stopped buying her jams? She was tired of the way they scrounged just to make it through hard times.

Mr. Al-Halif called out to his wife, Yasna, and daughters. The urgency of today's petition to Allah required *jama'ah,* as prayer in congregation was more likely to win Allah's favor.

Lemon lowered her head. "I know it is haram to end a life."

"It depends. Islam is a religion of compassion."

Like Lemon's father, Mr. Al-Halif was a hafiz, and had memorized the Qur'an. "But we are told in 6:151 'you shall not kill your children because you cannot support them.' "

They did their ablutions — the washing of face, hands, forearms, and feet — and prayed the Salaatul Istikhaarah for guidance. On the walk home Lemon remained conflicted.

Ten days later, May-Belle opened the door and beckoned her niece inside. For weeks she had dreamed about it, waking up agitated, mournful, and unable to tell a soul about it. Now all the signs proved it. Lemon's face was fuller, her neck a smidgen darker. "Ain't no worry over the tansy and rue," May-Belle said, removing a pinch of herbs from a small canister. The tea would make Lemon sick as a dog for three days even before she started to bleed. "You best let Ennis know what you fixing to do 'cause it's as much his as it is yours."

A gust of February wind rustled papers jammed between the logs of the cabin as Timothy rolled onto his side weary from a fitful sleep. Since the death of his friend Junior and Junior's father, strange habits had taken hold of the Williams family. Momma used to be all peace. Now when Papa moved from the bed out into a day of God only knew what kind of danger, Timbo could hear her say, "Come back to us, you hear?" Delivery of her jam stopped. "Folks who want them just gonna have to come get them." She wasn't about to have Ivoe on the road alone with her little red wagon. In the last week, Papa didn't have two words for anybody. Timothy looked outside to see how much snow remained. The ice he'd seen caked on the roof the night before — when they heard strange noises and Momma sent him out to look around — was melting. The bucket in the corner of the room was nearly full. He hated to rise so early, but like everybody in Little Tunis who now tended to business at strange hours, he figured getting out with the sun was the best way to see it rise again.

Many would miss Mr. James Williams. He had a business in town, gray in his head, and friends. But Junior. Nobody knew his friend Junior like he did. When the milk sickness had Timbo bedridden and vomiting, it was Junior who told him whose titty he'd squeezed behind the church on Sunday, or how he'd made dice skitter across the floor. Junior was convinced one day their fortune would be made in craps games. Then they would have any woman they wanted. And with bond money too, they might even tell a cracker to go to hell. Junior wasn't scared of nothing. Timbo hated to think how scared his friend had probably been at the end.

Timbo warmed himself by the grate in the

kitchen. "How you sleep?" he asked his mother, who was cooking breakfast.

"Pretty good," Lemon fibbed. "Can't let it end you. The living got to keep on living." She pulled at the front of her tight housecoat, carrying a plate of eggs and fried potatoes to the man-boy slouched at her table. She watched her son eat, wondering when he would sleep through the night again. The tragedies of last week had taken more from him than he would ever know. "Need to set up the peppers and radishes for spring. Getting orders already." She nodded at the boxes of soil on the floor across the room. "When you go into town this morning, pick up my seeds. We out of coffee. Better get a tin of that too."

Timothy reached for his coat. "And take that" — Lemon pointed to the croker sack in the corner — "have them ground it up for me." A moment passed, then, thinking of her spring yard. Lemon jumped up from the table, waddling swiftly to the door. "Baby, my mind ain't but a minute long these days," she called out, shaking her head to show her forgetfulness was a personal nuisance. "Better get me some petunia seedlings too. Be sure to fetch Ivoe from school. And, Timbo, don't let the sun set on you."

■ ■ ■ ■

Junior and his father had not heeded the warning. Sunday, after people stood up to share what they had seen or heard, Reverend Greenwood said the boy and his father had paid the price for taking the long way home. Didn't make sense to try to put the pieces together, Timothy chided himself. Facts were simple: most Negro men lived till somebody saw fit to kill them. One day his time would come too; the why and the how of it didn't matter. Feeling bad about it was foolish too, especially when he needed to pay attention like Papa always told him, so he could steer clear of potential trouble like now — an old woman reaching out to touch his arm. She fumbled with her pocketbook and asked for his help right there on Main Street.

Across the street two men observed.

"Look over yonder. What you suppose that boy got to talk to Lady Henderson about?"

"Can't say. I reckon she asked him something."

"I reckon she ain't done no such thing."

The threat of the woman's victimhood made the men walk with an elastic step.

"Howdy, ma'am. Everything all right here?"

"Everything's fine. Sometimes I'm just a silly ninny. Went off without my specs. This boy helped me by reading the address on this envelope. I can manage just fine now," the woman said, patting her thanks lightly on Timothy's arm.

Ssth. Lemon sucked her teeth. "Just ain't right — James and James Junior both gone. Say before they was shot they took a mighty beating. Found them both half-naked," she continued to Ennis, who made the stew his excuse for the lunchtime visit when they both knew he had come home to make sure she was safe. Lemon stopped stirring and waited for him to say something. How he could lose a friend — brother, really — and keep so quiet about it worried her. She was glad for the cooking so she didn't have to look at him, because then maybe he would see how much it weighed on her. Couldn't be helped. Life ought to feel heavy when secrets piled up so high not even a crack of light could get through. Made a soul dark is what it did — all the untelling.

That morning fifteen years ago, when James Williams came by with the firewood, Lemon had been thinking of her parents in the cold, cold ground when James put the bundle down and asked where Ennis had gone. "To see about work," she told him. Funny how the truth of a thing could change, depending on who said it. When Ennis had said it, somehow it sounded right, but coming from her mouth — well, she felt foolish just repeating it. James wondered if Ennis hadn't run off like his momma had. And she didn't know any better than to let her doubt show. Doubt told James he could take her in his arms like that and give her something she could believe in. Timbo didn't come out looking like either one of them, but he was black, black like both men. It shamed her when Ennis held the baby for the first time talking about "My son."

A bottle slipped from Lemon's hand and crashed against the floor, making the room reek of tamarind and chili peppers. "Don't know how this gonna taste without the Worcestershire sauce," she said, turning away from the bubbling pot, the house of the unborn baby leading the way. "Cora about ready for somebody to carry her on away from here. Can't say I blame her. If something happened to you I'd sit down in that chair and try my best to rock on away from here. Yes, I would. Ivoe said the girls wasn't at school last week. And you know it ain't like me to meddle but they children. They can't rightly see to each other. I went over there this morning. Look like Cora been beat from head to toe with a worry stick. Hair wasn't combed. Dress soiled. I cleaned up a little bit, combed all they heads and fixed them something to eat. *Ssth.* Take a woman's husband and her only son. Don't make no kind of sense."

Lemon rubbed her belly and blamed the pear. Last November, she had intended to start the ridding process once Ivoe left for school because she didn't want the girl to see her in pain from the cramping. And the bleeding could be messy. She waited on the herbs until lunchtime when Ennis showed up unexpectedly. Wearing that boyish grin, he held out cupped hands, wiggling and carrying on until she pried his fingers open. She laughed that it was only a pear, then grabbed the golden thing, sinking her teeth into the ripe flesh as syrupy juice trickled down her chin. Ennis pulled her close, pressed his head to hers, and kissed the sweetness from her lips. She inhaled him deeply — sweat mingled with the hint of clove in the shaving cream she bought him — and fell against his chest. The sleeve of his shirt couldn't catch her tears fast enough. In their bed she told Allah she was fine with another mouth to feed just as long as He showed her how to do it.

Ennis didn't cry for James Williams like a brother because he had lived with him only a year at Paw Paw's place, but his head hurt him just the same. Maybe it was the catfish stew Lemon was preparing, which James had liked so much, or maybe it was the dwindling pile of wood near the hearth that brought his friend and the morning they shared last summer so near. Sitting on the riverbank next to buckets full of sunfish, anybody could see James had a lot on his mind. Ennis waited until Timbo and Junior put down their fishing rods to go for a swim before he spoke up.

"Seem like when we was boys time was lazy. Just stretch on out before you like this here river. You remember, James? Seem like time wasn't never gone end."

"Yeah, Ennis, we mens now. My family, we not no little people. We hardworking and we not no little people. I want to see big things happen for my family. I want to see it before my time is up," James said.

"Ain't a man in Little Tunis ain't done felt how you feeling now."

"A man supposed to be able to put his family up in a good home. Leastwise that's why we work. Didn't Paw Paw tell us the only way we was to live and die mens was if we worked and made good homes? Well, Ennis, dammit, I'm doing that but it don't matter none if my wife afraid to leave the house or afraid to come back to it once she gone," James said, wiping his eyes.

It was the first time Ennis saw a grown man cry and it stirred something in him.

"Ain't so much the house as it is that sawmill of yours — up there in *they* neck of the woods."

"They neck of the woods my foot. Been hauling that devilish timber since I was them boys' age. Shit, after all them years I knowed what he know, why wouldn't I go into business for myself?"

"Seem to me you can't stay up there with them, James. Just ain't safe."

"Been thinking on that, Ennis. Been thinking on it hard. You remember when folks used to talk about Kansas? You probably didn't pay it no mind."

"Boy they talked on Nicodemus so tough — like it was some kind of heaven," Ennis said, wistful. "Nicodemus, Kansas."

"They say we owns all the houses, all the businesses up there, everything. Down here they wanna work you half dead then pay you with that company scrip. Soon as I crawled out from one hole and dust my knees off good, I crawled back into another one. Took a little time and we did without. Now we got our own outfit and doing good. Got all the colored business."

"They gonna make you pay for it, James. Watch yourself."

"I ain't watching nothing. One more year and they can have all this. You and Lemon oughta come go with us."

"I'll run it past her. Don't think I ain't thought about it. I could smith anywhere."

"But a colored town . . . boy you can't beat that with a stick."

Ennis and James washed down the lunch Lemon packed for them with whiskey, watching their boys climb the trees along the muddy shore, crawl out on the limbs, and dive into the river with a mighty smack. At one point James said, "How them boys expect us to catch anything making all that noise?" But Ennis knew, like James, they both found the day's only comfort in their sons' laughter.

Presently, Lemon had a hard stare fixed on Ennis.

"And you wonder why I don't want you building me nothing. What I want a little shack for? Or even a stand? White folks ain't ready to see colored folk have nothing of

69

they own. No, sir. I'll keep right on selling my jams from my kitchen 'cause soon as they see you doing all right — doing for yours like they do for theirs — they go and do something like this. Opening a business is one thing, but to leave Little Tunis? You know, Ennis, I believe if James had kept his family down here he would still be with us. That was mistake number one — leaving Little Tunis."

"Naw, mistake number one was being born colored."

Not even the brutal cold could cool the heated blood of those mourning the 266 killed in the blast aboard USS *Maine.* Seized by the fervor of war — the nation's first in foreign territory — the men of Burleson County practiced chivalry at every turn. Small boys marched down Main Street, going out of their way to open doors for women or to catch a toddler before it fell. Young men joined the National Guard and army with hope to deliver a blow against Spain worthy of a spread-winged eagle suspended from a red, white, and blue ribbon.

Held up against the silent war at home, Havana Harbor was an afterthought for those gathered in the shop of a carpenter who described the scene witnessed a week ago: a Negro boy reading to Old Lady Henderson. Where did the boy and his family live? Did anyone remember a few years back in Snook? Derisive guffaws broke out among them. Treading a path to Little Tunis, one slipped, having caught a boot in the hem of his robe, and tumbled down the frozen alabaster pasture. The more surefooted made giddy strides in the blistering cold until they came upon the white edifice shimmering silver in the moonlight. An hour later they would still be found there, feeding the blaze.

Ivoe listened with her classmates before a heap of charred wood. She tried to understand, but like jamming the wrong puzzle piece into an almost-finished puzzle, she couldn't make the picture in her mind fit with Miss Stokes's words. Why would anybody want to burn down a schoolhouse whose benches left your behind full of splinters and none of the inkwells ever saw a drop of ink?

The tallest girl among them began to cry. "Can't we all just come to your house?" Or can I come by myself? she thought but did not say.

"There is not enough room to accommodate all of you," Miss Stokes said.

A small boy piped up cheerfully. "Is school finished for good?"

"Certainly not —"

"But us ain't got no books. No papers. No nothing," said a small girl.

Ivoe thought of the books: *Golden-Haired Gertrude, One Thousand and One Nights, Gulliver's Travels.* She drew a shuddering breath, picturing the dictionary somewhere in the heap, and began to cry.

"As soon as I gather some materials and find a meeting place," Miss Stokes began, fighting to quell the anger in her voice, "we will continue with the business of your education. In the meantime, read whatever you can and practice your ciphering. I am sorry for our loss."

That spring, "sorry" seemed to follow Ivoe everywhere. She walked too heavy, ate too loud, made too many messes. Everything she did required an apology to Momma. In the weeks since the school burned down, she had worn out most of her mother's nerves and was now on her last one. On account of her baby brother stretching and growing (the unborn baby had to be a boy), the only time Momma stopped complaining was when Papa came home. Everybody knows a growing belly makes you tired. While Momma slept in the afternoon, Ivoe cleaned up the kitchen and thought about what she liked about school and now missed — like playing drop the handkerchief or leapfrog, where she could best the tallest girl in class, whose legs were longer but who did not bend enough at the knee before she leaped. She was fond of spelling bees and even handwriting, despite her poor penmanship. How many times had Miss Stokes handed her a scrap of flannel to erase and start again. She did not miss multiplication or trips to the recitation bench at the front of the room, where each pupil was called to talk through an arithmetic problem, the worst part of school.

Most days, time could be lazy and barely move at all. Ivoe liked to take a pair of shears to the old Sears, Roebuck & Company catalog Susan Stark brought when she came to buy jam. Cutting out pictures of items she wanted seemed to nudge time forward till Momma fussed, "Make this the last time I see you sitting around with wish books and pictures of things you'll never buy. Instead of studying on things you want, study on what you want *to do*." Momma had also gotten after Miss Susan about the catalogs because one day she brought a bundle of books. After morning chores, during the long middle of the day and then again before bed, Ivoe rode the hills and valleys of Sheffield County alongside her favorite knight. No challenge was too great since her bravery equaled the hero's. She had defeated the Caddo girl just as Ivanhoe had beaten Sir Brian. Even more than the camaraderie found in the Waverley novels, she was rapt by the stories' allusions to love.

Love was a curious thing. Love made her mother harp about the ways she should act. (She ought not be boastful or call attention to herself.) Love had Papa and May-Belle remind her of the light she carried that was hers to shine. (She should speak her mind, share, and be brave.) Sometimes late at night she could hear love in the next room — Momma's whispers, Papa's laughter (in the morning there would be extra jam). Love was all around though no one ever spoke of it. In this way the Waverley books were the greatest gift she'd ever received; she could read all about the bold things love made a hero do.

The *click-clack* of Lemon's pestle was the only sound in the cabin. To the fine cornmeal she added a spoonful each of vinegar, vanilla, and cream, then stirred, the fat of her upper arm shaking, as she reached for the cup of soft butter. She folded in four eggs, brought in that day, one and a half cups of sugar, a packed teaspoon of lemon zest. Her pinky finger skimmed a taste from the side of the bowl. Like fairy dust, a pinch of her secret ingredient floated into the mixture she now poured into the pie shell as a knock landed on the door.

Out of all the parents in Little Tunis there was no question of support from Ennis and Lemon Williams, Zilpha Stokes thought. They were staunch advocates for Timbo's education and continued in the same fashion for Ivoe. She needed only to shore up their faith in the Little Tunis School. She returned the warmth of Ennis's greeting, but before she could give a proper hello to Ivoe, she had scurried off with her coat and hat. Divine aromas piqued her curiosity as she glanced around the cabin. She could see where Ivoe's sense of organization came from and smiled to note several pieces of her schoolwork propped up on the hearth.

Dinner for Miss Stokes was a lavish offering of corn pone, Hoppin' John, hominy casserole, roasted chicken, and the chowchow Lemon was obliged to serve since the teacher had ordered plenty. She placed the jar of relish next to Zilpha's setting and approved her table, recalling one of her mother's sayings: "All good meals call for some sacrifice." The last of the crowder peas, canned at the end of summer, had gone in with the rice and onion for the Hoppin' John and the cracker pudding had finished the cream. She peeked into the oven to see if the pie had puffed, pressing her fingers gently across the top, listening for the crackle. The chess pie was golden brown and perfectly firm, her finest.

Moments of quiet eating pleasure marked by soft murmurs and the occasional scrape of cutlery against glass plates made the hostess content.

Zilpha watched Lemon turn the pie as though the taste depended on the knife's point of entry. Juneteenth picnics, church celebrations, weddings: simple ingredients and a few easy steps meant every woman in Little Tunis made custard pies. Zilpha had eaten them all her life. None rewarded in such creamy comfort as this one. She wished for a smaller fork to stretch the sweet moment.

"I tip my fork to you, Mrs. Williams. I've never had a pie so fit for devouring. How did you come by lemons in March?"

"In the summer, after you've made a batch of lemonade, pack the peel in a jar with about an inch of salt at the bottom and on top. Turns the peel a little orange but otherwise it keeps fine. Nothing to this pie," Lemon said, shooting Ivoe a serious glance.

Ivoe read her mother's face and knew she had better not fidget at the table any longer. She excused herself from supper, disgusted that she would miss anything Miss Stokes said. She was fond of the young woman for many reasons — the way she spoke, how she often reached out to touch you in the middle of a sentence where a comma might go and smiled at the end where a period belonged. Miss Stokes had interesting things to say because she had studied at college and traveled. Miss Stokes was not like Momma and May-Belle, and Ivoe meant to study all of her differences and try them on for size. She hurried to and from the outhouse, only glancing at the bucket of water kept on a hook for hand washing. Still, something important had been missed; it showed in the look on the teacher's face when Ivoe took her seat again.

A shadow of disgust broke across Miss Stokes's face. "Mind you, it was four weeks before the Department of Education sent anybody. When the man finally did show up — with a box of chalk, a bucket, and a dipper — I was truly outdone. I said, 'Mister, what good is chalk without a board? I need assistance in quenching the minds of my pupils, many who are fine readers without books.' Lest he go away thinking Negro students draw from the bucket and play all day. I let him know the department's so-called relief would never do. I sent him on his merry way back to Galveston with the message that the teacher from Burleson County wishes to teach and therefore requires materials — books, pencils, paper. Didn't do a bit good. That's when I posted the signs in town."

The call for magazines and books nailed to every post on Main Street had impressed Ennis. He especially liked the part: "Help me champion the children of Little Tunis whose lives require the power of education if they are to mold their individual character and become sound citizens and able leaders."

"Then yesterday a curious thing happened. I awoke to a barricade of newspapers on my front porch. Stacks as tall as you, Ivoe," Miss Stokes said. "This solves the problem of books for the children. If they can read a newspaper, they can read anything." Pushing aside her clean plate, she withdrew a paper from her bag and handed it to Ivoe. "The next time I see you, I expect you to have read this entire paper and to have written a report on one of the articles. You are one of my best readers and surely up to it."

"Surely she is," Momma said with a look that held the double message: *Take the paper* and *Don't talk back.* "Now, excuse yourself, missy. Teacher gave you an assignment. Get to reading. Let grown folks talk."

Over coffee Miss Stokes's hope dimmed. "I'm losing them. Two of my boys are at the county jail."

"I heard about Peter's boy," Ennis said. "Who the other one?"

"A woman caught Brown's boy kissing a girl behind the train depot. The girl didn't know any better and sassed the woman." Miss Stokes dropped her head a little, her cup catching most of her words.

Ennis shook his head. "You tell them things but they forget. I'm always reminding Timbo about the etiquette laws. He knows holding hands and carrying on in front of white people — even with his own kind — is asking for trouble."

"Those not in trouble are in the fields. Parents are starting to depend on the bit of money the little ones bring in. I mean to get the night school running as soon as I can before I lose them all to sharecropping."

"Where you plan to meet?" Ennis asked, impressed with the teacher's thoughtfulness.

"Lord willing and the creek don't rise, Old Elam Church — if they don't burn it down too. Reverend Greenwood has designated some of the deacons to stand guard outside while the youngsters get their lessons. I do hope you'll send Ivoe back. She is full of so much promise."

In the next room Ivoe crawled into bed with the *Starkville Enterprise,* her mind a tumult of excitement as she pored over the headline above a reprinted letter: "The Worst Insult to the United States in Its History!" Her hunch said the letter, signed by the Spanish ambassador, had something to do with all of Timbo's talk about Little Cuba's troubles. She pulled the covers over her feet. For months she had kept her stolen newspapers a secret. Now she could be seen with a paper any time and no one would wonder how she came by it.

3
COMPANY E

The brisk walk to church filled Ivoe with questions. After Papa told a story or when one of Momma's pies was baking, the quiet felt just right, not like breakfast that morning. She couldn't remember a time the cabin felt so heavy. Papa knew better than to ask Momma to join them for church, but sometimes knowing better and what you want don't jibe and you try anyway. Momma said it wasn't a thing at Old Elam that she needed and Papa should stop meddling her about it. Papa said the word going around was that the preacher had something important to say and this one time she should be with the people. Momma rolled her eyes and mumbled something about the word of Little Tunis.

Only one other time did Ivoe remember her parents put out with each other over religion. Papa reasoned that bringing the children up Momma's way, and by Mom-

81

ma's way he meant Muslim, would make them lonely and children needed lots of folks interested in them. They talked so long, so hard about it till Momma cried. She had asked Momma why she didn't marry a man who loved Allah like she did, and Momma said wasn't none to be married and Papa was a good choice because he was honest and fair and knew how to love. Papa got the same question in reverse. Allah was God, Papa said, "no different. Your Momma think it is and I respect her but ain't no difference." Momma showed her a piece of paper to the contrary, written in a hand Ivoe couldn't recognize. "That's Arabic. Your grandmother Iraj wrote this down for me when I was half your age, working in the cotton fields. Wore it on me every day. It says 'The Holy Qur'an, Surah 2:255: There is no God but Allah, the Ever Living, the Eternal One. Neither slumber nor sleep overtakes Him . . . He is the Most Exalted, the Most Great.' " After that Ivoe got tired of going back and forth between them. She didn't mind parents with two different gods, but she did wonder how the gods felt when Momma and Papa didn't act like spoke and wheel and go along smoothly.

The latch slipped and the church doors flew open. Eager congregants filled the oak benches. Built on the worst of the wetland, Old Elam called for the sturdiest wood for flooring. The trade-off — benches instead of pews — ensured enough blackjack for the tongue-and-groove boards that sloped from the vestibule, through the sanctuary, down to a raised chancel on which the pulpit was located and where the preacher had just closed his Bible. The closing of the Bible at the start of a sermon struck Ivoe as peculiar.

The minister eyed the congregation the way a teacher took silent roll call.

"Church, for a long time now we been shut out of sight, forced to eat in the kitchen — America's most loyal servant hid away from the company. Well, I'm here to tell you it's time to come out of the kitchen and show what it is that we're really about. Not too long ago we was forced to toil at the plow . . . take up the hammer, the hoe, and anything else there was for us to take up. My daddy's traveled on to Glory but I can still see his back bent from where he hauled bales from here to yonder —"

Hands waved, heads nodded, sighs escaped the mouths of elders rocking from side to side, a common gesture whenever they heard the pleasing sound of truth. Everyone watched the country preacher whose hard memories showed in his face.

"— and the blisters all over my mother's hands where the thorn of that devilish stem tore her flesh when she snagged the cotton from the boll. I remember it well. Now, y'all hear me. Any time you're made to do a thing, that thing don't count for much — do it?"

Reverend Greenwood scanned the congregation.

"Sister Fanny, when that niece of yours, Roena, does something for you and you ain't asked her to do, it surely puts her in your favor, don't it?"

"Amen," Fanny said.

"And when you got to tell her to do it even when she do it right it just don't move your heart the same way, do it?"

Fanny shook her head.

"Now in Ecclesiastes, Solomon reminds us that wisdom is better than war, but I believe the president's war can be the great leveler. Church, we can't wait to be asked. We must join in the fight for America, even if she ain't all that she could be . . . 'Cause it just might be our ticket out of the kitchen. Y'all hear me? Don't it get hot in the kitchen?"

Someone shouted, "Yes!" The preacher stood silent.

"Now to shame the devil, I got to tell the truth. Some of us have put the question to ourselves and to each other: Is America any better than Spain? Some of us thinking, If the white man fail in this war, Cuba might be a free Negro republic. And won't that help us a little? That's dangerous, church. We can't fix our minds and hearts on such questions. As Christians we called to a duty. As Americans we called to a duty. We got to serve God and country too. Can't serve one without the other. My name's not Ezra and I'm no prophet but I see this thing clearly: the colored man got to pick up the same gun the white man use to defend his family and country. Then we might stop finding our husbands and sons floating in the creek and hanging from the tree where they ain't got no business being. Church, I say to you: Let us be ready and willing even more than others in the hour of our nation's peril. Thus shall we reaffirm our claim and our right to equal liberty and protection."

Ivoe pulled back her blankets, imagining the big red *E* circled at the top of her paper denoting excellence. She was thinking of her assignment and the comment Timbo made. He said all the talk about war had started with sugar — as important to Little

Cuba as cotton was to Little Tunis. Spain — Timbo told Ivoe to think of the country as Cuba's overseer — was angry that many Cuban sugar plantations did business with the United States, so it imposed high tariffs and that was the root of the trouble. Her brother was good about painting a picture and coloring it with details to make you see it all clearly. During supper Ivoe could hardly eat for listening to Timbo talk about brown-skinned and mulatto folks rebelling against the Spanish. He got so excited talking about the Cuban Liberation Army Momma had to tell him to "hush!" Ivoe asked Timbo why the Cubans were destroying their own land and fighting to death — on account of they were dying of all kinds of strange-sounding diseases. She had never heard of malaria, dysentery, typhoid until Timbo described them. She imagined Little Tunis full of people with chicken pox and measles, which she had already suffered. Timbo said that dignity and freedom would cause you to do anything, even die.

"This will be our first war overseas."

"Remember the *Maine*! To hell with Spain!" Ivoe shouted, reciting a headline from the paper. "Timbo, why do you want to fight?"

"You heard what Reverend Greenwood

said. It's good for a man to help his country."

It was the first time her fifteen-year-old brother called himself a man, and in the light of the lantern that evening Ivoe thought he was beginning to look like one. Later that night she read her letter many times, pleased by how well she had followed Miss Stokes's direction to think of someone specific when writing. Her questions about Little Cuba and the safety of her brother resulted in a letter to the commander in chief himself.

An invasion of the fattest flies he'd ever seen put Timothy off his breakfast. He left the mess tent, patting his breast pocket holding Roena's letter, and ruffled his hair the way she had done the last time he saw her. Bet she wouldn't want no parts of you now, he thought. His hair looked like a feather bed and he smelled like a rotten onion from the neem oil he used to ward off chiggers. The men in his company called him Sweetie, teasing that the only reason those chiggers were after him was because he had too many girls sweet on him back home. Not too many, but one special. Roena had listened to him go on about the expectations and doubts he had for his life until the train whistle sounded. As the first sergeant ordered the crew aboard, he took the train steps by twos, moving down the aisle to his seat with Roena following along on the platform outside, waving frantically.

"Timbo, you forgot my good-bye kiss."

"Ain't it just like a woman to say that after I been kissing on her all day?" He leaned out the window for her hand, catching up her sleeve instead as the train lurched forward, causing him to tear away her button.

"Even if them Spanish don't get you Fanny gonna kill you when you get back. This here's my best dress."

"Least I got something to remember you by," he said with a wink.

The train thundered to a slow pace. Soldiers spilled over him for a last look at the crowd, resounding with cheer. It was more colored and white folks together than any of them had ever seen.

Company E was held at Lakeland, Florida, the first and last site for most colored men who had enlisted to fight. War would have been easier — even if it meant dying — than the backbreaking labor that greeted them. Timothy spent the first month rolling hogsheads because the convicts working cane on the prison farm down the road were too puny to move the barrels, several hundred pounds of sugar each. A week later he was draining the swampland on the estate of someone important. His hands and feet were blistered and torn from long hours slogging through gator holes and pulling dead cypress trunks out of foul water. The list of lackluster chores for all-colored crews was long, but jugging and jawing about it wouldn't increase the three dollars a week he earned, or give him the big adventure stories Roena expected. His letters were short since he left out the truth: he had come a long way just to scuffle with peckerwoods for talking to him any kind of way. The closest he'd come to battle was when a screeching red egret, protecting her eggs, flew out of a mangrove and flailed him with her wings. The thought made him chuckle as he followed the trail of low-grumbling voices behind the tent.

A pair of dice held the gaze of huddled men. Whatever amount of money was covered by the fat hand had made them careless. Gambling so near the sergeant when the beach was half a mile away was foolish. After a while he cussed the heat, laughed at a few jokes, then volunteered to be the fader so that all six could play and he could spot the competition.

They counted the money twice before handing it over. On what was about to be the winner's fourth roll something James Junior said on his sickbed — something about keeping his eye on anybody who threw seven after seven — came to mind.

"Wait a minute," Timbo said, taking his hands off the money, raising them in the air for emphasis. "I believe this rascal done rung in the peeties." Growls passed among the men. A gaunt man turned to the offender and drew his razor. Someone grabbed his arm. "If Sweetie right, ain't no need in you exciting yourself about killing no Spanish. 'Cause you and me fixing to have war right here." The man snatched the dice for inspection, casting a wild-eyed glance that told the cheater he had a minute to leave with his life.

"Give Sweetie the dice," someone called out.

"Ace caught a deuce!" the gaunt man yelled at Timothy's come-out roll and slapped him on the back. "Just stick with it," he advised, "sooner or later that ill wind gonna blow in another direction."

That evening, Timothy chipped at the clay clumps on his boots thinking on the path life had blown him onto. No need in pretending that he was fighting for the same cause as the white boys, who had already left for Tampa on the ship bound for Santiago. No matter where the wind blew Company E it wouldn't be in the direction of battle. Not when they could use them for shit work.

In a few years, he'd leave the cornfields for the mill. He couldn't smith like Papa and had no interest in sawyering like Junior had. Share-cropping hardly allowed for a man to keep his wife and children looking decent. Boots aside, he removed a pair of dice from his shirt pocket and practiced setting them. His throws were short. He could hear Junior say, "You scooting them across the ground instead of letting them tumble and glide like this. You got to control your roll. Tumble and glide." When he could set the dice without looking, he worked on his toss: a rhythmic roll, *tap-skip-tap-tap-skip* to the same mark time after time.

Sundays brought Timbo to Palmetto Beach, rubbing his lucky button, rolling the bones for high stakes. Big winnings and a growing bankroll had made him popular since he could lend money to some of the players. For every three dollars lent, Timbo collected four. "Hi-lo," he bet. Two or twelve, he thought as he shook the dice and let them fly.

"Boy, you take away that kitty, you have enough to build your woman a house," someone said.

The first die skipped twice and landed on six. A six and he had the game. The second die took its time, a pirouette with a triple rotation.

"Corn rows!"

Six and six.

In the unlucky hour that found Timothy with no money, including what he'd put aside for Roena's ring, a loud thud woke Lemon. She nudged her husband. "Ennis, something's going on out there." Maybe one of the chickens had gotten loose. Lemon crawled out from the wool blanket and the heat of her husband's body and threw his coat over her shoulders. In the kitchen she groped blindly for the shovel somewhere in the corner. She crept toward the garden fence, straining to see and tightening her grip on the shovel. "Go on away from there. You hear me talking to you? Go on. Get now. Get!" she hissed, drawing the animal out into the moonlight.

A dog, or something quite pitiful that would be a dog again someday, reclined on its haunches, its rib cage pressed against fur like garlic against its own papery skin. "I guess you don't believe fat meat is greasy. When I say get, I mean —" The mangy thing sprang to his feet, bounding in the opposite direction as the coat slid from Lemon's shoulders to the ground, where she caught it underfoot, stumbled, and fell. "They say hunger pains messes with the mind. It's done surely messed with yours. When I get up from here we gonna find you something to eat. And you welcome to stay. But if you plan on staying we got to get one thing straight: you can't be messing in my garden."

Timbo and Ivoe had both been born in September. This pregnancy came at the worst possible time — when Lemon's garden was not in bloom. To worry a wrong situation into rightness, she took long walks down by the creek, but not without a word from Ennis. "It ain't summer. You fixing to fool around and catch your death out in that cool air." She grabbed at her hips. "Ain't enough cold to freeze all this here meat on me." She had gained more weight with this baby than the others; this too she blamed on the weather. "Nothing to do but sit and eat," she presently complained to May-Belle, who was staying with the family until the birth.

May-Belle chuckled. "Sitting and eating ain't all y'all been doing."

Lemon smiled to herself. With her other pregnancies, by the sixth month she could barely stand Ennis's eyes on her let alone his hands. This time she blamed the baby for the extra sprinkle of sugar in his morning coffee, the care she took with his supper, the gentle filing of his nails. Countless times without knowing how or why she wound up on his path, she arrived at his work cabin, rucking up her skirt as soon as he opened the door.

Lemon glanced over at the woodpile. April's unusual cold called for nightly burning of the hearth. They were down to their last logs. Struggling to fasten the coat over her belly, she wondered about Timbo. "May-Belle, I'm gonna take some air."

She came to a dry gulch lined with sticks and stones as fire shot across her lower back, forcing her legs out beneath her. She crawled into a position that offered little comfort. As soon as the pain lessened she would head home and have her baby. Bunk drew in close, his wet nose against her cheek until he turned his full attention to the drupes scattered on the ground. Not long after his feast began, Lemon let out a high-pitched yowl.

■ ■ ■ ■

Bunk barked at the door.

"Where's Lemon?" May-Belle asked, holding the door open.

Bunk walked backward a few paces.

"Where's Lemon, Bunk?"

He whimpered and shook his body, flinging hulls of a nutlike fruit from his dense cinnamon coat. May-Belle bent down and stared at the porch. She grabbed up a few things and followed Bunk to the hackberry grove. "Look like this one about ready to join us," she said as she and the dog closed in around her writing niece. She put aside the heavy quilt and withdrew a small metal box from her bag, then helped Lemon to her feet. Holding her belly from the underside, Lemon chewed the black cohosh from the tin as she walked to a tree, put her back against it, and squatted over the quilt. May-Belle knelt beside her, tearing off the wet bloomers and kneading the center of her belly. "This baby's right at the door of life." May-Belle never knew the premonitions to be wrong. Even on the walk to the birth site, she had batted away chilly visions. She had not told Lemon or anyone the peace this baby had taken from her, how often dark dreams rended her from sleep in a prickly sweat. The child would have virtue — others would struggle to keep theirs in her presence and she had seen the losing battles.

"Soon come, Lemon. Soon come."

Bunk barked then squealed, digging into the cool spring earth as Lemon's breathing changed to hisses and finally a long, deep groan.

"What we got?"

"Bless your heart, 'cause it's gonna break for this one. Another split tail." May-Belle placed the baby on a square of jute, swaddling her.

Whatever Ivoe intended to say vanished when she saw the baby cradled in her mother's arms. What color was it? Did it have hair? She could hardly wait to see if God delivered the right baby to fit her plan: a little brother brown like her with hair softer than Timbo's — whose hair hurt your wrist just pulling a comb through. With a baby brother, she would remain Papa's only girl, because even though he was tough on Timbo she could make her father see things her way and a little sister would only give Papa too many choices to think about. Baby brother would grow up to be like Timbo, another somebody Papa could wrestle and talk manly to, another somebody Momma could love, and someone she could play with and teach. Just thinking of all the reading aloud and new games she had to play with the baby made her tired.

"Come on in and see what we got," Momma said, staring down at the bundle in her arms.

Ivoe halted. She had been so busy planning for the little fellow she had forgotten to ask God for the most important thing — that he not be born the same color as the Johnson children, who were called a lot worse than Alligator even though they always dressed clean and were smart. She crept to the bed. Please, God, don't let my brother be black as tar — and ugly.

"Them others didn't have no hair, did they? Where in the world did this child get all this hair? That's what I want to know," Momma said to May-Belle as she raised her cradled arms.

"What we gonna call the baby?"

Momma demurred, as though she had forgotten that babies required names. "You know, Ivoe, your momma ain't paid no mind to a name for your sister. You got any ideas?"

A sister?

May-Belle had prayed for this baby like

she had for Timothy and Ivoe, but their prayers were easy because she knew to ask for a strong will for Timbo and courage for Ivoe. She had intended to pray for the infant's peace, yet when she opened her mouth, a crying plea for safe pathways tumbled forth. Now, May-Belle was sure of one thing: "Lemon, look like the way you miss your momma, Iraj is about all you could name her. Give the girl some of her grandmother. She gonna need it."

Late that evening, after delivering her mother a cup of pennyroyal tea, Ivoe returned to the kitchen, where May-Belle stirred a simmering pot: "I know something you don't know," she said.

"A whole lot of folk got more in they heads than May-Belle. Now, what you know good?"

Even her auntie told white lies, Ivoe thought, because it was impossible that anyone knew more than May-Belle, who had mixed the barefoot root with lard and cooked it down to a salve that fixed her sore arm and made the cherry bark tea that brought back Timbo's hunger last autumn. The mayflower balm that, along with time, had healed Papa's burned hand was also her doing.

"Momma named the baby Irabelle."

■ ■ ■ ■

Lemon's mind was full of all she needed to do. "Sugar and jars. Jars and sugar. These folks keep me busy, little one." She took a small handful of peat from a canister and added it to the baby's diaper for absorption. "Either got your momma on her knees planting seeds or on her feet in the kitchen. You think I'm about to work myself into an early grave for these folks?" The words of her complaint curled, revealing the delight with her new orders. In spite of themselves, one by one the women of Little Tunis had given in, especially to her tomato jam. In the beginning it was "Just one jar" from Ivoe, who pulled the red wagon down their road every Saturday morning. Behind closed doors, they made up a rule: Lemon's jam would be eaten when there was nothing else. Nothing else arrived a day or two later. Seals were broken, lids popped and spun off, releasing a delectable aroma. Fingers and spoons dug into the mottled ruby pulp to taste what the dicty woman was all about. No one admitted it to herself, or to each other, but Lemon knew her business. Nothing made a biscuit or cracker taste better or satisfied both a sweet tooth and the hankering for something savory. Worse yet, nothing they themselves cooked made their children behave or their husbands cheery. The problem then became how to get more of the stuff without anyone finding out. They told their children to find Ivoe alone at school — only then were they to give her the money. At church, women grabbed Ennis's hand, placed their hard-earned coins inside, and whispered what kind of jam in his ear. Those childless and without religion took sick so May-Belle would pay them a visit; then they could send the message through her. No one spoke to Lemon about her jams but the orders kept coming.

Lemon pushed her buggy past the mailbox at the edge of the yard and shook her head. No word from Timbo in how long? Her mind traveled all the way to Florida then back to Ivoe. She wanted her to have something nice to wear at the town assembly. For a calico back button dress, she had settled on a floral print and some mint-green material for an apron chemise. With the baby and several new orders to fill there was no time to give the dress an eyelet trim, so she would be sure to buy a ribbon for the girl's hair. She was deciding whether to shop for her cooking or sewing first when two women called out and waved her down.

"Lemon. Lemon, why you all the time in such speedy-hurry? How you doing?" the nosy neighbor said, knitting her eyebrows at the carriage.

"Fine."

"Lemon, you know Annie Faye, don't you? She just come down with her family from Oklahoma."

"We've howdyed but we ain't never shook. Pleased to meet you."

"Ain't no great big secret why you don't know nobody, Lemon. You know how you is. We been trying to friend with you for years. Can't nobody confidence with you 'cause can't nobody catch up to you."

Annie Faye fidgeted with the strap of her pocketbook, then said in a smoky drawl, "God know He love Texas 'cause He surely made His sun to shine bright on us, didn't He?"

Lemon's head started to throb; she ached to run a hand across her abdomen where pools of sweat had nestled beneath her breasts. Who's the bigger fool, you or them? she thought. Standing here fixing to stroke out running your mouth to women you could take or leave. Leave, mostly.

"I see you done finally had that baby."

"Um-hum."

"What the good Lord give you?"

As if you don't already know. "A girl."

"Girls sure is blessings."

"Blessings my foot. They just a mess is what they is. You have a hard delivery?"

Lemon acted as though their steps went unnoticed as she leaned over to pull the cover over the baby's face.

"Can't say I did."

"Well, all three of mines liked to killed me."

Annie Faye laughed.

"Well, y'all, Miss Stokes asked Ivoe to read something she wrote in school at the town assembly. I got to get after some material to make her a new dress for the special occasion."

"Before you go, Lemon, let us see that baby."

"Yes, honey, let us see."

Lemon pulled back the cover, causing Annie Faye to gasp and draw up a hand to cover her raggedy mouth. This was the moment when one or both women should say, "What a pretty brown baby," because that was the compliment all new mothers were given in the Bottoms. Only not a speck of brown was found in the infant's milk skin. This was the season when tiny bumps covered every child in Little Tunis. Why had the sun smiled on this one? Spared her the heat rash. And all that hair. The two leaned in closer, making Lemon stifle her laughter at the picture before her — two grown women climbing into a buggy. Irabelle cooed prettily then. As if she could sense their gawking, her eyes fluttered open. Stunned by the large, glassy eyes that looked blue one second, brownish the next, then purple, the women withdrew themselves abruptly, bumping heads and rocking the carriage. Lemon rolled off with deep satisfaction. Now they knew she and Ennis made them smart and beautiful too.

Soft bustling charged the cabin and excitement clung to the faces of the Williams family. Irabelle cooed. "Even the baby carrying on like she fixing to talk to a crowd." Hearing her father — dressed like the preacher but much more handsome — call a thing like it really was — "talk to a crowd" — made Ivoe nervous as she thought of the day ahead. May-Belle tied her chemise strings in a bow and patted her on the back. Now, with the exception of one, they were ready.

Ivoe watched her mother wrap a long bright green shawl around her shoulders and then cross it over her breasts. She looked every bit the lady as she took up her pocketbook. So as not to muss their finery in the heat, they walked at a leisurely pace, past the shriveled cornstalks and downy fields, along the cracked dirt road that eventually turned into Main Street. As her father opened the door to the town hall, he leaned down to whisper to her, "You smart as a whip and pretty enough to frame today."

Ivoe did not recall ever seeing a Negro girl in Little Tunis with a dress like those she admired in the Sears, Roebuck & Company catalog. She had never looked so fine in her life, down to two braids instead of the usual four, the ends of which were tied with ribbon and, with the aid of the humidity, turned perfectly under. She walked to the front of the auditorium and stood before the lectern, far away from the last seats, filled with the people who mattered most. Shifting from one leg to the other, she flattened her hands against the podium to prevent her voice from trembling, but it was no use. "Dear Mr. President," she began in a voice scarcely heard beyond the first row. She opened her mouth to speak again but the words within her stopped short. What good did it do to know the letter by heart when the muscle inside her chest was too busy pounding away to give up a single word of it? She stared down at the paper as if she had lost her place rather than her courage. Soon it would be lunchtime. Over sandwiches and lemonade everyone would wonder what the letter said that made it so special. She looked up, surprised to see another person standing in the back of the room. May-Belle's eyes shone pure satisfaction the way Papa's had all morning. Ivoe started again, catching the sound of her words and liking it.

The corpulent man wiped sweat from his brow a third or fourth time while congratulating Miss Stokes. As mandated by Texas law, each year he traveled from Austin to attend the assembly in order to judge the teacher's success by her students' abilities. And each year he found her work irreproachable. He was impressed by a teen's dramatic recitation of Paul Laurence Dunbar's poetry and the Caddo boy's memorization of all forty-five U.S. states, but the thoughtful letter to President McKinley read by the little girl before him had moved him most. Her plea that the commander in chief never forget the effort of her brother and men like him and her ideas on how he might protect them overseas were a marriage of simple facts and opinion born of heart. He invited her to read it again at the all-state educators' conference later that summer. "The teacher usually travels with the student to Austin," he said. "We pay the train fare. It's a long day. Sure to be a hot one too. But a day I reckon Miss Ivoe will remember."

Ivoe's eyes widened at the thought of a train ride anywhere, while the beaming Miss Stokes agreed to chaperone her, assuring the man that the invitation was not wasted on a student who possessed enthusiasm, imagination, and diligence. She had noticed the way Ivoe took great pains at getting things right when called to the board; how she deliberated when asked a question; the care she gave to handwriting even though a sentence poorly written could be erased and rewritten, giving the final product a dimensional aspect as if the scrawl might float right off the page.

To keep herself from smiling Lemon shifted the baby from one hip to another, saying, "Well, you want to go? Come on now. Folks got better things to do besides stand around in all this heat while you make up your mind."

"Yes, ma'am. I want to go."

"Fine then. Miss Stokes say she'll take you — I guess that means you going."

Ivoe knew from Sunday school that pride was not a virtue, so she smiled down at her second pair of new shoes in a year. They were white and shiny smooth with one strap over the ankle and a sparkling silver buckle.

Finally, her own news worthy of a headline: "Letter to President Wins Girl Austin Trip!"

4
HOOD, BONNET, AND LITTLE BROWN JUG

JUNE 1905

Slivers of light through the heat-soaked outhouse shone on the smeared purple clot. Ivoe hissed through clenched teeth at confirmation of the ache drawing her abdomen into fitful spasms. She bundled her skirt in one hand to clean the mess. Usually a morning like this found her in the grove — a quilt pallet under a tree, the sun dappling shadows on the pages of a good book or the newspaper. But the day ahead and its ruckus left no time for the novel that had vexed her all week.

At seventeen, she was well practiced at drawing out a book long after its last page. Conversations with the characters in her head helped her hammer out opinions on why the heroine had chosen the wrong lover, or the hero deserved his victory. None of that was possible with *The Clansman,* whose pages shone a light on a dark memory lurking in the back of her mind for years.

She remembered how heavy the house felt back when Mister James and Junior were found dead — how quiet Papa and Momma had been and especially Timbo, who all of a sudden turned manly, coming and going at odd but regular hours. Miss Stokes had given the agonizing read as a graduation present, so she had pressed on with a troubled mind and particular longing to know Reverend Thomas Dixon Jr. — to shake him till his eyes popped from his head. For writing such degrading drivel, he deserved worse. Dixon's Negro characters were shiftless and depraved, when anyone could see that her people had been holding up the sky while white folks walked through the world for a very long time.

Her veil had been lifted. Papa and Momma deserved a prize for shrouding the shameful truth of their lives. Borrowed copies of the *Colored American* and the teacher's recent gift helped Ivoe to see what had been hidden during childhood. Negro life was the worst. Certainly no cause for celebration. She slammed the outhouse door and frowned at the day ahead.

Juneteenth was the high point of summer in Little Tunis — plenty of jugging and jawing about slavery, freedom, and how far they had come. A bunch of hollering up a creek and whistling down a well, if you asked her. The view from their porch was enough to put doubt in anybody's heart. Freedom didn't look any better than this? Up the road in Starkville, now that was another story. The county seat of Burleson County was now home to the largest cotton gin in East Texas. The *Enterprise* boasted that Starkville had ten times as many cotton gins as Snook, yielding a daily output of two hundred bales, but in the drive for profit Ivoe knew of many colored families left behind or lost to poverty. At a sharecropper's graveside Reverend Greenwood would say, "Up the road he was a cotton picker but down here in Little Tunis he was a friend." Adolescence had shown her that a funeral could be a classroom. She learned what a cry meant: family members left behind cried from exhaustion, the increased labor already felt. Sometimes their cries sounded like a wish to trade places with the one in the ground. Scared to death of the future, some wept for tomorrow.

Those who told Earl Stark exactly what they thought of his contracts (impossible rents valued in dollars but figured in cotton like so: one bale of cotton a day, six bales a week, for three rented acres) watched their belongings get tossed into the road, their cabins axed to the ground. Little Tunis homes were fewer, down from forty — when Ivoe was Irabelle's age — to twenty-two.

Juneteenth my foot, Ivoe thought.

The screen door banged shut.

"Somebody think she on vacation," Momma said. "Cooking's almost out the way. Still got three pies to bake so I need for you to bring some coal home from Papa's shed. Make sure you take your sister with you."

Ivoe rolled her eyes. Irabelle's name was never mentioned without nagging duty. She had not minded so much until the Starkville Lyceum granted admission to colored people for two hours on Saturdays, a day most worked, but where on occasion she had seen as many as two brown faces. With no borrowing privileges, Ivoe cherished her time at the lyceum, but it was impossible to get any decent amount of reading done with a seven-year-old.

"Don't you roll your eyes at me. I told your sister she could go see where Papa works today. Timbo took you when you was about her age. Make sure she know the rules before she go in there, you hear? And hurry on back — he ain't gonna be there too much longer 'cause I need him to come finish this brisket . . ." Momma's voice trailed off as she drew up a hand to shield her gaze from the sun. ". . . I ain't got enough to do?" she said as Susan Stark's carriage pulled into the yard.

"Ivoe, that sure is a long face for June-teenth. Lemon, when do you plan on getting a telephone so I don't have to come all the way down here?"

"Well now, Miss Susan, I can think of one solution that don't have me buying something I can't afford and won't put you out neither."

"It's just that I hate to bother you — and on y'all's holiday too," Miss Susan began, holding out a bag. "I brought some of my best things that require mending. Minnie can't sew worth a lick. Get around to them when you can, no hurry. Of course, I'll pay you for your time."

Ivoe shot her mother a hateful glance when she accepted the bag.

Miss Susan drew a hand under her bonnet, dabbed at the corners of her forehead so that when Ivoe brushed past and bumped her arm, the bonnet fell to the floor.

"Momma, I'm gone."

Ivoe paused to consider their route. The shortest way, by Deadman's Creek, would take them through the marsh, but at least she wouldn't have to look at people she had gone to school with, standing shoulder to shoulder with cotton and corn stalks on a day so hot thinking was hard to do. Her time to get away from the Bottoms couldn't come quick enough. She was tired of seeing people drudge, get sick, and die. (Sometimes, as with Mister James and Junior, they were struck down for no reason.) Tired of yearning for the woman she wanted to become, someone who moved through life with self-designed purpose. Conversations with Miss Stokes had helped her uncover her inner world as a source of solace when the outer world presented contradiction and strife. Their chats had emboldened her imagination and helped her to carve a plan. The obvious means to secure the ticket to her future was education. Miss Stokes believed education served those in pursuit of an original life, one that truly suits, so Wiley College and Prairie View State College — known for teacher training and home economics — would never do. Even a life like that of Miss Stokes, whose energy and ability she admired, was not the life for her. The two-year course at Willetson Collegiate and Normal Institute offered commercial courses in typing, shorthand, book-keeping, and, of particular interest to Ivoe, printing. If she worked hard enough, one day she might operate a press at a newspaper as far north as Chicago, as far east as Boston.

"Why we come this way?" Irabelle asked no sooner than she spotted something jutting out from the underbrush. Momma was learning her to whipstitch. After she washed the dingy gore and made it sparkly white again, she could make a jam for Dollbaby. She had soaked the green husk of Dollbaby's face in coffee grounds until she was as dark as Papa, then used honey to glue on corn silk for hair. But no matter how careful she was, by day's end Dollbaby was baldheaded. The least she could do was make a dress for her, Irabelle thought, slapping the cloth against her skinny leg to remove the dirt.

Suddenly, Ivoe lunged at her.

"Stop messing with things that don't belong to you," Ivoe snapped in such a way Irabelle knew better than to challenge it. Instead she took off running because nothing burned up Ivoe more than having to chase her.

Ivoe tossed the hood to the ground and took off after her sister. Hearing a woman's

114

wail, the two stopped. Soon there were other voices, which they followed beyond the cypress trees to a gang of black-skinned women swinging axes under the glaring sun. Their axes dropped against the chopping block in harmony. Falling wood chips syncopated the voices singing, *Let your hammer ring! Let your hammer ring!* "You better watch-a my timber!" a voice boomed. *Let your hammer ring!*

For Irabelle the day was full of excitement: her first visit to Papa's shed, where he disappeared for too many hours, coming home like a boo-hag or something that terrified little children when they got out of hand. The picnic promised all kinds of sweets. And now, the sawing, piling, chopping women whose voices made her want to dance.

"Sure is some pretty singing. Why you sing like that?" Irabelle asked, though she meant how do you sing like that.

"Got to — make the time go by more faster."

"Takes you away from here," someone grumbled, raising her ax to the wood in perfect measure.

"What y'all doing?"

"Minding their business," Ivoe said.

"Earl Stark building his own private

115

railroad to haul cotton over to Brazos County. We got to scatter this timber so the mens can lay new rail. Without piling, them tracks just gonna sink 'cause this here swampland."

Soiled cotton would serve Earl Stark right, Ivoe thought, gently pulling her sister away. "Come on, Irabelle. Don't have no business in a smith's cabin no way," she said when they were back on course.

"It ain't your business nohow."

"It is my business when Momma takes my time away from me to carry a certain black-eyed squint someplace she don't belong."

"I can stand more trouble than anybody your size."

"Girl, do you remember the rules?" Ivoe said, half exasperated, half tickled. "Last thing Papa need is for you to rub against something and hurt your fool self."

"Number one, all tools are sharp and will cut. Number two, all work pieces can burn. Number three . . ."

Lemon pulled down the oven door to cool the pound cake.

"That Miss Susan leaving when I come?" May-Belle said.

"Yeah. She had dresses to mend. Talking about Minnie can't sew worth a lick."

"Well, she knowed that when she give her your place. They having troubles?"

"Is eggs poultry?"

May-Belle laughed as Lemon wiped her hands on her apron and picked up the letter. Eight days ago when the package arrived from Willetson Collegiate and Normal Institute, Ivoe had skimmed the letter, letting it drift to the ground while she took off like a bolt of lightning out the door for Miss Stokes.

Lemon carried the letter out to the yard, where she sat against her favorite tree and read it over until she knew it by heart. No orders were filled that day; she was too excited by the catalog she now showed to May-Belle, who sat picking greens. "My head ain't big enough to wrap around all what's here. No telling what Ivoe fixing to do. Don't look for her to be no school-teacher. Too flighty to sit in a room of books like a librarian. Ain't got the stomach for sickness, or the heart for the way being sick changes a person. Can't be no nurse. Listen, May-Belle. Listen at this." Lemon read from the catalog, all bright and singsongy, " 'Students should dress for health and comfort and not for show. Special dresses for special occasions are not necessary. This institution does not wish to encourage expensive dressing.' But that still leave . . . What this list say? One sheet, pillow slip, dresses — at least four — one skirt, underwear, two nightgowns, an apron, shirtwaist, towels, and handkerchiefs."

"What we can't make you'll get one way or another," May-Belle said.

A picture she'd seen a thousand times flashed before Lemon: Ivoe in the kitchen reading, sometimes putting the book or newspaper aside to stare out the window. God only knew what the child thought about. Sometimes the tomatoes needed stewing, or Lemon needed to get to the table to cut something up, but she just hated to bother her. Not that Ivoe took up much room, long and skinny like she was. Just seemed like her thinking needed all that space. She didn't care what it took; Ivoe would show up to Willetson with everything on that list. But damn if she knew how. "Already sent a money order down to Austin so they can hold a spot for her. The scholarship nearabouts covers it all. *Ssth.* May-Belle, I tell you, if I had known that nearabouts would leave so much to come up with I might've told that girl to fix her mind on cleaning houses or something. That bill what come here liked to made me faint. I showed it to Ennis. He give it right back to me. He say, 'Ivoe can wait awhile — she ain't got to go just yet.' Say Ivoe already got more schooling than most folks in Little Tunis. Well now, May-Belle, don't tune up your face. He right about that."

"What what other folks got and what Ivoe need got to do with each other? If it ain't up to you and her papa to see to it that she get what she need, who it up to?"

"I know you right. It's not like she don't deserve it. Times I thought I'd forget how the child looked — face always stuck in a book. Folks been good enough to pay up front for orders because they know Ivoe be leaving soon. Running out of room out there just planting for the orders let alone planting for us. Ennis say it ain't right to make the whole family suffer for Ivoe's schooling."

"What did you say to him?"

"I told him we don't all the time have to agree but on this here he got to stand with me on the side of right. It'd be wrong not to let that girl go. Just don't seem right, though, Ennis's money carrying us the short distance it do."

"Life ain't nothing but a peck of trouble to a pint a joy," May-Belle began. "If you can handle your garden and my little plot, seem like you'd have plenty then."

Lemon sifted sugar into a wooden bowl holding soft butter and vanilla and started to whisk. "I appreciate it. Won't be no peace around here until that school bill's paid. Owing peoples ain't never sat right with me. Can't rest good when I do. Them devilish taxes got me feeling like some big bear after me. Ennis the same way, excepting when he owe a man he commence to acting ornery. A person can't do or say nothing right around him. I asked him once why he got to gripe so. He say, 'A dollar's no different than a shackle. Owe one, you in the other.' Well, with your garden and mine too I can feed my family. That fix the future. But what about the present? Ivoe ain't got but two dresses. One ain't fit to wear out the yard — poor thing been darned and mended to death. You love your children more than they can ever know. I mean, they can't never best you in the loving department. But they sure can make you proud."

"You stop carrying on about how she gonna get everything. Look how far we done come," May-Belle said, pointing to the letter. "Look how far we done come."

May-Belle's memory stretched back fifty-five years when she arrived in the Brazos River Valley with her husband, Bukhari; his second wife, Iraj; and twenty-eight bonds-women and men who survived the hellish passage from the Kebbi River to America aboard the *Clotilde*. Starkville was nothing but a seed in the spring of 1859 when Alfred Stark was contracted four leagues and a labor of land (17,890 acres), which promised plentiful corn and cotton, in exchange for bringing sixty German and Moravian families from South Carolina and thirty-one Arabized Africans from Alabama.

In Alabama, Stark paid no mind to Bukhari's true name. He studied the scars — three lines from forehead to chin on each side of the face — looked at the ledger, and called him Booker. Took a lot of calling for Bukhari to step forward. Stark clamped the pliers he would never be seen without on Bukhari's bottom lip and pulled until his eyes welled. When they arrived in the bot-tomlands, many more bondspeople lived in small shacks along the river, but they spoke in the same tongue as the white men lash-ing them. Sunup to sundown confusion — dangerous fear, fights in the cotton fields whenever the *Clotilde* Muslims ceased work to pray. (Her first learned English words had been "Pick up your sack.")

Stark hired Booker out to the Snook foundry, where he could fetch more fitting metal than he would picking cotton. Booker was the only town bondsman Stark had. After the drowning of the twenty-eight, after some time had passed, he took white-folk-decent to him: "This ain't Hausaland and I ain't none too keen on friending no Muslim. Things be all right if you act right . . . same holds for your women, Iraj and Mehriban . . . Don't let me hear you talking that talk." Stark let him keep a dollar or two of his own money and fixed it so Booker's women worked in the big house and picked cotton only half a day during harvest.

Her name was still Mehriban the first year. Alone with the trees, studying their bark, tasting the leaves, she watched trade ships up from the Gulf unload dry goods in exchange for cotton until Bukhari arrived with the portion of his love meant for her. He gave a different part to Iraj, whose only child she birthed their first December in Little Tunis. The Kebbawa called a girl born at night Leila, but this one was the color of a lemon.

Word carried on the wind in April 1865 that Negroes were free. One of Stark's bondswomen took the rumor to heart and tried to set fire to the cotton field. They had a way of dealing with the wild ones. They were all marched to the creek that swallowed the twenty-eight in 1860 to watch a white man drown her.

The truth came again on the nineteenth of June — high cotton time. Everybody had to work the fields. Iraj, Mehriban, and four-year-old Lemon were the first to lay down their sacks and watch Pete, who'd brought the freedom word, jumping through the field. Iraj took Lemon's hand and headed for the blacksmith shop, where she found Booker at the bellows, wiping sweat from his face, the blue black of a ripe plum and just as smooth. Her words fell like drupes from a sugarberry tree. *"Ashhadu anna Muhammadan rasul-ul-lah . . .* Bukhari. We are all free." At the same time, the cook untied her apron, laid it on the counter, and vowed to find her mother somewhere in Georgia. Iraj agreed to cook for the Starks so long as Lemon received tutoring with the Starks' only child, Earl. Bukhari struck a deal with Mr. Stark. He promised his best smithing if Stark allowed him to earn the house he lived in and the little bit of land Iraj made pretty with flowers and vegetables. He wanted the same amount of land and the hut by the river for his second wife, Mehriban. Stark agreed but his trouble was far from over.

Stark was used to getting good labor from

a mean word or the shake of a noose and was surely put out by negotiating with freed people, who were beginning to see share-cropping for what it really was. Many left the Bottoms unsure if they would survive the journey to God only knew where. After the Freedmen's Bureau refused rations for those who refused to work or couldn't, the strong ones lived off the land for as long as a seed could be found. The elders suffered till death, bewildered that they had lived to see freedom and would die hungry because of it.

Many expected that part of the valley to perish and did their part to help death along. Soldiers stationed to ease the transition took food and anything else they could carry away, including girls and women. Little Tunis made a ruckus till they found Black Pete, the logger, floating in the creek with a pair of chicken feet where his eyes used to be and his thing stuffed in his mouth. At Old Elam Baptist Church they mumbled that the Good Book had lied; the meek surely wouldn't inherit the earth.

If not the earth, in 1905 it seemed they had inherited some other fortune, May-Belle thought. Today marked forty years of freedom. Lemon was forty-four, Ennis forty-six. Timbo wasn't in the county jail.

Despite her visions, Irabelle was a happy child, beloved by other children, so maybe she didn't notice when grown women sucked their teeth or rolled their eyes when she passed. And Miss Ivoe was on her way to Austin, proof of something they used to say back in Alabama: "Sometimes it takes generations for opportunity to come, but if you keep on living, it will show up."

Balancing an armful of pies, Lemon glanced around her yard. Three children, each having their own way with her heart: Timbo twisting it in worry; Irabelle stirring it in wonder; and Ivoe making it beat wild with pride.

"Got a lot to be grateful for this year," she said to Zilpha Stokes. "Our girl's on her way. And don't think I don't know it's 'cause you been more than a teacher to her these years — you been a friend. Me and Ennis appreciate you taking the time with her, telling her things we don't have half a mind to tell her. Helping her to school and all."

At that moment, she saw Ennis welcome the Al-Halif family as they entered the yard.

"Mrs. Williams, Ivoe was made at home. You and your husband did all the molding. The most I ever did was clear the bramble off her path," Zilpha said.

Irabelle ran laughingly between her mother and the teacher, chased by the Al-Halifs' daughter and a little boy with skin like a bruised peach and golden hair. He belonged to a Moravian family newly arrived in Starkville.

"Times sure have changed, ain't they? Go on and fix yourself a plate, Zilpha. Plenty to eat," Lemon said, as she watched Timothy pull something from his shirt pocket and wave his hand before two young men she did not recognize. When they started away from the house she called out, "Timbo, time for you to eat. Say good-bye."

"They just some fellows passing through from Bryan," Timbo said, as he crossed the yard in her direction.

"You talking sugar but you giving salt. Just 'cause they both white don't mean they taste the same. Passing through, my foot."

"All right, Momma. They just come to tell me about a game. The dice level out my thinking."

"Boy, you grieve me. All the time chasing the wrong things so the right things can't catch you. Papa told you. I told you. Leave them devilish dice alone. Don't play with Roena, Timbo, that ain't the thing to do. Gonna fool around and lose that girl."

A gleam in his eye brighter than the North Star, Timothy tucked a coin in her apron pocket. As long as luck was with him, that boy wouldn't pay her no mind. Afraid to try but not scared enough to lose and he didn't even know the difference.

"I done said what I had to say. I'm gone away from it."

Later that evening Lemon stood on the porch between Ennis and May-Belle with a little brown jug.

"Zilpha, you want a taste of this whiskey? Maybe that one over there will fetch you a glass. You ain't in Austin yet, missy," Lemon called across the yard to Ivoe, reading the newspaper.

Before Ennis could put down the jug, Irabelle was at his feet, tugging on his pant leg to remind him of their routine. The first taste belonged to her, but because it was Juneteenth he nudged the bottle with the toe of his shoe to say she could have the last swig too. Irabelle jumped off the porch, her hair flowing like raven yarn. She twirled and blew into the empty jug, thinking of the women loggers down by the creek. Everyone clapped except Lemon.

Irabelle was a pretty child with few traces of her or Ennis. Except for the creamy skin of golden corals she was every bit of Lemon's mother, Iraj, down to the small mouth and pronounced cheekbones. Her beauty was the easy kind. Folks gave themselves over to it quickly. But quick as looks caught them, looks could lose them. She wanted her daughter to cultivate something besides the accident of features, something that would earn loyalty, kindness, and make the right people want to be around her. Irabelle craved no more attention than her other children had at that age, but she was too young to know the trouble beauty brings. Beauty cowed folks too weak to resist it, embarrassed those shamed in their own skin. Irabelle was courting envy, inviting confusion, and didn't even know it.

"All right, all right now," Lemon gruffed. "Folks didn't gather on this pretty day for you to entertain them." She beckoned for the jug and rolled her eyes at Ennis. "I don't know what you give it to her for. Ain't done nothing but made extra work for me. Come morning, I'm liable to find that jug in pieces all over the yard."

Irabelle slipped past her mother's reach and scampered over to Timothy and Roena.

"You best give it to Momma, lessen you want one of them boo-hags to get you 'cause you at the age when they like to snatch little girls bald," Timbo said.

Irabelle's eyes grew big as saucers.

"You seven, ain't you?"

"Yep. Old enough to know ain't no such a thing as a boo-hag."

"Just wait and see."

"Ivoe?" Irabelle said anxiously.

On the pallet beneath the fig tree, Ivoe was reading the paper. The headline gasped: "Shocking Incident in Snook! Negro Man Robs Widow!" A complete account of the crime scene included a full description of the perpetrator, who sounded to Ivoe like every man she knew in Little Tunis.

"Ivoe!" Irabelle repeated.

"Don't pay Timbo no attention. The butter slipped off his noodle a long time ago," Ivoe said.

Roena chuckled.

"Some folks all right till they get two pairs of britches," Timothy muttered in Ivoe's direction.

"Papa, ain't no boo-hags that take girls' hair, is it?"

Ennis tore off a piece from the hunk of brisket on his plate, looked down at Bunk waiting expectantly, and flung it. "Well, let me see. How good is your ciphering? When was Ivoe your age?"

"Nine years ago," Irabelle chimed.

"Far as I can remember your sister never

did lose no hair. Leastwise not to no boo-hag. I believe once she might've lost a bit wrestling with some Indian children."

May-Belle and Lemon laughed.

"That rascal Timbo just pulling your leg. 'Cause even if it was a boo-hag after you, Papa would just get a ghostdog to take care of it. Papa told you about ghostdogs, didn't I?" Ennis sat his plate on the porch, leaned forward, and rubbed his knees the way he did every time he was about to settle in for a story.

Irabelle shook her head, cautiously eyeing Bunk as he stretched out. Sometimes the boys in the churchyard talked about haint dogs, she recalled, climbing into her father's lap.

Ivoe closed the paper and sat up. To hear her father tell a story was to witness great art. His voice resonated with power, wrapping itself around the listener like a quilt on a cold night, while his big hands painted vivid pictures to match his words, sturdy like oak — words you could live in until the warm baritone caught fire; then you were sure to burn in excitement.

"Used to be Saturday was the day cotton pickers would come from all around and have a slap-bang-up time jugging and jawing just like we doing today. While the sun was making up its mind on when to set, somebody would commence to playing on the banjo or the fiddle. Nobody never did the musician no dirt about paying him neither. He could count on getting at least a dollar for the night. Sometimes we danced till the rooster crowed on Sunday morning. May-Belle, you remember what we used to say? We had us a saying back then: 'If a white man could be a Negro in the Bottoms just one Saturday, he never would want to be white no more.' "

May-Belle let out a lazy laugh where the first note was drawn out like the final whistle of a freight train.

"Once, a fiddler was late getting off from Snook on account of he brought his baby brother with him. See, they momma had just died and they daddy was working all the time, so the fiddler had to keep the little one with him."

Irabelle nestled against her father's warm chest that vibrated when he spoke, tickling her back a little. Momma had just the right words to fit Timbo. Even if he didn't mind her all the time, he listened. May-Belle and Ivoe had their own special talk; you could tell it by all their private laughter. But Papa melded words just for her.

"Well, they's traveling and the fiddler's

getting a little tired, but he don't wanna stop because he worried about reaching the Bottoms late. See, he don't want nobody bird-dogging for the dance he fixing to play for. Well, the fiddler's baby brother commenced to looking real pitiful and starts in with how his little legs is aching him. Fiddler know he can't hardly make it with the boy, but where in the world can he leave him?"

Irabelle curled her fingers around one of Papa's ears, burying her other hand in his coarse hair.

"The fiddler scratched at his head." Ennis scratched his own head. "What was he gonna do? That's when he noticed an ole cottonseed house a piece-ways down the road. He was plum tickled about finding a place to leave baby brother, so he snatched the little rascal up like this here" — he grabbed Irabelle around the waist, holding on to ensure she didn't fall from his lap — "and took off running. When they reached the house his tongue was hanging out his mouth just like a dog what been chasing a rabbit. He takes his brother by one hand, his fiddle in the other, and climbs up the ladder and through the window. Cottonseed piled so high in there — almost to the top of the ceiling — that baby brother barely have room to stretch hisself out. He finally get fixed so he can lay down. Fiddler gives him a paper sack with some ginger snaps in it and tells him he'll be right back. Now, the fiddler ain't been gone but a minute when baby brother hears a puffing noise and raise his head to see what the trouble is. What you reckon he saw?"

Irabelle hunched her shoulders. She couldn't bear to delay the story with guess-work.

"A great big ole puff of smoke come through that window and scared baby brother, so he commenced to shaking like the front wheel of your papa's cart. Took him a long time to get up enough courage to look. What you think he saw this time? A great big white dog was looking down at him. Scared him so bad he started in to hollering and peed hisself too. He thinking that dog gonna bite him for sure, maybe even carry him off somewhere and he won't never see his big brother again. But the dog stayed right where he was. Didn't budge an inch. Didn't make a sound. Finally, the little boy see the dog don't act like he got any interest in biting him so he doze off. His brother's fiddle wakes him up. Ghostdog still standing over him too. But before the fiddler reach the house the dog turn into smoke again and floated out the window. When the fiddler climbed in, baby brother told him what happened. His brother allowed that the dog was they momma what done come back from the grave to keep a watch over the little one so he could earn a little money playing music for the cotton pickers to dance."

The Williamses lounged beneath a cornflower-blue sky all afternoon. The chickweed grass, coarse and brilliant green, gave the earth a spongy feel beneath Ivoe, who lay stretched out with the newspaper over her stomach. The branches of a blackjack oak stirred a slight breeze for Roena and Timothy while they played cards in the fleeting twilight. Lemon crossed before Ennis's chair, causing his eyes to light up like stars as he reached out to pat her behind. Irabelle, playing in May-Belle's hair, watched a jaybird flutter away from the fig tree just as Bunk rolled onto his stomach, extending his forepaws on the porch he dusted with a fanning sweep of his tail. For a moment nothing stirred except now and then the call of a screech owl. They didn't have much but this happiness was their own.

Momma could look at a long face all day

without it getting to her, Irabelle thought, but Papa was different. A poked-out mouth and droopy chin did the trick. "Come on then — with your sad face on." Her first time away from Little Tunis marked a special occasion. Momma had even let her wear her best Sunday go-to-meeting dress — pink polka dot cotton with scalloped red-work trim — to escort Papa to Snook.

After Papa's business, they strolled about town hand-in-hand. On Snook's Main Street she heard the sweetest sound coming from the shop on the corner. Papa must've liked it too because he stopped to listen. On account of the hawthorn hedge, which she recognized by its little white flowers that would give way to tiny red berries come fall — one of Momma's favorites — she couldn't get close enough to the window, so Papa picked her up for the first time since she was five, two years ago. Together they watched the wood box with a plate spinning 'round and 'round beneath a giant golden bellflower.

"How you think them tiny people got in there? See, it's iddy-biddy people no bigger than your pinky toe down there making that pretty music come out."

Irabelle let Papa pull her leg while she wondered about the music. This was noth-

135

ing like the singing and moaning she heard at Old Elam Church — no banjo plucking, or whining fiddle either. The shopkeeper said it was an *a-ree-ah* from an opry called *Bow-He-Men Girl.* She didn't know what a Bow-He-Men Girl looked like or did, but from that day forward she was going to be one — unless Ivoe told her that was no kind of thing for a colored girl to be. Ivoe was always telling her what she ought to want to be and do.

"That right there sounds like the wind whistling pretty to me," Papa said. You could tell he didn't know about opry either. The shopkeeper said a clarinet made that pretty whistling sound.

"I want a clarinet."

Ennis recalled Juneteenth when Irabelle had played the little brown jug. The tax bill was coming due but his decision was made. "Sir, how much for the music and that what you play it on?"

The clerk glanced at the money in Ennis's hand and laid his newspaper aside. Generally he didn't do any dirt by Negro customers because their money spent like anybody else's. The *Snook Chronicle* was to blame. Every day for the last week some Negro's face was blasted on the front page accompanied by a story about a robbery, a fire, or some kind of mischief. He told Ennis to hold on while he got everything together and disappeared to the back room. In his call to the sheriff, he described his customers as well-dressed Negroes with more money than a Negro ought to have. He wrapped the Edison Home Phonograph and returned to the front of the store.

There was the usual hem-hawing about the heat between the shopkeeper and the deputy while the sheriff studied Ennis. His hands were blistered and calloused; he'd picked enough cotton for three people. "A Victrola's mighty frivolous, boy." He eyed the pretty little girl whose legs, the color of wheat stalks, put him in the mind of a beautiful boy he knew in his youth. The sheriff turned Irabelle away from the phonograph and patted her head. Hair as soft as Ory's had been. Squatting at her feet, his gaze met with the most extraordinary dark violet eyes. He tried to soften his own face to coax a smile from the child, but she only stared back at him, twisting the ends of her dress. He unfastened each finger from the dress bottom and, gripping the edges himself, pulled the dress taut.

Irabelle wobbled a little.

"You like music?"

Irabelle turned to look at her father. Papa nodded so she did the same.

"You got a name?"

"Irabelle," she whispered.

The simple action of rising to his feet seemed to require effort from the sheriff. He had been at the jailhouse very late last night keeping watch over two colored boys. Then, like now, his lust had surprised him. Instead of pouring out for his wife, it seemed only to spring forth for the most pitiful. He yanked Irabelle in front of him, his hands on her shoulders like heavy weights, and looked at Ennis.

"Who are you, boy?"

"Ennis Williams, sir. That's my youngest child there, Irabelle. We from Little Tunis." Wasn't no shame in being a colored man, but it sure in the hell was tedious at times. For every question they asked you, you better give at least three answers.

"What's your business in Snook?"

"I'm a blacksmith, sir. Come to collect my pay on a job I did for Mr. Jacobson. My baby girl ain't never seen these parts, so soon as my business ended we set in to take in your town."

The county jail never stayed so full as it did in June, thought the sheriff. Something about Juneteenth made Negroes step out of

138

line. "Whereabouts you say you from?"

"Little Tunis —"

"Them darkies that live in the bottoms of Starkville," the deputy added.

The sheriff leaned down to Irabelle's ear and said in a kindly voice, "Your daddy's fixing to buy some music so you can listen at home. I bet you'd like that. Wouldn't you?" The sound of her "yes," bright as a bell, could have belonged to Ory. He gripped the bony shoulders too hard before turning his attention back to Ennis. "You say you was here doing work for Jacobson?"

"Yes, sir. A little ironwork out at the ranch."

"He pay you enough to buy all this here? Deputy, you ever knowed Jacobson to pay so much?"

"Well, sir, I'm doing all right for myself. You ask anybody in Little Tunis they vouch for me. I'm a hardworking man. And I never goes nowhere without no money."

"I bet you is what they call a hardly working man. Ain't no need in worrying about money 'cause what you can't earn you can just steal. Ain't that right?"

"No, sir. I don't steal and my family don't steal. We works for what we needs and what we wants."

"Deputy, name me one Negro you know

above lying."

"Can't say I can, Sheriff."

"You see, boy," the sheriff started in Ennis's direction. "We had us a most unfortunate incident here in Snook a week ago. A widow had her wedding ring stolen, her finger plum tore off by a thieving Negro man. A hardworking blacksmith like you, after you melted it down, I imagine you fetched a pretty penny for it. Ain't that right?"

Ennis gulped. From the corner of his eye he saw the deputy reach into his holster. If he grabbed Irabelle and ran, they'd shoot him. And Lord only knew what they might do to her.

"Now, sir, I wasn't nowhere near Snook a week ago. I only been here once this year and that was on May twenty-seventh and May twenty-eighth." His voice was soft and steady. "I got my own money what spend like everybody else's. We don't want no trouble."

"I'll tell you how this is gonna go. I'm fixing to have my deputy check to see if you got the ring on you. Maybe you come back to return it 'cause you got some kind of conscience. I'll search the child myself."

Irabelle lurched toward her father but the sheriff pulled her closer, his hands trembling as he groped her back and shoulders.

It was very long ago but the sheriff remembered still. Running down to the smokehouse every Saturday evening after ten long hours in the fields with the other orphans. The colored boys he picked cotton with numbered six; he was the only white one, which meant he got special attention or none at all. More than anything, he liked to watch what went on behind the smokehouse, where arguments over who would touch whom ended in a group circle. Colored boys were something to look at. They came in all colors and sizes, but none was as perfect as the youngest, Ory — an angel from the Bible, except he was better than pale (too deathlike), he was the color of butterscotch. Whenever the sheriff closed his eyes there was the picture to beat all pictures, still: Ory with his britches midthigh while the others worked to make that angel face break. By his fourteenth birthday, the sheriff had the courage to demand his turn with Ory in the circle. He trembled in delight as Ory unbuttoned his pants, oblivious to the gunshots. Three or four rang in the air like angry church bells while someone yelled, "Get — you nasty boys." He didn't care about meeting his maker if it

141

meant he could touch Ory, but the boy took off.

"Please, sir, we didn't come for no ugliness," Papa said, twisting in the deputy's hold.

Irabelle felt the buckle of the sheriff's belt knocking against her back.

"I ain't got nothing she ain't seen before or won't see soon enough, pretty as she is." The sheriff pulled her head back and shoved two fat fingers into her mouth. He poked under her tongue, along the sides of her jaws, the back of her throat, making her gag while Papa did nothing. If the sheriff had asked she would've told him she would never try to eat a ring. At school a little boy had choked on a marble and almost died. The belt buckle clanged faster. She was going to get a whipping in a store by a white man and Papa wasn't doing a thing about it. Her knees felt weak. Maybe the sheriff's did too because he gripped one of her shoulders even harder now. Papa's growl sounded worse than any sick animal she ever heard. He sobbed words she did not understand. And then the sheriff released her.

Papa groaned as the deputy let him go and Irabelle ran over to him.

"No ring."

A few miles beyond Snook, Papa drew his cart to the side of the road. "Don't you never tell nobody about what happened." He squeezed her shoulders, forgetting his strength, until she began to cry. "You hear me?"

"Yes, Papa."

Everything about the trip was horrible, Irabelle thought an hour later as her father lifted her from the seat down to the ground in their yard. Now Papa hated her dress. No spills or dirt anywhere, but before she could reach the steps, he made her take it off. She stepped out of the dress and ran to the cabin. She wondered why Papa lied to Momma that evening. She had not torn the dress so badly that it was beyond mending.

September nightfall brought no reprieve from the heat. Ennis hammered the ground, blinking back perspiration. He dabbed his forehead with the back of his hand, turned his head, and caught the full length of the man's body. The man must've been blind to miss a boulder that big. Must've been driving the horse too hard and fast 'cause when Ennis came up on the cart it was a pile of lumber and the man was crumpled up against the tree. Looked like his arm and leg were broken. "Take my horse, go into town, and get help," the man said. Horse was hurting but it would be all right. Ennis thought about ripping the shirt off the man's back to plug the hole bleeding from his head when he saw a small black case on the ground near a wheel still spinning on its axle. In fits and starts, the man explained that he had been on his way to Caldwell to play at a circus.

Ennis screwed the three wooden pieces together, but blowing into it didn't sound like much of nothing. "This a clarinet — ain't it?"

Ennis wondered if anyone had seen him leave his shed that evening. Wasn't nothing for a Negro to up and disappear, but sooner or later they'd come looking for this man.

"See, you can't all the time do what you got a mind to do, even if you thinking with your right mind. You laying there thinking I'm studying on you with my wrong mind. It ain't that. Can't take you to May-Belle's. She liable not to be home and ain't gonna do me a bit of good to get caught with a ailin' white man. I could tell it just like what you and me know to be true and they still gonna find some wrong in it. Can't help you, sir."

He couldn't end the man's life or leave him there to rot. It took a few hours for the

144

bleeding to kill him. Ennis used a rock to hew out a grave, took the clarinet, and started for home.

5
GUILLOTINE
SEPTEMBER 1905

Motes of dust rode a beam of autumn sunlight through the train window. Hardly an auspicious beginning, Ivoe thought, as she twisted uncomfortably, careful not to snag her skirt on the splintered bench. Her long legs dangled over a battered leather valise the color of burnt butter, stuffed with books and every item on the Willetson list, including three long dark skirts made of poplin and pongee, donated by Miss Susan, who had once been twenty-six inches at the waist. Her seatmate (wide as a safe) reached into his vest pocket, poked her in the ribs, and decapitated several flowers from the bunch laid across her lap. *Push, push, went the rude man, fumbling with his tin of cigarettes.* By the time they reached Austin, the porter would have to peel her off the window. Colored people paid the same fare as whites, yet they were packed into a filthy passenger car half the size of the adjoining coach for travelers of a fairer hue. (And with the added indignity of no lavatory.) Yet when the white coach overcrowded, a white man traipsed past her to an old colored man who gave up his seat with no prompting. How did colored people live with the brunt of these inconveniences posing as law? Ivoe wondered as she leaned against the window, nearly tasting the fig jam that sealed her memory.

Seven years ago when Miss Stokes shared her Newtons during the train ride to Austin, Ivoe quelled her excitement by sweeping her tongue against the roof of her mouth where the soft, sweet cookie had melted. Now she swept jittery nerves into a corner of her mind with a bundle of memories woven tight like the finest of her mother's homemade brooms. After reading her letter to President McKinley at the all-state educators' conference in 1898, they had strolled Congress Avenue, teeming with streetcars, shops, and fancily clad people. At the Soda Fountain they could not enjoy their drinks in the cool of the parlor, so they stood beneath the awning, escaping the sun's glare but not its heat. Between sips of Vernors ginger ale, Ivoe peered through the window at the whirring fans cooling white customers, listening as Miss Stokes went on about promises. "If you make just one to yourself and keep it, it will be a lifelong comfort to you."

A return to Austin seemed as good a promise as any. Now as the train rounded the curve, shutting Starkville from sight, she thought of her last moments with her family. When Timbo passed the house on his way to work, she was feeding chickens in the backyard with Irabelle. His jump-atcha gave her a fright that made her holler. He teased her about being so scared all the time; she called him a fool and they laughed too loud for so early in the morning. Before leaving, Timbo told her about something he'd seen years ago on a Florida beach. "You can't see the end lessen you cut it down. The sun can't wither it, fire can't burn it, and moss can't cling to it. When a strong wind come, it just bends — lays all its fans out till the wind lets up. You remind me of that cabbage palm, Ivoe. You might have to bend a little but you ain't never gonna break." That's how it was with Timbo. Lord knows he could act foolish and ornery, but whenever her brother said she could do something she believed him. The ride into town with Papa and Irabelle was silent — creaky cart wheels on a dirt road. Momma waited by the tracks at the train depot, a bunch of yellow primroses in her hand. "Probably wilt on the train in all this heat. You be in my thoughts much longer." She hugged her tight and whispered, "Baby, you going places I didn't have sense enough to dream about."

Once again, heart and head thrilled to the excitement of Congress Avenue, where Ivoe hailed a colored livery. Her stomach quivered as if one too many butterflies had flitted in. Whose orders did she have to follow now? Who would she talk to when she was excited, scared, or just plain lonely? With timorous step, she approached the main gate of Willetson Collegiate and Normal Institute. A man took her luggage and welcomed her with a map and his assurance that her belongings would be sent to her room. For years to come she would remember the next moments of quiet joy; she felt soothed and embraced by the terraced hills of lush, shimmering grass and a blooming mandevilla arbor. Now here was a place to think — no hint of strife, no untidiness, nothing ugly staring her down. At every turn were mounds of lavender and sassafras bushes. She followed the redbud trees, like sentries, along the narrow path to the main buildings — fine masonry of russet-brown and orange clay — and thought of May-Belle. She climbed the hill behind Allen Hall, where she watched the Colorado glimmer through town. Two years surrounded by books and beauty.

The nature of joy was her first lesson: how it loses savor without anyone to share it with. She had won a round or two in the fight against loneliness, remembering her family's advice. Papa had squeezed her tight and chided, "A colored man crave flesh. He don't wanna be hugged up on no gristle. Don't be the last one to eat 'cause the only man what want a skinny woman is a man what can't afford to feed her." Momma meant for her words to be called up on some lazy afternoon when she said: "Keep a hold of that bed and see what happens. Because while you got a hold of it, white folks got a hold of a book and they somewhere reading and thinking. When they come to you, they done already thought twice about how to use you. Study hard. Bring me some good marks. Don't you bring me no big stomach. Keep my nose high."

Leaning against her favorite redbud, Ivoe smiled to think how proud her family would be as she copied her schedule in her first letter home:

*Willetson Collegiate and Normal Institute
Course of Study, Fall Term, 1905*

14 Weeks, Class Hours per Week	
Printing	5.5
Typesetting & Basic Press Operation	3.5
Renaissance Literature	4
History & Civil Government	4
French	4
Domestic Science, Cookery & Lab	2.5

A glance at her watch and quick thumbing to the end of the book made Ivoe's heart sink. Less than ten pages of the Pauline Hopkins novel remained but there was the convocation to attend. She smoothed her skirt and buttoned the top of her blouse, listening to the chatter outside her window. A week had passed and she had not learned the name of a single classmate. There were smiles, a door held open, directions given to Beard Hall, the usual politeness, but not the makings of real friendship. She was the apple fallen from the lemon tree, having inherited from her mother a lack of female companionship. Failure to arouse anyone's

151

interest made her feel ordinary. Now in the midst of small groups making their way to the assembly hall, she fell behind, lacking all gumption for introductions.

As the convocation began, she took a seat in the empty first row. The Willetson choir sang; a Methodist minister prayed; the president made his address. "At Willetson, we wish to impart a liberal education to women whose sole objective is to harness character and gain intellect." He spoke of the school's founder and bade their attention to the music of Schumann, performed by one of their own.

The young woman entering the stage was oblivious to their snickering, a metallic buzz like the swarm of locusts. No feature of her frock adhered to the mailing — "A plain white cotton shirtwaist with high neck, a long dark skirt, and dark shoes should be worn to all special programs and classes." Her dress, a dull shade of green-tinged yellow, was hemmed by tattered black lace that drew eyes to the cracked white button shoes so stiff with polish a single step more and the leather might crumble off her feet. Ivoe pitied the dress but not the model. If only she had walked the planks of the Little Tunis schoolhouse like the girl gliding to the piano with a confidence that made one forget her shabby appearance.

There was confusion — a thunderous roll on the keys against the quiet commotion in the corner of the stage, where the heaving tremor from the piano's ragged melody agitated the president from his seat. A wave of soft rustling rippled behind Ivoe as others adjusted to the unexpected rollicking tempo. Ivoe tapped her foot along with the strong, marchlike *boom-chick, boom-chick, boom-chick.* The pianist was a flurry of hands, swaying side to side, pounding the pedal on the far right with a surprisingly sturdy shoe. Head reared, a smile blazed across her face. A high-pitched laugh of pure pleasure erupted from the stage. Watching her was like feeling inside an old mattress and finding a newspaper.

The sun beamed through a rift in the clouds that morning. On Fridays, Ivoe made haste for the printing department. She was disenchanted with history and civil government, which was compensated for only by Rabelais (so funny she could not read him before bed, or else sleep with a sore belly), and embarrassed by French, the vocabulary of which felt strange in her mouth. Nothing felt strange in the printing shed, where her time was divided between three stations —

the composing room, the pressroom, and the bindery room — trial and error, possibility and adventure. After a month, she knew grades of inks and paper and was practiced in different styles of magazine and newspaper folding — practical training in the everyday work of a printing office, all under the tutelage of Miss Durden.

Miss Durden stood out for her fiery intelligence. On the first day she warned her students that the gentlemen of Wiley College were not likely to know them. Printing students did not lollygag; printing students belonged in the shed, at work on the weekly publication of the *Willetson Herald* or producing the college's programs, stationery — all printing needs. She was the kind of teacher who gave herself completely, connecting seemingly disparate ideas, presenting a knowledge so whole, so shockingly simple in its complexity, as though you were fated to find it out. Reports of kindness about the teacher clung to students' tongues like honey: This girl received a graded test along with a discreet envelope, making possible her visit to a sick parent. Another girl, told to wait after class, was the recipient of a much-needed coat. How many times had Miss Durden escorted a student to the dining hall, whispering into the matron's ear before leaving the girl to eat?

The clink of silver greeted Ivoe as she passed the printing shed's wall of "Perpetual Visitation," where a jungle of hands opened cabinets and dipped into trays. The first cabinet housed the whole-word types used with great frequency — *the, what, for, but, so, and.* Subsequent cabinets each held two shelves: cases of capital letters on the top shelf, lower cases on the bottom. A few feet away from the metal cabinets, worktables of quiet camaraderie set print letter by letter. Ivoe often fumbled with the cases and fell behind the others in typesetting speed. Some girls handled the chase and stick as naturally as a knife and fork — not Ivoe.

Observing the position of Ivoe's hands as she worked the press bed, Miss Durden often gave a comic groan and pulled the girl's hands away in the nick of time. "Father up in heaven," she muttered.

Cracked shoes and a shirtwaist stained from too much bluing failed to render the figure in the dining hall entrance anything but invincible. Ivoe recognized this girl's regal bearing. Since the convocation, she had gone out of her way to pass the music building, unsure of what she would say to the girl — a shade too good-looking for life's

155

most awkward stage — if their paths crossed. She waved to the pianist, who looked back at her, unsmiling, as if determining whether Ivoe was worthy of her company.

Ivoe removed the books from the chair beside her and admired the girl's hair, clustered in rich dark waves and pulled together at her nape in a chignon. Conversation was easy when you started with the truth. Ivoe said she had never heard piano playing like that.

"Mister Tom Turpin's 'Buffalo Rag' instead of their Schumann. I lost a week in the practice room on account of devising my own program, but it was worth it. Now listen" — she leaned in close to Ivoe, as if about to tell a secret — "I would know very little that our people have accomplished in the ways of music, poetry, literature, if I had not found it out for myself. I suppose Willetson is like every other institution for learning in America. Even when the teacher is colored, don't expect to be told anything worthwhile about yourself. Most teachers here are white and they love to hear about how great they are. Can't shut them up on talking about it neither, as if they made the world on their own. Makes my ass hurt. But commence to talking about how great you are and you'll be talking to yourself. I imagine you'll do fine. You're polite enough. I bet you can recite all kinds of facts about what they've done — Edison, Einstein, and them. They'll love you for it too. But will they love you when you tell them about Douglass and DuBois? If you're not careful, they'll teach you to despise yourself. And you can't do nothing worthwhile unless you feel good about yourself. When I play Mr. Turpin, I feel good. Going to feel good again when they finally let me back in that practice room." Berdis winked and broke into gales of laughter like silver rain tapping on broken glass.

In Berdis Peets Ivoe recognized the flare of heroines she had met in her literary solitude. Conversations with her never seemed to go in the expected way. Berdis didn't care two straws for the latest fashion but would go without eating to buy music. She was indifferent to clothes and the attention of boys. Neither did money hold her interest; never having had any she never spoke of it. Punctuating her musings with a gesture — a soft stroke down the arm or, if sitting, a pat on the thigh — Berdis spoke excitedly about traveling the world and playing music, descriptions so vivid that Ivoe could hear and see the concerts happening in Vienna, Budapest, Paris! Passion for music gave Berdis an original life. In this way, she reminded Ivoe of all the women she loved — her mother, Aunt May-Belle, Miss Stokes — each had certain talents that seemed to dictate her womanhood. Conversations with Berdis were full of the girl's saucy tales peppered with outrageous antics. She liked to give the white man hell and refused to give them the satisfaction of knowing they had wounded her. Like the time a white woman would not sell her a Rachmaninoff piano concerto: "You think you've done something? You're not the only music store in Austin. One is bound to take my colored money, you old ugly thing you." She reminded Ivoe not to kowtow to white folks in her unconscious ways. "You've got to act as high above them as cake is over shit."

Berdis Peets came from a family of coal miners in Bastrop, Central-By-God Texas. Five brothers followed Daddy into the mines while she was meant to fill her mother's washerwoman shoes. Berdis could rinse clothes in plain water just fine, but adding Mrs. Stewart's Bluing to the laundry brought on a fit of sneezing. "Can't hire her out — won't be able to whiten nothing."

She attended school, but nobody gave a damn about ciphering and reading. Only the work her brothers did counted for something since it brought in money. What counted for Berdis was school, where the teacher played piano and took her as far as she could in music lessons. All efforts to persuade Daddy that he should put her under a proper music teacher failed.

"No kind of rearing, you see? No tenderness," Berdis said in the midst of reading one November afternoon in Ivoe's room. They were at the stage of their friendship where stories were prompted by everything. Dickens held Berdis enthralled; more than once that day Ivoe had seen her eyes well with tears while reading him and she had loved her for it.

Berdis laid her book aside and Ivoe's too. Her daddy had raised them like crops, she said, only the crops got more tending. Sometimes it was all Daddy could do to pace the floor cussing, knock one of the boys upside the head, pinch her titty too hard, anything to keep from filling their beds with coal and lighting a match. Things like that happened in Bastrop every so often when a parent's mind filled with visions of a life that could never be, or when a child's laughter sounded too sparkly and sweet.

Daddy got old quick, Berdis said. Kept letting them overwork him even when Mother took sick, lay down and stayed that way. One day Berdis came home from school and found Daddy pacing out in the yard. "Your momma wanna see you." One brother was on the floor outside the closed bedroom door, holding his head and crying. The door creaked open and two more brothers came out, raggedy voice trailing behind. "Where Berdis at?" The woman in the bed was too small, too frightful looking to be her mother. Rough gray scales gone past the chance of softening had replaced the satin mahogany skin. And she smelled very bad. Her mother gasped for breath and her chest rattled. She gave an openmouthed cough. Some of the phlegm caught in the corner of her mouth, most of it stuck to the front of Berdis's dress. For a long time Berdis would think of that cough, what it meant: Death was looking to move in, about to sign the lease. Death was slamming doors, creaking on bone floors, displeased that it had to live, if only for a little while, in such a hellhole. "One day . . . you'll wisen up . . . find yourself a man . . . Never been bad looking . . . don't know how long . . . that's gonna last . . . Better pick up . . . a needle and thread . . . an iron . . . find work

160

with . . . somebody in town . . . find yourself a man . . . a husband . . ." Then she opened her eyes, gray and pink where the whites used to be. "Find you a husband, girl. Nothing's gonna come . . . from that music mess. Nothing."

After they put her mother in the ground, Berdis's mind filled with all kinds of strange thoughts. Finding a husband, though, was no more near to her than the moon. (If Mother couldn't love you, who would? And even if they surprised you with all the trying, still wouldn't be a love big enough to fill the spot where Mother should have been.) Bastrop's Ebenezer Baptist Church took pity on the girl who played so beautifully during service. They donated money for continued piano studies and would pay her tuition in exchange for her promise to return to Bastrop to teach after graduation. "Thank God for sickness and death," Berdis said in a wry tone. "Losing a mother and gaining music is a better deal than most." They both knew she was right. "A hen will dip snuff before I set foot in Bastrop again."

In the last five months, Ivoe had given long hours to the printing shed while Berdis labored at the Steinway. Berdis's practice hour often turned into three, and Ivoe lingered at her special place at the library — the round oak table beneath a plaque bearing President Abraham Lincoln's quote: "I am not bound to win, but I am bound to be true. I am not bound to succeed, but I am bound to live up to what light I have." She liked to read at the table closest to the glass bookcase from which she withdrew the untaught books — *Incidents in the Life of a Slave Girl, My Bondage and My Freedom,* and, a favorite, George Washington Williams's *History of the Negro Race in America from 1619 to 1880.* Time away from the press, the library, and the practice room, Berdis and Ivoe became for each other what both had missed growing up: a best girl.

Around this time Ivoe began to think whites and Negroes inhabited the same country but lived in different worlds. Whites enjoyed a world of opportunity, freedom. Colored people trudged along in a world of retribution rooted in something as ridiculous as pigmentation. She tried to explain her feelings to her friend one afternoon.

"What you huffing about?" Berdis said.

"I've been thinking . . . white people must be remembering something bad about Negroes. The memory's all wrong but it's nothing we can do about it. If you look on down through history . . . take the Romans. They killed everybody. I mean everybody. We got some Italians in Starkville. They marry the Moravians, the Germans, all kinds of folks. Folks want to hire them — they building everything. Never mind all the killing — down through history — of everybody that wasn't them. Take the African. What Africans do you know — down through history — that killed a bunch of Europeans? What did the American Negro ever do to anybody? They're remembering something on us that isn't right, holding it against us. And seems like they can't ever forget it."

"You the one all in their faces, talking to this one and that one. There are a thousand better things you'll catch me doing before you ever see me up in a white person's face or letting them in mine," Berdis said.

"Merely putting my education on display," Ivoe said in a tone she heard in her head whenever she read about English royalty.

"What's the advantage of that?"

"They should see we possess great intellect and are worthy of their respect."

Berdis frowned. "All those colored people in the fields and you think white people thinking about you like that? You said so yourself — can't change what they remember. And why would you want to? Why would you even want to be involved? They're hateful. Maybe not the exact one you talking to but his daddy is, his momma is, and that means the hate's right there in the blood. They eat their own, Ivoe! I was reading a book where all the cannibals were white . . . and they're the civilized ones!"

Ivoe laughed. She felt a peculiar comfort and trust in Berdis's contempt, which leaked out like a bad smell whenever she felt slighted or was in a good mood. "You don't have the sense God gave a bird!"

"I got more than you got."

The joy of having a close friend gave Ivoe confidence. From the chatter of other girls, she knew Berdis also needed her. Playing piano didn't give her the right to be so dicty, they said. Who did she think she was refusing to haul wood and coal in the winter months? Glad to see Strange Bird go, they said, after Berdis left the post assigned to all scholarship recipients in exchange for room and board. She now lived with a wealthy colored family, looking after a toddler, which she said was a heap better than doing anything for Willetson girls. Dicty and stupid, Berdis called them. Ivoe wondered what qualities she had that made her Bird's inevitable confidante.

That was the Williams girl outside Beard Hall, thought Ona Durden. Ivoe's features weren't perfect and Ona could see how, in a sullen mood, she might even be unattractive, but inspired by passion, Ivoe commanded your full attention. During instruction of the Mergenthaler linotype, her cheeks flushed, her large brown eyes sparkled. While other pupils stepped back, cautious of getting burned, Ivoe went to work moving letter forms into place, watching excitedly as the machine spaced the line, then poured molten metal that cooled into a single line of type. Now, here she was on a Saturday afternoon, more eager than a basket of puppies when most girls were ironing their skirts for the week ahead.

"Miss Durden, you said the new press was arriving today and we could come see it."

"That was one invitation I thought no one would take me up on."

A great clattering rig of iron caught Ivoe's eye. Except for the water motor in the place where the old press had a crank, turned manually by two students, she quickly identified each part of the Cottrell cylinder press, memorized from the catalog Miss Durden had shared with her.

Miss Durden flipped the switch and the contraption slowly started to move. "A motorized drive passes the ink rollers up to the platen," she shouted over the rumble. "You can't see from over there. Watch the platen where the rollers collect the ink. Then it goes down over the type. When the platen closes, the pressure forms the impression of the wood block on the paper. Now, come over on this side. That's where the printed sheet will come out."

"The Cottrell is faster than the old press by nearly thirty minutes," Ivoe said, taking the bulky practice papers from the steel frame and carrying them to the guillotine, where she released the lever at just the right angle.

Miss Durden wiped grimy hands on her gingham smock.

"You ever think about writing something for the *Herald*?" she began casually. As with many of her pupils, she had sensed in Ivoe a need for special encouragement. "You do a fine job of printing programs and things. I'd be interested to see if you can write."

In the printing shed Ivoe felt calm and happy, feelings she laid to a childhood made infinitely brighter by the press. And there was a sense of excitement she could not describe but knew had something to do with her future. "I-I never thought about journalism . . . mostly I enjoy putting the paper together," she stammered.

"Father up in heaven, she can set type for a paper but can't imagine writing for one." Miss Durden cut a wicked grin and rolled her eyes at the ceiling.

As usual with the teacher, there was instant courage, motivation to want to do more and better. "I've loved newspapers all my life. It just never occurred to me that I could write for one. I don't know that I can."

"Well, maybe you can't but I don't see the great upset in trying." Miss Durden removed her smock. "All right, Miss Williams, you've got other studies and I have a thirty-minute trip home."

"I know tomorrow's Sunday but I'm free to practice on the press," Ivoe said.

Miss Durden removed her glasses and laughed a quick, knowing laugh. "Fine, then. Let's make it noon."

How vast the gulf between consuming words and making them! Reading had always enlivened Ivoe but writing was death. Where she had cherished books for their company, writing was a lonely endeavor she was not suited for. Her first contributions

167

to the *Herald* were written in her habitual passive voice. "On the way to progress, we make self-discoveries," Miss Durden encouraged. For Ivoe, the blank page was a looking glass. In writing she came face-to-face with her truest self. She could speak her mind without worrying about who it offended. She was a gardener like her mother, planting seed for thought in a reader's mind. Like Papa she forged the right word on the anvil of her mind.

Watching Berdis go up the hill, Ivoe stepped wrong into a ditch over-grown with tiny yellow flowers. She stumbled and pitched forward into a sprawling vine of nettle. Oh — the sting! She could hear faint laughter as she scrambled to her feet. "I'm gonna get you, Berdis." Climbing the hill in such heat was not for the weak: she drew on the energy left over from the early-morning excitement. From seven until noon she had set type, stopping only at Miss Durden's insistence that she enjoy some of her Saturday when Berdis poked her head inside the printing shed. "Go on. Give the others a chance to get as good as you have become." It was Miss Durden's first time remarking on her work. Now she could barely stand to be away from the *clink-clank* of metal, the rhythm of the steam-powered press, Miss Durden's laughter.

Ivoe was still deciding whether she should spend the evening studying for Monday's French exam or begin the essay for literature when she reached the overlook. Her gaze followed the winding rusty ridges of bluffs banded in splendid reds down along the narrow gorge where Barton Creek joined the Colorado. She squinted against the sun trying to make out the figure; Berdis was climbing down.

A bee flew off a thistle, fluttered, and disappeared inside a claret. Hidden in a cove full of tall crimson cones, Berdis snapped off a clover and pressed it to her nose before tossing it to the ground. "Took you long enough," she said, sliding her skirt down. Ivoe followed the curve of her back, looking away from her buttocks snug against her slip. "Well, we didn't come here to keep company with the flowers. You waiting on some fancy invitation? Sorry, ma'am. No post out in these parts." She raised Ivoe's arm, let it drop like a rag doll's, and ran off. "Take your clothes off and come on!"

Jumping, twisting, laughing, splashing — and the frigid cold of the creek — delighted Ivoe. Shuddering in a clinging petticoat, she was catching her breath when Berdis kissed her long (greedy as Gargantua, patient as Pantagruel). Ivoe froze. She could run a list as long as the Colorado on what might happen if they were caught. She thought of losing her place at Willetson and pulled away.

Berdis grabbed her. "I've been coming here since before I knew you and I've never seen another soul down here. No place else for us to go. Life sure was wasted on you if you're going to be so scared about everything." She gave the water a great smack.

They crawled onto the bank giggling. Bird gathered their skirts and flung them over a floor of cream-and-purple petals. She pulled Ivoe down on the bed of wild plum, where they shivered in the sunlight, hands entwined, palms soft and warm against each other.

"Ever notice how we never study on menfolk?"

"I talk about Papa and Timbo all the time."

"They're your daddy and brother. You know what I'm talking about."

"I've never done any courting. Unless you want to count the little bit of kissing I did with the Indian boy."

"Hush up with them tall tales."

Ivoe folded her legs under her behind so that her knees bore uncomfortably into the ground, a welcome distraction.

"I don't study on boys because when you study on them then you start encouraging them. And I don't want to encourage them."

Berdis inched closer. "They need encouraging too. Don't they? Claim to be so brave. Shoot, I've never come across one who could best me out of bravery. Not a one. And I got five brothers."

"That does not surprise me, Miss Peets. You'd stare down a bear moving in your direction."

"And it does not surprise me, Miss Williams, that you didn't get no further than kissing with your shy self. But it might surprise you to know," Berdis intoned magnanimously, "that I study on you. Yes indeedy, Miss Peets studies on Miss Williams every day. All day."

The sun slanted over Bird's shoulder, drawing Ivoe's gaze momentarily to her nipples, like gossamer figs, and quickening a sense of dread. She could no more study on boys than give up every leisure hour retracing her steps with Bird, whose cool hand now lay on Ivoe's thigh.

"Now what, Miss Williams, do you say to that?"

"I don't have to study on you 'cause you're always there. It's like you send yourself to me. I won't be paying you a bit of mind. I'll be at the library, or thinking on typefaces, or reading by my redbud, and here you come. Seems like you found yourself a good hiding place in my mind. When I least expect it you're tiptoeing around in there making me smile and think all kinds of foolish thoughts."

Before, Berdis had acted tall in the saddle — big throaty laughs and sass — but now something cooled in her. She hadn't chosen her family so she couldn't help it — eighteen years is a long time to go without loving anybody. Her eyes softened. "Well, you don't have to be George Washington Carver to understand it," she drawled womanly. "Don't be so scared, girl. It's only . . . well, shoot, Ivoe. What is it?"

Ivoe's heart raced. Damn if she knew what to say, what to do to turn the world right side up again. The sweet, heavy scent of bricklebushes made her dizzy. Bird leaned in, licked the tip of her nose playfully. All manner of kissing went on as Berdis gently pushed her down. The touch of cool fingers spreading her legs, drawing her pleasure up tight, tight like the skin on a drum, forced her eyes shut. The light shower against dry leaves made her wonder when the rain began and how it missed them. She gripped the smooth shoulders as her pleasure intensified. Orange, green, purple mingled behind closed eyelids. She cried out, opened her eyes to a bush that quivered with caterpillars. One, alone on a branch, contracted and came a distance, leaving a silky trail. The rest of that long afternoon no impulse was denied. A touch from Bird and she was an ancient tree — hardened flesh peeled away by the persistent, nimble stroke of . . . love, a curious thing.

Ivoe lay on her stomach, feet crossed at the ankles, heels in the air, watching the orange ribbon of horizon turn purple, as Berdis traced the slope of her buttocks.

"I'm not studying on Adam, but you're my rib, Ivoe. You made something different out of me."

The voice, so soft, made Ivoe turn around to see Berdis's eyes wet at the corners. She thought of their closeness, how brave she now felt, and laughed.

Berdis loved it when Ivoe laughed all deep down in herself. "What's got you so tickled?"

"Momma always told me not to show no man all my teeth. She said you can't smile at them too wide 'cause then they know they got you. She didn't say nothing about showing my teeth to a woman."

Berdis pulled Ivoe close enough to kiss. "I got you?" she said, too serious.

"Yeah. You got me."

Two months of orange-colored skies and purple horizons had sped by. Yet in a moment like the present, Berdis wondered exactly who had whom. Ivoe was always too glad when a chance meeting put them on the path of *that* woman, walking in their direction now.

Though the teacher was obscured by a steel-gray felt hat, Ivoe had recognized her from afar. Ona Durden carried the added weight of dignity that comes with hard-won achievement. Her clothes were always of an interesting cut and texture, in bays and browns; colors becoming on few others were somehow chic on her. Ivoe felt at the nape of her neck where her hair had gone back.

On a good day, with the help of a pressing comb handled by one of the girls on her floor, Ivoe's hair lay smooth and shiny, pulled back into one plait down the middle of her head; the style remained from Thursday evening until the start of the week. On Friday and the weekend Miss Durden saw her at her best. By Tuesday, her hair reverted to its natural state, as if to say five days was long enough to live a lie. Today, the fine, once-straightened hair had snapped back into a tight coil, the braid fuzzy and loose.

"Miss Williams, I was just thinking about you," said Miss Durden, acknowledging Berdis with a nod as she reached out to touch Ivoe's arm. "I have received the unfortunate news that my editor is not returning in the fall. Would you have any interest?"

A look of determination took shape around Ivoe's mouth and her eyes flashed. "Yes."

Watching the two riled Berdis, who was unaccustomed to spending time with a person she cared for the way she did Ivoe, and not fond of sharing. She hated the way Ivoe turned greedy for every little thing Miss Durden had to say. The fun had gone out of their togetherness, replaced by Ivoe's writing for the *Herald*. This month it was something to do with a colored woman held at the county jail without food or water, an article that took a week to write. As editor it would be worse. As though she were looking right through Berdis, Miss Durden extended an invitation to discuss the editorial post over dinner.

A week before the end of her first year, Ivoe paid the conductor a quarter and walked to her seat, a package tucked under her arm. The small brown box had arrived in the nick of time that morning from Reynold's Apothecary in Dallas, the only colored druggist in all of Texas. Naturally, Ivoe's forehead was riddled with heat bumps along with the painful pimples marking her face like a calendar for the world to see she had her monthly. The whole week her abdomen ached, the cramping slowing her down, so she made no extra jaunts around campus except to the dining hall, where she had begged a few lemons off the large cook whose eyes slid from side to side when she spoke. "I'll give 'em to you but watch yourself." Ivoe knew "watch yourself" referred to the girls who believed old wives' tales and sucked lemons ad nauseam to "dry up" the blood, increasing their fun with the boys down the road at the Agricultural and Mining School. The only thing she wanted to dry up were the pimples. She had followed May-Belle's direction to wash her face with lemon juice, cover it with honey, and rinse with cool water. Miss Durden had been privy to her hair gone back, her skin riddled with bumps, her worst look ever. On Friday night, only her very best self would sit at the teacher's table.

Berdis took the brown package and welcomed Ivoe inside her bedroom, where the chair from her desk was already pulled out, the desk itself prepared with a bucket of water, towel, comb, and brush. She tore open the package. All this trouble for Miss Durden, as if the teacher were the Queen of England. Chores at the house demanded her attention and there was the piece by Liszt she had purchased and had not played once.

Ivoe thumbed through the *Colored American*'s special issue on art and fashion and found the advertisement that had started it all. Berdis had stolen the issue from a Negro shop in downtown Austin. Their excited perusal saw them tearing through the pages like little girls, pausing only to read to each other (in high-toned ladies' voices) the silliest advice. But the page-long advertisement that looked like a newspaper article had caught Ivoe's attention. She studied the two distinct oval-framed female images. Above frame one, which held a woman whose profile most resembled her own, Ivoe noted the words *Before Using*. The model's hair was a few inches long and wild like her own when not straightened with the hot comb or rolled with cotton at night. The woman in the second frame, with the words *After Usage* beneath, looked more like Berdis, whose hair fell to her shoulders.

Now, as Berdis poured Miss Lincoln's Medicated Hair Tonic over Ivoe's head, she read aloud from the same advertisement: " 'You owe it to yourself, as well as to others who are interested in you, to make yourself as attractive as possible . . . Positively nothing detracts so much from your appearance as short, matted curly hair.' " Without asking, Berdis added all of her Curl-I-Curl: A Cure for Curls tonic, rubbing vigorously as Ivoe chatted on about things she hoped to write about in the next issue of the *Herald.*

Ivoe's scalp tingled and began to sting. The odor emanating from her head was stronger than anything she'd ever smelled. "You think it's time to wash it out?" Gently, Berdis leaned her head back into the bucket, combing her fingers through the hair to rinse away the tonic. Berdis dried the hair with a towel, then removed. The short tresses had sizzled down to nothing. She lifted a finger to feel — an act more of inspection than compassion — the patches of woolly mats and pink stripes of tender scalp, now burned and bald.

Eight years of teaching at Willetson and Ona Durden had never invited a student to dinner, but she had greeted the idea to cook for Ivoe cheerfully. She was drawn to exchange ideas with her. Whether they knew it, Ivoe's peers had her to thank, for even when a shortcut was possible, Ivoe compelled her to her most generous teaching. In Ivoe she found someone whose inquiring mind reminded her how much better life was when you returned something to it. In the last year, she had dusted off the little mimeograph machine once used to print the memos for the Texas Association of Colored Women's Clubs and returned to the meetings that had often left her feeling hopeless about the race.

She opened the drawer in search of a music roll befitting the occasion. "Rosebud" — jaunty, springlike, perfect. The pianola began to play just as she remembered the flowers and dashed out to the yard for some of her rhodies to stand in a glass on the table. After removing her apron, she inspected the settings, excited by the empty dishes waiting to be filled with the food she prepared best and with joy.

Ona had the distinct impression that the green scarf Ivoe wore and the fumes tickling her nose during their embrace had something to do with dinner.

Ivoe was a bundle of nerves when she sat

down at the table for two, constantly patting down the length of her skirt to smooth the wrinkles; touching her nape to check the scarf; pressing chin to chest to eye the front of her blouse for specks of dirt, dust, anything. She admired the crisp napkin folded on a plate adorned with a restful design of rose sprigs on a white porcelain background as Ona filled the glassware gleaming to perfection with water.

While cooking, Ona heard about Little Tunis and talked about Lincolnville, the Saint Augustine, Florida, enclave where she was raised by an aunt after her Seminole Negro father ran off to fight in the Texas-Indian wars. She had come to Austin from Jacksonville, a product of Edward Waters College, "a gift bestowed on colored Florida by the African Methodist Episcopal Church."

Ivoe watched Miss Durden carry a small iron pot from the icebox, recalling a favorite saying of May-Belle's: "An ole black pot can't be beat when you craving something good to eat." Miss Durden ladled a smooth brown sauce into a small bowl. The aroma was scrumptious. "This is how we do in Florida — pour some of that peanut sauce over the red rice and shrimp. Take more.

There's plenty." Succored by the meal and Miss Durden's calmness, Ivoe found it easy to talk about everything.

Miss Durden put her in the mind of Momma, who had a way of saying no more than she thought might be heard. Yet Miss Durden was savvy in the ways she hoped to become. Her conversation hinged on matters of real consequence. Her ideas were sensible and hopeful and moved the heart of her listener. The questions she asked Ivoe were the most thoughtful she'd known: What was she going to give? On the subject of friendship, she cheerfully discussed what she had learned or accomplished because of the help of others, praising the women who had "helped to make" her. What was Ivoe going to do with what she had? She spoke of living to work, not working to live, and knowing the difference. Working to gain prestige, or worse yet, money, was a sad life. Only work fueled by passion promised a life worth living.

"What work are you doing for the race?"

She had done nothing for the race. Only in the last year had she understood the importance of joining a cause, any cause to improve Negro life, Ivoe intoned, regrettably. Barred from the Anti-Saloon League because she was colored, when Miss Durden was her age she had picketed juke joints in Lincolnville after some women were so badly beaten by drunk husbands they could not stand up to cook for their children. Temperance remained a cause she believed in: "Colored people have not yet acquired enough to be so frivolous as to drink it away. The saloon is one man's dream — the owner. And it is his goal to strip his brother's last nickel from him . . . It is schooling — not juking — that's going to help us."

From hearing about the books Miss Durden read in the Hypatia Literary Society to her involvement with TACWC, whose current project was the establishment of a home for Austin's delinquent colored boys, everything Miss Durden said and did sent Ivoe's admiration soaring into inspiration.

As the teacher prepared the dessert plates, Ivoe took courage.

"My articles . . . what begs improvement?" She touched the edge of the sweet potato pie lightly with her fork; it yielded then proved soft all the way through. Toothsome. Momma would approve even though Miss Durden's was sweeter and had a good deal more nutmeg and a smidgen of something that did not readily come to mind — root beer? Shaved pecans in the dough gave the crust flair in its speckled design. She could make a home in this pie.

"You're coming along." As usual, the teacher was sparing with compliments, having seen how they snuffed out potential greatness. "You know, a sentence is like a race. You can't possibly win it unless you end as strong as you began. Good journalists understand that the last word is as important as the first."

Ivoe dallied at the open front door where the air was sweet like honeysuckle, and Miss Durden drew her into a tight embrace, touching the knot of her scarf in a way that prompted Ivoe to look her in the eye.

"Father up in heaven. It's what's inside that makes you shine, girl."

Excited to death by everything that evening — the meal, the editorial post, the faint scent of Floris White Rose perfume that lingered on her dress from the long goodbye — Ivoe climbed the steps to her room, three at a time.

6

A Gratuitous Insult

Exiting the Austin train station, Ivoe was about to step off the curb when a curious scene unfolded.

Congress Avenue teemed with colored people moving in silent droves. Many held picket signs — SEGREGATION & NEGROES DO NOT MIX: TROLLEYS NEED A BETTER FIX! Two streetcars passed, both entirely free of colored passengers. A cardboard sign hanging from the rear of a packed conveyance read, FOR COLORED ONLY. The world-weary look on the faces of women burdened by heavy loads and the stern quality of the men toting large bundles signaled the obvious — Jim Crow had reared his ugly head, again.

The world beyond Willetson never enjoyed a concert between the races, but the ordinance requiring colored passengers to board using the back door and to sit in separate compartments on streetcars was a gratuitous insult. According to the driver who helped her into his dray, the boycott had lasted forty-two days. Among the riders conversation was of no consequence — cravings for dinner, the heat — then someone complained about increased travel time to work. A domestic shared that when her employer reprimanded her tardiness she had responded that she'd rather quit than ride a Jim Crow streetcar. She leaned over the aisle, placed both hands on Ivoe's shoulder, and drew her head close to whisper that every woman she knew had threatened to boycott the men of the race if they dared to "Jim-Crow" on a trolley and Ivoe should do the same. One passenger thought Negroes ought to form their own transportation company — "completely separate from whites, owned and operated by us." He reminded them that the white man's conscience was not in his heart or mind but in his pocket, and it was there they must strike to the quick, again and again.

"Nothing like a robust welcome of southern hostility," Miss Durden said, sliding a box across the table in Ivoe's direction. "Old issues of the *Houston Post* with articles on their boycott, two years ago." While Ivoe looked through the papers, Miss Durden recounted the events that led to Austin's boycott. Protestors had faced violent intimidation from Austin police during the initial weeks of the protest. Three young colored women had been the first to test the new ordinance, unaware that conductors had been granted judicial power. Most drivers were not eager to confront a man, but with women they asserted themselves with brute force. One woman had been thrown from the trolley so hard her arm had broken on the fall. A colored delegation petitioned the city council and a meeting date was set, yet on the meeting day the council refused to hear the delegation. "Nevertheless, out of the humiliating disgrace of Jim Crow something exciting is stirring — rejection of second-class citizenship," Miss Durden said.

Boycott articles from the *Post* made fine examples of tone, but Ivoe wanted more coverage of Austin to provide context for her articles. Where were copies of that summer's *Democratic Statesman*? "The *Houston Post* and the *Democratic Statesman* are very different papers," Miss Durden explained. "Arrests and court records are criteria for a Negro to appear in the latter." The colored community's large but silent protest was not illegal and was therefore ignored. Not one of the local white dailies devoted ink to it. Whitecapping and the Black Codes and countless discriminatory tactics proved the white race spent extraordinary thought on the colored race, yet nowhere in Travis County's press was there ever any mention of black life.

"If not the newspaper, where do we turn for information?" Ivoe asked. A question not even Ona Durden could answer. A failed boycott against the Nashville Street Car Association had inspired the launch of the city's first colored newspaper, the *Nashville Globe,* Miss Durden said. "If we're lucky, the same will happen here. They're boycotting in Savannah, Georgia, right now for the same reason. I subscribed to the *Savannah Tribune* so we can follow its development."

For Miss Durden, the outcome was not as significant as the protests themselves, which she credited with the changing definition of colored life in the South. But she was concerned about the workaday needs of her Wheatville neighbors, domestics, and laborers in Austin's booming construction sites "more than a few miles away." "Each and every protest is a wave that moves us beyond the stagnant waters of servitude and oppression toward the shores of self-respect." Her stance and the position of the *Willetson Her-*

ald was clear: Willetson women must be urged to walk with colored Austin.

FIGHTING "JIM-CROWISM" IN AUSTIN'S STREETCARS:
A HUMILIATING DISGRACE
By I. L. Williams

Beyond Willetson's gates the color line, as ordained by the city council, was drawn on the streetcars for the first time on Wednesday morning, August 1. The innovation was not relished by the Negro population of Austin and resentment was demonstrated in a general boycott by the race of the streetcars, which commenced on Monday morning, August 6. Owing to the light travel by colored people, the traction company set apart only the last two seats of each car for Negroes. The presence of a Negro on the cars is a rarity, the boycott being for the present most complete. It is stated that at all the colored religious meetings word is passed to keep off the cars and the injunction is obeyed. Here and there a colored passenger is seen and every once in a while some colored man who declines to go into the reined-off portion stands on the rear platform. It is the position of this organ that

Willetson women walk with the race. Save your self-respect and your money and boycott the streetcars. See Miss Ona Durden in the printing workshop for schedules of dray service.

Ivoe put aside the third draft of her first article of the school year, certain that it also missed the mark. There wasn't time enough before her meeting with Berdis to begin again. Frustrated, she collected the pages, shoved them into the drawer, and pushed back from her desk, going over the events of yesterday with Miss Durden.

For nearly an hour they had haggled over the title and debated when Ivoe could not explain from whom she had procured her quotes.

"I don't recall if it was at the church or during the silent march. And I don't appreciate being accused of fabricating material," Ivoe said. "I'd just as soon not write for the paper."

Miss Durden's eyes never left the page.

"You've got what my mother used to call natural smarts — the ability to look at something and form the right question. You've got love for the written word, everybody else's more than your own. If you combined those two and cared a little more —"

"I care."

Miss Durden read a passage aloud that Ivoe was especially proud of and pointed out two misspellings.

"I'm lazy then."

"Not lazy." Miss Durden sensed Ivoe, anxious and seething. "Miss Williams, you are careless. And defensive. Neither will serve you as a journalist." She continued to read. "Refrain from paraphrasing. You are the voice of a community, use people's exact words . . . Otherwise, these bad habits will leave you open to factual errors, misrepresentation. Neither belong in the *Willetson Herald*. Or any other newspaper for that matter."

Ivoe hesitated for a moment of painful embarrassment, and in a sudden crude motion she reached over the teacher and snatched the paper from her hands. She brushed against Miss Durden so hard she mussed up her hair but withheld apology and turned to leave. A touch on her shoulder from behind made her tremble. She felt foolish, vulnerable, found out. She was no writer; she was a reader who ingested too many words, some of which spilled out, leaving a mess.

"Miss Williams, kindly return the paper. I am not finished with my comments," Miss Durden said softly.

Without turning around, Ivoe handed her the paper. *The woman was determined to drive her in this unpleasant manner.*

Miss Durden's fealty to the best story curbed any desire for Ivoe's favor. Empty praise and flattery were a writer's enemy. She read on, circling an idea worth keeping, a well-crafted sentence, but by the end suggested starting from scratch.

At the sight of Berdis's swaggering air, Ivoe jumped up from the bench and flew to her. They laughed and rocked each other wildly in their embrace.

Berdis plied her with questions about the summer: "Tell me everything you did . . . and with whom."

Summer in Little Tunis had dragged on without incident, Ivoe explained. She had worked in the Al-Halif family store from eight until one and spent the long, idle afternoons and evenings reading. She was home two weeks before it got around Little Tunis that she could come and go from the Stark house whenever she pleased. She had been seen on the road headed home with books bound in leather. "Girl, how you go up in they house like it's a Negro library?"

people from Old Elam Church asked. "Turn the doorknob and walk right in." Interaction with Miss Susan — a quiet pass in the hallway, or a silent dance around each other in the library — was far less exciting than the townsfolk made it out to be unless their literary tastes collided. Occasionally, Miss Susan paused her at the door to check a book's spine — not for accounting purposes but to see if she had read it. Ivoe enjoyed the way they spurred each other to their best articulation on plot, character, style. They exchanged reviews on global literature, formed alliances over certain titles, disputed others. On Ivoe's recommendation the singular book by a Negro writer in the Stark collection — Paul Laurence Dunbar's *Oak and Ivy* — was read by Miss Susan (twice) and now traveled among her friends. "You must read the Negro Shakespeare," Ivoe once heard her say.

Visits to Susan Stark's library, sometimes as often as four times a week, were a passport to the world. Europa opened her arms wide and enclosed Ivoe in British romances, Norse mythology, and the translated tracts of German philosophers. She rejected southern white men's narratives of beguiling warmth and Negro characters possessed of sunny dispositions but read everything by northern white men: Mr. Hawthorne and Mr. Melville never bent a fictional truth, a fact she laid to the abolition movement. But the greatest flutter of heart she found in Irish drama. One evening, Miss Susan had requested she read aloud with her Lady Gregory's *Spreading the News*. Language and laughter powerful and extravagant rendered an Ireland so real that Ivoe scarcely remembered she was sitting in a parlor in Central East Texas. A singular passage had heightened her spirit and wed her to every character on the page. For the rest of the summer Miss Susan's parlor became the Abbey Theatre, where they delved into Yeats and Synge.

Her summer of lavish reading nearly ended without consequence until that dangerously hot day Miss Susan insisted she not embark for home before the sun went down.

The glow of the mottled amber lamp was cozier than the glaring sun, shut out as Ivoe drew the curtains. She plumped up the scarlet pillow, admired the brocade ticking and silk braid trim, and settled upon the divan with *Moby-Dick.* Minnie delivered a tray of cucumber sandwiches and iced tea and whispered an odd question about the jailhouse, quickly waving her hand to dismiss it. Ivoe had eased off her shoes and was about to enter the Spouter-Inn with Ishmael when she heard the front door slam shut. Earl Stark called out for his mother and began pacing the floor. Despite every effort to ignore them — closing the doors of her mind then the library door — she caught Miss Susan's voice, taut like the skin of a drum: "You did what without my consent?" Then, disgusted, "What about all those families in Little Tunis?" Earl remarked plainly, "Well, Mother, they will have to move on."

That evening Ivoe found Miss Susan lying back on her favorite chaise with the *Saturday Evening Post.* Her face showed a mind taken up by worry as Ivoe stepped onto the verandah with hesitation. "Miss Susan, it may be indelicate to ask but I heard you and Earl talking about Little Tunis. It concerns me."

"Earl's quitting cotton."

Sharecroppers in Little Tunis had complained about the steady decline of cotton for the last few years, but Ivoe asked, "Why now?"

"I don't understand it . . . with the cattle ranch and the mill we'll be fine, but if we don't crawl from under this crop-lien system it'll bankrupt us. Earl says the convict leas-

194

ing program will ensure our wealth and Starkville's."

"We don't have a prison."

"About to — the Burleson Prison Farm."

Ivoe felt her stomach drop. Her family, Miss Stokes, and the Al-Halif family were the only people she knew not dependent on sharecropping. During their exchange, Susan had patted the cushion and motioned for Ivoe to sit beside her but she was unmoved.

"Now, the plain fact is some of your people are unwilling to work. They'll never save enough to buy their own land." Miss Susan's eyes fluttered, her face registered disappointment and embarrassment. "The way Earl sees it, he's the victim because he stands to lose the most. He never once turned his back on them. They've turned on him . . . defaulted contracts, unpaid loans. When he gets after them about it, well, some of their responses are downright incendiary."

Ivoe bristled. Colored people were supposed to be maltreated and cheated without so much as a word of protest.

"If the prisoners pick all the cotton, how will the people who've been picking it for years, for generations, make a living? Or doesn't your benevolent son think obliterating a community's only means of survival counts as victimization?"

"I will excuse your tone because of your usual tactful manner. Nothing can be done about it. He's signed the papers and everything."

"When —"

"Now, Ivoe."

Ivoe returned an incredulous stare and said with sudden force, "When are they building the prison? When does Earl plan to tell the sharecroppers?"

"I don't know any more about it," Miss Susan said, shaking her head like a disgruntled child. "The *Enterprise* knows more about my son's affairs than I do. Nothing for you to worry about." Susan's disarming smile enraged her. "Lemon owns that plot — unless she's planning to sell it and you and I both know better than that. But, I'll tell you, those families behind in rent, they'll be the first to get evicted."

That summer's great mistake was telling her parents about the conversation with Miss Susan. Her last weeks at home, prison farms were the only subject to ignite her father. Day after day, not a word reported on it in the *Enterprise,* but Papa's questions persisted and made him cross. He asked customers about prison farms in other counties and drew Momma into serious talks. "They put a jail here, you mark my words, Little Tunis won't be fit for no kind of living at all. We ought to think about leaving here." He harped on Kansas or anyplace west, as he had done when Ivoe was a child. For the first time in her life, she had seen her parents argue in close vicinity. Papa towered over Momma with hurtful eyes and said in a quiet voice seething with regret, "Land what don't come with peace ain't worth having." Still, Momma had the final word: "They can build a prison all around me. They not gonna build it on Booker and Iraj's land 'cause I ain't selling it."

Despite the surprising letter from home, climbing the dormitory stairs Ivoe felt rankled by her conversation with Berdis. For hours they had argued about the boycott. Berdis complained about the streetcars; dividing lines painted on the floor were no longer good enough. They had added screens about a foot tall on top of the back of the seat — so cumbersome that when the trolley lurched heads banged; hats tumbled to the ground. "I feel like a damn caged animal . . . Gentlemen and hoodlums heckle the entire way while the conductor does nothing. I count it as luck if I can ride without an insult." All the more reason she stay off the streetcars, Ivoe had shouted. Impossible, Berdis claimed. Without the direct route of the streetcar, dray service added an hour to her Willetson commute. She could not walk nor would she use the colored conveyances, which were "inconvenient and tiresome." While Ivoe appreciated a different perspective, she questioned Berdis's allegiance. Did she have any? For anybody? Last year she had admired her friend's tenacious drive for music but recent conversations showed how selfish she could be. "I don't recall leaving it up to the church to decide for me," she'd said as Ivoe passed along information about the boycott from Miss Durden. "As long as I can afford it, I will Jim-Crow to school — if that's what you want to call it — and when I arrive to the music room I won't smell like a horse and will have strength enough to play." Ivoe said the difference between them was that she understood that any society accepting of a colored woman concert pianist must also allow for colored patrons to travel to the hall in first-class accommodations. There would never be the one without the other. The steeliness in her tone silenced Berdis for only a moment. "Colored people choose the wrong things to be proud about.

We're barred from the best music shops, pay the same entrance fee at theaters . . . to sit in the buzzard's roost, muss ourselves entering and exiting establishments through back alleys . . . Why is a damn trolley seat so important? At least they haven't doubled the fare. Must every step for colored progress wear our heels down?"

While they were fresh on her mind, Ivoe jotted down the reasons Berdis withheld support from the boycott. She would use them to frame her next article, calling attention to the heroes of the movement, the colored hackmen, who for the past two months had lowered their quarter fare to a dime. Some drays and delivery wagons hauled workers into town free of charge. She would turn a critical eye to the Austin police, exposing their latest tactic — employment of crooked county humane officers to pursue colored hackmen on false charges of half feeding and working to death worn-out horses — and conclude the article with a clarion call to Willetson women: "Do not trample on our pride by being 'Jim-Crowed.' Walk!"

Little Tunis, September 30, 1906

Dear Ivoe,

I hope you are studying.

You are an auntie. Your brother and Roena are parents of twin boys. They named the firstborn James, but at half the size of his brother and with beady eyes, Junebug seemed a better fit. The second baby, pudgy with big eyes that make him look wise, made Papa think of the King of England until Edward stuck his little finger in his mouth, then I called him Pinky and that's the name that took.

You would think fatherhood would make Timbo want to act right but that boy won't stand straightening. I wonder what make Timbo think he can cheat life. Seems like I raised you children better than that. He ought to know sooner or later you got to pay with something — your mind, your heart, your sweat. Something. He's in for a rude awakening. I just hope the cock crow before it's too late. Roena fusses about his gambling but your brother got some hard bark on him. Can't tell him nothing. We got lucky with you. At least you will listen to somebody.

There have been a few other changes around here. It was a year ago when you first went off to Willetson that your sister commenced with the clarinet. She reminded Papa of the promise he made to her if she stayed with it. He sure had a hard time finding somebody to give her lessons but he kept at it. Finally Meyer's daughter — a music teacher in Bryan — said she'd do it so long as Irabelle comes in the evenings so folks don't see that she is taking up Negro students.

If Irabelle is not practicing she don't go far lessen Papa's with her. Always up under him. You sure was different at nine. To help with the lessons I raised the price on my preserves to fifteen cents. Folks don't seem to mind.

May-Belle is doing fine. Papa's worrying himself sick over this jail business. He told me to send you this from the paper.

Keep my nose up. I pray for you.

Your Mother

Inside the envelope was a clipping: Earl Stark on the front page of the *Starkville Enterprise* with the president of the Texas Board of Prison Commissioners. The headline: "Seeds of Change Planted at Prison

Farm!" Stark had not renewed any share-cropping contracts. His cotton would be picked by convict labor leased from the prison in Bryan. The Burleson Prison Farm covered four thousand acres and housed 280 inmates. The plan called for the clearing of two hundred acres — from cow pasture to every cabin on the north side of Little Tunis's Main Street. To expedite his plans, sharecroppers were paid to leave the Bottoms immediately and encouraged to integrate Starkville's "more established" communities. Many had taken the deal, "or were themselves twice taken," Ivoe blurted out to the empty room. From what the article left out she surmised a harrowing revelation. Her neighbors had been enticed by paltry sums and signed contracts they didn't understand. The rents, let alone mortgages, for homes in the German and Moravian enclaves would break them in less than a year. Her parents knew better than most that no colored person ever made out well in a business deal; nevertheless, should Papa be tempted, she expressed her concerns in a note.

On a quiet Sunday morning made for sleeping in, Ivoe rose early and looked out the window at the heavy spring rain. For a handle on anything affecting colored Austin, she knew where to go. She dressed in a hurry, forgoing the usual breakfast of hominy and toast since even on a good day the passenger carriages closest to campus kept infrequent schedules. The fetor of wet horses and hay directed her to the nearest hack line. A ride to New Hope Baptist Church in Wheatville, where Miss Durden and many colored Austinites lived, cost five cents aboard a double horse wagonette that seated about twenty.

The preacher admonished his congregants for any show of violence: "Those who did not know any better than to stand in solidarity with the race must be left alone to ride the trolleys." Streetcar conductors, now sworn in as deputies by the sheriff, arrested any Negro who heckled riders as they attempted to board or disembark. The preacher had used church funds for the release of four members jailed after pulling two boys from a streetcar. Murmurs and sighs of displeasure rippled through the congregation. Someone shouted, "What about *them*?," in response to the tragedy of last week when reportedly a drayman had driven too slowly in front of a streetcar, prompting the conductor to leave his car and club the colored man's head repeatedly. Within an hour, Wheatville blacks stormed downtown Austin, many with hunting rifles and makeshift weapons. The Texas Rangers joined the police force to contain the posse, resulting in fifty-seven arrests for weapons possession. Those who witnessed the attack of the drayman said little more than a bag of pulp was left between the man's shoulders.

Ivoe laid her watch on the desk. She was behind in homework for most subjects but wanted to give more time to the *Herald,* to bring the requisite clarity and truth that led to equal rights for black Austinites. Her articles included detailed accounts of white backlash. Stories like the successful colored businessmen issued fines by the city for fabricated infractions. Craft came easier now but the subject matter troubled her mind and sometimes broke her heart. The last six months of covering the boycott had brought a revelation. Journalism was more than a talent to cultivate, more than her life's calling; it was social justice.

WALK A LITTLE LONGER
By I. L. Williams

The colored people of this community are

still exercising common sense and demonstrating the enviable quality of self-respect. There are forty thousand Negroes in Austin, and we believe we are safe in saying that the streetcar companies do not haul one hundred of them in the course of a week. We are purchasing buggies, carts, horses and mules; and in cases where we are not able to purchase any of these things we are taking the time to walk.

The Negroes of this city are more united in efforts to discourage "Jim-Crowism" than they have ever been against any project of any kind. Men, women, and children are fully determined that we will not ride until the Union Transportation Company, a Negro business enterprise that came into existence for the purpose of affording relief, has turned loose the motor cars for our accommodation. Five of these cars are now on the road, and as soon as the patronage warrants it as many more will be purchased. The Willetson woman who rides on the "Jim Crow" streetcar for any purpose after these motor cars have been pressed into service is, to all intents and purposes, an enemy to her race.

We desire to live peaceably with our white neighbors. They have passed the law creating the "Jim Crow" section. We do not wish to violate the law, and we are certain that we will not violate it if we stay off the cars. Most of the streetcar conductors have no respect for women; they delight to insult and make attempts to humiliate us. Many streetcar conductors feel that, because they are white, they have the right to assault women. There has been trouble of this kind already. We do not wish for more.

The *Herald* admonishes Willetson women to stay off the cars by all means. The motor cars will arrive in a few days; the Negroes will be afforded the relief that we so much desire, and we will all be further removed from the possibility of insults and friction, on account of the iniquitous "Jim Crow" law. In view of such relief, we can afford to walk a little longer.

"Excellent," Ona said of the article. "I wouldn't change a word of it! And that reminds me . . . I have something for you." She reached into her bag for the May 1876 issue of the *Austin Gold Dollar*. The newspaper, yellow from age but still legible, had thrived for four years in the Wheatville area of the city. After the death of an elderly neighbor, Ona had acquired several copies found in the neighbor's possessions. Ivoe drew the paper up to her face, inhaled deeply, and laughed.

In a flash, Ona glimpsed an image of the child Ivoe had been. Strong affection tumbled forth. Her arm brushed against Ivoe's as she moved her chair closer, pointing out every aspect of the paper she had analyzed. The plainest typeface had been chosen. Extra space had been inserted between each single letter — "to decrease reading difficulty but also to encourage the illiterate." Editor Jacob Fontaine focused his journal on the needs of freed slaves: advice for reestablishing family ties, education, moral and religious discipline, and racial justice. She was most touched by the brief editorial on the front page. A twenty-year separation from family, caused by slavery, had ended in rich symbolism when the paper's founder received a gold dollar from his sister at their reunion.

Side by side, Ivoe tried to ignore the pull of blouse fabric against Miss Durden's bosom. She studied the beautiful slender hands turning the pages, suppressed the urge to cover a hand with her own. The impulse to confess how she had thought of the teacher every day, often multiple times and with great pleasure, perched on the tip

of her tongue. She feigned incredible interest in the newspaper. Repeatedly leaning
into the teacher made her feel warm and
sweet like the inside of a favorite room filled
by a butterscotch sun.

As Ivoe prepared to leave the printing
shed, Ona seized the moment to share an
opportunity she could recommend to no
other student.

"The University of Texas is once again
opening a few spaces for colored students
to attend a journalism camp this summer.
In previous years, one or two students from
Willetson were accepted. You should apply."

Ivoe smiled before a look of doubt took
hold. "My parents were hardly able to make
up the difference of my scholarship. We
can't afford any extra schooling."

"Don't worry about that. We will take up
a collection among Willetson faculty if you
are accepted. If that doesn't solve it, I will
solicit the clubwomen. To live with dignity
and also find work that brings a little joy is
almost impossible, but something tells me
that you, Ivoe, specialize in the wholly
impossible." Noting the nervous look on the
girl's face, Ona reached across the table and
grabbed her hand. "On our best day none
of us truly knows how great our potential

208

is. We are so much more than the selves we doubt."

"I wish I had the courage you have."

Ona looked unflinchingly into Ivoe's eyes. "You will have it when you need it. It's in your character."

For weeks Berdis had looked for Ivoe in their love and saw her nowhere in it. Ivoe had attended only one recital the whole school year and had arrived late to her final concert. While others celebrated graduation, she had failed to pull Ivoe away from the newspaper, or keep her from running to Miss Durden with drafts of the journalism camp application. Not even promised trips to their creek distracted. Now, standing in the doorway of the printing shed, she felt foolish for leaving her last music lesson early. The old hen knew how to keep Ivoe by her side. She watched Miss Durden lean across the table to brush her thumb against the ink smudged on Ivoe's cheek and draw Ivoe's face close to whisper in her ear — something that made Ivoe break into peals of laughter. Without waiting for Ivoe to collect herself, Miss Durden announced her return that evening to celebrate their last publication for Willetson, nodding to Berdis on her way out.

Ivoe smiled to herself, tempted to swap her article for the comical story Miss Durden had just shared. Last week a meeting had convened at New Hope Baptist Church. Maps were disseminated, marking stations along each beautiful tree-shaded avenue in Austin's exclusive Hyde Park, where deeds prohibited Negroes from renting or buying property. Hackmen received notice to feed their horses a generous dose of alfalfa mash and Epsom salts. Those who drove foals and stallions were especially encouraged to participate since their drays defecated twice as much as mares. Draymen were advised to assemble in pairs outside of businesses. Directions ended with: "Pray for rain!"

On a typical spring day the sun would dry out the mounds as quickly as they were laid. The following morning's shower started as a drizzle, but by the time draymen were in place, the clouds had burst. Residents watched in horror as manure — kept fresh by the rain — flecked their neighborhood. Patients from the nearby State Lunatic Asylum were agitated by the odor and doctors feared facility unrest. More than a hundred policemen were deployed to the malodorous scene yet no arrests were made. Where would they put the horses? Handed a ticket by an officer at the Hyde Park

Presbyterian Church, an Avenue B drayman uttered a now-famous line: "Been paying a poll tax since 1902. A shit tax this one time won't kill me."

Now, as Ivoe worked on her final *Herald* issue, she amused herself with befitting headlines:

"Locust Swarms Migrate to Heavenly Hyde Park — Attracted by Manure Mounds!"

"Colored Dray Horses Shit-Out White Residents!"

"Shit! Shit! And More Shit for Wealthy Hyde Parkers, Cries the Colored Hackman!"

She was laughing to herself when she felt a hand on her back.

"Finished soon? We don't want to be late," Berdis said in an upbeat tone that disguised her sulkiness.

Ivoe read her watch — a quarter past noon. She had planned to be finished in time to attend the picnic but now felt rushed and resentful. The typesetting of her article and several others lay ahead. She wanted to tell Berdis that the issue was taking longer than anticipated and — her speech rehearsal ended as Berdis sat down beside her, cupping her chin in her hand.

"One more hour," Ivoe snapped. In the

last few months she had grown irritated by Berdis's insistence that they do all things together and be all things for each other. "Maybe two. Really, you shouldn't miss it. Go without me — Bird . . . wait!" She lurched to her feet, envelope in hand. "I hardly deserve to be in your good graces but my application has to be mailed today and I'll be here . . . who knows how long."

"Of course." Fabricating a necessary trip to the post office, Berdis pocketed the two cents. On her way to the picnic, she threw the envelope in the trash.

7

TO WALK IN SILK ATTIRE AND HAVE SILVER TO SPARE

JUNE 1907

The mailbox lid slammed shut. Ivoe waved to the postman in hope that he had delivered a letter from Austin. For two weeks she had awaited news of her camp acceptance. Agitation pushed against her optimism: in haste she had miswritten the address, or Berdis had forgotten to mail it. She found no envelope in the mailbox, only a bundle of last week's *Enterprise* from Miss Susan. She settled back on the porch with the stack of papers.

A series of shrill barks pierced the quiet, sending Bunk to the edge of the porch to gaze ahead and growl. A hundred yards from the iron fence and a team of blood-hounds, a curious construction had held her attention for days. The structure was too small for a work shed and lacked ventilation for a chicken coop. Today they had painted and closed the entrance to the big black box that, according to Papa, was eight by ten feet. A search for a clue in every paper on her lap turned up nothing.

James Williams's family and other neighbors once lived across the road. Now a look in that direction made Ivoe think of a mouthful of bad teeth, gaps where cabins used to be. From the clipping Momma had sent to her at school, she had envisioned a crude prison built of rough lumber like the one-room county jail in Starkville. But in the distance was a crenellated castle, the grandest building in Burleson County. A round turret with a conical roof encircled by a pressed metal cornice gave the prison a fairy-tale air. The jailer's family residence occupied the ground floor; the second and third stories contained the infirmary and cells for 280 inmates. According to a member of Old Elam, a deliveryman who transported dry goods to the prison and claimed to have received a tour, a trapdoor was included on the third floor, to be used as a hanging gallows.

Ivoe despaired at the fact that Little Tunis's only point of interest was the prison. Choices for social interaction that expanded the mind were few: a sewing circle or the juke, where Timbo claimed drinking too much corn likker imparted as much wisdom as any Willetson teacher. In her first week home, she had tried the Hagar Sewing Circle, but found the conversation unbearable. According to the circle, the only places a woman ever heard or felt anything worthwhile were during prayer or in the bedroom. They were a chorus with only two notes — men and church — but the life she envisioned did not hinge on these things. She craved the company of women who read and talked about books, knew music other than the spirituals; women who aspired to go to Paris — France, not Texas. Her idea to start a literary society like that Miss Durden belonged to mostly fell on deaf ears; its sole recipient was Miss Stokes, with whom she exchanged views regularly. Her common complaint: their embarrassing reliance on a few scriptures and a hymn. They were too content to moan and gasp and call on Jesus while colored people in Austin protested and formed fraternal organizations to aid themselves in the struggle for rights and protection. How many conversations had she suffered where a woman shared a problem only to silence her solutions with: "I'll put it in God's hands." "If Jesus don't fix it, it'll stay broke." Or her favorite: "If it's the Lord's will," as if they had no will of their own. She didn't know which was worse —

blind faith or the sanguine thinking of Sister Brown, who was just biding her time on earth because she would reap her true rewards in heaven. It didn't matter that Mr. Brown beat her and frightened his children half to death. Worse yet were the ones who loved to tell you how good God was while they made do with as little as one could imagine. Colored religion was the white man's most clever tactic yet. A new form of Uncle Tomming. It burned Ivoe up. Lord, woe is me — instead of pulling together and doing something to change the course of their lives, like colored Austin and their boycott.

There had been no way of knowing the trouble that a rigorous education brings. Her ideas had nowhere to go in Little Tunis. She mourned Willetson and Miss Durden, who had been from day one both pin and cushion. When would she — where would she — ever encounter someone who knew how to prod her and the precise moment and manner of necessary help? She longed for laughter with the teacher. Ona Durden's laugh hit you like the Galveston Giant in a match against Joe Jeannette. If sitting when struck by something comical, she would slap her thigh, the table, any surface. If standing when something funny struck, she bent her knees a little, as if about to dance, and pitched forward, rocking back on her heels. Either way, a warm golden sound, shrill around the edges, wailed from her throat like a trumpet. Her eyes lit up and she covered her mouth, embarrassed for taking all the joy out of the room though her laugh returned it tenfold.

The wild scrawl on the envelope jolted Ivoe.

South-By-God, Texas, Near Matamo-
ros, Mexico
June 30, 1907

Dear Ivoe,
On the trip to Louisiana I had the most wonderful fortune of meeting my husband. I have never known a colored man like him. He is completely uninterested in owning anything. With hands more beautiful than my own, he is very opposed to physical labor. He plans to see the world in his capacity as a manager to the finest musicians. I am the first musician he will attend to. Exactly what it means to have myself attended to I will devise shortly. He promises that I will play in all the great concert halls in the world, starting in Mexico City.

Let us hope the Negro is better treated there.

Your Bird

A sense of despair overcame Ivoe that had little to do with the marriage. Soon audiences in foreign countries would hear Berdis play while further study — let alone a career — in journalism eluded her. She had no clue how or where to begin the life Willetson had prepared her to lead. She was stuck and lonely while Berdis was on her way to becoming a woman of the world, making good on their graduation vow to each other to walk in silk attire and have silver to spare.

A week had passed since Miss Durden's disappointing news: she had appealed to the university to consider a second application from Ivoe but her recommendation was not enough. Still, the teacher's letter had ended on a note of encouragement:

. . . Austinites boycotted so effectively that notices were sent to all the colored churches notifying us that we may ride in any portion of the car we desire. The Statesman reported on the rescinded ordinance (enclosed). It should not be forgotten that the defeat of the "Jim

Crow" car bill was aided in no small part by your articles. You may have arrived at Willetson a Little Tunis girl but you departed a race woman.

Off to water my rhodies — so beautiful you almost have to lie down on the ground when you pass them.

Carry on . . .

Ona

Crinkled lavender blossoms rained on Ivoe along the wooden sidewalk of Main Street. At Planters & Merchants Bank, a well-dressed man alighted his carriage as a distant rumble changed to a passing roar and, finally, to the low hum of the twenty-mile railroad transporting cotton-filled locomotives to Houston. In the spinning wheel shop, a carpenter emptied a box of spokes on a table while heaps of laundry awaited folding by the colored maid at the boardinghouse. Behind the Church of the Epiphany wild rye, blown by a rare morning breeze, hovered over three fallen peaches as Ivoe stepped inside the office of the *Starkville Enterprise.* She stood, unnoticed, at the first desk, thinking of Miss Durden's recent letter — she should assert herself but not clamor for opportunity. Too much clamoring might drive it away, like a person

219

you love too much and put at a distance.

"Ma'am, I am here to see about a job," Ivoe said.

Edna Standish, secretary and wife to the paper's owner, wondered where the girl before her had gotten the notion that the newspaper was hiring — and a colored person at that? Before she could ask, Ivoe handed her a letter of reference, several clippings from the *Herald,* and a recent essay in response to *A Fool's Errand, by One of the Fools,* Judge Albion Tourgée's fictional retelling of his experiences in the South during Reconstruction. Pluck and graceful carriage earned her an invitation to sit down while Mrs. Standish read the fancy scrawl over fine stationery. Zilpha Stokes hadn't changed. The voice that championed her students on signs posted around town after the colored school burned down years ago — the same voice that compelled her to donate newspapers — now spoke to her from the page in elaborate detail about the virtues of Miss Ivoe Williams. She'd have to wage an unnecessary battle with her husband, but the girl spoke well enough. If she was as clever as the teacher claimed, or as she herself evidently believed, what harm could it do?

"Errands . . . and some of the unpleasant

duties the office requires. The pay certainly won't give you bragging rights."

Unlike many newspapers that sprung up to advance a politician's campaign then dissolved after Election Day, the *Starkville Enterprise* had longevity and a steady pool of subscribers. For a small-town paper, its reputation shone like polished silver on account of solid news coverage and editorials reprinted in the *Caldwell Post* and the *Bryan Daily News*. Ivoe's duties with the press that held the distinction of "oldest democratic newspaper" in Central East Texas belied its progressive beliefs on equality between the races. (She filed papers, answered telephones, complied with any thankless task.) A newspaper founded on the republican ideals of Lincoln and Douglass might've been a better fit, yet she felt kindled by the office chatter, the buzz of fast typing, the clatter of the press machines beneath rattling floorboards. She relished hauling heavy boxes, or any chore that brought her to the lift, where she could hear the pages humming off the press bed. She pushed the call button, waited until Wendell, the colored lift operator, loaded the freight and reversed its direction, driving up a gust of ink-scented air that reminded her of Willetson.

■ ■ ■ ■

"It's a start," Ivoe explained to her mother that evening. She was already meditating on the letter she wanted to write to Ona, scratching her left hand so hard welts appeared like ripples on a pond.

Lemon looked at the pile of okra and grabbed her daughter's hand. "Where is your mind? You fixing to scratch yourself to ribbons. Get some of that camphor before you touch your face and start itching all over." The look in Ivoe's eyes she had seen earlier that summer. After the graduation ceremony Ivoe had none of the calm satisfaction that came with achievement. She was oddly quiet and fidgety until the teacher joined them on the lawn. Talking to Miss Durden seemed to perk her up.

Children ought to know the wishes their parents hold for them. Lemon held a special one for Ivoe. She hoped that a person would come along to go the distance with her, help Ivoe run the race in her and Ennis's stead — and with the same devotion. Timothy had found his One, now who would love Ivoe on the road to her life's purpose? On graduation day she had thought she would meet a nice young man from the school down the road, but in the shade of the red-bud tree, hope faded. Watching Ivoe and Miss Durden she saw something curious — perfect tenderness of the teacher's hand as she swept a curl from Ivoe's forehead. A funny feeling came to her watching Ivoe's eyes when she accepted the teacher's gift, a clothbound book with a fern-green slipcase with gold embossed writing: *A Dream-Alphabet, and Other Poems.* She'd never seen Ivoe embrace anyone like that or look at a thing the way she read Miss Durden's card ("May your road wind to where the heart leads . . . Love, Ona").

"You get a letter from your friend lately? Imagine you can't wait to write and tell her about this," Lemon said.

Ivoe wiped her hands and reached for plates to set the table, wondering what her mother could possibly know about it.

"I imagine finding words to say what's going on with yourself, putting it all down, and sending it off for another soul feels good. The only letters I ever wrote were those I sent to you. No need in me lying. If I ever sat down to write to somebody all what's on my mind . . . well, I probably would still be writing."

The cabin was still that night when Ivoe

thought again of the letter she received that afternoon, as if Momma had talked it up. Reading Ona's letter for the third time, she paused between sentences, taking her eyes off the page to imagine everything Ona described, savoring each stroke of pen like a glad eater who lays the fork to rest during an exquisite meal. She clutched the letter to her chest, sighed for all its subtle niceties, and returned it to the special box under the bed. Peanut hulls on the little table brought to mind the only time she ever missed a class at Willetson. For a week, she had braved the interminable cold with the boycotters. After two days of missed classes, someone rapped on her door. The only proof that she had not hallucinated a benevolent phantom came when Miss Durden touched her head.

In and out of fevered sleep, she was fully jolted awake by a smell so divine she wondered if this was part of her delirium. Miss Durden peeled off a snow-dusted coat and ordered her to sit up. She watched the teacher pull a small iron pot from a box. Moments later she held a magical bowl of velvety amethyst. Sweet and creamy, the purple yam soup was unlike anything Ivoe had ever tasted. Even the thought of it now in still midnight heat roused her. She imagined Miss Durden at home, before she entered her tiny room that winter's day — the beautiful slender hands assembling ingredients, eyes that held tenderness gazing over a recipe. An unexpected breeze rustled the fig tree limbs outside her bedroom window as she pictured Ona in a lace slip, arms opening to embrace her. She breathed in the musky scent of fruit, heavy and succulent, turned on her stomach, followed the curve and line and pressed the arc with patience until her nightgown, damp with sweat, clung to her back. Such sweet rhythm, her song for Ona crescendoed in silence. She held the notes deep in her throat where they melted and trickled like fresh honey from a comb to the hollow of her belly.

8
THOU ART SO NEAR AND YET SO FAR

At the last oak tree before the Stark house Ivoe followed the slate path to the fountain. Inside a fluted cement bowl on a terra-cotta pedestal stood a cherub cast from ebony with a pitcher of flowing water. As a child, Ivoe had found the fountain a great source of intrigue, not for the sweet black figure poised on tiptoe but for the monstrous bird etched on the angel baby's chest. One traversed an identical black eagle, painted on the porch, with outstretched wings, a scepter and orb in each talon, to reach the front door. This coat of arms was stamped inside each of the Starks' books, embroidered on their linens, etched in the center of the rockwood bench where Miss Susan sat dressed in denim trousers and a short-sleeved shirt, a shapeless sun hat balanced on one knee.

"That's a face that's holding something in. Go on and laugh. I know I look like a funny ole scarecrow. Don't I know it?"

A few stairs delivered the giggling women into the garden.

"You ever see trumpets that golden? You can almost hear them they're so loud. I know Gabriel's up in heaven fit to be tied! When Mr. Stark built this garden for me, he chose narcissus because they're sturdy and are supposed to bring domestic happiness. Any wits left at all tumbling around in this skull, I lay to these flowers — a little peace on loan from God."

Susan knelt on the ground and drew a finger to her lips. She looked over her shoulder, leaned forward, and unscrewed the lid of the DaysO Work tin. The plug of tobacco daintily packed between her bottom lip and gums, she winked. Ivoe wanted to laugh. If Miss Susan prided herself on this secret, she needed to find another one; everybody in Little Tunis knew she dipped snuff.

"Now, I told Minnie good to snap the bulbs apart before she planted them. This morning she told me she forgot. Figured I'd work on this overcrowding here — so they don't grow tangled — while you tell me what it is you came to say." She slid a small shovel under the clump, careful not to knock the bulb.

Ivoe didn't know where to begin. She was twenty-two and life was going on without her. She felt tired and disgusted, just marking time on Little Tunis's roads that winded nowhere.

"Do you know anyone who needs a secretary, assistant of any kind — maybe something to do with books? I need work. Meaningful work."

"Aren't you still at the paper, or has Edna Standish made it impossible for you to work there?" Susan took a rag, spit, and folded. "That woman could irritate Michael the archangel."

"For four years I've done nothing but menial tasks at the *Enterprise.* I've pleaded with Mrs. Standish to give me real work. Proofreading, fact-checking, anything. Each time I mention it she waves it off, like's she's swatting a fly."

Susan sat up straight and still. Nearby, two bees landed inside a flower's corona. She lowered her voice. "Hand me that rag. Sweat makes bees aggressive. They don't usually bother with narcissus — it's early yet and there's little in the way of pollen. They'll take what they can get. Go on —"

"I've asked Mrs. Standish more times than I care to think to let me write. I bring her good ideas for stories to report on. A couple of days'll pass and the story I proposed is printed — sometimes on the front page and not written half as well as I might have done."

"Go right on blaming Edna or the *Enterprise* if you want to but you'd be wrong as two left shoes 'cause neither of them is confining your life, Ivoe. You are. Finishing at Willetson — that's tall cotton. You ought not to give up."

"Give up?" Ivoe's voice escalated. She thought of Willetson's annual alumni bulletins in which each year the number of her former classmates, now married to sharecroppers and working in the fields, grew. White southerners held it against colored people for not accomplishing more when they went out of their way to devise their greatest impediments. "It may be possible for a young white woman to carry off her career plans without incident, but for a member of my race and sex — even with credentials — it proves difficult, if not impossible."

"Help me up from here. I've had my sun for the day."

Susan grabbed hold of Ivoe's hands and struggled to her feet. "Who told you to stay in Texas?" Her eyes brightened with devilment as she leaned closer. "Why don't you get out of here?"

Shaded by the pecan trees, on the path to the house Ivoe traced the reasons she had stayed in Little Tunis: "Paltry earnings — and no savings." And the mailings she received from Ona every month — clippings from the Negro press that included warnings to overzealous migrants to the city. Without a job or friend waiting in the new destination, she couldn't even dream of leaving. "Not that Momma would ever let me."

"Let you?!" Susan's eyes were full of wild wonder. "Well, I sure did waste a whole lot of envy on you."

Ivoe could taste the blood from a tongue bitten too hard. Why on God's green earth would a white woman, who owned more land than a thousand men could plant in a day, be jealous of anybody, least of all a colored girl?

"How do you figure I have anything worth envy?" Ivoe said, climbing the porch stairs.

Susan bored in on her but there was warmth and kindness in her bearing as she sat down and motioned for Ivoe to do the same.

"Being white don't mean I've been done right by life. Now, the Negro is the last person I expect sympathy from — and that includes you — but you need some facts to balance out those assumptions." Miss Susan's face balled up; her searing blue eyes looked like the ocean about to spill over, a face that grieved the world, at least the South.

"I wasn't born to cotton. Daddy was no planter. We didn't own slaves. Daddy was a hardscrabble upcountry yeoman farmer and a piss-poor one at that. He only had about twenty-five acres and a whole heap of debt. Failed at raising tobacco. Eventually, he got a little corn crop going. That was around the time Mother died and he took to the bottle. He used to fuss to high heaven about having three daughters and no sons to help with all the work. We did our share but it wasn't enough. In town one day — I must've been around ten — Daddy met a young man who was signing up families to take west." Susan paused to look about the porch — every surface was bare. No cool beverage awaited her. She rolled her eyes and rang the bell for Minnie.

For as long as Ivoe could remember, she had wondered about the coat of arms. Now, sitting a few feet away from the black eagle, she settled in. By the time Alfred Stark fled the Prussian province of Westfalen for South Carolina with thirty-two Prussian and

Moravian families in 1859, cotton profiteers had depleted the backcountry soil. His plan for a Piedmont cotton empire had failed before he dropped anchor. Fortune grew westward. Stark brokered a deal with the governor of Texas to lead a gang of yeoman families and Muslim bondspeople from Alabama to the cotton frontier.

"Stark put it to Daddy straight: Central East Texas was wild country but the soil was good. Well, that was more than Daddy could boast. He collected his daughters and packed up the household. The journey was hell. Daddy had damn near pickled his liver but couldn't stop with the drink — only the German Evangelicals didn't allow it. He sweat and cussed and fought the whole way. In Georgia, one of my sisters turned back. Said she'd rather die alone in South Carolina than head into the unknown with a drunkard."

Susan looked at Ivoe and wondered how much of her own history the girl knew.

"We picked up thirty-one Africans from a ship in Alabama and there were at least that many waiting when we arrived in Texas. The Alabama Africans were different and they weren't long for Texas. Whenever chastised — beat — they cried out to Allah. Refused to convert. They spoke Arabic and some other languages the whites had no knowledge of. Alfred couldn't trust that the Alabama Africans prayed to a God he didn't know anything about, and so many times a day, like your mother. 'Cause your grandfather Booker brought in money with his smithing, he was the only man Alfred spared, along with his two wives Iraj and May-Belle. That business with the Muslim slaves haunted him all of his days, though he never would admit it. He'd be figuring on something, push his paper over to me, and ask the obvious: 'That right there say twenty-eight, don't it?' Every time he dealt in money, seem like the sum was 280 . . . 2,800 . . . 28,000 — couldn't get away from 28. That's how many Africans they drowned in the creek."

Ivoe recalled wartime and the burning down of her schoolhouse. On one of those long winter days with Momma she'd asked her why she hadn't married a Muslim man. Momma told her there wasn't none to marry but she had not said anything about the twenty-eight. There was no telling, no counting the loss her parents had known that she would never know about.

"In Louisiana, I lost another sister. Ran off with a fella. I was fourteen years old when we landed at the Brazos. Daddy died a few weeks later. At his funeral, Alfred Stark, then a twenty-five-year-old widower, told me to come work scullery in the big house. That's how I came to know your grandmother. I heard awful stories about cotton pickers — how it destroyed the hands and back — different from the Negro rice planters of Carolina with legs and feet blistered and swollen where they worked the marshy rice fields fifteen hours a day. At fifteen, I took sick with Stark's child — bedridden with fever. After I finally came to myself, Iraj told me Stark had married me for fear that I would die. If I died a fornicator, well, that made him one too, and he didn't want it on his conscience. My baby girl died in infancy."

Ivoe flashed on the mysterious tombstone she had discovered in the garden while playing as a little girl: THEDA SUSAN STARK, FEBRUARY 10, 1860–FEBRUARY 23, 1860.

"That December I gave him Earl. Your mother was born the same year. If you really want to know the truth, Ivoe, ain't nobody free. The whole business of living is mismanaged by a few who are long on money and short on common sense. In the matter of all that living I just told you about I didn't have a say in a lot of things," Miss Susan said, her voice catching a little. "That's what it means to be just a woman — no say. But an educated woman has a say and choice! Ivoe, you've got more education than every white woman I know. And a sense of duty, a life's purpose . . . I never did find mine."

"Every month I write to the editors of the *Bryan Daily Eagle* and the *Lone Star Ranger.* I have even offered to write for no money with the hope that more clippings will prove to Mrs. Standish —"

"You'll fair better in a city — someplace north. Now if you don't want to leave that's another story, but don't put that on Lemon. She'll understand and if she doesn't — well, you just keep talking until she does."

"I don't know anybody anywhere else."

"Well, I do." Susan straightened up and regarded Ivoe with earnestness. "If I let you borrow my name — to see if it'll open doors — will you make the most of it?"

Before she could answer Susan had hurried into the house and returned with eyeglasses and a leather book.

"There was a woman in Chicago who had a temperance organization. Maybe she could help. Alfred's people are known all over the state of Missouri. You write to this man in Kansas City. I believe he owns a couple of papers, or knows somebody who does — tell him that you know me. See if he can do anything for you."

At that moment, Ivoe nodded to Minnie, carrying two glasses of iced tea.

"I put a ham up for tonight's supper, Miss Susan. Ham be all right?"

"Minnie, that's the third time you've asked me that today," Susan snapped. "You ought not to fixate on one thing. What about the silver? Is it polished? You know I have the ladies for tea tomorrow. And my hats — did you go into town to pick them up?"

While Minnie's scolding continued a bee landed on Susan. Ivoe wondered if the fine hairs covering the woman's arm like fuzz on a peach made her oblivious to the bee, or if she was like May-Belle, who sat rock-still to encourage flight. Only a queen bee would cakewalk like that, syncopating each step with her stinger — once, twice, and again. Sturdy as a jonquil.

"Shiiit!" Miss Susan's hand came down on her arm like a cleaver on a chicken's neck. "It's my own damn fault. I know better than to sit out here — Minnie, run, bring me some lemon to clean this with." Susan studied her arm, scowled after the help. "Today! Not tomorrow." She whispered to Ivoe, "I have half a mind to fire her. She never was any good and now that she's gotten old, she's worse."

236

"Miss Susan, I better get on home," Ivoe said.

"You remember what I told you. Write to Kansas City."

From the road Ivoe heard her shouting to Minnie to call the doctor.

Earl Stark never knew his mother was allergic to bee venom.

The Williamses paused before the walnut coffin to take in the nest of brown-and-gray curls piled high on Susan's head, the pearl earrings dangling from her fleshy earlobes, the dress. "She always did favor that one," Lemon said of the bodice of beige lace over a skirt of brown silk. She looked at the smooth hands, remembering the final chore of each day when she delivered a toddy on a pewter tray, retrieved the liniment of rose petals and wild cherry bark, and disrobed her mistress, carefully kneading her limbs as a mother rubs her ailing child.

After Earl's eulogy, a small boy was deployed to hold the music while Irabelle played "Du Bist Mir Nah und Doch So Fern," a song cherished by Miss Susan, who had often recalled how beautifully her husband played it when he returned from the war.

For many from Little Tunis, the funeral of

237

Mrs. Stark meant they would finally see inside the Starks' manse, whose stories of grandeur had lived for generations in the Bottoms. A long line wended from the porch down into the famous jonquil garden, with two butlers ushering visitors into the parlor. Though they were barred from other rooms, some paused in the foyer to glance up the staircase, craned their necks for a view of the dining room and the kitchen where Minnie claimed to get her fill of sweet cream and pie or cake every night after supper. But there were also those who would pluck out an eye before lingering on lavish furnishings; they couldn't leave quick enough: "Ain't a house in all of these United States worth what we been through picking cotton to an early grave."

Minnie and the Williams family were the only colored guests to remain for the reception, during which Lemon eyed the silver for spots. None. The china gleamed. Minnie had done her best. Even the tomato aspic with homemade mayonnaise almost tasted like something.

On the way home with her family, Ivoe thought about the small kindnesses of Susan Stark — the books given to her through the years, the skirts and dresses she had taken to Willetson and still wore. The best gift had been their last conversation. The talk with Miss Susan had the uncanny ability of strengthening her backbone. Once again she had assembled her articles from the *Willetson Herald* and a letter in which she spoke of her education and eagerness to write for a newspaper or to print one. Yesterday morning, before Minnie brought the news of Miss Susan's passing, she rose early to mail the letter and those addressed to the colored *Texas Freeman* and other papers in Oklahoma, Nebraska, and Missouri — none sealed with as much hope as the envelope bound for Kansas City.

"Far as whites go, Miss Susan wasn't all bad," Papa said.

"*Ssth.* Wasn't all good either."

Papa cleared his throat. "Well now, Lemon, hold on. My Good Book don't say you got to be perfect to enter the pearly gates. What yours say?"

May-Belle chuckled. "If Alfred Stark up there and she headed that way, I know he ain't none too pleased about it. Couldn't get a word in edgewise when he was alive. She liable to talk him to his second death."

At that moment Irabelle realized the feeling of loss had nothing to do with Miss Susan's death. She pictured her clarinet on the piano stool in the parlor a half mile away. Papa said it could wait until tomorrow, but Momma meant for her to learn responsibility. "Ivoe, you go on with her," Papa said. But Momma meant for her to learn responsibility alone: "Ivoe don't need to go. Ivoe didn't leave nothing."

"Can Bunk go with me?" Without waiting, she gave a sharp whistle. Soon, Bunk arrived, wagging his tail.

Momma patted Irabelle lightly on the behind and watched her take off. "Get on back here before it gets dark."

For weeks Irabelle had not put the instrument down except to play with the twins, only four years old but clever and funny as anything. At thirteen, she was learning to feel pride for something apart from her parents and siblings. The clarinet was hers and all her. She loved the weight of the dark shiny boxwood, the feel of the twenty-four keys that made her think of nickels, the way the bell blossomed like her mother's flowers, even the mysterious way it had come to her six years ago.

Papa had come into her room late one night. With Ivoe away at Willetson, it took her a long time to fall asleep, so she lay there with her eyes closed but not sleeping, "playing possum." He gave her a soft nudge.

"Sit up. I know you ain't sleep." Whenever Papa put a match to the lantern he meant business. "You remember what I told you about that day in Snook?" His voice was shaky and cracked. "You never did tell nobody did you?" She shook her head. "A secret like that too heavy for a little girl to carry, but Papa brought you something for you to tell that secret to and any more you pick up along the way. You put your mouth to it here and when you blow it'll talk back to you."

For six years, she had scarcely let the clarinet out of her sight. Relieved to have it back in her possession, she could almost see her cabin when her music drew the attention of a pair of boys.

The younger boy squinted up at her, the skin on his nose and shoulders so badly peeled she had a mind to take him to her aunt to get fixed up. She asked the boy what kind of fish they had caught, but he just stared. The tall boy with hair the color of burnt hay was not as old as Ivoe, though he spoke in a deep voice.

"Play something for us," he said.

Bunk bared his teeth and growled.

"Well, if you ain't gonna play, give it to my brother. He might as well have it. You want it don't you?"

241

The little boy nodded.

Irabelle clutched the instrument close as the older boy lurched, grabbed hold of the clarinet's end, and gave it a hard yank. Each direction he pulled his half of the clarinet, Irabelle followed. Even when he kicked her, and she went down, her grip did not loosen. Bunk scrambled over her, stepping into her face and chest to get at the boy. She heard the hard kick, followed by Bunk's keening. The boy swore as she bit him but pinned her arms down anyway, lowering his face close enough to kiss her. She could wrestle with Timbo for hours and never get tired; this boy felt heavy as lead. He gripped both her wrists with one hand and, with the other, drew a knife from his trouser pocket. He kissed her softly on the lips.

"Be still," he said, drawing the tip of the blade along her cheek. Only his brother would know he kissed the most beautiful girl in Burleson County, but the scar would be a constant reminder. A mere prick was all he intended but the girl beneath him writhed more than a snake and jerked her head in the opposite direction, carrying the blade an unintended distance.

Ruby clay puddles where her blood met the dirt road scared the boys off. The wetness of her cheek and a crimson hand made her scream. Bunk's nose was cool against her arm, where he started to lick as she felt around for the clarinet. There was pain in her knee when she tried to stand.

As she drew near the faint cry, May-Belle made out the long braids of her great-niece in a crumpled heap. With so much blood she could not tell what had been done. The blouse was torn; the skirt bore a bloody hole; one bruised leg jutted out awkwardly. She pressed against the leg to make sure it was not broken: "Hold on." She hooked her arms under Irabelle's, pulled her to her feet, and started for Lemon's.

From the front porch, Ivoe's voice could be heard high and frail: "Momma, I can't hold her. I can't —" Ennis came through the door to a scene he did not understand — a moving table, arms and legs flailing in the air. Blood had dripped onto the floor. Lemon and Ivoe tried to hold Irabelle, whose pain lent her surprising strength. May-Belle had something in her hand.

"Can't you do nothing besides stand there?" Lemon shouted.

He changed places with his wife, his big hands firmly placed on Irabelle's shoulders, pinning her to the table.

Between the sobs and wails of his wife and eldest girl and May-Belle, Irabelle screamed a mercy roll call: "I-voe, please . . . tell them to stop . . . Momma it hurts . . . Papa help me." Blood squirted from the gash in their child's face that ran from the side of her nose across the plateau of her cheek as May-Belle guided a needle into its soft pliant flesh.

The tea of valerian and licorice root finally took its toll on Irabelle.

Ennis left her to sleep and found Lemon scrubbing the stain on the kitchen table. She had done her best, and now in the midst of a soft cry that jabbed at his heart, she complained that the blood would not lift from the wood.

As she looked at the handsome couple, a queer thought entered Ivoe's mind. Any colored person seeing her parents on the street today would know something serious had happened, because the only time Negroes dressed this fine in Little Tunis was for a funeral, or to solicit the help of a white person. In this case, both were true. Something had died inside of her sister. Ivoe saw the evidence late at night when she turned up the lantern to dab at the pus that seeped from the coarse black thread woven across

Irabelle's face. Now, watching Momma size the knot in Papa's tie, Ivoe was seized by a pang of hopelessness. Even if the young perpetrators were identified, she was certain nothing would be done. She handed the written description of the boys to her mother and was about to ask her what she planned to say when Irabelle appeared in the kitchen doorway. Her eyes were red-rimmed and moist as she drew a shudder-ing breath. "Can't Papa stay with me?"

At half past eight on Sunday morning, Ivoe and Lemon set out for the sheriff's, where Ivoe's face was known on account of the errands she ran for the *Enterprise.*

The deputy inquired as to the nature of Ivoe's visit in a friendly manner. She stated that they wished to file a report. Three and a half hours later, during which time the heat allowed only the most necessary mo-tion, the sheriff emerged to take his lunch.

"I don't know if the deputy told you . . . We are here to report a horrible —" Ivoe began.

"Ain't this the gal that makes and sells them jams?"

"Yes, sir. This is my mother. Leila Wil-liams."

"Now what's that you say — something done happened over at the newspaper?"

"Nothing's wrong at the paper, sir. It's my sister —"

"Sir, my child, she ain't nothing but thirteen and two boys —"

The sheriff cut in front of Lemon for the fountain, where he took his time drawing long sips of water.

Lemon thought it was very likely she might faint before getting her story out. "Yesterday my youngest child, Irabelle Williams, was on her way home after retrieving her clarinet from the Starks' house. She was minding her own business and along come these two boys who wanted to take her clarinet. They asked her for it, and when she wouldn't give it to them they — they cut her. They cut her face from here to here." She drew up a finger and demonstrated on her right cheek the design of the gash.

"Where did she get a clarinet from?"

"My husband, sir. My husband give it to her years ago."

"And where did he get it from?"

Ivoe tried to quell her anger by clearing her throat.

"Can't rightly say. You know my Ennis. He smiths around here and yonder — in Snook and Bryan. Sometimes he don't get paid proper. Meaning, he don't always get cash. Some folks barters with him. I figure Ennis got the clarinet the same way."

"You say your gal refuse to let the boys see it?"

"No, sir. They didn't ask to see it. They tried to take it from her. We have a description of the boys right here."

Lemon riffled in her pocketbook.

"Now, you said it was two boys?"

"Yes."

"Must be a mighty strong gal you got to be fighting off two boys." The sheriff chuckled. "What you feeding her?"

"She didn't fight them, sir. They cut her."

"Well now, it's terrible how these youngsters fool around. They ain't meant no harm. Seem to me that gal of yours ain't telling the full-out truth. She was probably acting high and mighty 'cause she had something two white boys ain't got."

"No, sir. Irabelle was walking with the dog . . . and they come up on her. And they cut her."

"For the trouble this gone bring on you, you be better off if you just get the girl another clarinet."

"They didn't take the clarinet. After the boy cut her he and the other one took off."

Indignation showed on the sheriff's face and his growing impatience was heard. "If y'all got the clarinet what can I do for you?"

"You saying it's all right to just go around cutting folks? I know that ain't what you saying. We appreciate if you find these boys."

This was an uppity Negress. "And do what with them?"

Ivoe tried to hold her mother's hand but Momma jerked away and cut her a hateful look. At home, in Little Tunis, even in Miss Susan's house, her mother was a mountain of a woman, strong and brave. Only once had she seen her mother wilt — for a minute — when Timbo was ill and Miss Susan expected her to cook for her husband's funeral. She had expected her mother to cave under Susan's demand, when all of a sudden Momma grew ten feet tall. This time was different. The law hefted more weight. Her mother was slivered by injustice.

"I reckon it ain't for me to say."

The sheriff poured the cup of his hand around Lemon's elbow and led her to the door. His voice had a tense edge.

"A lot of folk come here thinking we can find this one and that one. Had one fellow come to say somebody stole his wagon. And you know what he asked me to do? He asked me to find them and punish them. I told him — a white man — just like I'm

248

telling you. We here to protect but we ain't in the finding business."

Lemon took the sheriff's hand from her arm. "I come here to report a crime and ain't taking another step till there's a writ account of what's been done to my child."

They waited until six o'clock that evening, when the sheriff invited them to spend the night in a cell because he had to get home to supper.

Distracted from every chore at home and the newspaper, Ivoe thought incessantly about the incident at the sheriff's office. Two weeks of hard regret (she should've reminded her sister about the clarinet during the repast, she should've accompanied Irabelle on her walk to the Starks) had passed when a box arrived from Ona Durden.

She opened the letter and smiled because it was a long one, funny from the start, warm and charming to the end.

In the best possible way she felt chastened by the one-line note attached to her gift — "If purpose was a snake it would've bitten you by now" — and thought of it as she struck a key on the secondhand Underwood typewriter, smaller than a picnic basket. The scar on her sister's face and the hatred surrounding it flickered in the fire of her soul as she typed. Who could they blame? The Ku Klux Klan, the Red Shirts, the Knights of the White Camelia, the White Line? Not even — their young sons now terrorized with impunity. In the blink of an eye her family had been changed because a white boy wanted something he could not have. Papa was short on patience and plum out of language, cussing at the slightest irritation or dead silent. His silence created a void not even Momma could breach. She tried to talk to him, drawing in a deep breath as if her words required extra force to reach him, but Papa would shake his head or walk away before she finished. When the words fell back into Momma, her chest jumped a little like during a hiccup, or like a child who, at the end of a heaving cry, sucks in his hurt and humiliation. An odd sight to see, such a proud woman taking sips of air to quell the rage that swelled inside of her. Who could blame Momma or Papa? General Granger had issued the proclamation nearly half a century ago, but so-called free colored lives were still up for grabs, with no real claim to safety, no judicial ear to whom they might cry.

Ivoe wrote with a fervor she had never known, drawing lines through superfluous sentences, consulting a history book, until she held her despair in two pages. On the final read-through, she struck the word *judgment* and wrote in *justice.* In the margin beside the last two two paragraphs she drew question marks, before placing the essay in an envelope bound for Austin.

At the sound of her sister sleeping, Ivoe left the bed and dressed. She grabbed the lantern and the envelope from Austin. Ona's suggestions had improved the work, yet it was the five-word message at the top of the page ("Find a way to publish!") that had kept Ivoe's mind in the devil's workshop. In the kitchen, she patted Bunk's head and whispered for him to lie back down. A quiet tussle with the door and a leap across the creaky porch landed her in the yard. She turned the lantern up. No one from Little Tunis would be stirring at this hour.

The other plan, to be carried out in the light of day, would have cost two people their jobs. She had seen how she might approach the lift operator with her essay and a forged note that gave explicit directions for the compositor to make space and include her article in the morning edition. Discovery of their crime would bring on their fury and prompt her firing. The white compositor would be at another paper within a week, but what would happen to the lift operator? Fact or fiction, reputation of distrust made it impossible for a colored man to secure work. Of the two plans she had chosen right.

For the last two years Edna Standish had entrusted her with a key to the office. Usually, Ivoe arrived at the office at 7:30 A.M. to check the basket for instructions on early-morning errands. On choreless days, she answered the telephone, took orders for advertisements, read old issues — once as far back as the winter of 1898. Not a word about the lynchings of Junior and James Williams Sr., but plenty of letters to the editor adumbrated their deaths all the same. A Starkville businessman expressed dissatisfaction with James's lumber business, more lucrative than any in Burleson County. Under Local News, the schoolhouse fire that same year had earned two short lines: "Negro school catches fire. Teacher to establish night school at Old Elam." A thousand days of waking up too early was going to amount to something. Neither the sheriff nor his deputy had used a drop of ink about Irabelle in their "reports," but they were all going to read about it just the same.

Ivoe knew the exact number of steps from the top of Main Street to the newspaper office but turned the flame high to prevent suspicion. A passerby might wonder at a colored person's confident walk in the dark, as if she were embarked on a long-planned robbery. Should anyone stop her, she was armed with a lie: Mrs. Standish had sent word that she check on the presses because someone had called to complain of strange noises emanating from the office. Alone on the street, she hurried the lock as punitive scenarios flashed before her — arrest, jail, and worse. In the basement, bundled and stacked on dollies near the freight elevator, the morning paper awaited delivery. She glanced at the clock. At five thirty, the printer would arrive to press two thousand copies of the noon edition. She had less than three hours.

At the composing table she pored over the dummies, mock-ups of story and advertisement placement. She knew better than to tamper with the front page. Letters to the editor were too short. Spacing for an article on Bryan County's prison farm on page three came in at six hundred words. Perfect. Unlike Willetson, where she type-casted by hand, she had no stick to fill with letters, no column line to pad out or justify, only the level and the keyboard. Four years had gone by since she last sat at a linotype. She stared at the fifteen columns, remembering finger placement: the index finger of the left hand typed *s* and *a;* the second finger typed *e* and *t;* the third pressed the large space bar; and so on. Ona Durden's reprimands rang clear: "Forearms parallel to thighs . . ." Fingers that rested on the keys caused letters to drop into the machine, a costly mistake. Two hours of slow, deft keystrokes and the new page three dummy held her column.

Rumbling machines greeted her later on that morning. The paper had gone through stereotyping and was now on the printing press. Whatever the consequence, she thought as she sat down to her desk, her article was condign publication for the apathetic sheriff and the journalistic assignments Edna Standish had denied her.

Ivoe appeared too busy to care about the noon edition. She stammered through important phone calls, spilled ink on Mrs. Standish's desk. She had accomplished very little when Edna Standish came to her that afternoon. "Ivoe, if you expect to be paid for today, you'll need to stay late. Finish at least one of the tasks I have given you." The phone calls started shortly thereafter. By two o'clock a line of angry subscribers was out the door: no democratic organ should publish the likes of page three.

Strangely excited by her firing, Ivoe grabbed a stack of newspapers on her way out of the office, then wondered who, other than Ona Durden, would care to read it.

ON THE SAFETY OF COLORED GIRLS AND WOMEN

The Negro female is made the test in everything pertaining to American civilization; its high principles of religion, politics, and morals all receive a shock when a Negro woman's head appears, upsetting all theories and in a conspicuous manner proving that the structure of American civilization is built higher than the average white man can climb. Denied the limited judicial protection offered to white women, Negro women have no recourse when they are victims of assault, maiming, and rape.

From whom, then, shall the Negro woman seek help? As this is unquestionably the woman's era, the question is timely and proper.

Every race and nation that is at all progressive has its quota of earnest women engaged in creating for themselves a higher sphere of usefulness to the world.

This fact is now seen in the struggle for woman's suffrage. In 1910, Washington gave woman her vote; this year California joined the ranks of those states that insist upon the necessity of a higher plane of integrity and equipped woman with the ballot. The place occupied by woman and child is said to be the best test of a people's advancement, yet the Negro race is denied the fact of its sacred womanhood. In Burleson County, Negro women and girls are accorded neither protection nor the preservation of their own integrity in this land of their birth.

On the evening of April 27, in the unincorporated enclave known as Little Tunis, a few miles from the county seat of Starkville, a thirteen-year-old Negro girl on the cusp of womanhood met with danger in the short distance from her home. The Negro girl was accosted by two white boys of the approximate ages of ten and fifteen, who demanded the girl give them her musical instrument. The victim was not killed or raped for refusing to relinquish her most prized possession — a clarinet — she was gashed in the face and left to bleed on the road. It is neither plausible nor possible to launch an investigation of the alleged event, the Starkville sheriff concluded to the victim's mother. It is a case when a custodian of the law turned his back on the defenseless condition of a victim when he should have provided her his best defense. The presentation of such facts is not flattering to the two white boys or their parents (presumably ignorant of their sons' vengeful act or else why have they not come forward in the spirit of atonement as civilized persons do?); neither are the events pleasurable to the colored family of the girl victim. Nevertheless they are facts that must be considered.

It is with feelings of respect when members of the Negro race reflect upon the great work that was accomplished in the nineteenth century for the Negro by truly good men and women of the white race. Now the twentieth century is confronted with the sobering fact that there remains yet more work to do, for the progress of the human race depends on each group giving its best energies to the uplifting of all people. The twentieth century in its infancy is striving to grasp what it pleases to call the "Negro problem," when it is in reality only a question as to whether justice and right shall rule over injustice and wrong for any and every man regardless of race in this boasted land of freedom. It is at this stage of American existence the question must be asked: To whom will the Negro girl cry "Help"?

— I. L. Williams

9
IN THE GLOAMING
JUNE 1911

"Looked to me like that girl learned a thing or two in Austin," Lemon said, laying aside the *Starkville Enterprise.*

"Ain't done nothing but told the truth. I just hope them crackers don't come looking for her. Can't go running off at the mouth like that to them people in they own paper," Ennis said.

Lemon shook her head. For weeks her husband had barely talked. Never heard nothing the first time — had to tell him things three, four times. He was gone. Just gone — first his speech, then his listening. She hesitated to tell him what was on her heart when it used to come so easy.

"Who is you, now, Ennis? Who you supposed to be? I just don't know you no more." Dead silence. "You full of hell is what you is. Can't say a right word around you. Can't touch you. About the only thing I'm good for is to cook and feed you. I'm

259

wondering how long till you recognize you ain't the only one around here carrying hurt?"

"Life ain't fit to live is all. Well, maybe up there in Starkville, but this here we living ain't fit for nobody. Don't matter how hard I work — if I can't see to my family what bit of good do it come to?"

"You got yourself so twisted up you ain't thinking straight."

"I'm thinking straight for the first time in a long while. Colored man so used to doing what everybody say, he done forgot how to change. Things got to change for us, Lemon. Lessen they do ain't no future in tomorrow."

"Change?"

"Damn sick of life testing me. How much can you stand? How much can I take from you? I wants to be the kind of man what gets tested another way. How much you want? How much can you get?"

"That sounds like the white man's test. You ain't had the proper schooling for it."

"Should've left when I first had a mind to. Now that girl ain't never gonna be right. When I look at her . . . when I got heart enough to look at her . . . They took something from her, Lemon. Maybe next time they core her like an apple. Leave her for dead."

It had taken weeks for the swelling to go down, the plum bruise on Irabelle's face to fade, yet it seemed to Ennis that the scar had spread all over her.

Neither rotted corn piled high in the cribs or the blood of slaughtered cattle baked on the land outside the smokehouse could be blamed for the rancid odor. The revolting stench blowing in their direction came from the prison farm, where that morning three colored men had been carried out of the black box. Why they were put inside and for how long they had been there no one knew, but the cause of death was simple: with the temperature well above a hundred, suffocation came quick.

A few neighbors had heard the confined convicts scream for help, but according to the *Enterprise* that afternoon, the guards had no reason to think the inmates were in distress or suffering. The commissioners' investigation found that the guards had not violated any laws or acted negligently. They had "exercised poor judgment."

In 1907, when Ivoe started at the *Enterprise,* she began to pay attention to prison farms like the one in Starkville. Each discovery of a new farm sent her to the large swath of butcher paper hanging on her bedroom wall. Four years after she'd first used Momma's sewing pins to plot a marker, pinheads dotted the entire map of Texas. Silver clusters showed the counties with the most convicts — Houston, Robertson, and, now, as she pushed the fifth pin into place, Burleson County. From conversations at church she learned that in places like Snook and along the Old River, prisoners did more than pick cotton. Private companies rented convicts for labor associated with corn, coal, timber, and granite. Reverend Greenwood had asked for a show of hands from the people who knew somebody at a prison farm. Her family and one other were the only people without raised hands; some raised both.

Little Tunis, May 27, 1911

Dear Miss Durden,
  Angry letters and a steep drop in subscriptions secured my speedy firing after the publication of "On the Safety of Colored Girls and Women." It was well worth it. Strangely, apart from my family, you and Miss Stokes remain the essay's only advocates. Not every share-

cropper reads but many do, and no one in Little Tunis has offered so much as a single word about it, including the preacher. I don't know when I'll return to Old Elam. I am convinced their only aim is to deafen their pie-in-the-sky God with lowly prayers of strife and tribulations. Not one of them seems interested in lifting a finger for change — only for cotton!

No word in return for the letters of employment I send out to newspapers every month. Mediocrity dressed in pants regularly sees his name in print when no one will so much as read one of my sentences and consider my potential. Convincing any paper to hire me seems as likely as scratching my ear with my elbow. And I am most needed now. Three colored men were murdered at the prison farm. The details are thin and no one among us has any authority to demand answers, least of all your journalist-in-waiting.

I have taken work at a boardinghouse in town, making beds, emptying basins. These acts fill me with such bitterness I can scarcely write about it.

Yours (in the wilderness),

Ivoe

Austin, June 18, 1911

Dear Ivoe,

I worked so hard today that I thought if death should come, I would be grateful. For hours I joined neighbors in sweeping, bagging up trash, then hauling buckets of water to scrub down the sidewalk and streets — in hundred-degree temperature, mind you. And the worst part: there is no place to put the garbage. The city refuses to take it away. We have designated the backyard of an abandoned house — most upsetting for neighbors in close proximity.

Austin has passed more building restrictions designed to affect Wheatville residents based on a survey that blames us for the accumulation of garbage and waste in the streets when it is the city's garbage wagons dumping trash in our neighborhood. I have been busy organizing community meetings, writing letters, placing phone calls — none of which are ever returned!

We are in for a tiresome battle. Many feel we are being forced out, or rather east. I do believe if I were ever to leave Wheatville, I'd leave Texas altogether.

How much time has passed since we

laid eyes on each other? Do you think you might be able to meet me in Dime Box?

Keep the faith!

Ona

Before she had time to gather her thoughts for a reply to Ona, Irabelle entered the room. The trousers she wore bulged a little at the hip where she kept the sheath from plain sight. With her hair cropped close and skin bronzed by the sun, Irabelle reminded Ivoe of Gauguin's Polynesian boy soldier as she handed her a single piece of mail. No sender's name. Truxillo Street. Houston. The *Freeman*'s editor was impressed by her submission, but before she could saddle up to hope, the word *apologies* stood out like an unwanted penny. Apology number one — for the delayed response, caused by a fire that had destroyed their offices. Her letter had been slow arriving to the space the newspaper now occupied in Houston's Light Guard Armory. Apology number two — the cryptic return address, a tactic employed by many colored newspapers to protect against organized white vigilantes. With great regret, the editor could not do as well as the *Enterprise* in offering a job.

"Ivoe, somebody's bound to want you

soon," Irabelle said, glancing at the pile of clippings from the editorial she inspired. She admired her sister for wanting to help colored people and to set the record straight for whites. If anyone asked her, civilizing the white race would take a lot more than words. Irabelle couldn't understand why white people instigated so much trouble when they lived better, had more opportunity. Let them tell it, they had created the world and everything in it, so why meddle with the lowly Negro? Why not leave him alone to his own ruinous ways? It was enough to sow confusion in anybody's head.

To straighten out the tangled contempt, Irabelle played her music and devised ways to protect herself. She kept the scissors to her hair — wearing it short would draw less attention and give them nothing to pull. She grew long nails — for clawing. Each meal reminded her of the great work her teeth could do. After Timbo gave her "something to cut with" she practiced on everything from fish to trees. She tore out the fear she had lived with since that day heading home from the Starks'. White boys grew wrong. They grew into terrifying white men, She nurtured a lustful eye for men like her father, men the color of the sky before dawn, obsidian black, ink black, oil black, raven black, devil black. Well, if white boys and their fathers were God (and they were, according to the pictures in the Sunday school books), she wanted the devil.

Little Tunis had a few of these men. They talked loud, laughed louder; you could always hear them coming. They worked hard, but on an off day you could find one on the porch or out in the yard delighting everybody simply by breathing. A beer drunk too fast brought a belch, and his children fell out from laughter. Undercooked crowder peas made him fart, and his woman cut her eyes and called him trifling in a tone you might call prideful. The old men dreamed as young men do — of big satin thighs, fluty-voiced laughter, a good swat on the behind. "Good God," he praised in a whisper, whenever a young woman just learning to carry her beauty passed him. Sometimes it was his own woman walking by his porch chair that he caught by the hem and pulled close so that her behind was near enough to bite. Children or whatever company he had snickered. Who could tell if his pull or their snickering tapped her hard bark, but "You . . . so . . . *naaa*-sty" trickled from his woman's mouth in a syrupy drawl. No child anywhere had ever been given such a sweet

reprimand. He could act ugly too. Sometimes the cabin's wood frame bulged, the
sagging windows rattled, the porch shud-
dered and shook, his voice boomed and she
screamed. But walk past the same cabin
later and hear it hum. The humming told
who had won, the fight settled between her
legs. Like everything you love too much,
these men were feared. Why else would
there be so many pins on Ivoe's map and a
black box a hundred yards from their door?

For two weeks Ennis's mind had been fixed
on the journey but breaking the news didn't
come any easier.

"Any time you can haul three dead colored
men out a box and not a damn thing is done
about it . . . something got to change. You
see Al-Halif gone after what they done. Just
up and took his family. Didn't leave it to
prayer neither. Left his business and everything."

"Yeah, well, you blame him?"

"Naw, I don't blame him. I want to be
right behind him. He did what he was supposed to do."

"I know why Ivoe wants to leave — two
years of city schooling and she's biggity, but
you, Ennis. We done been down this road
before. We might not have much but what

we have we own. We gonna be colored wherever we go. I don't see what leaving's gonna fix."

"I've decided I'm going on without y'all."

Lemon stopped busying herself in the kitchen. "You got to take me with you then . . . Ivoe and Irabelle can make do. Timbo will see to that. Ain't nobody getting sick around here long as there's breath in May-Belle's body. Take me with you." She could already feel it, emptiness too heavy to carry.

"Easier for a man to find work when he by hisself."

Lemon opened the cupboard and reached behind the flour for the jug of whiskey. "Where you thinking on going?"

"Kansas. It ain't just them, the children, what supposed to make us proud. We they parents. Ain't they supposed to know some kind of pride for they papa?"

"They love you, Ennis." And you know I do.

"Loving and priding is two different feelings. I can't even protect them. How you think that makes me feel?"

Something about the way Ennis turned his glass let her know he was already gone. She sank, wounded, into a chair. Here she was worrying, planting, cooking, cleaning, and he had been planning his escape. She took a swig, set her glass down hard on the table, and looked him straight in the eye. "What you talking is foolishness. We done seen our way clear of ugly before. We gonna see our way clear of this. You not going nowhere."

"Lemon, I'm fixing to hurt somebody real bad if I stay around here. Already watched a man die."

"*Ssth.* I feared something had a hold of you. How you living with that? How you take a man's life and not tell me?"

"I ain't took his life. Just didn't do nothing to help him get it back when I saw it getting away from him. That's why you got to let me go. I ain't no kind of good for y'all no way. Restless in my mind . . . and can't feel. Can't feel you. Can't feel the children. Only person I feel for is myself. Wrong for a man to feel like the only life he can save is his own. He just got that in him. God put it in him to want to see to others." He would work until he raised means to buy a plot and send for them. A year, maybe two, he figured.

With the gloaming came dread. Lemon turned away from the kitchen window, where she had watched Ennis talk to Timbo

270

out on the porch until her head began to throb. No use in him telling the boy how to look after them when Ennis was the only one fit to do it. Didn't he know that by now? All week a bad feeling had seized her. No other way to describe longing for somebody not gone, grieving somebody not dead. That evening during their last family supper she felt as light as dandelion dust. For thirty-one years she had studied that man, knew how to care for him, how to leave him be, how to love him. What if he needed her? Or didn't he think he would?

In the next room she could hear her husband talking to Ivoe and Irabelle. "Be a while 'fore folks know y'all here alone. I want it that way, that's how come I'm leaving tonight. Let peoples think what they want. When I left, where I'm gone, and how long I'm staying ain't nobody's business."

Irabelle doubted the horse's night vision but he assured her the mare could see better than him. And he wouldn't drive her too fast. Lemon felt her stomach drop. His feet were like lead walking to their bedroom, where he stood in the doorway a long time just looking at her. When he finally closed the distance between them, he pulled her chin up and kissed her.

Before he opened the first drawer she

knew the things he would take and why. Her chest tightened as she watched him pick things out, knowing for certain exactly how he weighed them in his mind. Traveling fast meant traveling light. He filled a gunnysack with his razor and strap, a few tools, two clean shirts, and underwear. "Afterwhile somebody gonna come to you about my shed. Don't worry about what's in there. Go ahead and rent it. Should fetch you a few extra dollars a month." He took the small bronze carving etched with her image off the wall, explaining his plan one more time. He would find work, live cheap, and save money. Once he set their new world to spinning in a town where colored people could live in peace, he would return for them. He promised.

"Till I get back, don't give away nothing you know I love."

They watched Ennis rattle to the end of their road, stop his horse, turn on his wagon seat, and wave. After Ivoe and Irabelle went inside the cabin, Lemon eyed the chair, his chair, in the corner of the porch. If she sat down, she might not get up. Before she could go inside, she had to figure out what came next. The answer was in front of her like the flowers at the edge of the porch bending this way and that. Her feelings were all in the blue sage the night breeze was having its way with. If life could treat a flower like that, why should she be any different? Stand. She just had to stand. But how when the only somebody to prop her up was gone? She leaned against the cabin, wrapped herself tightly, and looked out into the night sky, taking the journey with Ennis in her mind — past the cornfields . . . orchard . . . beyond Starkville . . . on the road to Snook. She had never been farther than that. It was pitch black when she started reciting the eleven verses of the Surah Adh-Dhuha to ensure her husband's safe return.

Ennis. Ennis. Ennis.

News of Ennis's flight spread through Little Tunis like water on a grease fire. The Williams family was living proof that working hard and sticking together was all a colored family needed to get by. So, why did he leave? Where did he go? For a little while the boisterous banter of children and guffawing of grown women happy at the heavy thud of their men lumbering down the road at day's end was silenced by these questions that hung on the tongue as if rooted there. Some said they understood his leaving, what with that uppity wife and the bitter fruit she bore him. That man-boy of theirs was about as handy as a back pocket on a shirt. Couldn't be depended on for shit. People hated to see him coming, talking about he had something to sell you. And owed everybody. Fanny should've known better than letting Roena marry that boy. And that oldest girl was strange as snow in July. Went away for a couple of years then come back asking folks to stand they irons up, stop folding clothes — to talk about a book. Who had even seen the inside of a library with them changing the hours for Negro admission whenever they got the gumption? Ruining that pretty one with music. What Lemon think? That she could keep Ennis cooped up in that strange house forever? Probably talked down on him too much. Or acted like that thing of hers was too good to share. Big ole man like Ennis, you can't be stingy with your stuff, you got to satisfy. Shit, the man was probably tired of resting on a mattress every night when he should've been settling down deep between warm thighs. More than a few were willing to oblige him but he never asked. Lemon had her something too, didn't she? Faithful and honest and didn't owe nobody nothing. Never seen him gambling or drinking up the family money. Didn't beat on her or the children.

About the worse thing anybody could recall Ennis doing was cussing a little. Hell, what more she want? Now they would just sit back and see how high and mighty Lemon was when the door was off the hinge or the roof needed mending. They could help, but shit naw, they wouldn't.

10
MONKEY-WOMAN BLUES

"Anything with a heart still beating when it catch afire and burn up bound to stank," May-Belle said to Junebug and Pinky, when they asked why the dead chickens smelled so bad. Her craggy face bent in disgust, she moved about the squash pen, reaching for any gourd not scorched, whispering, *"Ash-hadu anna Muhammaden rasul-ul-lah."*

"Nobody was hurt. That's the only thing that matters," Roena said, sweeping up the shards and soil from a broken pot.

Beneath the scent of singed feathers, Lemon detected the hint of sulfur that precedes a storm as she canvassed her garden: disheveled flower tubs and trampled vegetable beds. Pots and pans used to carry water a few hours ago were scattered over the yard. She watched her children try to order the chaos and cupped her hands over her mouth to stifle her cries.

In the wee hours of the morning she had

rolled over, looked out the window, and seen the outhouse in flames. There was no time for modesty; head uncovered and robeless she shook her daughters: "Ivoe, Irabelle, get up. Hurry now. We on fire. Grab something for water. Timbo went to the well yesterday. Water's on the back porch. Hurry now before the fire spread to the cabin." Lemon had tried to salvage her garden — the tomatoes, peppers, okra. Pounds of sustenance for family and business had been set afire. She ran to check on her daughters. There was no way to breach the blaze. The chickens trapped in the coop were fully engulfed. "Y'all do something before we lose everything!" Frantic, they drew water from the washtub, spilling most before they doused the flames.

The screeches of the chickens stopped long before the fire was out.

A few days after the fire, Lemon rose early to visit May-Belle. She was greeted by jars of her jam, stacked high and in neat rows on her porch. Some of the jars were half-empty. She carried them into the kitchen and was filling the cupboard when Ivoe entered.

"Just as long as nobody asks for their money back."

"They don't want their money back, Momma. They want us to leave," Ivoe said. All week Irabelle had reported the loud clucking of old hens at church. Not since the schoolhouse in '98 had Reverend Greenwood posted deacons outside the church to keep watch during service, "less they do us like they did Lemon's chickens." It had been years since they'd had any trouble out of white folks. Stood to reason one of Lemon's children would be behind it. Didn't she know any better than to write something like that?

In the five years since Papa left, life in the Brazos Bottoms had gone from bad to worst. In 1916, the Starkville City Council issued a series of mandates. A new curfew was set, prohibiting colored people from holding evening fraternal meetings and worship services. They were banned from the Starkville post office every day except for Tuesday, between the hours of noon and two, when most people worked. Now Ivoe had to travel miles, usually on some neighbor's wagon, to post a letter to Ona. She never ceased her inquiries to newspapers. Occasionally she received a short note with praise for her work, but more often her query was met by this painful question: Did she have more recent clippings to submit? Hostage to a dreary life, she often wondered about Berdis, imagined her playing in a London or Paris music hall. The pages of her calendar turned slow until September.

Once a year, at Labor Day, she took an early bus to meet Ona in Lee County. The hunt for venues accepting two colored women for lunch depleted their time the first year. Thereafter, each hauled sweets and savories especially chosen for the day. As bus stations go, the depot in Dime Box was amenable; they lunched in the small area designated for coloreds, which lacked the clean tables and chairs of the white section but held benches. After lunch they braved the steps of the Presbyterian church, where they took a bench, held hands, laughed and talked. (Ona dared anyone to bar them from the church. If they tried, she was prepared with a letter that stated her affiliation with Willetson, built and maintained by the Cumberland Presbyterian Missionary.) The four o'clock bus always arrived too soon, as Ivoe searched for words . . . "Stay near."

In the harvest of 1916, the screen door nearly rattled off its hinge, causing Lemon to jump and May-Belle to shake a little, then return to carving out biscuits from the dough rolled out on the table before her.

"Ivoe, you done always been crazy about the mail. But this here is getting to be too much. Knocking folks down, running out of here when you hear the man coming . . . then bringing the house down when you come back empty-handed. Whatever it is you expecting . . . What are you expecting?" Lemon said.

"A word from any newspaper that will have me can't come soon enough. I can't wait to get away from here. Folks walking around just as lost as they want to be. Looks like it's bound to stay that way. Little Tunis — land of the lost colored people."

"I'm still waiting to hear what running's going to prove," Lemon began, her voice coming out hoarse. The world was broken. Seemed liked patience had slipped through the crack and run off somewhere. First it carried away Ennis. Now it was fixing to take Ivoe. "Sometimes you got to bend low to follow through."

"We already bending. Can't we just follow through to someplace else? Momma, there's nothing for us here. Even the mill's closing. Now what you think Timbo's going to do when it close — but take the dice back up?"

May-Belle looked up. "My, my, ain't you running off at the mouth this evening. Mind who you sassing and remember where you sitting. Your feets is still under your momma's table, girl. Hush with all that foolishness about going away from the only home you got."

"Not for long."

"Ivoe, I'm not fixing to sit here and let you cross-talk me," Lemon said.

This evening, Ivoe could not back down. The last nine years in Little Tunis had taken her hope and her patience.

"Momma, surely you don't expect me to stay here. I've been home nine years . . . I'll be around here old as Methuselah doing the same meaningless chores."

"Grow you some patience, girl. Always take longer than you think to make things better."

"I can grow all the patience in the world. Life for me will not play out in Little Tunis. And if you think Ira—"

Lemon rose, bristling. "Irabelle is a child —"

"Irabelle is eighteen and ready to charge hell with an ice bucket. You think she gonna stay here for much longer?"

"Hand me them onions. And what you suppose we all gonna do in this left-for place? We don't know nothing about living no place else. Besides, when something belongs to you it's more than a notion to just walk off and leave it."

"We can go to any city we can make it to, Momma. In the city they make and sell everything anybody could possibly need." Ivoe tried to keep her voice even. "We'll find jobs. We'll make do. And before you know it we'll have more than we ever had."

"Listen at you. To hear all them grand plans somebody would think I'm talking to the Duchess of Windsor. I'm too old to start over. Don't know nothing about no city living nohow. White folks made cities — just another place for us to work indoors. The country belongs to us."

"Show me a paper that says anything around here belong to us."

"Girl, I'm not studying on no papers. That's between white folks and they God. Just 'cause you put a price on something don't mean you own it. Paying for it don't make it yours neither."

Ivoe already regretted what she had to say. "Momma, what if Papa never comes back . . . because he can't."

"He ain't dead," May-Belle said, flashing Ivoe a stern look. "He done lived in two places. Left the last place on a white sun. They took him on a yellow sun, and they letting him go on a red sun. When he come back won't be no sun at all. A person don't always come back to you the way he left or the way you remember him. He ain't dead."

Listening to old people talk was a little like trying to catch and hold on to the rain, Ivoe thought. Your hand got wet but you couldn't carry it far.

"If he is dead, it's Momma's fault," Irabelle said. "We could've left with him if she didn't go on and on about this little shack. I wanted to go with him."

"Irabelle, start the stove for me," Lemon said. "I don't want to hear no more talk about Papa or leaving, less they giving away money wherever it is y'all going." She looked at the clock. Ten after six, but before she could begin to worry the twins shot past her and Roena closed the door behind, yelling after them: "Draw Bicey a picture . . . Touch the typewriter keys gently . . . Leave the clarinet alone."

Lemon wiped her tears with her shoulder.

"Let me finish peeling the onions, Lemon. You ain't looking yourself. You all right?" Roena said.

"Every time I stand up, my mind sits down. Doing too much is all, but like they say, ain't nobody ever drowned in sweat." Lemon sat down with a large wooden bowl in the vise of her knees, peeling potatoes she tossed into a bucket at her feet. Ivoe sat close to the grate reading her newspaper. Roena and Irabelle sat at the table playing cards with Junebug and Pinky. It was nearly seven; they expected Timbo to show up with more coal for the grate at any moment and then they could prepare dinner.

"Roena, you quiet tonight," Lemon said.

"Your son —" The veins on Roena's temple swelled as she took a handkerchief from her pocket and wiped Junebug's nose with unnecessary force.

"What he do now?"

"— we didn't have no business marrying is all. Well, Lemon, it's true."

"Can't put the rain back in the sky," May-Belle said.

"He a fool. I say to him, 'Timothy, don't you want to go somewhere? Don't you want to see something? Don't you have no interests other than dice?' He don't pay me no mind. Still chasing down a game."

"What game?" Pinky said in a deep tone, groggy from sleep, that made them all think of Ennis.

"Lemon, you think the time gonna ever come when you ready to leave here?" Roena said.

Ivoe looked up from the paper.

"*Ssth.* You too? You and Ivoe the most

leavingest gals I done seen. What make y'all generation so restless?"

"Just ain't you, Lemon. That's all," Roena said with sullen politeness.

Lemon stopped peeling the potatoes and turned around: "What ain't me?"

"In the eight years me and Timbo been married and the ten years I watched you before that, I've always known you to tend to things. People too. Some of us was put here to do that and you one of them. I am too, that's why I watched you so. You always been able to see a thing before it rightly reveal itself. So I know you see ain't nobody 'round here thriving no more. Nobody. I don't mean you no disrespect. All I ask is that wherever you go, you tell Timbo to gather up his family and come go with you. We can't stay here. Naw. Sure can't. Time for a change."

Lemon heaved a sigh. How quickly age had come for her. She blamed it on change. At fifty-five years old she had never heard so much about change. What did any of them know about change? She had felt some change of her own — the way Ennis took up less space in her mind, Ivoe's impatience, and Irabelle, the way she walked around you'd think nobody had ever lost anybody but her. What more change did anybody

285

expect from her?

Pinky climbed down from his chair. "Bicey, can you tell us a story?"

Lemon was nobody's grandmomma, big mama neither. She was Bicey. Soon as the twins commenced to walking good, they'd climbed up her porch steps, flung open the door, and ran in her house just like it was theirs. No hello or nothing. Went on like that for a few years on account of Timbo not raising them proper — just letting them grow up like corn. She couldn't keep a quiet tongue about the twins' behavior but had sense enough to make her peace in a way that wouldn't make Roena feel bad. "Junebug and Pinky just taking over — I don't know what to think" became the official grandmother's hello. Come time for the boys to leave, well, they left just like they came, slamming the door, running wild out in the yard. Soon as they got up some size, she pulled them off to the side. "Rascals, that ain't no way to leave nobody's house. You walk natural-like so you don't make folks feel they ain't hosted you proper. Don't go running like you can't wait to be gone. Any time you leave my house you supposed to say bye, see?"

"Tell a scary one, Bicey." Junebug grinned,

revealing a gap where two front teeth should be.

Time wasn't the only truth-teller. Blood will also tell. When Junebug smiled, he was every bit his grandfather, not only in name. "Bicey fixing to cook you something to eat. Irabelle, tell them babies a story."

"Y'all just don't know. Papa was the one that could get a story told. Couldn't he, Ivoe? Y'all ever hear about the ghostdog?"

Lemon looked at her daughter. She didn't have sense enough to keep memories out her mouth.

Junebug shook his head. Pinky crossed his legs like an old man and sucked his thumb with an alert expression that made Irabelle giggle. "It's a real good story but scary, scary."

"Irabelle, go on and tell it if you gonna tell it. I'm not fixing to do all this cooking by myself. Not when it's two and a half grown women sitting here with me."

Lemon had Ennis on her mind when she started to peel the last potato. She understood the reason he left them, but what was keeping him so long? In the five years since he'd left only one letter had come, September 1911: "I am gud. Wurkin in Okluhomey. To old to work lik this. Soon wil leev for Cansus. Soon wil come for my famlee lack I promussed. Lvoe, Ennis." He did well with just the little bit of tutoring she had given him when they first met. Now, for the first time, she wondered if anybody had helped with the letter, if he had found a friend, or . . . She hated to question. Questions made it harder to keep a promise. Before Timbo came to the world thirty-three years ago wasn't nothing for men to just walk off, looking for whatever they thought freedom owed them. She was wrong not to know better, wrong to think Ennis wouldn't return. After his return and Timbo's birth, she was wrong for not sitting both men down — asking her husband's forgiveness, telling James about his son. About the only right thing she did was to make a promise to herself to never doubt Ennis again. The way she saw it, they both had promises to keep.

"Once a fiddler was late leaving Caldwell. It was way past dark when he finally reached Little Tunis because he had to carry his baby brother with him. They daddy had died so the fiddler was in charge of his baby brother and his momma too."

"That ain't the way the story go."

"So, the fiddler and his baby brother were going along."

"They got a au-to-mo-bile?" Junebug wanted to know.

Pinky slurped on his thumb and grunted, "Naw, they walking."

"You gonna let Auntie tell this story or not?"

The twins nodded.

"The fiddler and his brother are marching along when the fiddler's stomach starts grumbling like thunder right before a twister touch down. He figured his brother was hungry too but he didn't want to stop because he was worried about reaching Little Tunis, where he was getting paid to play for a dance. Since his daddy died he had more than himself to look after. He had three mouths to feed."

Lemon twisted in her chair, trying not to catch the *misbaha* beads hanging from her hip where she'd worn them the last five years, praying in a steadfast manner that some nightrider hadn't snatched Ennis up and turned him loose where he didn't belong just to collect a dollar or two. It was so easy to steal a colored man, erase his past and darken all the days of his future. She tried not to hear the story Irabelle was telling. Ennis had made it out of Texas. It had taken him a while to gain people's trust is all — a colored man traveling by himself, no wife, no children — and at his age. Sure as she was sitting there, he was somewhere working hard, preparing a place for them. Who was Irabelle to think otherwise?

Lemon let out a long, tired sigh. "If you gonna tell the story, tell it right. That ain't how it go."

"Who's telling this?" Irabelle snapped.

The wooden bowl of sliced potatoes smacked the floor when Lemon sprang to her feet. "I'm awfully tired of your sassing."

Irabelle's sudden rise upset the table. Veins bulged along her neck. "And I'm tired of you acting like he left on account of what happened to me. Maybe he ain't no different than these other men that leave when they want to."

Lemon kicked the bowl from her path and flew into Irabelle with a hard shove.

"Momma!" Ivoe lunged after her but missed and fell.

May-Belle called on Allah. Roena's voice was frail: "Y'all, don't do this —"

"Get her off me!"

Lemon's fists were like hammers. Each blow against Irabelle carried the pain she'd felt since her man left. Not even the wailing of her grandsons stopped her.

At one point, Irabelle thought it would be okay if she never turned nineteen.

When they finally pulled the women apart, Lemon stood across the room breathing hard. She took off a slipper and hurled it against the wall before dropping her head in a weepy groan. She spoke in a low, shaky voice: "I won't stand here and say he ain't wrong for staying gone so long. Instead of being angry with him, worry about him . . . I don't know, maybe that'll bring him home." She wiped her tears with her shoulder. "Now, I don't never want to hear no more talk about Papa's leaving. He did his level best by this family. His level best."

Timothy closed the door.

"Momma, that roof on the henhouse fixing to fall in. I'll fix it for a little change," he said, and winked. "Somebody dropped this in the yard. Ivoe, it's for you." He put the envelope on the table, careful-like, not flung, and sat a bag of coal on the floor. He looked at Ivoe, rock still with watery eyes. He looked across the kitchen where Irabelle was balled up in the corner and noticed the trouble on his wife's face. "What's going on?"

Terrified by Bicey's rage, the twins ran to their father. Each one grabbed a hand, eyeing his grandmother with a little fear.

Ivoe took her time opening the envelope, certain that like all the others this too would end in rejection. Her eyes scanned the letter. Her lips parted and her voice shook as she read aloud, " 'Your experience and specimens were the most satisfactory sent.' " Her eyes rested on the words *fact-checker.* In the same paragraph a date was given for when she should show up for work. She tried to hand the letter to her mother, who turned her back. She crouched beside Ira-belle, placed the letter before her eyes, and spoke in a whisper everyone could hear. "Soon as you finish up school, come join me."

"Where you going?" Roena said.

"Kansas City" curled off her tongue with pride. "Kansas City here I come!" Ivoe shouted, doing a bunny hop that made the twins laugh.

"When they want you?" Timbo said.

"In three weeks."

"We going too?" Junebug said.

A week later, Lemon thought about her grandson's question. *Ssth.* To live with three grown children and her grandsons under one roof — how? She missed Ennis beyond hurt. Might've been short on money but plenty peace abided. She and Ennis never stood for fussing and fighting. "Leave that ugliness outdoors," Ennis used to say when-ever the children meddled with each other. "We keep peace indoors." Not every word

292

that passed back and forth between them was all the time pleasant. How could it be with a man thinking one way like he do, a woman thinking another, but together they had kept peace indoors for thirty-one years. She laid her head down on the table Ennis built. For a few days she had not taken food or water between sunup and sundown. Fasting would strengthen her prayer request — forgiveness and traveling mercies. The visit to the county clerk had been short. A man shuffled loose pages of an unbound ledger where the value of their land and house had been blotted out, next to it a far diminished sum penciled in. After the sell, there was enough money for five one-way tickets and a little something left to help them start again. She ran her hand over the bloodstain in the center of the table and thought of Irabelle. The outside world had come in.

The last call issued from the station speaker as Timothy helped his wife aboard the train. "I got more years than all of y'all put together and know full well how to see to myself," May-Belle said when Roena's aunt Fanny and Zilpha Stokes promised to look after her. Bunk thumped his tail against her leg like he agreed, then sprang back as Ivoe grabbed May-Belle, tears rushing from her eyes. Irabelle joined their embrace, their soft farewells swelling to a hurt jumble of thanksgiving and promises. After her daughters climbed aboard, Lemon and May-Belle stood in silence holding hands. Bunk moved under the swaying bridge of their arms, wagging his tail.

"No, Bunk. You can't come with us. You got to stay right here and see after May-Belle. You got to do a good job too 'cause she's all the grown-up love I got."

"Ain't so," May-Belle said. "Your children got love and they not afraid to work. Let them help when you needs it. Let them help."

The conductor's final whistle blew. Lemon released her aunt's hands and drew her in close. She rested her face in the curve of her neck, inhaling deeply the scent of pennyroyal oil. Finally, she squatted to talk to Bunk. She cradled his face between her hands, pressed her lips into the soft depression of smooth fur between his eyes. "I left something special for you in the garden, you rascal." Bunk rose on his hind legs and whimpered. Quickly, Lemon turned, grabbed her valise, and disappeared up the steps.

In the train car a fat woman told two well-dressed boys, who were eating their sandwiches and tossing the crusts on the floor between their stubby legs, to "Stop kicking and be still." She toed a bag at her feet from which a long stick protruded at a jaunty angle and the boys sat still. Across the aisle from the Williamses a man in a straw hat, dungarees, and a wrinkled jacket drummed his fingers on the backside of the guitar across his lap. At the third stop he began to play and sing in a gravelly tone:

Going to Kansas City
Sorry that I can't take you
Going to Kansas City
Sorry that I can't take you
'Cause ain't nothing on Vine Street
That a monkey-woman can do.

Lemon watched the blues man, who seemed to favor the strum of sad strings over the happy ones. As she listened, she realized questions could burden a heart as much as the wrong answer. How did she wind up on a train without her husband? She looked out the train window beyond the reflections of her family, slouched and bent in peaceful sleep. Didn't have no business leaving behind everything she knew. Like the little furniture they owned, cut from trees by James and made into a little something by Ennis. The wood was a record. Held the big and the small: Timbo's sweat after his first real day of labor and all that he wasted on those devilish dice, the ink from Ivoe's fingertips, Irabelle's blood. Didn't have no business leaving Texas. Her soul and the soil were one, tilled together. She had marked fifty-five years in the Brazos Bottoms, land that knew her better than the people she loved. What did she know about the city? She had borrowed somebody else's trouble and left hers behind is all. A storm was brewing and nothing about the future she saw in her mind's eye could chase the clouds away. Somewhere out in the velvet black night was her star, brighter than any of those twinkling up the sky. If she called him, maybe he'd light the way.

Ennis. Ennis. Ennis.

■ ■ ■ ■

PART II

■ ■ ■ ■

11
MEDITATIONS
OCTOBER 1916

Wisps of fog hung over Kansas City's Union Station as the Sunshine Express blew a noisy tuft of steam, rousing Ivoe from a dream. She was more excited than anybody had a right to be. Three days until her life as a fact-checker began at the *Kansas City Palladium.* Tomorrow, after unpacking, she would find Twelfth and Wyandotte and plan her route to the newspaper office. Momma pulled on her shoes. They had been traveling for two days and Junebug and Pinky were fast asleep. Timothy woke them gently. Irabelle and Roena gathered the toys that had amused the ten-year-old twins on the journey. Ivoe was the first in the aisle, slipping into her coat. A gentleman in a derby hat with a bright green feather held the door open as they entered the station's grand hall, where a chandelier shone bright like her hope. Lord only knew what stories awaited her in the city.

A gloomy Sunday in Kansas City could put New Year's Eve in Little Tunis to shame. Telephone and trolley wires crisscrossed a sky teeming with tall buildings; electric streetcars rumbled along, causing the ground to shake beneath their feet. A colored boy with a face of joyful mischief dodged the grasp of a white man. Horns honked. From every corner someone shouted the sale of wares. A man holding a crying toddler haggled with the owner of a vegetable cart. A woman in a faded green coat got out of a taxi. And someone gave a terrific whistle. The city in motion! Ivoe clutched the map in her hand. "Come on, y'all. The house is close. Let's save the carfare and walk."

Where a left turn was necessary, Ivoe turned them right into a street of dreary flats that eventually spilled into Whittier Lane. The Williamses stopped to gawk at the half-naked women sitting in windows knitting, reading, or staring blankly ahead until a taxi drew near. In unison, the women commenced tapping their windows with coins until the men from the taxi approached. Sporting women would never get Timothy's money, but a sign above a storefront where men shook dice right where the whole world could see caught his eye. A game or two would square the debt back in Texas. The church on the corner was an easy marker for the Spinning Wheel — money, cigarettes, whiskey, and God only knew what else was in there. At the corner of West Twelfth Street and Pennsylvania Avenue, the air turned a putrid odor — rotten food and dried blood. Ivoe consulted the map again. They were back on course.

"These big houses for just one family?" Roena said.

"Look more like castles from a picture book," Irabelle chimed. One day she'd live in a house just like that one — with a man as handsome as the one who made eyes at her each time he walked down the train aisle, all the way from Texas. In one hand the porter had two bottles for the twins, in the other a bottle for her. She memorized the numbers on the napkin wrapped around her cola.

In the part of Mulberry Street that had once been beautiful stood a maisonette whose odd symmetry and melancholic feel seemed out of place amid the apartment houses. Measly shrubs, tall as Lemon, looked like they never did see a leaf. Even in spring she didn't count on them shutting the house off from the street like they were supposed to. She bore her heel into the ground then raised it to fleck off and feel the soil. No count. She touched a tree of sickly brown leaves and snags of wool and thought, Somebody went off and left you. We a good match. A narrow path delivered them to the Queen Anne, whose numbers matched the address in Lemon's hand. Lemon ignored the mural in the foyer (touched only by Ivoe because the patina reminded her of the art at Willetson) and led her family through a dark hall. On the fourth floor, she opened the door to a kitchen much smaller than the one back home, but they were paid up till spring.

Five of the hardest years without Ennis and I did the best that I could do, Lemon thought, as she opened a box. The carving done by her husband was laid across the dishes, its bark gnarled and rough. The smooth side of the oak showed his tree-woman, the top half a likeness of Lemon, the bottom half all roots. Lemon turned to Ivoe unwrapping a plate that had belonged to Big Momma Iraj and exhaled.

Lemon crossed the room and cracked the window, frowning at the stench. "What you say they call this part of town?"

"West Bottoms."

"You mean we moved from the Bottoms to the Bottoms? Y'all have to help me with this one. What kind of sense that make?"

Roena chuckled.

"You don't want us to be rent-poor — broke after paying the landlord — do you? We can always move once we've started working and saved a little," Ivoe said, sweeping aside her mother's logic to make room for the city's opportunities.

"What plant you know thrive changing pots all the time?" Lemon took Momma Iraj's plate from Ivoe's hands and put it in the center of the table. They hadn't unpacked half the boxes yet and that child was talking about moving again. That's how city folk lived. How many steps had she climbed? Forty? Fifty? On the trip up she had lost count. "Give me that pie." Ivoe pulled the leftover sweet potato pie from a shopping bag and thought of Ona. "Been a while since we could leave a pie on the table. Wonder how my Bunk doing." Lemon looked out the window. "You say peoples like living this way? Peoples call this home? These iddy-biddy rooms and a couple of windows?"

"We had the same amount of space in Little Tunis."

"Ivoe Leila Williams, don't you know nothing about where you come from? Indoors you might've lived in just a few rooms, but outdoors you had nearly an acre, girl. And all of it was yours. When you could hardly stand yourself or had your fill of one of us, you could march right out the door and where you be at? Home. You could sit yourself down, lean against a tree, and your behind was on top of your very own piece of ground, leaning against your very own tree. Home, girl, where the work you do in the garden you don't mind doing since any seed you sow gonna yield what's rightfully yours. And even if you don't feel like the room is yours, the tree is yours, or the ground is yours, when hand bring to mouth that thing you growed and you gets yourself a taste, you think one thing: *Home.*"

Ivoe thought, between a garden and her career, it was more important that the latter grow. And there was no chance of that in Little Tunis.

A trolley ride and a short walk delivered Ivoe to the *Kansas City Palladium.* Inside the lobby, she frowned and plucked at her stockings, flecked with gray mud, some of which dotted the hem of the hunter-green gabardine dress handed down by Miss Susan years ago. She followed directions to a room at the end of the corridor and settled in for the inevitable wait that seemed to accompany her race and gender. This link seemed as true in the city as it was in rural Texas; she had witnessed in a number of establishments how well-dressed colored men received attention, or at the very least a greeting, sooner than a colored woman.

An hour had passed when a man came out and asked what she wanted, as if neither he nor anyone he knew expected her. Learning that his paper had hired her as the new fact-checker, he welcomed her inside his office, where another man, older, more distinguished looking, rose to greet her. Awkward silence hung in the air followed by a series of questions. Why had she signed her correspondence with initials? Was she often in the habit of trickery? Had she written or received considerable help with "On the Safety of Colored Girls and Women"? What kind of paper was the *Enterprise* to publish the writings of a Negro woman? Did she have any idea what work at a city newspaper required? This work demanded long hours, they said. The acuity and mastery of the English language, rules of grammar, were better suited to men whose wives tended to domestic chores while they focused on the page, they said. "Why, I bet you pressed the dress you're wearing," the older gentleman said through a wry smile, as if ironing precluded one from the verification of information. When it was clear she had lost the job at birth, she tried to secure another post at the paper. She apologized for withholding her gender and reminded them of her introduction letter, which had detailed her experience setting type and working multiple presses. Men filled these positions best, they said. "Faster work, fewer accidents." She might consider other jobs, more suitable to a colored woman's abilities.

On the street Ivoe was too angry and frightened to sit and wait. She walked past the #17 stop, pulled up the collar on their collective best coat, and commenced a chilly stroll that lasted nearly an hour. Vine Street's colored businesses thrived inside handsome two- and three-story redbrick buildings. Scarcely a dozen steps delivered you to all your living needs, a claim she had tested and found true her first full day in the city. A dress purchased at Lady's Ready-to-Wear Emporium could be fitted around the corner on Highland Street at Dibble's tailor shop and cleaned just up the way on Vine at Green and Sons, across the street from the graceful stone colored library.

At the lighted candy cane pole she slowed her pace to look inside the three-seater barbershop and tobacconist filled with men like her father. For those hard on luck or faith, pawnshops and storefront churches dotted the four corners of Eighteenth Street, where she crossed for the northern end of Vine. She averted her gaze from the women's stores. Shop-window cajolery. The thought of things she could not buy would only make her feel worse. Four weeks of trolley fare, meager lunches out, and new stockings had added up fast. Less than ten dollars of the money saved in Texas remained. Worse yet, Momma had taken none of it. "Girl, keep your little money," she had said whenever Ivoe tried to help. Humiliation and worry were enough to drive her into hopelessness as she opened the door to Ruby's Five-and-Dime.

The woman at the counter nodded hello over shimmying saucers and the clink of silverware. "Cold out there, huh, baby? Coffee or tea?" Ivoe felt a knot lodge in her throat as she quickly batted back tears. She had been tossed by harsh winds all day, needed a soft place to land and had found it. "Tea," she said, smoothing her dirndl skirt across her lap as she took the stool. She removed the stationery purchased at Halls Brothers earlier that week from her pocketbook. Thoughts of Ona arose like the steam curling up from her cup of tea. There was no sense in fighting the urge to tell her everything — even what shamed her.

Kansas City, November 14, 1916

Dear Ona,

I begin with a pitiful and funny story. We are three women with one decent coat between us and a little luck from Father Time, since Irabelle is still in school, or else the following scheme would never have worked. We decided that Momma should wear the coat daily because the family she cooks for lives on Ward Parkway, a boulevard that surpasses all other streets in Kansas City and is, according to the Star — the city's organ of reputation and record — the greatest parade in America. It would not do for Momma to be seen coming and going in a tattered coat. Today I wanted desperately to make a fine impression at the Kansas City Palladium, so I rode the trolley out in the afternoon to pick up the coat, with a mind to return when Momma's workday ends. In just an hour I will execute the final part of our master plan (I will wear my raggedy coat on the journey home with her). All the day's luck was spent on the scheme of the coat. The I. L. Williams the newspapers expect to meet is clearly of a different gender and should be a much fairer hue! My own articles are routinely flashed before me as I am asked whether I wrote them. I have been urged to consider janitorial work and frequently respond that I came to this city to write for a paper, not to mop the floors for one.

Kansas City is starting to feel more like a dead end than a crossroad. Timbo still can't find work. And Roena can't work while keeping house for us all and caring for the twins. Irabelle is hoping to bring in a little money playing music, but Momma (with good reason) won't allow her in any club until she has graduated. Everything costs much more here. Momma returns from the grocery disgusted with the price of food that, in her words, don't taste half as good as the dirt it grew in. I want so desperately to shoulder some of this burden, but how? The beautician needs a license and requires equipment (and really, think back to my first month setting type — should I wield a pressing comb in the direction of any woman's head?). I never learned to sew and cannot train to become a dressmaker — a good living, so I am told — nor can I teach. If I try to enter the vocations in which white women are employed (secretary or saleswoman), my would-be employer stares at me blankly: "But I didn't advertise for a colored girl." Surely by now I have racked up enough lessons in degradation for the dean of life to confer upon me a degree in bitterness.

I am downhearted and wishing to be near you. A word from you would lift me.

Yours truly,
Ivoe

Austin, November 20, 1916

Dear Ivoe,

In your long silence I feared you had forgotten me. I have been thinking of you and wondering what you are about. When has it not been true that a colored woman has a hard row to hoe? The path to livelihood is by no means smooth but let this be no impediment! You might consider joining any number of women's groups (NACW) that have helped to stabilize our people. You would benefit from those women and they, no doubt, would benefit from you. Have you visited the YWCA?

No need to write that any word from you brings long-lasting cheer, but there you have it, along with my wishes for a letter from you, soon.

As ever,
Ona

The newly mopped hallway of the YWCA reeked of pine, but Ivoe's hunger and nervousness were to blame for the uneasy flip her stomach made. That morning she had buttered the last slice of bread and reached for the jam when Irabelle grabbed the toast up. She'd looked at her sister, books under one arm, the clarinet case in the other hand, and let her keep it. Together they listened to Roena and Timothy bickering in the next room. "You say we ain't been here long. Timbo, even a chicken know to run for cover when it hears thunder. Now we fixing to have real trouble if you don't find no work." Timbo told her to stop worrying. Roena said she was long past worry. Worry had gotten tired and gone off somewhere. "Can't you find something?" Irabelle said to Ivoe. " 'Cause Momma can't do it all." Presently, Ivoe's mind lingered at her sister's question as she strained to keep her attention on the girl inside the office.

The job placement coordinator noted the sleeves of Ivoe's coat — a little too short — and her long legs. She was certain of the match; Lois Humphrey could use Ivoe. The YWCA had deployed dozens of young women — runaways from crazy men, desperate mothers, or those just itching for a scratch at city life — to numerous jobs. She couldn't figure out which type Ivoe was, distracted by the way she talked. Educated, even if it didn't sound all the way like it. Texans had a funny way with *r*'s. Sometimes they disappeared altogether, like how she said "*shoaly* appreciate any help you could give me." Other times the roving *r* crept in where it had no business being. When questioned about hygiene, Ivoe responded about the care she took in "warshing" and pressing her clothes.

Tall, willowy girls fared best with Lois. The short and stout ones returned a week later, "too slow" or "tardiness" given for their dismissal. For an especially good match the forewoman at Alton Clover donated butter, sugar, flour. Sometimes flavored extracts found their way into the YWCA pantry. Over the years, praise for the branch increased. No other YWCA in the city served cake daily. "Be smart," the coordinator said, handing Ivoe the address. "Park bench turn awfully cold at night."

There was a bustle and a roar on the corner of Vine Street. A man in a grimy coat with jaundiced eyes snatched up a toddler, yelling at the driver of a Model T whose face registered the almost-accident as Ivoe climbed the trolley car steps. The threat of rent due made her resolution swift and easy. Whatever job offered, she'd follow every order, do every task better than well. Across the aisle from her a woman combed her bangs to cover the scar on her forehead. "Lye," she whispered. "Got to be careful with it." At the next stop a man with a wooden crutch tucked beneath his arm hobbled to the seat vacated by a dark-skinned woman in an ermine coat. In the city, even the maimed and crippled were on the move, and Ivoe was determined to move right along with them: south on Paseo Boulevard, left turn into Twelfth Street, straight to the corner of Main.

She stepped into a drone of whirring machines, asked for directions, and headed to the back of the fragrant loft. The handsome woman in a gray lady's dress with white pinafore was fairer than her mother, fair enough to pass, but Ivoe knew a Negro woman no matter the brightness of complexion; it had nothing to do with pigment and everything to do with carriage.

"Williams?" the woman said in a funny, earthy drawl distinctly not southern. "I got a call about you."

Papa used to say when a person looked you straight in the eye that he was bonded by his word. If she could make the forewoman like her — for whatever reason — she might have an ally. In the country family and neighbors were enough, but in the city she needed alliances. Ivoe smiled at the forewoman, pulling her hand slowly apart from their handshake. "Yes, ma'am."

Lois Humphrey eyed her with curious satisfaction. Ungloved in this weather? Poor but not city-poor. Not desperate. This girl had never dashed out of a restaurant midway through the meal, or noticed the style and make of a woman's pocketbook for a clue to its contents, let alone fainted before a copper just to be brought indoors. Lois had forgotten how many nights she had escaped the streets, laid up in a hospital in Beacon Hill. Who knows, if the hospital had permitted one more night she might still be there dealing with a winter far worse than this one. But a woman on her hospital floor had pointed her out to the police. She remembered the accuser's bag — maroon ostrich. Tremont Street.

The paddy wagon doors flung open to a gang of sporting women and a nun. Grateful that her daily round had yielded one white among the fallen colored women, Sister Adelaide listened to Lois's story and proposed she join the Oblate Sisters of Boston to serve God instead of time. The gloom of the convent suited. Mother Superior remarked on Lois's tranquillity and placed her at the boarding school. A dark-haired Irish girl with bangs sharply flattened against her face touched her with a sensuality that shook her. Merciful Savior. Up the stairs to the choir stall in the chapel's nave where there was no pew, Lois begged for salvation's release against the cold tiles. Who knows, if the door to the chapel had not been left open that afternoon she waited in the gardens for the Irish girl to run away with her, she might still be there calling on Jesus. A gold crucifix caught her eye, along with the brass chalice and silver communion trays. The habit suited the crime. In no time she was beyond the gate.

Clean nails. At least the country girl knew that much. The coat had seen too many winters and was dump-ready, but underneath her brown skirt molded nicely to narrow hips and long, shapely legs. A second and third mention of Willetson was supposed to impress her. Studied long and wrong was what she'd done, filling her head with grand ideas, working for newspapers and such.

There were more than a few reasons why the woman before her was not a good hire: she was new to the city — likely to struggle with transportation; she was no dipper (only girls with petite hands were any good at bonbons); she was dicty and stuck-up (knowing how to operate a press didn't benefit Mister Clover); and she had no children — those who did said so right away to increase their chances of getting hired. She preferred family women. Women with families worked harder because there is no heartache like a hungry child or a man whose own work is not enough to take care of you. This one in front of her was a dutiful daughter or sister, helping out. In a month or two, she would walk away without giving a thought to who would cover her shift. Still, there was a hint of something Ivoe shared with the others. Yes. There was one thing Ivoe might do well and it had nothing to do with her fine diction, polite ways, or candy. She slid a blank card and pencil across her desk. She disdained weak women. Had no patience for complainers, whiners, fools. But a woman who managed to do what her own mother never could — face the world, take what she needed from it or die trying — well, she admired the type. There was a sense of urgency about Ivoe. She was trying to do something.

"We're getting ready for Valentine's Day. I need to know the shifts will be filled."

"If you give them to me, I'll fill them, ma'am." Ivoe softened her eyes. She had seen a look that reminded her of Ona Durden. For too long she had been Ivoe the help, Ivoe the daughter, Ivoe the sister, Ivoe the auntie. Not since Willetson had she truly felt like Ivoe the woman. A love like Berdis's hadn't existed in Little Tunis. She hadn't known where to find it. But in the city . . . She returned a gaze that said she felt Mrs. Humphrey's once-over and didn't mind.

"No latecomers. And I expect you to work until that whistle blows. Better get yourself a pair of comfortable shoes." Lois told her the rate of pay and made her fill out a medical form while she looked for a uniform. "See you in the morning at half past seven. And you can stop with all that damn ma'aming. It's Mrs. Humphrey until I like you. Then it's Lois."

In the city politeness didn't pay. If anything it reminded white folks that you knew your place and that they should treat you accordingly, Lois thought. Her mother had made the same mistake, no-sirred and yes-sirred herself from the domestic's room into his bedroom. The photographs of her parents told the awful fairy tale. Mother had done the worst. She had accepted the invitation to the white ball not understanding she was merely the entertainment. Whites would never accept her and colored people would never trust her — either she looked down on them (not even the lowest man wants pity), or she found greater comforts in the white world (who was she to deserve them?). One was worse than the other, but both were grounds for keeping her and her funny-looking children at a distance.

Folks said Father did right by her, married her and everything. But it was never right. Mother married into money but not into kindness or compassion or any of the goodness she herself came from. After the trip to the altar, the marriage went to hell. Mother privileged Father and all he came from. You could tell by the food she prepared, what she read, how she prayed. Reached so far outside of herself — and for so long — she couldn't feel for what truly belonged to her. Aping his manners, his vocal inflection, his everything, she would die lonely from all that reaching because she was not interesting enough to be accepted by any of the women he charmed in her presence. Colored women denied her their easy, pleasant smiles — wouldn't dream of breaking bread with her. Why should she be trusted with their recipes for fixing disaster, mending broken hearts? — especially since she didn't have any of her own to give in return. White or colored, no lady-friend of Mother's ever brought her warmth and big laughter into the house for a visit. Lois counted it a miracle then that she knew how to love women.

After Ivoe left, Lois tried not to dwell on the quality that landed Ivoe the job, because the last time it had ended very badly. The girls called it a catfight when the puny colored girl with strong arms from stirring chocolate all day flipped a switchblade and cut the Polish blonde from packaging and receiving. Both had been bragging about the raise she had received. Both claimed to be Lois's bulldagger. And both would do in a pinch. Really, the extra two cents she gave to each was not about all of that. Both worked hard for Lois at the factory and at home. Homemade pierogi and collard greens were worth the raise alone. When they carried the blonde out on a stretcher, cussing so much she foamed at the mouth like a rabid dog, Lois understood something about women: no matter how tough she was, a woman was made to show her love.

Lois Humphrey ran a tight ship, the proof of which was all around Ivoe as she followed her through the factory. Fruit and flower juices and extracts used to flavor the candy sat cheek by jowl in the storeroom like the bottled herbs in May-Belle's cellar. The pans and kettles shone like noonday sun. Sieves and trays sparkled clean as did the floors and white caps worn by all the girls. Her gaze followed Mrs. Humphrey's finger to wooden trays of freshly molded candy centers, packed tight and smooth before delivery to the dippers. In a closet-sized room, four women worked over cherries piled high and bowls of creamy pink paste. "Almonds," Mrs. Humphrey said, pointing across the hall to the costliest bonbons. "Be a while before you good enough to be in there." The next door opened to a cavernous room filled with large marble-topped tables where girls sat in rows, each with a pot of melted chocolate before her. Ivoe's eyes wearied at the rapid motion of more hands than she could count dunking tiny white balls that came out lusciously brown. "Williams, this is you."

Kansas City, January 5, 1917

Dear Ona,

I write to you on stationery from money I earned. The IW in the corner of the page you now hold is the same font once embossed on the perfumed yellow paper of Susan Stark many yesterdays ago back in Starkville. As a child, I coveted that paper, the envelopes, the unknown destinations they were headed to. Now I have my own, paid for by labor not sweated on behalf of the Starks — like my mother and her mother — progress!

You may blame the five-week lapse since my last correspondence on an unjust world. I hesitated to write without good news, but now that I am convinced a colored woman must sweep her crumbs of happiness off other people's tables, there is no need to wait. Hunting a job has bruised the ego Willetson had no small hand in raising up. I have wasted nearly two months writing letters and placing telephone calls to the K.C. Times, Post, Border Star, Far West,

Liberty Banner, Liberty Tribune, K.C. Gazette, Kansas City Kansas Globe, Kansas City Kansas, and Wyandotte Herald. Except for the Kansas City Star, where I cannot acquire so much as an acknowledgment for my inquiry, every newspaper in this city and the next has turned me away. My new employment in a downtown candy factory brings with it a hard lesson and new empathy for the vast portion of the world performing jobs they've no heart to do. As for my family, they are fine. Irabelle enjoys her music studies at the high school (and a nameless young man I believe she has her eye on there); and today Timbo started his job at a meatpacking plant. Of course, Momma will never appreciate working for somebody else's family though they are decent. By age twenty-eight I had hoped to be much further along in life than I am and in much better spirits. I am friendless in a city I hoped would befriend me and without any meaningful thing to do. If I went without drinking for days and someone arrived with a canteen and a letter from you, I would reach for the letter first, sure that it would quench me. I long for your correspondence.

Yours,
Ivoe

Austin, January 24, 1917

Dear Ivoe,

At today's newspaper meeting I half expected you to show up. This term's crop of minds is keen as ever. As for crumb snatching, I say make your own table. If you feel that what you do does not matter, do what I hope Willetson has had a hand in teaching you: find a way to do what matters not just to yourself but also to others. In the meantime, what joy are your pursuing? I recently acquired a book of verse by Paul Laurence Dunbar — Oak and Ivy. The poems are delightful. Between teaching and the poems there remains plenty of time for me to feel discouraged with myself. Tomorrow I will turn forty-two, and along with added age comes the feeling that the chance for untried things has slipped away.

We two are a pitiful pair!

Write when you have the chance. You cannot imagine what pleasure I take in your letters.

Love, your old friend,

Ona

Kansas City, February 7, 1917

Dear Ona,
I have been too discouraged by my
family's need and my own to write. I am
lonely but it is not a friend I crave. You
are nearer to me than you know — than
I know what to do with since I cannot
reach out and touch you.
I am lonely yet there is never a moment alone at home. Momma and Irabelle bicker constantly, as you might
expect when wisdom and youth collide.
Timbo, Roena, and their boys are suf-
focating. Each one speaks of his or her
want hourly. You'd expect this from the
children; it's the parents who must learn
to do better. Still, it seems everyone but
me has someone to talk to.
I have been remembering Papa several
times a day. The remaining hours I
spend wanting this, wanting that — good
food to eat, a newspaper to write for,
proper lady's shoes of the latest fashion,
a good book to read and someone to
discuss it with, someone to talk to and
touch. If you passed me on the street

you wouldn't know me. The load has sagged for all this want.

> Yours (in dire need),
> Ivoe

Austin, February 18, 1917

Dear Ivoe,

Sometimes in life you have to bend low to follow through on your dream. As soon as you are able, straighten up. In the meantime, the city you couldn't wait to get to awaits your discovery. Get out of doors, walk around, discover . . . I enclose a book, Pauline Hopkins's Of One Blood — quite a bit of my soul reflected in its pages.

> We remain near to each other,
> Your Ona

12
"Mammy's Chocolate Soldier"
FEBRUARY 1917

Ivoe has been a dipper at Alton Clover twelve weeks when her name issues from the loudspeaker in the room that smells of cocoa and bergamot hair grease, where she dips nine hours a day across from a sullen girl Ivoe is sure lost her smile to the bruises peeking out from the collar of her dress. It is the worst kind of job, monotonous and requiring total attention. As in all piecework, skill and speed count, and she has neither. What she has is a cold metal stool at the end of the row, where all lefties are seated, and a small instrument with a bowed wire at the end just large enough so that the bonbons do not slip through; with this she dips each ball of cream into smooth chocolate and sets it on the parchment-lined tray. Getting the balls to stay where she places them is hard enough but the final step is next to impossible. She can no more make the little fold of chocolate over the top, the

326

trademark for the pricier bonbons, than Timbo can give up gambling. Her bonbons are a mess, as though her trays are intended for the Smudge Company. "I know the girls by their trays," Mrs. Humphrey had said on her first day. At the second call of her name, Ivoe thinks that she is not long for this job.

Drawn shades and Mrs. Humphrey unbuttoning her shirtwaist surprise Ivoe — but just a little. It has been five weeks of warm hands against her back, ample bosom pressed against her head while her tray is inspected, and greedy glances whenever the forewoman enters the commons where the hefty girls from packaging and receiving take their lunch. (They are not friendlier than the dippers but they are louder, which gives the same effect.) There are things about being a colored woman in the city that she can learn from Lois. Ivoe likes the way she says "Williams" in that funny accent, the hooded hazel eyes, and all the small ways she is generous — invitations for overtime, packs of cocoa powder slipped into her coat pocket (later used by Momma in cakes). She appreciates the advice: which banks cheat Negroes; where to get the colored livery when she misses the trolley; which beauticians can't press hair worth a damn; the church all striving Negroes attend.

There is nothing furtive about the forewoman's touch. She pulls Ivoe close for a kiss, slow and gentle. She unzips the uniform, bites the back and sides of her neck, cups her breasts from behind. Down and under the slip, she probes between her legs in a staccato rhythm that ends in a surprising deluge.

Ivoe thinks of Ona, backs Lois against the desk, pushes up the sides of her skirt. She takes a seat in front of her, leans forward. She thinks of stew meat for supper instead of beans. Soft hands cradle her head, lead her to a heady scent. "Sweet, sweet," says a voice like velvet. She keeps at her business — pleasant enough — until Lois arches against the noise of steam whistles. Afterward, Lois erects herself, hand-brushes loose strands of hair in the direction of her upsweep. She knots Ivoe's apron and pats her on the back. Ivoe takes the two-dollar bill from under the can of pecan brittle on the desk, pops a piece of candy into her mouth, and returns to work.

Six months after their arrival in Kansas City, Ivoe sat the heavy valise on the ground, rubbing where the handle had left a red depression across her palm. Everything she owned had fit into the suitcase and three hat boxes, carried by Momma, Irabelle, and Roena, who were farther ahead, each striving with all eagerness. "Y'all wait for me. I'm the one with the key," Ivoe called out. She shook her head at their excitement to see the little house the Stranger's Rest minister had given her permission to live and work in. Last week, after ironing out the arrangements, she had visited the house alone — little more than four walls and a roof on empty Cherry Street. Only the kitchen came furnished, if you could call the rickety table and chair shy of one leg furniture, but there was no one to hurry out of the bathroom, no one to share food with, and no one to consider late at night when she needed to type. Best of all, no one to talk to, no voices to crowd out the one in her head.

"Clean it up and it'll do," Momma said, while Irabelle's eyes lit up. "Shoot, girl. You got as much room as we got — and it's just you." Roena stood in the doorway, looking out into the small yard. "You know anything about the street?"

Momma and Irabelle talked over each other with suggestions for how she might fix up the little house. "Saw some decent things at the Salvation Army." "I'll tell your brother to keep a lookout for furniture on the street. It'll be good as new once you wipe it down." All she needed now was a little hot water, salt, and vinegar to clean the windows, the typewriter set up in a comfortable spot, and a little peace. As Ivoe pushed the Williams women out her front door, a shadow of worry crossed Momma's face: "Don't forget us over on Mulberry, you hear?"

Ivoe dipped the sharp pointed nib into the inkstand and begin to write in her favorite hand, delicate copperplate.

Kansas City, April 10, 1917

My dearest Ona,

Reading a letter from you is like settling into a large comfortable chair. Braced by your encouragement, I seized an opportunity worth celebrating. It so happens that the minister of our church has his eye on a public office next year. Learning of his plans, I shared an idea hatched from your advice to find a way to "do what matters to me and others." I told him that a newsletter would galvanize his congregation and the West Bottoms and be a giant step toward his political goal. I offered to write on the community's social concerns and to attend to the church's printing needs. I'll keep making bonbons for Mr. Clover because the church job carries no pay. However, as editor of the newsletter, which I will call Meditation, I can live and work in the little church-owned house where there is a printing press — used now only to print the Sunday bulletins. I invited Momma and Irabelle to stay with me, thinking Timbo, Roena, and theirs might spread out in the Mulberry apartment. Momma reminded me that she is saving for her own home and encouraged me to take the house for myself. At twenty-eight, I am finally living alone in a home I do not have to share. You can't imagine how this encourages me.

Through with feeling lowly and helpless. I will be a journalist and live an original life — see if I won't! As always, nothing seems as if it has truly happened to me until I share it with you. Please take note of my new address and the tiny aromatic box.

I remain your loving friend,
Ivoe L. Williams
1810 Cherry Street

Kansas City, MO

Austin, April 21, 1917

My Loving Journalist,
   What words are you bringing to the congregation to help wartime K.C.? When I am in bed, I think of the men scattering like chickens at the sound of sniper shots. I worry about your brother finding himself face-to-face with a German.
   No time to write a long letter. After receiving yours, I aim to be your first mail in the new home. Let me know if the old homestead requires anything. And PLEASE do send your Meditations my way. I am more eager for them than I can write, more proud of you than I can say.

Love,
Ona

PS: I received the chocolates. How anything this divine arrived intact is no small wonder. Many thanks, many kisses.

The door to the past flung open, Ivoe was joined by two unwelcome guests — regret and doubt. Errands and answering the telephone for the *Enterprise* did not take her far, but they had placed her in the midst of her dream. What good was the newsletter she had no time to write? Every morning she awoke determined to write a paragraph for the week's *Meditation.* She left the house by seven in the morning; her shift lasted from eight until six. By ten in the morning, she had taken three, four lavatory breaks to scribble down ideas, phrases. Around noon her eyes began to blur from the hundreds of balls she had dipped. Late afternoon her stool felt like granite, causing her spine to curve like the letter *C.* (She had been taught the right way to sit in order to make left-handed penmanship legible — shoulders rolled back, forearm straight, not bent in a ninety-degree angle, which always caused the hand to smudge the slate as she wrote across it. She now sat wrong all day.) Despite weary eyes, a tired ass, and a sore back, on the trolley home she perked up again. She was unaccustomed to work that exhausted the body while the brain remained charged. At the kitchen table she studied the jumble of folded paper and scraps of notes emptied from her pockets, but in a tired haze none of it made sense. She mulled over ideas before pulling out the little portable Underwood — usually around ten. She pecked out three or four sentences. Sometimes she imagined May-Belle at the table quilting, or for inspiration that simple command spoken so often by Ona Durden: "Carry on."

From the corner, Lois Humphrey watched Ivoe with hungry intensity. Her candy girls ate lunch in their respective workrooms. Williams belonged across the hall with the rest of the dippers, but there she sat alone on a bench in the commons, known turf for the girls from packing and receiving. Conversations were in full swing: Who'd seen what picture show at the Gem Theater? Or cut a rug at the Ozarks Club on Saturday night? Ideas and invitations for the weekend flew back and forth, not a single one caught by Ivoe, whose food went untouched as she greedily eyed a letter. Sal, a loud girl with shiny black pin curls, laughed in a loose sort of way, stood up, and walked over to Ivoe. Hand or machine packing — it didn't matter — two-faced Sal could do it all to a fare-thee-well and still stir up enough she-said to keep the factory rocking. A week ago she couldn't stand "dicty hussies from Texas." Said it loud enough for everyone to hear. Now she interrupted Ivoe, paying her a phony smile for half of a sandwich. Whether Ivoe knew it, feeding the backbiting chippie had probably done her some good. Someday Sal might remember the edge taken off her hunger and tell someone not to steal Ivoe's coat or pour chocolate in her shoes — a good thing since Ivoe wasn't hard enough to make it without a friend, nor was she about to pretend that sitting in a theater balcony melting over some dandy in too much cologne was entertainment.

Away from work, Lois tried not to think of the wide-eyed girlishness and warm southern manner, the long legs and full lips, but these things kept Ivoe on her mind. "Williams!" she shouted above the lively chatter.

Ivoe looked up, a degree of annoyance crossing her face.

Lois watched as Ivoe's face opened wide with pleasure. She grazed and tugged the blackberry nipple with her teeth then gave it a pinch. They moved from the floor to the chairs, where Lois lit a cigarette. As usual when they sat across from each other bare-chested in half-slips, discussing this and that, there was no mention of the ring on Lois's left hand.

Thirty-four hours after boarding her train in Boston, fifteen years ago, Lois Brady left Kansas City's Union Station on the heels of a well-dressed crowd. At the club she picked the darkest berry on the vine, an elevator operator at the Jefferson Hotel. He wore his need tough. If not the little ones, he answered the big desires; he made her a wife and a home, and she felt protected within a community where Mother and brother would be welcomed. After a little while he understood the bargain. Not to worry, she assured him, one man was plenty. Apart from her job and their too-quiet home life, she had neither the time nor the money for dalliances. He learned to ignore strange perfumes, lipstick, the scent of another woman whenever he brought her hands to his mouth to kiss.

Lois drew from her cigarette. "What's going on down there on my floor?"

"Work. That's all."

"Shit, work ain't never *all*. Somebody's mad at somebody. Somebody's sick. Somebody owe somebody money. Somebody sleeping with somebody she ain't got no business sleeping with. And all that mess affects my floor."

When Lois's eyes went flat like that, a sharp wave of desire tore through Ivoe. She watched Lois roll the stocking up her leg, snap the garter. She had a figure to beat the band.

"Well, I wouldn't know anything about it. I keep to myself."

"Um-hum. Busy reading letters." She fit one breast and the other into the cups of a lilac brassiere. "Hand me my blouse. I read your *Meditation.*"

"Was it any good?"

"Preachy. Didn't tell me nothing I don't already know. Or knew and forgot 'cause it wasn't important the first time. You got me scratching my head on this one, Williams. If you can't tell me what's going on here, how are you writing a newsletter?"

Not very well, Ivoe thought. Copies placed in the vestibule before church ended in the ladies' room, blotted with lipstick or scribbled over with more pressing news. Some littered the hallway floors or blew over the outside steps. Her opinions and the little insight gleaned from the occasional chat with the church secretary and minister (who knew very little about the lives of his congregants) wasn't enough for members of Stranger's Rest to carry the *Meditation* home.

Lois stubbed her cigarette out and stepped into her skirt. She would've put money — hell, the whole factory — on this bet: Ivoe had never sat to any woman's kitchen table having her hair done or playing cards, nor had she seen the inside of a pool hall. No wonder the people couldn't see themselves in her writing, all dressed up in Willetsonese. "If you listen out there like you listen in here, you'll never find out what's going on."

Ivoe tossed the wrapping from a pecan brittle into the wastebasket, then leaned over to remove the *Boston Guardian* from the trash.

"My brother sends it from back home. Go on. Take it with you. Better make your trolley. I wouldn't want to be caught out late in the West Bottoms by myself on a Friday night."

Ivoe gripped the rope suspended from the trolley ceiling transfixed by the newspaper's cover photo. The caption read: "Sold to the *Boston Guardian* by a member of the attending party." Nothing about the onlookers hinted at the atrocity. Their wardrobes — Sunday best. Their faces — blank. What looked like two blackened thumbprints hanging from a tree had once been colored men. She nearly missed her stop — neighborhood problems, muckraking, police raids, and violence. So much violence. As in a Hearst scandal sheet, too much space was given to crime news. Not one word devoted to racial self-help.

In the summer of 1917, Ivoe kept her ear to the Vine. An acquaintance at the YWCA apprised her of a new city chapter of the Prudence Crandall Club. As a guest of the Ivy Needle club, she learned about the special concerns of young colored women in the city who were protected neither by law, father, nor husband. To fill in the other half of black life in Kansas City, she used her brother's name as a calling card when venturing boldly into billiard halls, gambling dens, any place men congregated, including the basement of the YMCA, a temporary home for the Negro Leagues' baseball players. She inquired about people's lives in the city: What did they want? What weren't they getting? What did they struggle with and hope to change?

After a day on the street, she turned out the light in the wee hours satisfied, only to awaken and read over the steady, uneven product of the night. On the disgusted ride to work she tried to shine a light inside her mind, blast away the dark thoughts. The less time she gave to moping about the *Meditation* — remarkably unhelpful — the sooner better ideas showed up. If she concentrated on words rather than chocolate and if Lois left her alone, by midmorning she could draw inspiration from everything from girl gossip to a radio tune.

Sophie Tucker's "Mammy's Chocolate Soldier" filled the airwaves that summer, but the constant refrain — *Pickaninny cute in his khaki suit . . . Come and lay your kinkey head on Mammy's shoulder* — sugarcoated the fact that draft agents worked overtime to prune the Vine of its men. Doors to several colored businesses were chained and locked, their owners drafted. The firing of colored men had become common practice, as was their arrest. She had looked into the draft registration, worried by some of the changes. At thirty-four, Timbo had aged out of the previous two registrations. He was no longer decrepit by government standards. The third call to duty accepted men as old as forty-five.

Kansas City, August 6, 1917

Dear Ona,

This morning I watched as a well-dressed Negro man was questioned for twenty minutes about his travel plans. When the police finally let him go, he shrugged and said that was the second missed appointment this week due to "special inquiry," a term the KCPD employs with great frequency. The city, I thought, would be amenable to our race, but here you find store upon store push their wares to us while a colored person has yet to set foot in these same businesses as employee. In next week's Meditation I will suggest we do not buy where we cannot work.

Through a gentleman at church, I learned of an opening for a cub reporter at the *Kansas City Star* and immediately placed a call so that at least my gender would be known. I disclosed all: race and age and willingness to accept a cub's salary despite my experience. Imagine my joy when the conversation ended with an interview date — here, finally, my chance had come and at the city's top newspaper. Nothing could dampen my spirits, but when the hour came, my hope was dashed. Seated with me in the waiting room was a young man from Illinois who had just completed high school. He assured me the post was mine as he had only written for his high school newspaper and was equally interested in professional boxing. When they called me in, I asked the young man for his name. This morning an article by

Mr. Ernest Hemingway appeared on page two.

Next month I will turn twenty-nine. A dozen of those years I have tried to write for a newspaper. In Kansas City alone, thirteen papers have barred me from even the lowest position. If I am to succeed at a paper, I will have to leave this city and there is no guarantee of employment elsewhere. Remind me again of the virtues of black womanhood.

Your loving friend,
Ivoe

The apartment on Mulberry Street was quiet when Lemon let herself in. She stubbed her toe on the bag near the broom closet and chuckled. The sack of beans had started out in the cupboard, moved to the counter, and now that three of them were working, somebody had the beans on their way out the door. She could hardly blame them. She had boiled the beans with onions and carrots — bean soup; mashed the beans with a little egg and some seasoning and filled a crust — bean pie; added corn syrup and a little honey before they went into the oven — baked beans; even beans fried in chicken fat. She placed the letter from Texas on the counter and swapped her coat for the apron on the hook. Her children knew how to send a message, all right, but she wouldn't pay them any mind. Long as there was war those beans wouldn't budge an inch. But today, with the little money Irabelle made playing in some band on the weekends and Ivoe's pay, there was enough for canned peaches, a pitiful substitute for the heavenly drupes she'd picked from May-Belle's tree. She opened the cupboard for spices, the mail from Roena's aunt Fanny visible from the corner of her eye. For a spell, preparation of the surprise cobbler took her mind off the letter. Her mind had trailed off to Ennis, like it always did in a too-quiet moment, when her daughters laughed themselves into the apartment, play-fussing and teasing Irabelle about something.

"You tell Momma about him yet? Well? Don't put your pity face on. What she say?"

"Ivoe, you act like me and you didn't come out of the same basket. How long you been knowing Momma? She ain't about to let me move in with some man she don't know nothing about."

"Bring him around then. How old is he? He mean well by you, don't he? You grown now. Only babies in this family are breaking up something in the next room," Roena

said. "Just make sure he wants to marry you
— and take you home with him. We filled to
the gills around here."

Lemon put her cobbler in the oven, picked
up the letter, and called everyone to the
kitchen. Junebug and Pinky shot through
the kitchen, eager to tell about their adventure at Aunt Ivoe's. Junebug rushed over to
Lemon and held out the palms of his hand,
proud of the ink smudged all over them.
"Bicey, I was working on the typewriter."

"Bicey needs to get in these pots and fix
something to eat. Y'all go on in the bedroom
and let grown folks talk. I be in there in a
minute and you can tell me all about it
then."

A key rattled in the door and Timothy
bumbled in.

Roena cut her eyes at the torn package
her husband threw on the table. Shaking
her head, she snatched up the bundle and
carried it to the sink, muttering to herself,
"A boiling chicken when your mother asked
for a roaster."

"That's about the most pitiful-looking
bird. Tell you something twice but you don't
hear."

"Ain't that what you asked for?"

Roena's face was balled into a knot. "I
heard Lemon from the other room when

she said 'roaster'. How come you didn't and was standing right in here with her?"

"What Timbo do to get on everybody's bad side?" Ivoe said.

"Can't follow directions on what kind of chicken to bring home — but you let one of them fools call about a game they got going. That's the message he gonna take to heart down to the iddiest-biddiest detail. They see more of him at the Spinning Wheel than we do."

"I done told you — I been at the Spinning Wheel but not on no gambling."

"I forgot. You're organizing," Roena said in a mocking tone.

"Organizing what?" Lemon asked.

Roena glanced sideways at her husband. "Your son has taken it into his head that he's a union man. Anything so long as it don't involve no real work."

"I tell you, Timbo, if foolish was dirt you'd have four or five acres. Walk around here just like you ain't got a thing to lose," Lemon said.

"The world ain't never give me nothing, so what I got to lose?"

Lemon threw up her hand. "Timbo, you make my head hurt. What you got to lose? If you got to ask you worse off than I thought 'cause straightaway I can think of three good things. You better wake up and start using your head for more than a hat rack. You got a wife and kids to feed — striking, my foot."

Hell if Timbo knew where the thought came from that he alone could get colored men organized, but it was the first time in his life he had his own thoughts on something important and he was excited to see where they might lead him. Whenever he tried to talk to Roena his words were like spots on dice — all that fumbling and still didn't come out right.

"I been trying to tell you —" Timbo said in a tone like Roena was the reason his back teeth ached.

"You ain't tried to tell me nothing. Too busy walking around here full of the devil. Go on and run off this job to another one if you want to. Don't matter where you go, Timbo, you give people the devil they gonna give him right back to you."

"What's going on down at the plant, brother?"

"Them Krauts down there talking they talk — don't even know what they saying half the time — doing the same work we doing, getting better pay for it. Tell you what it do too — put hate in your heart. Slipping and sliding in pig guts what supposed to be cleaned up before my shift begin. And the smell. Don't nothing stank like a pig's insides. Cold months no better. Suffocate in summer, freeze in winter. Nobody should have to work like that and they don't want to half pay us."

Irabelle heard echoes of Odell's complaints about what Pullman porters endured. "It's not just Timbo's problem . . . Work these no-good jobs and your head is still barely above water."

Lemon thought none of her children looked happy. She blamed the city — not worth leaving her dog for. She had looked for signs of the good life Ivoe claimed were all around them but couldn't find any. Now that she knew what went on inside most of the buildings — overcrowded with people just like her who worked long and hard just to buy things — she was not impressed. Youngsters couldn't see how they had traded cotton for some shiny thing, fancy trousers, an automobile, but she saw it plain as day: the only thing the city had on the country was more stuff to keep you working harder, longer.

She opened the letter and began to weep.

13
CHERRY STREET WALTZ
AUGUST 1917

Kansas City, August 14, 1917

Most Beloved,
A great warmth has gone from life. Aunt
May-Belle has died.
Yours in my darkest hour,
Ivoe

The taxi from Kansas City's Union Station
let Ona out in front of a little blue house,
the front door of which was ajar to welcome
the summer breeze. Her heart raced while
she rapped a little and listened before pushing the door open. It was not every day you
stepped into a room about which you knew
the history. She smiled at the modesty of
Ivoe's letters; she had done more than
"make do." A dreary room that served as
office, parlor, and occasional guest room for
Irabelle was now a cozy den. Faded floral
wallpaper seemed to blossom beneath the

wainscoting, painted cantaloupe to match the trim of the bay window looking out over the small manicured lawn. She could see her friend's taste, hinted at every now and then through months of letters. There were the cheery green curtains of organdy and voile, splurged on at the Salvation Army shortly after she moved in. A maroon carpet with paisley designs of the curtains' green hid the ugly wood floor that had splintered her feet. Near the window stood the cumbersome brown armchair that took three men to carry. Big enough for two, it held three orange taffeta pillows; next to it, peonies in a long-necked amber bottle on some rickety stand. Draped over the shade of the floor lamp was the pitiful scarf she had knitted for Ivoe last Christmas.

Ona saved the room's best feature for last. Before her, Miss Industry sat waist-high in books, working at a shabby desk. Ona glanced at a stack of typewritten pages that lay next to the little Underwood she had had mailed to Little Tunis a decade ago. Light from the window illuminated four perfect marcelled waves as Ivoe tilted her head, drawing Ona's gaze to a nail above the desk from which hung a pair of prayer beads — May-Belle's. At that very moment, without seeing Ivoe's face, Ona knew exactly the expression she wore — lips pursed, mouth twisted a little in a moment of concentration.

"Howdy, honey, howdy," Ona whispered.

Ivoe laid her writing tablet on the desk and brought her hand up to her chest — a mallet ringing against an anvil! — and stood, shaking.

The salmon blouse and powdery pea-green skirt Ivoe wore revealed a few extra pounds at the hips. She was taller, Ona thought, noting the heel on the brown tango shoe. They looked at each other, watching the joyful rise of the other's bosom. Books toppled over as Ivoe pushed back her chair. Ona's kiss on the lips was mingled with peppermint. "Goodness," she whispered, drawing her closer.

Neither could say if they held each other that way two minutes or twenty. Enveloped in the scent of Floris White Rose, Ivoe nearly forgot what all the heaviness was about until Ona pulled away, cradling her face and searching it. "I just had to come see about you." And there it was, a look of love so fierce it began to melt the grief, thick and frozen like ice floes around her heart. She grabbed handfuls of Ona's dress to steady herself.

■ ■ ■ ■

For years Ona had practiced how not to be taken in but to remain steady when Ivoe gave her affection without reserve. It was a lesson the pupil herself had taught — deep emotions are best expressed by restraint. She had forgotten the exact month or day but was certain of the season her love for Ivoe bloomed. Bypass Road was alive with red wildflowers as she headed home, quickening her pace because of a hunch. She dashed through a brambly lane on a short-cut home and spilled through her front door, a letter from Little Tunis clutched in her hand. Later that night the pages called her from bed. She returned to the kitchen, reading the letter a third and fourth time. Only when she was satisfied the girl could never be any more near to her than she was at that moment did she return to bed. She tried to bully her desire back into a quiet place but fell into a kissing dream.

Ona was thinking of Ivoe with the same intensity now while she cooked and Ivoe wrote in the next room. She threw a generous pinch of salt into a small basin of cool water filled with kale and mustard greens.

She liked to soak them that way then throw in a handful of raisins to bring out the flavor. The secret was in the fire; they didn't need much, just enough to get the leaf nice and tender yet still bright green. The other dishes Ivoe had spoken of longingly Ona's first night there were not any of the things she prepared with confidence; but this meal she had traveled seven hundred miles to make. The chicken pie, red rice and okra, and peanut butter soup were May-Belle's specialties, as much a part of Ivoe's girlhood as stolen newspapers. No recipes to guide her, Ona tasted as she cooked — more pepper, a dash of sugar here, a capful of cream. She hoped the meal would tell on her: she wanted to stoke Ivoe's memories and make new ones.

Ivoe snapped open the linen, turning the sofa into Ona's bed as she had done every night of the visit.

"What do you think?"

"Fine." Ona indicated on the page where improvements might be made, but she was not about to give the whole evening up for the plight of her race. They didn't have to be race women all the time.

In the kitchen, they passed a glass of water between them.

"Good thing my train leaves tomorrow. Stay much longer and you'll be all twisted up like a pretzel," Ona said.

Ivoe would twist into a thousand knots if it meant more time with Ona, whose eyes held a strangeness she had never seen.

"I've been meaning to ask, you keeping company with anybody? You never mention in your letters."

"I wouldn't call it company. We met at the factory — the job I got following your advice."

Ona laughed a single high note as derisive as a magpie's. "Had I known I was fattening frogs for snakes I never would've mailed that letter. So, how do you and Ms. Alton Clover get along?"

To watch Ona's demeanor change from bravado to jealousy tickled Ivoe. She took the empty glass from her hand. Everything she thought to say was wrong, yet she was braced by the furtive touch on her arm. She kissed Ona on the cheek, chin, the little bit of collarbone peeking out from her dress. The most delicious sighs fell from her lips, spilled off the kitchen counter onto the floorboards to tremble and nestle in the cracks.

Ona tore back the curtains and gasped. It was a devil of a sky — the orange evening sun in one corner, a full moon in the other. She motioned for Ivoe's help. Together they pushed the little bed beneath the window.

Their breathing told secrets their bodies could no longer hold. Kissing, nuzzling Ona's breasts all over, Ivoe smiled at their beauty, moon-washed and glistening. She kissed down Ona's stomach, pried open damp thighs, pressed her knee against the coarse, wet triangle. Ona arched against the outside light and cradled Ivoe's face, moving against the knee — staccato breaths like steady puffs of steam. Ivoe shifted her body, crawling backward over her lover. "Ivoe —" Ona grabbed her buttocks, moaned like she was in full-grown love with everything she saw, and pulled her sex closer. Above her, Ivoe rocked against her face in perfect measure, kissing the inside of Ona's thighs until Ona thrust forward, eager. Ivoe's breath caught in her chest; against her belly she could feel the cage of Ona's chest expanding like the sails of a yawl. She paused before kissing her there, strained to see everything, batted back the tears. Both spread her legs farther apart.

"Ba-by."

Belly on belly, north and south: full vision. Their sound, the new scent of them, filled the room. Ivoe had been here in the sweet place with Ona, feeling this good, a million times before in her mind. Whispering in the dark with her now was something else. Could a heart break from too much tenderness? She slid over Ona's body, slipping one hand inside her while the other felt around Ona's mouth, where pleasure held her lips apart. Ivoe whispered, "You took me the long way" — deep — "down back roads and everything" — deeper still — "glad you did . . . 'cause only time could tell me how I love you like I do."

Ona Durden was not a woman who hankered for things, yet everything she owned she cared for with devotion. Like the hat she now placed over her bun, securing it with a hatpin, the end of which was a small pink pearl. She'd worn the same hat a decade ago at Willetson. Even then it was far from new. Ivoe flashed on a funny little thought: if Ona could love a hat that well, she could trust her with everything.

Ona leaned her head a little to the side; the grip on her pocketbook slackened. "Come on now before I miss my train," she said, staring with eyes so full of desire Ivoe could not meet them. She crossed the room to where Ona's valise stood. A moment passed before she felt Ona against her back, encircling her waist with both hands. It was impossible to believe that somewhere the building of skyscrapers went on; that tobacco, cotton, and peanut fields brimmed full with pickers; a fisherman emptied his net; little children sat to their desks about the business of learning — there was only the two of them in the world.

Many words came to mind but only one fit as Ivoe struggled against a sob that rose in her throat: "Ona —"

"I'm not rehearsed in romantic speechmaking but I know this: we have work to do — don't look so glum. We got some loving too. Make room for me."

The trolley began its slow clank and rumble. Ivoe rapped against the window for Ona's attention. She had turned in the wrong direction for the dry-cleaners. Ivoe had half a mind to get off the streetcar and escort Ona to pick up the dress she planned to wear for a talk before clubwomen. Instead, she shook her head, causing Ona to laugh, and pointed her in the opposite direction. Ivoe's disenchantment with the factory was no mystery. Happiness had ruined any ambition, at least for chocolate. Lois would not take kindly to her request for the afternoon off, but she would hold her ground. It was Ona's first time doing any- thing of significance in the city; Lois could like it or lump it.

Five minutes before the bell rang and she belonged at her station, Ivoe poked her head in Lois's office.

"I thought you had lost your way, it's been so long. Close the door." Lois enclosed Ivoe in a tight embrace that Ivoe did not return. "Tell the girls you had to see the doctor this morning."

"I do have to leave this afternoon."

Lois stepped back and adjusted her skirt. "Well, I can't lay eyes daily on something that don't belong to me. With Christmas around the corner, I'll have to hire your replacement in the morning."

"I suspected you would."

"You know what you doing?"

Ivoe nodded. After today Ona would have leads on who to solicit for printing needs — programs, invitations, cards and such. Without the factory work, Ivoe would have more time to devote to the *Meditation*. Money would always be little, but life was already rich and full since her ambition was safe with Ona, even if her job wasn't.

"I've been good to you."

Love is a curious thing. In her search to explain, Ivoe realized it no longer mattered.

"You've been more than good, you've been fair in a city that showed me no fairness."

She kissed Lois at the corner of her mouth and left.

A groggy Ona shuffled behind Ivoe with a cup of tea, the white sheet clinging to her round shoulders, caught where her back ended and her ample behind began. They sat down on the sofa side by side. An orange scarf held Ona's pin curls in place and a crease lay deep in her left cheek as she stifled a yawn. Ivoe snapped open the *Dallas Express,* one of several colored newspapers they subscribed to. Ona got up to put a roll on the Welte-Mignon pianola, her only possession moved from Texas they had struggled to make room for. The small Perfection printing press, a teacher's wardrobe, and the box of memories looked as if they had grown there. Ivoe read swiftly, encouraged in part by the jaunty rhythm of Blind Boone.

Any discussion of Ivoe's life now would sound like the worst bragging. For the first time she could concentrate all her efforts on writing. Mornings played out at a meeting or lecture. From early afternoon through the evening she worked on the *Meditation.*

Between seeking out printing jobs at neighborhood businesses, Ona kept house with small flourishes. Where Ivoe had washed and ironed the curtains, Ona sprinkled a dash of vanilla on the hem and tied the curtains with a floral scarf, bringing sweet cheerfulness to a once dreary room. Decorative fir branches in the vase on the kitchen table from last winter were now replaced by orange peonies, and the undergarment drawer was never without grapefruit peel.

No Williams dared to say it, but Ona's sweet potato pie rivaled Momma's chess pie. She had even impressed Momma with recipes like her aromatic amethyst soup. She could hold the twins rapt with story; inspire Irabelle with chapter and verse of exactly how her music made her feel; and draw a laugh from Roena's little pot belly (her figure had gone from string bean to pea pod, the fate of all women who weren't danced enough). "Take your woman out sometimes," Ivoe once heard Ona say to Timbo. "It's not so much that your wife wants to be seen, it's that she wants to be seen *by you* — in a different light." Roena talked about their night out for months.

Ona remained true to her calling of civic duty. She joined the Kansas City, Kansas, chapter of the NAACP and the Colored

Women's League, who worked to raise funds for the Paseo House, a refuge for wayward colored girls. On weekends she turned their home into a meeting place for spirited women who held the same moral and ethical concerns for the race. Every Saturday at four, Mr. Nixon drove up in the Ford Runabout — VINE CONFISERIE etched on the passenger door — and handed over the box of usual goodness: rose-scented tea and violet honey; pralines; the gooseberry-jam-filled butter cookies that Ona loved. Plated treats and pots of tea traveled around the parlor as the women buzzed with ideas and concerns: suffrage; the challenges of motherhood; domestic budgeting; better employment opportunities. No matter the subjects, every conversation included the queer observation and worthy question: The Kansas City Police Department was vigilant on the Vine, but for whose benefit? And where could they turn for information on law and order?

Ona enjoyed her new life's rhythm. Having taught classes that convened at eight for fifteen years, she now awakened at half past six and tended the house, picking up balls of paper around Ivoe's desk where she had settled down to write after supper until late in the night. She appreciated tidying up for the clues it gave her on what Ivoe was thinking. Ona spent late morning working on the neighborhood printing — cards, invitations, posters — always ferreting out some bit of helpful information for Ivoe. Late in the afternoon, she turned her attention to supper. If they required an ingredient, she made note of it on her way to the mailbox. Presently, she was thinking of potato salad to eat with the chicken when she opened the tin door and pulled out a letter. She eyed it curiously. Who did Ivoe know in Baltimore?

Berdis Peets Brown Wilson Diaz greeted them in a voice carrying but unmusical. She handed Ivoe a small white box crumpled from the twelve-hour train ride and kissed her with tobacco-tinged lips. Her face held fine lines; her wavy hair, cropped close, showed gray about the temples. She studied Ivoe for clues on the life she led. Where was the dull skin that no amount of rouge could perk up? The shoulders rounded and bent from carrying too heavy a load? No traces of hardship, not a single ounce of grown woman pain did Ivoe seem to carry. There seemed to be all about her a high degree of satisfaction — not even — joy! Berdis knit her brows at some vague recognition of the woman beside Ivoe. The name did not readily come, but a sudden painful and vivid rush of feelings filled her at once. Miss Durden looked exactly as she had a decade ago. Before her face could register shock Berdis excused herself, explaining the small box, *"Chrusciki.* The Polish call them *chrusciki."*

In the bathroom, she passed the gas knotting her stomach while the pus-filled ulcers lining her jaws induced her to spit. Raising her head from the sink, she was appalled by her reflection. Ivoe and Miss Durden had barely aged but she had grown old. No rouge or lipstick can cover the truth — your whole life shows in your face. She tried anyway, caking light Egyptian powder on the butterfly rash over her nose and above her sunken cheeks. She made her mouth a blooming rose, transformed her eyes into two smudges of dusky dark brown. Several draws from her cigarette helped to mask the rank mouth odor caused by pyorrhea. Oblivious to fallen ashes on the sink and floor, she tossed the cigarette into the toilet. A second once-over in the mirror showed no great improvement.

The cozy house was redolent of cake or pie. Berdis sat in the dimmest corner of the room until Ona pulled back the curtain and the sun shone in on her. Everything was bright and gay as the two moved about setting up afternoon tea. The white box was emptied, the cookies laid out on a green glass plate. Ivoe was different. The high-minded walk gave it away: stiff-backed but shoulders swinging, hips following in the same side-to-side motion.

"Never happier," Ivoe said, sucking powdered sugar off her fingers. She was glad to be out of Little Tunis, glad to be through with the factory, and more in love with life in the city and with Ona than she could say. Berdis offered a phony smile. Printing had always been a tonic shared between the two; nothing had changed. Ona chatted with ease about printing cards and advertisements for colored businesses, while Ivoe wrote and published a church newsletter.

"You say they call them *chrus-ci-ki*?" Ivoe said, aware that she and Ona had filled the room with too much of their joy.

"Angel wings too," Berdis said, boring a baleful glare into Ona's back while she filled their cups and asked in a tone that belied judgment, "What are you doing in Baltimore?"

"She gives music lessons," Ivoe said, recalling the letter received a month ago.

"I give private lessons to the children of doctors, dentists, professors from the university. Occasionally, a charity case, like the son of the Polish baker whose shop is next door to my house." She said nothing of the first husband, a lousy manager; or the few years wrapped in the embrace of husband number two, who neither awakened her senses nor knew enough to let them lie sleeping; or Beetleboy; or husband three, taken by Uncle Sam.

"When you wrote and said you were coming to town, Ona picked up something special," Ivoe said, placing the piano roll beneath the tracker bar.

"From the recorded performance of Mr. Joplin himself . . . 'Pleasant Moments.' "

" 'Pleasant Moments,' indeed!" Berdis said merely to say something.

Ona's eyes slid from Ivoe to Berdis, who smoked the way a squirrel chews nuts. She rose when the pianola started to play. "Shake a leg, Berdis. Sitting is the last thing you ought to want to do after that long train ride."

"Y'all go on. It's not every day I get to watch two colored women cut a rug," Berdis said, minding the piano keys that moved without her touch. Through narrowed eyelids, she watched the hostesses dance. In their hobble dresses the foxtrot was a challenge. Still, their quick-quick-slow-quick steps, the gentle sway of Ivoe's hip when the step was deliberately slow, made Berdis twist in her chair, away from the couple, toward the pianola as if she could engage it in conversation. She was thinking of something Ivoe had said earlier about their time at Willetson, a season of dreaming. None of her dreams saw fit to come true. Her one true love had been dangled above her reach. Anything you served the way she had served music ought to serve you back, but life had unfairly chastened her plans. Since leaving Willetson, she had not set foot in a concert hall to hear music, let alone to play, even though her first husband had promised she'd be heard by crowds in Mexico City, where high-minded folks could hear past the color of her skin. He brought a piano home to the little apartment of ocher-stuccoed walls on Avenida del Pacifico. A week after he left, they came for the piano rented in her name. Overdue payments and unpaid rent sent her back to Texas, where she took a room with the Wilsons of Galveston. Young Wilson proposed on his fourth or fifth visit to his parents, her landlords. Soon, there was a child. Finally someone she might share her music with. Except that the baby didn't respond to her voice, or his daddy's voice, or even a thunderous roll on the keys of the piano at church. That was only the beginning. Stayed on the breast too long, her brown baby boy did, so his belly grew and his face changed a little even when the rest of him refused to. Wouldn't coo, crawl, or chew. Sometimes when she passed the crib she looked twice: "Baby or beetle?" By his fourth birthday, still he wouldn't speak. Maybe he figured since she made him, she ought to know exactly what his thoughts were. He stared up at her from the crib. At least he could see. Who knew all the work that came with being seen and not heard?

When she thought about it, she had never craved anyone's company — not before Ivoe or since her. Marriage had only brought more feelings of estrangement — from husband and baby. Nobody knew her in Lake Charles, where a new school had just opened. One of the builders — C.J., they called him, for "Crazy Juan" — bothered her for a while. Before she knew anything she was Berdis Peets Brown Wilson Diaz, packing moss in the toe of a boot just like she'd done for Daddy the days he worked the mines; only Juan was headed to war. The telegram arrived before their sheets cooled. The money most used to set themselves up like proper widows she spent on a one-way ticket east.

On May 14, 1915, dressed in a white suit and carrying a saffron-colored leather valise of memories — a rattle, a harmonica, scores of music — Berdis boarded a mixed-passenger freight train bound for New Orleans. Nearly thirty, though the joint pain made her feel older, and still possessed of visions of a harmonious life, she changed trains and eventually arrived in Baltimore, all smiles and gratitude for an elderly colored woman who mopped floors at the conservatory in Mount Vernon. How beautifully her seatmate had spoken about the music she had missed during her travels. From Union Station, Berdis followed the woman's directions to a boardinghouse. A second word of advice brought her to the opulent Belvedere hotel. As she changed beds on the eighth floor several months later, a conversation in the hallway ignited a dream.

No instrument was better suited for its player than the ebony grand Bechstein she played on audition day. Rachmaninoff's *Morceaux de Fantaisie* called for a moderate tempo played with exquisite touch and feeling, which she had practiced on the hotel's piano. The elegy conjured Willetson and all those things the heart had worked to evict.

Ivoe Williams had not crossed her mind in years, yet there in the first three chords of Prelude in C-sharp Minor were the days at the creek with her best girl. Now here she was, guiding her touch on the keys in rich bass, a propulsive climax. Gasps of pleasure among the dead-quiet jury gave her confidence. She played the remaining movements precisely, as one should — control from the forearm, wrists hard as snakewood. Heavy applause. "Miss Peets, you are someone worthy of an audience," said a pale face flushed deep rose. There was some question of her age, where she received training. In the end none of this would matter. An honest review of her program, rendered in praise, ended in kind rejection: "Regrettably, the Peabody Institute does not enroll Negro students."

Regrettably, indeed.

A return down south was all she could think to do. She wrote to Willetson, requesting Ivoe's address. Ticket inquiry turned into employment aboard the Alouette. She landed in Fell's Point, which suited fine once she learned poor Europeans were friendlier than colored people because they had less to prove. The little room above the Polish bakery on Essex Street was home when she wasn't giving manicures and dressing hair, eighteen hours a day back and forth to Cleveland. Occasionally, it slipped to the right woman that she played piano and she was invited to entertain lady passengers on the Observation Room's Steinway. A view of the Allegheny Mountains with Joplin at her fingertips! It could go another way too. No tip from the women, who called her haughty and accused her of such outlandish tales: Who had ever heard of a Pullman maid classically trained on the piano?

Berdis returned her thoughts to the present moment. Ona wore a playful grimace as she raised one knee sharply between Ivoe's legs. Her lips parted like she might say something, then a sigh gave way to a smile and a funny, exasperated roll of the eyes. There was for Ivoe real pleasure in the way Ona moved. She thrust the upper part of her body forward with open hands, grabbed Ona around the waist, and swung her till they both laughed. Their movement slowed, yet they were gaining sensation in their hips as they dragged their feet to mark the same beats in the gentle bump, bump, and shove of their dance. They were impossibly close on an up-tempo rag, dancing on a dime.

■ ■ ■ ■

Berdis opened the shiny emerald tin, lit a Lucky Strike, and took a long drag. For the last few days she had tried to put her finger on what she felt since entering the little blue house on Cherry Street. Nothing was off about Ivoe — everything was too on, lit up, polished, smooth. Gone were all the little ways Ivoe seemed unsure of herself, even scared of life, the parts of her Berdis found vulnerable, charming. The woman she'd spent the last four days with didn't fear the world; she mastered it, as much as a colored woman could.

At that moment, Ona rose, passed behind the sofa, trailing her hand across Ivoe's back. "Want anything?" Without lifting her eyes from the magazine she read, Ivoe reached behind, touched Ona's hand to say, *No thank you.* Berdis uncrossed her legs, leaned forward, as if improving her vantage. There it was, as she now supposed it had been since Willetson, a kind of haughty air surrounding Ivoe; Ona's love — if that's what you could call it, and she supposed it was love — made her arrogant.

Loneliness boiled up inside her at the terrible picture before her. Across the room

Ona sat in her slip and stockings with Ivoe on the floor between her legs. Ivoe's head hung low while she held up the Walker's pomade. Ona dipped into the jar, drawing a finger along Ivoe's scalp, calling up in Berdis the urge to walk over and rub her cigarette out on Ona's hand. Berdis tried not to let it show, tapping her foot, bopping her head along to the pianola. She blew a thick ring of smoke, riled by what private things she could tell about the couple as thick and close as flies in a jar of honey. Berdis was reminded of being between her own mother's legs. Having her hair combed was the only way to get back to that place (Mother had always said she loved her children each for one day and one day only, the day they were born). Heavy hands and rough fingers were delicate only when they probed her scalp, plaiting patterns none of the other girls wore. Her favorite, meticulous zigzagged lines forming the letter *Z* all over her head, proved her mother could care. "Bad enough He gave me a girl . . . I will say this for you. You got some good hair. Easy to fix." Between Mother's legs, dark as molasses and sturdy as oak trunks, Berdis had felt safe from the world. You could fall asleep down there even though the scent was dizzying — bergamot oil, Mother's

371

musk, So-and-So's laundry (you could always tell the washerwomen in Bastrop: they sweat ammonia) — and dream a wonderful dream of the sweet bread and candied apples that only ever came on Christmas and Sister Sarah singing "Steal Away to Jesus" with her head reared and slipping your feet into Daddy's mining boots first thing in the chilly morning. To be yanked from such slumber was the worst feeling in the world. Without thinking Berdis would always draw a hand up to the spot touched so tenderly before, groping for the braid pulled too hard. *Swwwwaaat.* The wooden comb landed hard against her knuckles. "What you feeling it for? Be still." Where did the love go? She waited for the word that held all of her mother's impatience, disappointment, unending fatigue. "Gone." As in: *Go on away from here. Go.*

"You want to go, don't you?" Ivoe was saying to her now.

Not for money or peace would Berdis have them know their affection toward each other rankled. She growled curses at the ash falling from her cigarette.

"Go where?"

"My sister Irabelle's at the Ozarks Club tonight. Wait until you hear her, Bird. Sister really can play. Roena might let my brother out. You know Timbo's married with twin boys. They're eleven."

Three years older than Beetleboy.

Ona nudged Ivoe, who sealed the pomade then turned around, pulling herself up so that she was standing on her knees between Ona's legs. Her voice lowered to a whisper for no reason at all. "Wear the yellow dress. The one with the cerise trimming." Just below the lace hem of Ona's slip, Ivoe planted a kiss on both knees, as if to say no deed was too small to go unnoticed. Ona dashed from the room and reappeared in the yellow dress, which fit her perfectly and drew out a pleasing nod from Ivoe.

"Shoes?"

Had they forgotten she was in the room? "Wish I could go tonight. I'm leaving on the late train," Berdis announced, as surprised as anyone.

"Tonight? I thought you were leaving tomorrow," Ivoe said.

"Naw, honey. I really do need to get back — to prepare for my students."

Ona had never wanted so much to shout for joy. Anybody could see Berdis was in a world of hurt, still wallowing in bitterness, indulging insatiable selfishness. Early in the visit Ona had given patience and tolerance; they were the spars saving her and Ivoe from the abyss of unfulfilled potential that Berdis drowned in. She had felt enough quiet, outraged emotion, witnessed enough brooding, to know that a dream without love is the most dangerous weapon in the world. She managed a slight smile now, her voice sober and flat. "It was nice of you to come." Berdis excused herself to the packing she needed to do, slinking toward Ivoe like a starved cobra for a good-bye embrace. Now their home could return to its pleasant order, rid of cigarette smoke and gloom, Ona thought. She was grateful she had not lost control and ruffled the shady woman's plumage, as she had longed to do more than a few times that week. At the desk, Ona pulled paper from the typewriter's carriage and scribbled in haste. "Here's the exchange for the taxi service. Better to call well in advance to make the train."

The pianola played Berdis's favorite Blind Tom composition, a clever piece for the peculiar harmonics of the treble and the bass that rumbled like thunder. Inside a box under the small bed in Baltimore was music for "The Rainstorm," which she could play from memory. Alone, she surveyed the cheery little room through a haze of smoke, nauseated by its contents. She looked at several small pictures — groups of women. Above them, in a heavy oak frame, was a picture of Ivoe and Ona. A honeymoon look hung about the two. Ona had laid a smile down deep inside of Ivoe while her mouth curved up high on one side in a smirk, as if she had won a secret prize. They were right for each other and right together. Years after Willetson, life still made Ivoe drunk. She was interested in everything, patient, and thoughtful. And Ona repaid all this with her quick wit, humor, and knack for making the light leap from Ivoe's eyes. They were just that damned happy. For all of her trying to control her feelings, Berdis was nagged by want to share her rage with the hostesses smiling back at her. She sucked her cigarette long and hard to drive back her rising anger, then laid it on the edge of the player piano. She moved closer to the picture and stumbled over her valise. She found her cigarette tin, lit another, and after a long, slow exhale laid it across a stack of papers. She slipped into her coat, struck a third match, and walked to their bedroom, where she placed a cigarette in the middle of the bed as the taxi blew its horn.

Vine Street pulsed and writhed with people and music. Ivoe, Ona, and Lemon stood off to the side while patrons bounced out of the Ozarks Club. A man ushered them along a wall of windows covered with burgundy velvet to shut out the public eye. The unassuming space could accommodate thirty comfortably, but on a Saturday night twice that many jammed inside, their heads swaying to melancholy strains, their faces lit by pleasure's flame. Ivoe pointed to a table at the front of the room with an empty seat and gave her mother a gentle shove through the crowd.

What Lemon understood about city life couldn't fill a mason jar, but she recognized a dandy when she saw one. She sat down next to a hulk of a man wearing a gray Stetson, a sack suit with a lavender vest piped at the pockets in gray silk and black leather, and gray gabardine spectator shoes. He mopped at his forehead with a lavender handkerchief, nodding at her and the small bucket on the table holding bootleg liquor in bottles branded with fake Haig & Haig labels.

Great anticipation brought hands together in feverish applause. Chore and worry behind, the crowd was eager to go wherever the music carried them. "I knew y'all pickaninnies couldn't stay away for long." The MC spoke in a booming voice above roaring laughter. "Had to come get you some more of the Three Deuces. Each one of the players got two stories, one they tell and one they play. Y'all know his story. Uncle Sam dropped by his place talking about did he want to fight in the war? Pease told him to take his khaki suit and shove it where the sun don't shine. And for that, he ranks high around here. Put your hands together for Major Pease." The piano clopped then galloped into a stride. "Now the one on the drums, well, his dough ain't done. Went over yonder with Uncle and listen at how they sent him back." A fleshy nub crashed the cymbal and the drummer grabbed it still with his only hand. "Stump!" The crowd howled as the MC strutted over to Irabelle and took a bow. "Ladies and rascals, you don't need no Alamo when you can hold up with a sweet tune like hers. Our very own Texas Bell."

Irabelle gave a single nod to the audience and raised her clarinet like a wineglass. "We have two names for this tune: 'Send Me Away with a Smile' and 'Chowchow,' after that good sweet-hot Momma used to make back home."

Major Pease ragged the melody, his left hand letting up, pausing in out-of-the-way places while the right played a steady duple rhythm. The high hat was hopping, the snare sizzling, then Irabelle made the clarinet moan.

Lemon couldn't put her finger on it, but something told her the bullnecked dandy sitting next to her was all vines and no tomatoes. "That girl something else, ain't she?" he said through a wide, toothy grin, nodding at her daughter. Her ears pricked at his cadence. Texas but farther east — 'round abouts Polk and Nacogdoches.

It took Irabelle sixteen bars, plus the four she traded with Major Pease, to tell her mother she was wrong. Odell "Plenty" Smalls was not a Texan or Louisianan. He had denied coming from both places. Whenever she had asked him anything about himself, he grabbed her chin with the cup of his hand, kissed her hard, and slapped her ass. He didn't have a home, didn't have no people, but he had a woman and she was it. His eyes said it first, as the train crossed the Texas state line. In Oklahoma he'd handed her three colas, and on her first night in the city she had dialed the phone number written on the napkin. All the waiting — between that call and his showing up one week later outside the high school — was to blame for tonight's tempo. Plenty never raised a hand to her. He didn't even raise a voice, so everything she had worked to turn hard turned soft again. She was silky smooth riding a mile of steel. "Stop rushing it," he said in the only motel on Independence Avenue where colored folks could rent a room. "Damn, you a furnace," he said. "Stop rushing it." Forward and backward and upside down and, well, if she used a thousand words describing what it was like being with Plenty nobody would understand. She made them feel it in her music while the porter who had served them two years ago aboard the Sunshine Express patted his heavy foot against the floor. She hoped he wasn't saying nothing too crazy to her momma, first impressions lasting like they do.

"You gonna send me all right." Plenty slapped his knee and leaned toward Lemon. "That girl sure do make it whimper, don't she? She make it whimper like a dog." His tongue did a slow, deliberate sweep over dazzling white teeth. "You squeezing it, Texas Bell. Got a death grip on that thing. Let it go, girl. Let it go!" After that he settled back, his teeth a mean little smile of contentment. Up there getting them to feel like that, Irabelle carried a sad kind of beauty, Plenty thought. Her hair might even be pretty if there was more shine to it. He didn't care too much for her skin — too dull for a girl of twenty — except for the scar. It reminded him not to handle her so well. Helping himself to her pocketbook, he had only to think of it. What's a little change? And why should she have it? He couldn't be bothered with remembering a birthday or taking note of the things she eyed in store windows. All she really wanted was in that damn case. With no encouragement at all, she would open it up and start in to playing that sad shit she should have left in the country, right on the dirty ground where they cut her. He wasn't moved. But whenever she played for a crowd and the light fell on the scar like it did right now, there was one thing on his mind: Irabelle's ankles on his shoulders. He grunted. Never mind the dicty woman next to him who probably never had it the way Irabelle got it — a fuck that left her so hoarse that "goodbye" came out broken into tiny pieces when he left out the motel door.

It was a hard feeling to put into music: Plenty rocking above her like he would in just a few hours and, with any luck, for years to come. An impossible emotion was welling up inside Irabelle. To get rid of it meant to pluck at a memory rooted so deep it had become part of her song. Every song. "You too young," Plenty had said when they pulled into the motel parking lot. She wondered at the surprised tone of his voice, as if he had not picked her up at the high school. She stared at him with grown woman eyes, told him she knew things. Knew things? Like what? Like how to blow a reed until a tune sprang from it. But before she could finish, Plenty had brushed past her thighs and beat through the drum until she sang for him clear and sharp like crystals. He must have liked that sound crashing around his head because he wouldn't let up till he shaped another tune, louder this time, and ugly. She tried to think pretty thoughts while he made her body a song but they never came. She blamed it on the city. Plenty was his very own industrial revolution, a shiny black piston that knew no end, a locomotive rocking above her. He rode easy, not so much gliding into her as flying down smooth tracks toward some expected destination. She blew the clarinet for as long as the pleasure had lasted the night she came so hard the waves of her pushed him out and laughter raised her cheeks, hiding the scar in a perfect crease. Plenty had looked down on her, stopped pumping, and cussed. An almost perfect memory, a damn perfect note.

■ ■ ■ ■

The backs of Ivoe's knees sweat and her toes were pressed too tight inside her shoes, but she was delighted. Sure as she was standing there, her sister was in love. You could hear it in the playing, the end of which was perfection interrupted by some little commotion. A voice was calling her name high above the thundering applause. She looked in every direction, not recognizing anyone. The boy working his arm like an ax to get through the crowd said something but was not close enough to hear. Finally, she reached out to brace the boy, out of breath and horrified.

"Ivoe Williams? Ms. Williams! I come as fast as I could. Your house is on fire!"

For years municipal services had withered on the Vine. Infrequent garbage pickups made the area home to the fattest strays in the city. Nothing smelled worse than leftover meat rotting after a day in the heat, let alone a week. No one knew when the sewers were last drained. Blood from the packing plants, shit, and piss backed up so bad only fire could cut the stench. The nobodies who never picked up the garbage, or plowed the winter streets, and forgot to light the gas lamps at dusk also drove the fire truck. Neighbors gathered quickly, sucking their teeth, cussing, praying the flames wouldn't get greedy and start to nibble on what little they had. Children from three blocks over clucked their tongues about who had motive. "Miss Ivoe give me licorice." "Me too." "Miss Ona give me two pennies for hauling her bags." Even without a culprit, the midnight blaze was more thrilling than peach ice cream. Nothing that summer would come close to topping it.

From the corner of Eighteenth and Cherry, Ivoe and Ona saw smoke billowing out against the starry sky. They turned into their street winded and afraid, pushing past the small crowd watching the conflagration in awe. The hissing crackle of wood stunned them into silence. The little house and pressroom was now indistinguishable parched timber. "Your friend left," a neighbor said. "Um-hum. Saw when the taxi carried her away. Fire broke out not too long after." Each breath Ivoe drew extinguished hope. In a cold season a faulty furnace or stove might take the blame. What she could not unpuzzle was how the house caught fire in the middle of summer. *The Underwood typewriter; the pianola; their letters.* With all the paper and ink that burned like oil, not even cinders remained when the fire truck finally arrived. As a breeze kicked up a final gust of smoke, Ivoe bit down hard on her lip, trapping words that crisped on the tongue like the smoldering pages of a dictionary.

14
OAK AND IVY
JULY 1918

Waiting on Ona to speak to her was like waiting on the sun after a long, long rain. Ivoe scolded herself for having grown too dependent on Ona's perspicacity. Nobody's fault but her own that she couldn't refrain from drawing out Ona's perspective. "What do you think about . . . ?" came as easy as hello. Talking to Ona made everything possible; even when plans laid came to nothing, like now, it was all right. Private little joys found along their journey were enough to sustain her.

Somewhere in the ash heap on Cherry Street were notes for the *Meditation*. The most important stories Ivoe had recalled with little effort and typed up at the YWCA. She was headed for the printing shop when she encountered an old foe, Jim Crow. The printers' union had direct orders to decline all colored business, including that of churches. She devised to condense the news into a single page and type as many as she could, but the letter in hand now thwarted that idea.

Ivoe laid the money order aside and threw away the envelope.

"Well, no typewriter."

How to work with less — a smidgen of this, a piece of that — was no great challenge. Fragments and ruined things sometimes came alive with a little imagination. But how could the music of their lives take back up again when she was a writer with no instrument? She had waited weeks for the new Remington, paid for by the church, before today's disappointing news that production had been halted indefinitely in favor of building arms and ammunition.

"Did you hear me?" Ivoe said curtly, annoyed by Ona's silence, her tried-and-true manner of curbing and revealing her disappointment all at once. Equally irritating were the one-word responses and the way she moved around the apartment in a concerted, noiseless way.

The first time they'd fought Ona didn't speak to her from the early winter afternoon until late at night, when Ivoe lay with her back to Ona, crying, and sure Ona would return to Texas in the morning. This fight was worse. A week had passed since they had engaged in real conversation.

"Do you ever intend to talk to me?"

Ona lowered her copy of *Sepia* magazine, peering over the rims of her spectacles. "No. I'm just going to sit here while you summon doubt and failure like you've been doing." Though her voice did not betray it, Ona was anxious. Past disappointments had been valleys for Ivoe to rest in, to prepare for the journey ahead. Over the years she had learned to detect in Ivoe's letters whenever she was in a shadowy place, divided against herself, or simply tired. Living with her she had matched the signs with the moods. "I might as well just . . ." hinted that Ivoe needed another perspective. Chewing the inside of her jaw meant the day had been a little long, a little tough, and a little encouragement was needed. Repeated sighs were another way of saying *Do not disturb* unless they were accompanied by the rustle of pages, then it meant: *If you want to talk to me, this would be a good time.* "It's too cold in here," or "Nothing's where I left it," when the missing whatever was exactly where she had left it, was good news — she was nearly finished, a conclusion away from a very fine article. Perpetual sullenness was a new state.

"I've already told you what you should do. You came to the city to write for a newspaper, Ivoe. So write for one. Write for your own."

"You say start a newspaper like it's as simple as baking a pie. I can't even get a typewriter. Did you forget we lost the little press in the fire? With the printers' union refusing to work on behalf of colored businesses, how do you suppose I publish the damn thing?"

"You're looking at the question all wrong. It's not can you but will you."

This was the kind of woolly-mindedness that brought Ivoe up short, Ona thought, a sob gathering in her throat. "I figured you for a lot of things. A quitter was never one of them."

"Wish you wouldn't," Ivoe said.

"Every colored woman I know has compromised her dreams." A degree of petulance had crept into her voice. "You just giving yours up. That's worth a cry at the very least. Don't you think?"

"When you get a no everywhere you turn, what can you do?"

"Shit, you act like a press can't be bought. All it takes is money. Money ain't no big thing. We can both work. Now, the big things — the will and the courage — that's got to come from you. If you don't have it there's no need in me carrying on about it."

"A newspaper's got to extend beyond my writing. And I can't pay anybody."

"People won't work unless you pay them? You're the only one who cares about the race, huh?"

"It's not right to have people working and not pay them."

"You do it. I'm willing to bet you aren't the only one who would. And you know why?"

They were interrupted by a knock at the door. Three little girls, each with outstretched arms holding covered dishes, and a finely dressed dark-skinned woman offered boisterous greetings. The floorboards of the hallway creaked as the woman parted the children to step forward and removed her sun hat. It was then Ivoe recognized the minister's wife from Stranger's Rest.

"In case the members have been remiss in their Christian duty, we wanted to bring this by to make sure you and Sister Ona have plenty to eat."

"Chicken and dumplings," the smallest one said.

"Lima beans and ham hocks."

"And apple crisp."

"Goodness. Enough to feed an army," Ivoe said, taking each dish and placing it on the counter. "There are no words for your generosity. People have been really quite kind."

"You say there are no words, but we hope you find them, Miss Ivoe. We need the *Meditation.* It is not as though we have our own newspaper."

To spite herself, over the next few hours, a list of those who might help carry the idea further came to Ivoe: members of Stranger's Rest, nearly four hundred; the YMCA; the YWCA; Vine Street — these were people who said yes when she worked on the *Meditation.* They might say yes again.

"If we raise enough money, I can print the paper," Ona said. "At least until the circulation grows beyond our means."

"If I'm going to build a true paper it's going to have to reach beyond the pews of Stranger's Rest. We'll have to move beyond the church for subscriptions."

Ona grabbed a pencil and paper to write. "We'll invite people over and you can address everybody at once. Whoever wants to help can and those who won't won't."

"Won't what?" Lemon said, glancing at the clock as she reached for her apron. Before she could tie the knot she noticed the counter. "My stars. Where all that food come from?"

"The church."

"What y'all talking about?"

Ona looked at Ivoe with pride. "Lemon, you are looking at the first woman founder, publisher, and editor in chief of a colored Kansas City newspaper."

"Newspaper? Now, Ivoe, I knowed you to have some funny notions all your life. How in the —"

"We're short on money — when have colored people not been short on money? — but we've got just about everything else covered," Ona said.

"We're not talking about anything big, Momma. Just a small newspaper."

"You think colored folks fixing to spend their hard-earned money on a paper? To read about how Miss Ann trying to get the vote, or this war that don't have nothing to do with us?"

"Well, Lemon, you might be right, but somebody's got to bring the news to the people around here. Last week, I received an old *Texas Freeman* clipping in the mail. Back in December, thirteen black soldiers were hanged in uniform at a military camp outside of San Antonio by a mob of infantrymen."

"Now, Momma, you know when you're in the kitchen on Ward Parkway perusing the

Star you're not about to come across anything like that."

"These are the stories we ought to know about . . . Some of us are walking around here within an inch of our lives and don't even know it," Ona said.

Lemon wished for Ennis; he ought to know what a little sacrifice was returning not just to them but a whole lot of other people too. She bent over the large burlap sack and dug down deep, past the beans, until she felt the cool jars.

"Here. This ought to help."

In Texas she had only to plan meals and feed the Starks and their guests, but in the city the chores demanded of her tripled by the week. Along with cooking, she counted and polished the silver, washed and ironed the table linen, and scrubbed the floors of the pantry and kitchen. Since her children weren't babies anymore and she spent so much time at her employer's house, she brokered a deal: "If you let me keep a garden here, whatever I grow will be as much yours as it mine. Won't charge for seeds or nothing. Got my own supplies. I sure would appreciate growing the things for preserves my family and I are accustom to eating. I think you'll enjoy them." Spring and summer months, she gardened until the sun set.

In the evenings, she made use of all the pots and pans the big kitchen provided. She often spent the night in order to rise early to can what had simmered on a low flame while she slept. One taste of her tomato jam by the maid next door and orders started to arrive from all over Ward Parkway. Domestics averaged $4 to $7 a week. Lemon earned $7.25 — an extra quarter thrown in because Dr. Bacchus loved her chess pie, a staple every Sunday — but peddling her preserves she had doubled her earnings.

"Ivoe, look. Look, girl!" Ona gasped, unscrewing the brass-colored lids. "You know, Lemon, they let colored folks bank nowadays."

Ivoe eyed the fruits of her mother's labor. *Hope in a jar!*

"I'm not fixing to trust the fruit of my labor to hands what done mishandled me and mine for years and years on down the line. No thank you."

When Ona Durden arrived last December, Lemon didn't know what to think. Even when her children were all for uprooting to Kansas City, she had hemmed and hawed, but here was a professional woman, no spring chicken herself, who had picked up and followed Ivoe. She thought back to a conversation she had with Ivoe alone in the kitchen while they were making Christmas dinner.

"I don't understand it. Go everywhere together, even the church. She ain't your momma — ain't your sister. Who do you tell people she is?"

"Momma, you got three children. I don't rightly recall you ever telling Timbo who he could love. Irabelle neither. So I can't imagine you're trying to tell me."

"I don't mean no harm. I remember Cherry Street — how she made that little house a home. I see how she think the world of you — that much has always been true. I see plenty, but it don't help my understanding none. No need in me lying."

They were quiet for a spell — time enough for her to run cold water over the boiled potatoes and peel two or three before adding, "It's like she the oak tree and you the ivy — just wrapped yourself all around her." That's when Ivoe reached across the table and laid a hand on her arm and said, "Momma, that's exactly what it's like."

Shoulder to shoulder, the two counted the money. Lemon understood something about life. You can look at a thing wrong for a long, long time. She had looked head-on, right side up, and sideways, and still not until this very moment had she given the picture any true meaning. No man had come along and poured himself into her daughter and let his love take root and flower there. Miss Durden had come instead. Planted a seed deep down in Ivoe. For years it had blossomed. She couldn't dwell on her faith. Allah would have to harden her heart because it was impossible not to love Ona for who she was, her way with Ivoe. She would continue to pray for them, for the help they wanted to bring to so many.

Their voices rose as they talked excitedly about presses.

"Y'all fixing to write the paper and print it?"

"If you cut your own firewood, Lemon, it'll warm you twice," Ona said.

The two rowed the same boat. Now exactly where they was headed, they would all find out soon enough.

"When you finish with those," Lemon said, turning to leave the kitchen, "might as well count them in the broom closet."

Ona listened to the soft drone of Ivoe's sleeping and wondered where she had found a copy of the book of poems lost in the fire. She reached out to touch her. The evening had been very special, despite her dread at the thought of coming home. For days, and without pausing for air it seemed, Ivoe had talked about plans for the paper. To distinguish her periodical, instead of graphic front-page images — à la the *Boston Guardian* — or flashy headlines in bold red ink like those in the *Chicago Defender,* she would use dusty-rose paper for front and back pages and grass-green ink for the paper's name. A well-placed editorial in favor of shocking violence would keep readers' attention. Like the *Philadelphia Inquirer,* which gave careful, attentive coverage of the community, she would not totally venture away from church or social news but would also offer significant coverage on national issues affecting them. She hoped to do a fine balancing act — to speak to the small elite colored class while proving to all her readers that she knew exactly who they were, like the Murphy family who called for equal pay for colored teachers in their last issue of the *Washington Afro-American.* But it was the thorns on the vine, those no longer completely controlled by the domination of whites for the first time in their lives and a discredit to the race, that she would target. They had left their manners in the country. Through her column, Woman

About Town, she would voice opinions on self-help as a means to bring about improvements for the race.

Her first published statement would be a gentle reminder of etiquette — to say "thank you" and "if you please" when receiving service and to speak softly. They should refrain from loudness and public ridicule of each other because the loud and blatant were never trusted. They should take all care in matters of hygiene, which was to whites a signal of moral judgment. They should take care in wearing pleasant hair and having clean teeth, nails, and clothing, preferably in subdued colors. Since the outbreak of the war, people dressed in somber colors, nothing like the woman who lived down the hall and wore tight, loud dresses. The woman's rouge and lipstick were always too bright for her mahogany skin and Ivoe ached to let her know in some gentle way the rules of cosmetics passed along to her at Willetson: darker skin means lighter, not heavier. Publishing a list of comportment classes offered at the YMCA and YWCA would go a long way. The way they looked, spoke, and acted mattered — a fact that should be ever present in every colored person's mind. She would warn against excessive spending, including money handed over in tithes by devoted churchgoers who could barely sustain the cost of day-to-day living.

But that night when Ona made it to the last step at the top of the landing to the apartment they shared with Ivoe's family, she had no interest in listening when Ivoe threw open the door. "Got something I want to read to you," Ivoe said, all spritely. Without the heart to tell the city's most important newswoman that she was dog-tired from trying to convince folks to take a subscription for a paper that didn't yet exist, she followed Ivoe inside and sat down to the table. Where was everybody? she wondered. "Everyone's gone to see *The Homesteader.* Even Momma was excited to see Mr. Micheaux's handiwork. Couldn't for the life of her believe we finally got a picture show with real live colored folks in it."

"What do you want me to hear?"

Ivoe pulled out a book. "Like we used to say in the good ole days." She read until the part she loved best and could recite from memory. Closing the book, she pulled Ona up from the table:

Put my ahm aroun' huh wais',
Jump back, honey, jump back.
Raised huh lips an' took a tase,

Jump back, honey, jump back.
Love me, honey, love me true?
Love me well ez I love you?
An' she answe'd, " 'Cose I do" —
Jump back, honey, jump back.

As they lay on their sides, Ivoe cradled
Ona from behind, reading over her shoulder
from *Oak and Ivy.* She loved the feel of
Ona's face against hers. She traced the
hairline where silver was just beginning to
show and followed the curve of her cheek,
tilting her chin a little to kiss her full on the
lips. For the rest of the evening until the
wee hours of the morning they lay this way,
talking, laughing.

Rising from the bed, Ona kissed Ivoe on
both temples. Their speechless conversation
an hour before was meant to send Ivoe on
her way, but in case she needed more proof
that this was a journey for two, Ona opened
the top drawer of the bureau, carrying away
the new tray of fonts to the bed, where she
went to work laying her letters. Ivoe writhed
at the cold metal on her belly, running her
fingers across the word: *Love.*

15

Jam on the Vine

AUGUST 1918

Ivoe powdered her face and double-checked her purse for the bank passbook. The refulgent morning lifted her spirits — in the white sun even the brick buildings seemed to glimmer. At the corner of Vine, an elderly man with a smile as warm as the day reached out to her with a gentle touch. "Miss Ivoe," he started, "heard about the fire. I hope that doesn't mean the newsletter has ended." A jalopy's horn startled them both on their way. As she reached the other side, she turned around to shout thanks to the man, but he had already disappeared in the teeming crowd. She glanced at her watch — right on time. Waiting for her at the corner of Eighteenth Street was the cunning grin that belonged to Ona.

They peered through the window as the young woman unlocked the door of the two-story barbershop, now the Vine Street headquarters of Kansas City's first female-run black newspaper. Ona's savings paid the first year of the lease; with Lemon's money they had purchased a linotype press, set up a telegraph account at Western Union and a telephone. In a few weeks, the ground floor looked like a pressroom. Clubwomen visited with houseplants, lightbulbs, pencils. Lois Humphrey sent two women from packaging and receiving with stools the factory had replaced. "Bang out the dents and they'll suit," she said after placing an advertisement for a new dipper. The minister at Stranger's Rest took up a collection. "If you ever received an encouraging word from the *Meditation* . . . if you believe the newspaper will do the same . . . dig deep." Wood, paint, a hammer and nails were delivered free of charge, compliments of the hardware store around the corner. Ona hand-painted the sign on the glass door, an elegant black calligraphy that each passerby stopped to read:

JAM ON THE VINE
EST. 1918
NEWSPAPER. LINOTYPERS.

Ivoe pushed the rickety dressmaker's table donated by the YWCA along the sidewalk. (Until the telephone rang that afternoon, she had been an editor without a desk.) The city's cacophony was a welcome reprieve from the young YWCA women's endless excited chatter. One of their own writing about and for them! And Miss Durden . . . handling the print job on her own! Across the street a colored boy tossed a ball against a brick wall while a white man, wide as a hassock, languorously filled the doorway of the butcher shop, working a toothpick as he eyed the boy. Whatever the butcher said to the boy prompted him not to catch the bouncing ball. Instead, the butcher bent down for the ball and placed it in his apron pocket. As the boy began to walk away, Ivoe called out to him.

Thaddeus Talmadge Bunchee Knox the Third lived with a house of Jamaican men — a father and three cousins. His mother and aunt, as he explained it, were on their way to America soon. Yes, he agreed, he was a well-mannered young man. Yes, he could be trusted to carry his end of the table down the block without bumping the legs too much. Yes, he most certainly would buy a new ball with the change she could not afford to give him but parted with anyway. He thanked her and turned to leave when she called him back. One day he would be every bit Thaddeus, every bit his father and grandfather's namesake; his dark skin, pointy chin, and neatly trimmed hair already gave him an aura of sophistication beyond his twelve years. The pug nose, bright eyes, and full mouth that could not help but turn up at the corners made him her Bunchee. "Bunchee," she said, as though they had been friends a long time. "Soon I'm going to need some help delivering my newspapers. Do you know the neighborhood pretty good?"

He nodded.

"It might be a little while before I can pay you what you're worth. But there are other ways to be paid besides money."

Bunchee looked skeptical. "Like what?'

"Sometimes I go over to the YMCA. Do you know who lodges in the basement of the YMCA?"

"No."

"Colored baseball teams passing through to play our Butterflies."

He laughed. True fans called the home team the Kaysees, since they might have been as graceful as butterflies but they sure flew much quicker around the bases.

"Think of the games you might see, the autographs you could get as my paperboy."

Bunchee grinned.

"Now, if I'm going to depend on you, you

have to stay out of trouble. Don't play around any place you're not sure of. Any time you want to toss your ball" — she leaned into the brick of her own building — "you can do it right here."

The carpenter was sawing pine for shelves to line the walls when Ona turned the key. If she had to rank it, it was the happiest moment of her life. She and Bunchee had just finished door-to-door deliveries of two hundred newspapers of handbill size. On the way back to the office that evening, she had met fifteen more people inquiring about subscriptions. She greeted the man, took a copy of the paper from the pile on the table, and ascended to their living quarters. As stenographer, linotyper, secretary, and cheery greeter, Ona was exhausted. She operated the press, typing stories dropped off by columnists Ivoe hired to offer diversity of opinion — her one rule: write only what you can prove.

Ivoe darted in and out of the office between investigations, interviews, and advertisement solicitations, often too busy to share the slighest anecdote. Bunchee bumbled through the door at half past two, fifteen minutes or so after school let out. He made a beeline for the small black leather book hanging from a hook on the wall near the telephone. "How many subscriptions you getting today, Bunch?" Every day he picked a higher number, then braced by the challenge would be off.

As for her editorial philosophy, in the newspaper's maiden issue, August 6, 1918, Ivoe outlined exactly what she intended:

Dear Reader:

Thank you for supporting the inaugural issue of Kansas City's Jam on the Vine, a publication whose object is to set forth those facts and arguments that show the dangers and consequences of race prejudice, particularly as manifested toward colored citizens. The policy of Jam is not to publish stories of brutality and crime in the spirit of the cowardly journalist. It aims to assist colored people in maintaining familial and community bonds, strengthening economic ties, and fostering political-mindedness. With headquarters on Vine Street, the paper takes it name from the spirit of enterprise possessed by my mother, who sustained her family through the hardest of times by selling tomato jam and other savory preserves. The spirit of my mother, duplicated and coupled with forbearance, will guide our people out of the shadows into the full light of promise outlined for the American citizen in the Gettysburg Address. The policy of Jam is thus defined: It will first and foremost record important happenings and movements that bear on the great problem of interracial relations in Kansas City and in the world, especially those that affect Colored America. It is my hope that its editorial page will be looked upon not simply as the musings or meditations of the paper's founder but as an important expression of opinion that reflects on the rights of the colored race and the highest ideals of American democracy. Jam will be the organ of no clique, creed, or party and will avoid personal rancor and rumor of all sorts. Every week we will rake the news field for subjects that will be inspirational to the race and promote good citizenship. It is our responsible duty to let the colored man know the plain truth of how to better the race's condition. It will assume honesty of purpose on the part of all its contributors, aiming always to accurately and completely address the great national questions that agitate our race.

Yours in the struggle,
Ivoe Leila Williams

16
BROTHER, WHERE ARE YOU?

SEPTEMBER 1918

THE COLORED SOLDIER'S PROBLEM
By Ivoe Leila Williams

There has been a singularly ill-advised handling of the Negro soldiers ever since the mobilization of the American forces. Numerous "race riots" and outbreaks of greater or less seriousness have occurred as a result of quartering Negro regulars in communities where race prejudice might naturally have been expected to result in friction, if nothing worse. These occurrences, however, appear to have been controlled and there have been no special reasons for complaint for some time.

But the wrong lesson appears to have been learned by the government's military authorities from these occurrences. Ever since the registered forces have been in process of selection under the new law there has been evinced a seeming disposition to ignore the Negroes as prospective units of the new national army, with the result that a twofold injustice has been worked. In the first place, white men who would not have been called for months, in all probability, have been "advanced" in the lists while the Negroes have been held back. Let it not be understood that considerations of race or color should operate to relieve white men of any obligations that are entailed upon them as citizens or available soldiers or that Negroes, because they are Negroes, should be sent to places of danger ahead of white men. That is not the fundamental principle involved. Before the law all are equal in the matter of responsibility. But wholly unnecessary and wholly avoidable dissatisfaction is being caused by this injustice, which is being wrought in the case of the white men who are sent to the training camps, while Negroes are held back by order of the authorities.

There is also an unnecessary injustice wrought upon the tens of thousands of willing Negroes who ought to take their places in the ranks but who are deprived of that privilege. They are being placed in the position of men who are either unwilling to assume the responsibilities of citizenship or who are not regarded as worthy of assuming the burdens falling upon all alike. Either assumption is unjust.

In view of prejudices that exist and that cannot be consistently ignored, the problem of the Negro soldier will not be solved by promiscuous mingling of the two races and certainly not by sending white soldiers alone while Negroes are held at home. There is no apparent reason that these Negro soldiers could not be trained at one or more training camps devoted exclusively to soldiers of their race. The same fundamental results would be secured without the friction and dissatisfaction, which have already been caused.

Under proper conditions the Negroes might give us as good an account of themselves as soldiers of the white race and they should be allowed the opportunity of doing so. If it is not considered an opportunity by all the available Negro soldiers, they should be required to assume the duty devolving upon them as such. They must be credited, however, with having shown as yet no disposition to shirk these duties and responsibilities, and they should be invested with their proportionate share of the burdens of membership in the national forces.

Ivoe stood with Timbo outside of the cattle killing beds, listening as he talked about the slaughtering capacity of Ogden Packing Plant. "Three hundred cattle and five hundred hogs daily." A walk through a courtyard delivered them to a row of wooden buildings. He pointed to the dry saltcellar, the cold storage room, and the tank house, where they rendered the lard. At the cutting room, Ivoe remained at the door. Coarse voices floated over the cleavers slamming against wood, the chorus of the slaughter. Smoke curled up from the wooden roof of the next building. "We cure over there. Remind you of back home, don't it?" For a moment, the aroma of hickory covered the stench until a warm breeze blew in the wrong direction. Across from the smokehouse, her brother worked in the sausage room, where men cleaned and sorted by hand the intestines before feeding them to the grinders. Here, the odor was the most pungent. Ivoe's stomach wrenched. Someone's grinder jammed. The worker dug his fingers around, cursing when the machine started up again. "See, that ain't got not business being there," Timbo said of the

411

dried blood caked on some of the machines.

Unbearable heat and long hours added to the degradation of Timbo's job. From the animals' entrance to the last point where meat left the plant, levels of sanitation were deplorable. Butchering stalls stank to high heaven. At every turn machines sparked or combusted, and nowhere was there a fire extinguisher. The colored workers could talk for hours — legitimate complaints and sound ideas for plant improvement (ventilation, hygiene checks, and the like), but the bottom line was simple: shared deplorable conditions and equal opportunity for injury should account for equal pay.

OGDEN PACKING PLANT —
WORKERS STRIKE FOR SHORTER HOURS AND HIGHER WAGES
By Ivoe Leila Williams

KANSAS CITY, Mo. — For three days now the steam whistle at Ogden Packing Plant has not blown at 9 o'clock as its West Bottoms neighbors are accustomed. Instead 200 Negro men are found picketing along the blood-swept sidewalks. The trouble in Kansas City's meatpacking plants is entirely economic; the strike is the result of unfair wages and labor conditions. Second

412

only to Chicago's Union Stock Yards, stockyards have boomed in the West Bottoms because of its close proximity to the largest convergence of railroad in the country, where daily more than 300 refrigerator trains ship fresh meats to scores of distant markets. Since the outbreak of war, demand for American meat products has skyrocketed. Our meat-packers have exported more than 100 million tons of beef and 1 billion pounds of sausage to feed soldiers and civilians. Factories that hold government contracts such as that of the Ogden Sausage Company are required by law to extend a livable wage. However, the firm drives down wages paid to its colored packers. Migration north of Kansas City and the first draft have precipitated an intense labor shortage, giving those men who remain greater employment opportunity and leverage in negotiating wages. But when the word passes around that help is needed and colored laborers apply, they are often told by white union officials that they have secured all the men they need because the places are reserved for white men only.

If he is lucky enough to secure a position, the colored laborer's path to livelihood remains by no means smooth. Even as his hours increase and his work doubles, his wages freeze. Laborers would normally take such complaints to the union. However, most of the trade unions exclude colored men, and those at the meat factories are no different. Ogden's white union men deny exclusion, yet I know skilled workmen who were not admitted into the unions because they are colored. (Even when the colored man is allowed to join a union, he frequently derives little benefit, owing to certain tricks of the trade.) The colored men of Ogden Sausage Company need our support. Imagine a unified front of the colored men of all the city's meatpacking plants — over 5,000. Surely the voices of demand for increased wages and more sanitary work conditions would be heard. And perhaps then it will be understood that our work, our loyalty, is a prize to be won.

Ivoe turned on the radio and looked out the window onto Eighteenth and Vine. Sophie Tucker sang about her little chocolate soldier, taking Ivoe's mind back to a conversation with her brother the other night. The disappointment with which he had corrected her childhood impressions of his time with Company E (he had not been armed let alone a participant in any feat beyond Jim Crow's purview) had embarrassed them both. But when he spoke of the union and the strike, his eyes brightened and he sounded strong. For no other reason, she would go against Ona and attend the rally where Timbo planned to address the strikers and their supporters. That morning's terse discussion with her partner hinged on Ivoe "laying low." Ona told her to spend the day writing an editorial not in direct opposition to the *Kansas City Star Ledger.*

For weeks Ivoe had been embroiled in rebuttal articles. The city's largest paper attacked men like her brother. The strike was denounced, the strikers labeled unpatriotic in their willingness to deny soldiers the vital nourishment of meat during the greatest battles the world had known. When the *Star Ledger* indicted black male strikers as draft dodgers, *Jam* responded with a front-page article, "Why Fight for a Flag Whose Folds Do Not Protect?" And it devoted three columns to personal accounts of men denied registration cards from white postal workers all over the city, a practice dating back to May 1917. The *Star Ledger*'s "Performance Report Card," which exalted white soldiers and made no mention of black soldiering, was met with an article (sourced by a clubwoman who worked for the exemption board) exposing hundreds of white registrants discharged on the same physical grounds that had exempted only two black men from military service. Letters of warning had come with no return address and no signature, demanding she desist her "one-sided dialogue." Thereafter, she received an invitation to visit with the mayor and responded with a request to bring along her brother and the members of his union because they would benefit most from a meeting with Kansas City's boss, whereas she had little if any need for a social call. Mayor Pendleton had not responded.

Timbo's questions evolved with his desire to penetrate the underbelly of the meatpacking plants. He had ferreted out much more than underpaid labor: schemes that led to the mayor's office, a range of bribes and fraud that included meat for local restaurants and the U.S. Armed Forces. For now, Ivoe laid the puzzle out, reserved Timbo's information. Ona thought that such a story — if not factually ironclad — could sink their fledgling newspaper. They should wait for additional pieces; it was no telling how big the picture was.

That day her brother's concerns were not with the crooked. He addressed a quiet mass of nearly two hundred about the small battles the union had won in front of the Livestock Exchange Building. With more than four hundred offices for the Stockyards Company, it was the largest livestock building in the world and the crown jewel of Kansas City commerce. The events that followed made no sense to Ivoe. One minute applause rippled through the crowd, the next Timbo was carried off. Ivoe thought she recognized the black men who grabbed him as a fight broke out in the audience. She strained to see where they had taken him when she was encircled by two police officers. She pushed past the men, unsure whether her brother had been carried to safety or danger. "Timbo!" she cried out, but stopped at the feel of a hand squeezing her arm.

"You Ivoe Williams? Are you Ivoe Williams of the colored newspaper?"

Her hands trembled but her voice did not betray her. She projected above the crowd that indeed she was Ms. Williams, founder and editor of *Jam on the Vine*.

The paddy wagon coursed along the curb at 1125 Locust, police headquarters. The handkerchief tied around her head cut into the corners of her mouth. Morbid thoughts

417

about prisons had haunted her for years, yet she was more concerned about Ona than a night in the county jail. The officers led her past the cellblock, out the back door, along a high wall to the stables yard, and pulled her along the horse tunnel until they emerged at a stall occupied by three men in suits. The police left her alone. She immediately recognized the men from political events associated with the mayor. Mice took cover in a pile of dung-smeared hay as the men tied her to a post. Grunting failed to put off the two working at her dress. The groping of buttocks she could endure, almost expected; it was the third man's casual glance about the stall that frightened her. He wore the calm demeanor she imagined of Jack the Ripper. Finally his eyes landed on a bucket. The grooming tools landed at her feet.

" 'Clean her up' was the message we were given. Isn't that right, boys?" He kicked a brush in her direction. "Which one do you want me to use?"

What sounded like "please" in her head came out muffled, drowned out by the neighing of police horses. The yank of her dress to the ground nearly pulled her down; a firm grip around her neck steadied her. A breast was fondled, a nipple twisted hard.

418

An odd thought sliced through the worst fear she had known. The expressionless man in front of her was wizened, had a family or somebody. Even if there was no one, he had freedom, a thousand other places he could be. Where did it come from? The kind of motivation that said, *This now because I can.* She saw her father's face in her mind's eye, felt the warm sensation down her inner thighs. The man cussed, said she peed like a mare, left the stall and returned with another bucket. The sting of the cold water made her knees buckle as they ordered her to stand and choose her brush.

The face brush — the softest — was missing. Papa'd preferred horse grooming with corncobs, but he had taught her about the tools all the same. The bristles of the dandy brush were long and hard. She nodded at the curry brush with short metal teeth. The opening of a jar labeled HORSEFLY filled the stall with a pungent odor. She writhed and shook her head furiously to fling the insecticide from her body. He doused her until the bottle was empty and she had accepted her fate. He would set a match to her, sweep up the remains or leave them to the mice.

The man stepped toward her. So this was the helplessness and regret Papa had also felt. At that moment, she knew her father was dead. The man raked against her breasts as though cleaning a tough-skinned elephant. Through her desperate pleas, they took turns scrubbing. Before she fainted, Ivoe thought of Momma — her daughter disappeared like her husband. She would see the worst of her life as the consequence of leaving Texas.

The nagging question of why she hadn't just gone with Ivoe wrecked Ona. Tears trailed down her cheeks as she bent to kiss the top of her head. Were it not for the dress Ivoe wore, she would not have recognized the woman she found in the cell. Her face, legs, and arms were full of welts, her body a map of bloody lines. That evening she followed Lemon's directions to the tee: salve and collard green leaves were laid over the scratches. Ivoe slept the whole night and all the next morning. In the afternoon she refused food and water, asking for news of her brother. He was fine, Ona assured her. Timbo had been taken away by friends who only meant to get him to Fairmount Park on time.

Ivoe laid her head in Ona's lap. Ona could feel herself trembling as she spoke. "If we have to eat beans every day, I don't care, so long as you have an escort whenever you attend a rally or protest." The peculiar nature of victimhood was under way, preparing for foolproof safety, planning for her next attack. "If you are ever late — you can't be late, Ivoe. You must be where you say you'll be at all times. We need an attorney on retainer. We need a telephone tree with many different branches . . . members of the women's clubs, the church, the Vine's business owners. Everybody gets called until your whereabouts are known." Finally, spent of ideas, Ona cradled her tight. "We will file charges when you are well enough to fight."

In the year that followed, they never spoke of the incident, though Ona often mentioned leaving Kansas City. No, Ivoe said. She had to stay and fight. The trick was battle selection. If they pursued Pendleton's administration, they would lose what little resources they had; worse, she could lose her brother or her own life. The problem of proof urged restraint. She and Timbo had figured out who was connected to whom and why, which was the same as for how much. But what leverage did they have? Why would any white man offer incriminating evidence about the mayor? Timbo's strike ended (after eleven months) with better wages and a more hygienic workplace.

They put their investigation aside, not knowing they were bracing for another war.

"Miss Ivoe, I'm sorry to be late," Bunchee said, bending over to catch his breath. Usually his pride in delivering the paper made him walk taller than four foot nine. At school, his teacher kept a copy of *Jam* on her desk. And his closest friend had gotten a whipping for using the paper the wrong way. After fishing at Brush Creek he and Bunchee had wrapped the trout in *Jam* to carry it home. His friend lit up, telling his mother about the two big fish they had caught. "That's good, baby" had barely made it out her mouth when she saw the soggy bundle tucked under his arm. She hit him upside the head, saying he never paid attention and how many times had she told him to leave her paper alone? It meant something that Bunchee delivered *Jam*. He hated to disappoint and it showed in his face. "I'll work fast. Run if I have to. I promise to deliver every issue before dark."

The nature of Bunchee's running concerned Ivoe. He hadn't run into the office as though he might miss the broadcast of a baseball game or free ice cream at Swope Park. His had been a distressed run, revealed by moist eyes and a torn shirt with snot on his collar. She looked out the window for any sign of trouble — bullying children, a disgruntled butcher. "Anybody after you? Wait just a minute," she said, running up to the loft to retrieve their sewing box. In case the police happened by, she wanted his shirt mended. A few whip-stitches would do. "Bunchee, what happened?"

"My cousin left for Jefferson City." Ashamed, he left out the part about tearing himself from the clutches of the tall police officer, who held him while the others took Frederick away.

"Seems like every time we talk somebody you know is headed that way. Never mind the papers, Ona's already at it. I got a train to catch. Come walk with me to the station." Ivoe grabbed her summer hat. "One of these days I suspect you'll come in here talking about you're on your way to Jefferson City."

"Oh, Miss Ivoe, I hope not," Bunchee said, grabbing the handle of her valise.

The city was stinking hot that September, the worst climate for a train ride. Ivoe followed Bunchee through a crowd of men haggling before the colored entrance to Union Station. She felt weary from a journey that had begun in her mind a week ago with articles from the *Omaha Bee* — "Black Man's Fury of Rape Erupts, Its Molten Destroys the Flower of White Womanhood." Absconded from his home on Omaha's Bond Street one Saturday afternoon, Willie Baker had been placed in Quitman jail before a final move to the county court, ostensibly for safekeeping. Who knew how long his trial would last. From the tone of the stories in the *Bee* — which often alleged attacks on white women — conditions were being stoked for a riot.

Ivoe said good-bye to Bunchee, purchased a ticket, and glimpsed herself in a mirrored door. A bundle of black steel wool blossomed from beneath the summer hat whose strap cut into her chin. She and Ona had both put on a little weight — too much bread and beans. She'd gladly give up the poor woman's diet for a lean piece of brisket roasted in the pit for hours like Papa used to do every Juneteenth . . . succotash with fresh summer corn . . . mashed potatoes and gravy . . . the flaky, buttery crust of Ona's peach cobbler. Her mouth watered as she thought of the low subscription count. With *Jam* eating up every cent they had, it would be a while before they could have a meal like that.

The train station was hot and dusty, and she had forgotten her fan on the dressing table at home. Hungry and regretful for not having packed anything for the journey, she glanced at the clock. Time to run and buy something, but money spent now meant fewer words telegraphed to Ona later. She resolved to eat dinner at the boardinghouse. Removing from her bag a copy of the *New York Times*, she focused on an article from July 31:

NEGROES APPEAL TO WILSON,
CONVENTION IN PROVIDENCE ASSAILS RIOT-
ING IN CHICAGO

PROVIDENCE, R.I. — Race rioting and burning of Negro homes in Chicago were bitterly assailed by the convention of the Northeastern Federation of Colored Women's Clubs, in session at the Olney Street Baptist Church here. The following telegram, adopted as a resolution, was sent to President Wilson: "The Northeastern Federation of Colored Women's Clubs in convention assembled plead you as president of the United States to use every means within your power to stop the rioting in Chicago and the propaganda used to incite such; that all people, regardless of race, creed or color be protected from mob violence. We await your reply."

Her reading was interrupted by a pair of women who sat on the bench next to her, eating sandwiches and brushing the crumbs from their skirts. A man folded his copy of *Jam* and offered it to the ladies, drawing out an unnoticed smile from Ivoe until one woman gnashed her teeth. "Too snooty for my blood." The man waved the paper at the other woman, who rolled her eyes. "It's a dicty rag, all right. I don't hardly need to read up on how to strive to be like white folks."

"I've been following all the riots. And I know a few people who have found work in it," the man said.

"You don't need no paper to find no job. Shit, this America. When you knowed colored people not to work in America? That ain't nothing. Pay may be no count. Job might not be what you want, but somebody always looking to put us to work."

"I looked at it once. It's not getting my hard-earned nickel again, I tell you that much. Talking down on her own folks — telling us how to act."

"How to keep in the white man's graces —"

"And, honey, I don't care nothing about being chummy with no white folks. Only thing we need from them is for them to leave us alone. Now, she start writing something like that maybe I'll pick it up again."

Ingrates! Inside the *Jam* office that summer the atmosphere had been intense. On the West Bottoms streets of narrow tenements, a solemn mood prevailed amid the hustle and bustle of black people who had heard or read about colored communities besieged by white violence week after week all summer long. In the paper's inaugural edition, she had reported on the racial tension at a New London, Connecticut, navy base, where black seamen reported repeated attacks from white sailors. At a segregated beach in Chicago, rock throwing by a white man had caused the death of a colored teen, Eugene Williams. Chicago's riot lasted five days and culminated in the deaths of over two dozen colored people; hundreds more were injured. In the nation's capital that July, more than a thousand policemen and military officers had been deployed to restore order after a race riot was ignited by reports of rapes of white women. Last week when a riot erupted in Tennessee, Ona had pleaded with her not to "go chasing down the white folks planning to free the country of Negroes by hook or by crook, noose or shotgun." But the similarities between the cases of the Knoxville man and Willie Baker were too close. The mulatto man accused of murdering a white Tennessee woman had been awaiting his trial when rioters broke into the jailhouse, eventually shooting out residents of Knoxville's black community.

More journalists than she cared to count had misunderstood the inclination toward migration. Industrial jobs had received the credit when migrants had fled southern violence to northern cities for protection by a civilized police force. How many Negroes had met their death that summer without remark from the president or legislative action? On the heels of the Great War, where colored men had exercised the finest patriotism even while combating Jim Crow in their own camp, the betrayal was devastating, the colored American's seeds of distrust sown. As editor, she had tried to seize upon this moment to shift the focus on the colored community itself — to point out ways they might lessen dependency on white businesses, create infrastructure, and uplift the race in noble acts and deeds, especially in behalf of each other.

She practically grew roots at her desk from

working through the wee hours of the morning below a framed picture of Wayne Minor, Kansas City native and the last soldier killed in the Great War. Private Minor had served in Company A in the all-black 366th Infantry Regiment and died just hours before the treaty was signed. The *Star Ledger* had made no mention of his service. In the midst of war, the United States struggled to realize its own democratic claims for all its citizens. To look at Minor's picture reminded her to stay in the trenches, to fight the good fight even if the foe was Ona.

Recent disputes with Ona and waning subscriptions had left her self-confidence badly shaken. Interest in the paper dropped off after the third issue. The seventh issue had just gone to press, but whenever Bunchee made house calls to collect money, people canceled further editions or refused to answer the door. Ona counseled her to add more from her own life experiences as a means of giving tone and relish to her writing. She should draw more from her problems — the same as her readers' — in her editorials, which felt a little cold. "People don't care how much you know until they know how much you care." She reminded Ona that the work of racial uplift was not a matter of temperature. One afternoon in Belvedere Hollow hinted at some of the race's trouble. She had distributed free newspapers up one dingy street and down a worse one, noting tomfoolery on every corner from the Italians, Irish, and Negroes, but it was the latter group the coppers harassed. White officers dragged colored men into paddy wagons for no other reason than the men were loud and unkempt. "Did the cop stop to ask if the person in his grip was lukewarm or freezing? Heck no." She had tried to get Ona to see that a tone of chastisement was necessary to improve relations between their community and the KCPD. "Some of us have the rights down pat. We understand those, but what about our responsibilities? Some of us don't know the *c-i* in *city* stands for *civilized.*" Ona tuned up her face, as if Ivoe's logic had a sour taste. "That's dangerous, Ivoe, 'cause we're not the only ones reading *Jam.* You better believe whites are reading our paper closer than they do their own. It's a fine balance is all." Ivoe thought she was achieving that balance — newsworthy items and editorials that spoke to curtailing behaviors that courted white malice. What the readers needed, Ona contended, was to understand the city was not their friend. They needed to understand the traps of so-called civilization that didn't exist in the rural parts. Wary of a "how to beat the man" tone, Ivoe said the organ must teach accountability. Ona agreed: "But both parties have to be accountable. Whites in power — from the mayor on down to the trolley driver — have to be accountable for their treatment of citizens." Where in the paper was she going to address that?

Ona's advice, meant to encourage, had made her doubt herself all the same, but it was nothing like the two women talking now.

"Who she think she is?"

"Who knows anything about her anyway? She got a husband?"

"No."

"Children?"

"No."

"Growed-up woman living in an apartment full of other growed-up women ain't natural. Ain't supposed to be but one queen bee in a hive."

The woman wiped her brow with a monogrammed handkerchief — a present, no doubt, from her employer, as nothing about her suggested she cared on iota about initials.

"Got a brother. He stay in the streets. Need to preach to him."

431

"She can't tell me nothing nohow."

Ivoe recognized the brand of negritude on display. To her, theirs was the worst kind of race pride: it ended when complaining ceased yet did nothing to propel the race forward. They gave the white man and his evils over to Jesus and prayed for things they themselves might remedy, while Jim Crow stood with his foot on their necks. Well, go ahead, Mr. Crow, crush on. See if I care. The boarding call for the Rock Island line to Nebraska issued as Ivoe snatched up her bags.

In the dying light of summer, the train whirred past cattle in repose along the russet plains. Nature permeated glass and steel, filling the railroad car with the scent of dung on hot soil. Ivoe crinkled her nose as she angled the small mirror of her compact, as if vantage might erase her wearied countenance. Hours later, the scene in Kansas City's Union Station still rankled. Ona had prepared her for the slow reception *Jam* might receive but that it had come under scurrilous attack by her own hurt doubly. Any publishing anxiety was now exacerbated by their lack of understanding.

A clap of thunder awakened her. As the train lurched to a stop, pages of the *Omaha*

Herald slid from her lap to the floor. She bent to retrieve them, recalling the dream interrupted by the storm. A black hound was digging a patch near Momma's fig tree. No matter what she did to distract the dog from the spot, he returned. Then she noticed the hound had something in its mouth. She spoke to it in a soft tone, trying to relax its underjaw. She succceeded, but she recoiled in horror at what appeared to be a human hand — big, black, and calloused like Papa's. The hound howled as screams resounded from all over Little Tunis, getting louder and more numerous until the sound grew deafening.

17
Casey's Row
SEPTEMBER 1919

Dark clouds exploded and thunder crashed in prolonged, awful peals.

Ivoe drew up the collar of her raincoat against the downpour. On advice from an NAACP member, she took a taxi to 3110 Harney Street, Liberty Café and Boardinghouse. No sooner than she dined on a sandwich and tomato soup, the young woman who had checked her in delivered an envelope: "Ms. Williams, this arrived for you today."

Kansas City, September 23, 1919

Dear One,

I hate to see you go. On the other hand, when else do I have just cause to pen you a letter? Rest assured, without you around there will be little joy. Here's what you will miss: Bunchee's antics, mislaid papers, ringing telephones, my eyes peeled to the door for your return. Do come home to me in one piece.

All my love,
Ona

From two hundred miles away Ona had put the ground back under her feet. Returning the letter to its envelope, she missed her, terribly.

Casey's Row was no different from other black settlements built around labor. In Little Tunis the sharecroppers' and later the convicts' day was spent on cotton. In Kansas City the packing plants kept men like Timbo working to live. In Omaha it was the railroad. A community of Pullman porters and women employed as laundresses and domestics lived in the community north of the city. Everybody worked and had something to show for it: a Buick H-45, a new roof, rose bushes flanking the front door, a freshly painted fence.

By noon, Casey's Row buzzed about the tall, well-dressed newswoman from Kansas City. Little girls ran up to her, said hello, giggled, and ran off. Older men nodded in her direction. A bit of celebrity helped to ease her shyness. For three days she conducted interviews in the boardinghouse's café with neighbors roused from their dinner by commotion the evening of Willie Baker's arrest. The waitress delivered the day's dessert special; Ivoe blew ripples into her teacup and listened to stories about Casey's Row — unchecked white hostility meted out against the community over the years and people's impression of Mr. Baker and his love affair. Leading the rabble the night they took Baker into custody was an elderly white man, father to the woman Baker lived with. A janitor leaned across the table so that the toddler sitting next to him would not hear. "Ms. Williams, I heard everything the old peckerwood said to his daughter 'cause I live next door to Willie and come out on the porch as soon as the car pulled up. He told his daughter to 'turn that black scoundrel loose! Before I turn you over in a grave of hog slop.' "

Ivoe chewed her pie like it was meat and let her tea get cold as the story unfolded.

Men from two automobiles shouted demands at Baker, threatening his life if he didn't account for his whereabouts the night before. The woman's claim that he had been home with her failed to quell the situation, as her father accused Baker of raping his other daughter, a sixteen-year-old.

"I think I was the first one to call the police," a washerwoman said. "Don't know how many times I warned Willie about that gal. Told him when he brought her here . . . I told him, 'You gone stark mad bringing a white woman up in Casey's Row. They gonna lynch you for it.' He said they had quieted all that down and not to worry. But when them white mens pulled up, I wasn't so sure so I called the police. Told them to come and get Willie. I figured he'd be safer in the county jail than at home. They come get him too. Soon as I said he lived with a white woman they come quick. I think he's alive 'cause of me."

The following day, Ivoe sought out the Western Union telegraph office. Usually Ona handled dictations by phone, but the cost could not be added to the boarding-house phone bill. Ivoe handed the two-hundred-word message to Ona to the operator. "Can't you read? Sign says no service for coloreds. Niggras neither." Rummaging her pocketbook for the membership card for the Colored Journalists Association of America, Ivoe recalled one of Ona's sayings: "Colored life isn't necessarily tragic, but it sure in the hell poses a challenge at the most inconvenient times." The operator was unmoved by her evidence. He gave attention to a white customer whose telegram was sent in all eagerness and politeness.

Ivoe looked out the window at a shirtless white man in filthy britches and waited for the office to empty. "Sir, I don't mean to be exigent but you are in business to make money." She pointed to the window. "The man across the street does not look like he has a telegraph to send but I can assure you he does. In a few minutes, he will come in here and offer you five dollars to send a telegram exactly like this one." To give her words force of conviction, she opened her hand with the money, twice the general cost for a message that length.

"Like I said, we just don't do business with coloreds. Will he require a confirmation?"

Her transaction with the hobo unfolded like this: she gave him an envelope with money, her message to Ona, and the destination code. After the hobo returned with her confirmation, she followed him to Bond Street, where a man sold tiny bottles of hooch from a shoeshine stand.

That evening, armed with a fresh strawberry pie, Ivoe took the steps to the third house in Harney Street. Truth being complicated on the subject of racial mixing, she had saved the most important interview for last. "A Kansas City newswoman in search of the delicate truth" is how she introduced herself to Miss Jones, hoping dessert and a sympathetic smile would win her an old-fashioned sit-down, the kind that bared not only the facts of a situation but also the feelings. Two hours later she emerged with the history of Willie Baker and Savannah Jones, who loved him as sure as Ona loved her.

An eerie quiet hung over Casey's Row that morning. Ivoe took a hasty breakfast, unable to shake a nervous feeling. She went toward the story anyway, as journalists do. At half past eight she gathered her notebook and hailed a taxi outside the Liberty Boardinghouse for the trial that began at ten. She wanted to arrive early to note who showed up and on which side of justice. A crowd was growing outside the courthouse. She left the taxi, looked around for other black people and saw none. "Turn him over!" A young man broke from the throng, advancing toward her, and ran to meet the police car that pulled along the curb. The courthouse doors flew open. Several bailiffs waved their clubs to halt the commotion, moving to the street. Willie Baker could not have seen the writhing branches of the magnolia, the fluttering wings of meadowlarks that took off for more peaceful climes, or how pretty the sky looked that perfect September day; police officers shielded the defendant out of the paddy wagon as the angry crowd lunged for him.

The fate of Willie Baker relied on the integrity of an all-white male jury. Dressed in his army uniform, his face betrayed no emotion while his attorney argued his fine demeanor and moral judgment. Baker was a veteran, a porter three years on the job with no absences, a home renter with no documentation of late payments. He had a bank account in good standing and no children. The motion stated that he could not have raped the Jones girl because he was aboard the Olympian, Seattle-bound. Three witnesses gave testimony in the matter, including two porters who worked the same shift as Baker the night of the alleged attack. It was a poor case, lacking evidence and showing neither motive nor opportunity. Even the accepted premise of black men's uncontrollable lust for white women fell flat when Savannah Jones took the stand, detailing the slow, slow pace of their courtship and the fact that Baker had never met her sister, the alleged victim. Baker was firm in his innocence in a trial that ended in less than two hours.

The jury's "not guilty" cut through the

hue and cry of the overcrowded courtroom. Ivoe tried to catch up to Mr. Baker for a quote on the outcome of his trial but he was whisked away as murmurs of disapproval escalated. News of Baker's acquittal traveled fast. She had seen protests before — picketers at every trolley stop in Austin and those outside Kansas City's meatpacking plants. Outside the courthouse, excitement ran high among the posse, infuriated that a black man could stand accused of tarnishing white womanhood and go free to tell about it.

Ivoe wriggled past a group of bickering men and fell into a mob rushing from all sides of the building. A fusillade of bullets fired into the air failed to disperse the hunters, stirring the angry mob into greater frenzy. "Baker hangs or Omaha burns!" the crowd chanted. Several men overpowered the sheriff and his deputy and seized Mr. Baker, dragging him to the flagpole not twenty feet from the court. The whole weight of the crowd seemed to lunge at Ivoe's back. She took a hard blow in the side and doubled over from the pain of it, when a man grabbed her arm to steady her. "You best get on away from here."

Finally, she breached the crowd and ran.

For four days she had not seen one policeman. Now a cordon of officers brooded over the heart of Casey's Row's "Street of Dreams." Uniformed men raided businesses and homes, ransacking. The door to one house stood open; inside an officer forced a woman to the floor, his foot on her back, while a crying child stood nearby. The smell of gasoline was very strong against a rising incantation: "Come out or burn out." When a fire truck arrived, several white men pulled out knives to sever the hose. She darted across the street, ducked behind a house, climbed a fence, and found herself not far from the Liberty Boardinghouse.

Harney Street was quiet. The chalkboard inside the boardinghouse read: VERDICT SPELLS TROUBLE. SEEK PROTECTION. She took the backstairs to her room. With one sweep of her arm, she brought dresses and their hangers from the closet to her valise as a terrific crash sounded. A woman screamed. A man laughed. A shower of stones rained against the house. The loud crunch of broken glass in the hallway made her jump. "Any coloreds in here?" She eased the valise shut and hid behind the draperies, grateful for narrow hips, betrayed by the fine toe of her shoe.

A crowbar pulled the curtain back. The boy was no more than sixteen, his hands neither bruised nor bloodstained from the riot. Raggedy from head to toe with pitiful shoes, he was poorer than they had ever been. He opened a mouth of chipped, discolored teeth as a rattle of revolver shots nearly drowned him out. "Stay in and get roasted. Run out — they gonna get you too. My daddy say he gonna catch enough of y'all to make hisself good and tired." His grip on the crowbar was slight but he could give her up to the men outdoors if smoke didn't overcome her first. The air lumped in her chest and her eyes started to burn. Just then a deafening blast blew her to the ground, hurling window glass across the room.

As with all journalists, people often shared more with Ivoe than they intended. Earlier that week, the Liberty's owner thought little of removing the key to her safe box from the register, motioning Ivoe to follow her to the back room, where she pulled the cashbox down from the pantry shelf to deposit Ivoe's payment. "The lady who runs this place showed me where she keeps the money. Be a shame for it to burn too."

They flew down the back staircase to the dining room, past the windows crawling with flames to the register drawer — ajar and empty. The pit of Ivoe's stomach dropped as she glimpsed the chalkboard again. Whoever had written the message had probably taken the cashbox. She dashed for the storeroom anyway, the crowbar fast on her heels. She reached into the pantry shelf, behind the bags of rice, a shudder passing through her with an image of Ona just as her hand landed on the cold metal box.

"We ain't got no key."

"You've got a crowbar. Be quick about it before somebody comes and takes all that money from you."

A look of gratitude passed quickly over the boy's face as he snatched the box and took off. She was not far behind, her throat full of smoke, her feet lead weights. A choking cough seized her as she dodged the grasp of a man.

Voices were far enough away when she finally stopped to catch her breath. The houses here were larger, some had garages; she felt safe enough to duck behind one and rest. When she emerged a few hours later, walking the vacant and unrecognizable streets, she wondered where to go. She turned into an avenue that would lead her back to Casey's Row, hearing footsteps not far behind. She walked faster, wondering if she should run for her life or beg for mercy. A few paces more and she turned around.

A brigade of black boys carrying bricks and clubs made her sigh. What did they intend to do? In a stern voice she ordered them to give up their foolhardy enterprise and go someplace safe. "Where?" In times of trouble where had they always gone?

Flurries of black ash rained down on them but her gaze remained lifted. Frightened children lagged behind adults up the street where yesterday dogwood trees had flowered in the yards of row houses made of inexpensive yet sturdy clapboard. Efforts of the fire department had been extreme: take an ax and smash in — even where no fire had spread. She led the boys into an ash-smeared lane, opened a wood gate, and mounted the steps to the small-frame AME church.

Before the pulpit, an oil lamp burned on a table of meager provisions: water, bread, soup. As the evening wore on many came wearing fear and grief in place of their Sunday best. They rested on pews, under pews, packed like cattle in pens before the slaughter. At half past eight Ivoe alighted from the choir loft to ask the preacher, or anyone, for the afternoon newspaper. The facts of Baker's verdict were scant yet enough to give rise to rumor and more violence. In the morning, the preacher sat in his office awaiting calls from the chief of police, the mayor, the governor, while station 8ZAE's broadcast issued reports of increasing numbers of injuries and lost lives. At ten A.M., a mere four hours after all riot activity had ceased with the aid of the Twentieth Infantry, Ivoe thanked the minister for his help.

Outside the train depot a man sold goods from a flatbed wagon. He raised a box above his head and the small crowd jeered. Ivoe moved in closer, watching money exchange hands swiftly. What were the trinkets tied by a bit of rope? She backed away, hoping to get a better look from a distance. "What is he selling?" she said. A stranger explained the prices and his reason for parting with a whole dollar. Had he not told her what dangled from the tiny piece of rope she would never have known, so crisply cooked it was. She rushed into the station, pausing only for the newspapers hanging on wooden stalls. Copies of the *Omaha World-Herald, Omaha Bee, North Omaha Booster,* and *Jewish Bulletin* under her arm, she boarded the train. In the twelve hours it took before she saw Ona, the papers would calm and help to restore her. She settled into her read, disturbed by the headlines of each. There

446

was no getting beyond the second paragraph of the *World-Herald*'s "Frenzied Thousands Join in Orgy of Blood and Fire." All her life she had revered periodicals, until that morning. Reports from the Omaha press were untrue and unfair. She kicked the pile of Omaha papers under her seat. If they could defend lynching and distort facts, certainly an eyewitness account and the call for self-protection was grist for her newspaper's mill. When her train pulled into Kansas City's station there was a draft for the weekend's front-page editorial:

MOB KILLS COLORED MAN AFTER TAKING HIM FROM OFFICERS:
A WARNING
COLORED CASUALTIES:
32 KILLED — 81 WOUNDED — COUNTLESS ARRESTS
WHITE CASUALTIES:
6 KILLED — 13 WOUNDED — 0 ARRESTS
By Ivoe Leila Williams

OMAHA, Neb. — Today the grief and astonishment in Casey's Row, a black neighborhood in North Omaha, Nebraska, is overwhelming. On September 27, Grant Street, known by locals as the "Street of Dreams," housed black businesses and modest, well-kept homes not unlike those on the Vine. Today the neighborhood is burned out, the brains, limbs, and eyes of innocent people scattered like dung on the soil. The scene is hell's half acre.

On September 28, Tennessee native Willie Baker, a 41-year-old colored Pullman porter, who fought in the Great War and bore a proud and solid reputation, was killed by white mob violence just minutes after his acquittal at Douglas County Courthouse. Contrary to erroneous reports in Omaha's largest newspapers, Mr. Baker was not a vagrant. In Casey's Row, Baker shared a home with Savannah Jones, a white woman who vouched for his whereabouts during the time he was said to have raped Anne Jones, age 16. Here is a familiar story: the sense of dread regarding the black man's "savage pursuit of white women . . . his tendencies toward miscegenation that spoil the pristine white flower of womanhood" that permeates not only the Deep South but also midwestern and northern cities.

Following Mr. Baker's acquittal, when the court doors opened, avengers of white womanhood stormed the courthouse yard with bullet, knife, and flame, demanding Baker. Bailiffs had only revolvers while more posses emerged with high-powered rifles and a rope. Within minutes, Mr. Baker was apprehended. His ankles were tied together and he was hanged on the flagpole, head downward, and beaten with iron bars. Before the torch was applied Mr. Baker was deprived of his ears and fingers. Members of the crowd looked on with complacency, if not pure pleasure. Some howled with glee. Newspaper dispatches report that no persons have been indicted for complicity in the lynching.

You may wonder what role the police played in restoring order. A hundred officers did little more than disarm those trying to protect themselves and haul the most injured whites to the hospital. Preparing to leave the station for my return to Kansas City, I heard a cop say, "I arrested my share of Negroes yesterday. I arrested so many I let a paddy wagon of them wait for two hours while I took my supper."

At last count, more than two hundred colored people have been burned out of their North Omaha neighborhood. Some have expressed the determination to leave. Thirty-two are dead. At the train station your editor witnessed the selling of human remains. Small bones went for 10 cents; digits for a quarter; charred organs sold for a dollar.

Reader, I put the question to you: Would the citizens of Casey's Row have met with such casual deaths had their president and local leaders poised a watchful eye in a season of repeated mob violence? Surely President Wilson belongs to that class spoken of in the Bible: "which have eyes and see not; which have ears and hear not." When the so-called American isolationism was weakened in April 1917, President Wilson did not hesitate to address Congress asking for a declaration of war against Kaiser Wilhelm's Germany. "Make the World Safe for Democracy" became the slogan of his administration, when an essential element in the conduct of the war for democracy here at home — "A World Safe for Negroes" — remains curiously absent. Being both blind and deaf, President Wilson is guilty of perpetuating a national climate ripe for mob action.

The events of Casey's Row are but one example of how white mobs overpower police officers and take the law into their own hands. Omaha now joins Philadelphia, Chicago, Washington, Knoxville, Charleston — sites of a bloody spate of lynchings, riots, and the razing of black

450

communities. Our secretary of the esteemed NAACP has called this season the Red Summer, and it appears it may well lead to a Red Autumn.

Jim Crow is among us baring teeth. His henchmen wear badges, carry guns, wreak havoc, and murder in the name of justice. It is a foregone conclusion that the colored race will not receive equal protection by police. Heed the story of the unoffending Willie Baker, an upstanding member of his community, a law-abiding citizen, severed from his life. In our wide-open city, where men consume alcohol and gamble freely, how soon before the blood of black Kansas City runs through the West Bottoms? Let this record of the tragic fate of Willie Baker appeal to every colored Kansas Citian who has any regard for the sacredness of his own life.

Before federal troops are called to dismantle a hellish nightmare like Omaha in the Vine district, we must raise our voices with this important message: Whitecappers, Ku Klux Klan, police, and lynchers beware! The black worm has turned. The United States has done much to stoke the embers of unrest. But a race that has furnished thousands of the best soldiers that the world has ever seen will no longer be content to turn the left cheek when smitten upon the right. Vigilante rule shall not prevail in Kansas City. Mobs will have to pay the cost and pay it in lives!

18
NEODESHA

Ennis walked for miles in eerie quiet listening to the first sounds of freedom. Dimmed by the grueling journey without so much as a bone to sustain him, he approached a hen-house and set the birds to squawking as they closed ranks around him. A man came out of the cabin; his voice boomed and prompted Ennis to duck for cover, remaining until nightfall. Hunger gnarled his stomach as he slinked farther into the deep purple gloaming of a new day. The next morning, he milled around abandoned lean-tos — rusty tools, metal scraps, not a single crumb. So much for life on the prairie, he thought, scratching his beard on the recollection of the 1912 drought. The guards had talked about it all summer, hoping the prison farm's crops wouldn't rot.

The moon was directly overhead when Ennis set out from Little Tunis on July 21, 1911. He traveled for days just to empty his

head. Work seemed to follow him. If he
stood still long enough someone, taking in
his size and quietude, made him an offer.
Leaving his family had been the right thing
to do; for the first time in his life he was on
a first-name basis with "No," able to say it
without fear of reprisal. What could they
take from him? A knapsack? A few tools?
He reached Titus in early August. For two
months he shod horses. He thought of sending Lemon the money but decided it was
better to save it all for their plot in Kansas.
He moved on to Oklahoma, master of his
own fate. It might have continued that way
except for one gold pear near the top of the
tree filling him with such longing for Lemon
he had to stop and rest. Before he knew
anything the sun was going down behind
the strangest-looking man he'd ever seen.
The hair on his face and head had not been
shaved but plucked. He wore a patch over
his left eye, and from his left ear an orange
feather dangled. Blood or red paint was
drawn around the sockets of his dark beady
eyes. Ennis tried to make sense of him while
holding on to the last bit of his dream: he
had come up on Lemon in the garden.
"Shoot," she'd said, stomping the ground
with nervous laughter. "Big as you is, you'd
think I'd hear you coming." He laughed too,

picked her up, and took what he came after, a kiss. Now he watched the man carving something and realized it was the snapping of the dry branch that had woke him. After a while the man sat down and stared at him for a long time until finally he stood up and motioned for him to follow. Inside a strange dwelling that looked like a giant beehive made of grass, he learned the man's name. Misae's wife, Niabi, spoke English, but Misae refused to.

October in Little Tunis often brought hot days and chilly evenings like the one they were in now. Food was prepared. Ennis sat with the men in a circle while the women and children sat against the walls of the hut, waiting. After the men finished their meal, Niabi brought Misae an earthen jar. Whatever it was that tickled Ennis's nose, Misae drank it in one gulp and picked up his pipe. He filled the room with thick clouds of red-and-black smoke that made the women and children cough a little before he spoke. Ennis figured it to be a prayer. Misae took up his carved branch and bored a few holes on the top before handing it to the youngest child.

While the little boy blew into his flute, Ennis talked with Niabi. Her bronze face was serious and beautiful, her arms looked strong enough to lift a bale of cotton. In the middle of a sentence, she swung her head to scold one of the children, her long black braid flying like a lasso. Pointing to the patch on her husband's eye, she warned that the people beyond the forest on the hill could not be counted on for fairness in any matter. She asked Ennis if he was like the others northbound, expecting to find a land and a mule waiting for them. "No." It raised the question then: What did he hope to find? Honest work was all. He aimed to put down roots in Kansas where he knew colored settlements lived well out on the prairie. He should be sure to homestead near a river, Niabi said, looking him over. Strong. Misae and the other men left fieldwork to the women while hunting game, fishing, and logging. Ennis could work the field fast. For each pound of buffalo grass he picked she would give him three cents. Buffalo grass wasn't like other crops; they'd be harvesting clean up to December. Steady pay. After their talk, Niabi pointed him up the ladder where the children had disappeared earlier and where a straw mat was laid out for him.

In the morning, when Ennis awakened the children were gone. He climbed down, surprised that the men too were already at their hunt. Niabi's eyes told him to sit while she ladled out a porridge of corn and honey. She talked about the Christian missionary school the children attended, obliged him with paper and pencil, and agreed to post his letter to Lemon. Before nine they were through the latched straw door entering the fields, where the air was heavy and sweet. Bees fed on alfalfa, Niabi said. He should keep a lookout for hives in the corners of the fields. She showed him where to locate scythes and sickles for cutting the hay and how to strip the stem from the leaves, to smooth out each leaf and put the "rights" in a pile. Work commenced at sunrise and continued until sunset with the exception of one hour in late afternoon when Niabi called them in for a musty soup made from turkey carcasses. Ennis liked to watch her pound the hominy for the flatbread they dipped in the soup, her back flexing as she squatted on the ground, driving the big rock between her legs, thick and shapely like Lemon's. After lunch they returned to work. "Come on now. Roll away, roll away, roll. Roll!" Ennis called to stout women pushing bales. Long after the women had worked to a fever heat and collapsed inside one of the huts, he worked. Strong from lifting anvils and large scraps of iron, his arms and back were suited for anything, but this work also suited his mind. Out in the dark blue fields he couldn't help but think of Lemon. It comforted him to know she was out there, meddling in the earth, talking to the wind.

Miles of memory have no meaning in an alfalfa field. Ennis tried not to think of the distance between himself and his family. There were several harvests that season. Seemed like quick as they cut it down, it grew right back up. By December he had earned a fair amount, according to one of the ranchers whose wagon he stocked. One evening while burning the field for reseeding, he decided to work through the winter, when heaving was a big problem. Niabi seemed indifferent but she ordered a woman to sew pieces of wool together for a poncho that kept him warm while he dragged the spiked-tooth harrow across frozen fields. Ennis figured he'd cross the state line come summer, but fate tipped him over into Kansas sooner.

In December 1912 the town on the hill was hit by a flu epidemic. They killed the forest for coffins. Tombstones sprouted down the hill. As the graves crept closer water from decomposed bodies drained over Misae's land; all the wells were contaminated. Misae told the men to build barrels. They would have to journey for water to irrigate the fields. Two trains of six horses tied head to tail heaved the flatbeds carrying forty barrels each into Wilson County, Kansas. With nearly two hundred dollars in the pouch under his shirt, Ennis thought of leaving, but they had been good to him. Now that he knew the way, he could return. He filled barrels long after the others lined up on the creek bank to sleep. Glad about his prospects, he looked so long into the future he didn't see the two uniformed men and rifle commanding him to stop. The Osage slept peacefully while the troopers asked for proof of his water rights, yanking the pouch from around his neck. A year's wages gone. An army poised against him would have made no difference. He was ready to lose his life but the rifle pointed at him jammed. He struggled for it and threw it aside, pummeled the man until he no longer saw the faces of his family passing before him like fast-moving clouds before a storm, until the crack of wood on his lower back brought him to his knees.

Eight years later, they opened the cell door, and for the second time in his life someone told him he was free.

Ennis wiped his eyes and dusted the dirt from his legs. In 1911 when he last rode on

Little Tunis's roads, families lived on the strip of land before the prison fence. Gone. Replaced by a timber warehouse. Next to Starkville Masonry, in the lot where his home once stood, he found a brickyard. He pressed on to the little shack Timbo shared with Roena and the twins, trying not to think of all that could happen to a family of women. He left the abandoned shack with chest pains. Many trees later he came to May-Belle's cabin still standing on the knoll by the river. He pushed the door open to a dead place. He thought for a moment. Nobody should see him in his road-rough condition. He wished he could bathe, run a comb through his hair, before Fanny mistook him for a boo-hag.

You could tell time by the Texas heat. Early morning in the Brazos River Valley was the kindest since during the night the trees retained their moisture. But by noon hateful humidity amplified the heat. Pecan and red oaks commenced dropping leaves. Ennis recalled from boyhood that families on the move knew they had arrived in Texas when they saw an autumn ground beneath summer sun. Late in the afternoon you felt heavy, heavy all through your bones. Sometimes this was on account of wind so hot it burned the cornstalks. On the back porch,

Ennis took off his shirt, rolled it up and tucked it under his head. When he woke from his nap, Fanny would be home.

Ennis's head throbbed from the heat, causing him to stammer: "I-I never should've left them."

Fanny struggled to match the voice she knew with the face of the man before her. When it dawned on her who the bearded giant was, she pulled him in with surprising strength and bolted to the back of the house. "Have mercy on our souls." She was waving a newspaper, walking swiftly enough for Ennis to see that she had put on weight. Maybe the years brought a touch of senility too. She was handing him a newspaper to read without a plum word about his family. He unfolded the August 30, 1919, issue of *Jam on the Vine.* His gaze followed her wrinkled black finger as she read: "Ivoe Leila Williams, Founder, Editor, Publisher." He drew the paper to his chest.

"Lemon? Ira—"

They were all together in Kansas City — Missouri not Kansas — and doing fine, Fanny said.

Hearing about the people he had yearned for over dinner would make the last leg of the journey bearable, Ennis thought, as he watched Fanny prepare for supper. Fanny lit the stove and pulled out a plate of chicken from the icebox. "Got cornbread. I can warm up yesterday's chicken too, unless you want to eat it cold like I do."

In the morning, Fanny packed a little food for his travels, sorry he had come three days before her payday when everything had run out, or had its hand on the doorknob.

Clutching his copy of *Jam,* Ennis made his way to the Starkville train depot.

Arms full of grocery bags, Ona called, "Howdy, honey, howdy." She could hear Ivoe in the loft and missed her already. In a few hours her newswoman was leaving for Jefferson City. She glanced around the office. The mailings weren't finished; the billing book lay untouched. From halfway up the stairs, she saw no pots or pans on the stove. Ivoe had not started anything for the night's festivities, the twins' fifteenth birthday barbecue. Recognizing the black leather book in Ivoe's hand, she quickly put down the bags to study the ledger over her shoulder: 2,161 subscriptions, up 450 from the spring.

A quick kiss to celebrate before warning Ivoe of the train she was about to miss.

Ivoe grabbed the step stool and reached

on the top shelf for the valise. For years she had heard talk about arrests in the Vine district. Missouri maintained the most congested, most wretched penitentiary in the country, but there was much more to the picture. Hearing the trials of Bunchee's family had decided for her the next big story. The idea to visit the Missouri State Penitentiary grew more compelling when Bunchee's research turned up staggering information: of the 2,198 inmates more than 1,900 were black men. After reading census data against arrest records, she spent the last few weeks making phone calls to obtain an interview with the warden, a tour of the facilities, and a visit with Bunchee's cousin, Claude Knox. It was old hat that white men often spent a night at the county jail or served truncated sentences at the reformatory in Boonville for the same offenses that landed a black man in the pen. With a little luck, she hoped to delve deeper into the willful criminalization of black men.

Ona looked out the window as she filled two glasses with iced tea. "Irabelle's coming."

"Odell with her?"

"No."

"Shit. Least when he's with her we don't have to hear so much about him," Ivoe said, listening for the way the floorboards creaked. Whenever Irabelle walked heavy, she was worried about Plenty.

"Y'all, I'm fixing to be manless," Irabelle began, sitting down at the table dejected. "Or tuneless. Odell's tired of me and my cornfield ditties."

"Irabelle!"

"Well, that's what he calls them. He said, 'What kind of woman prefer playing music in a honky-tonk full of men to raising a family?' He wants me to have a baby and I think I just might give him one."

Ivoe rolled her eyes only for Ona to see. She hated the way Irabelle was withdrawing from the world. She performed less, saw fewer friends. Surely a baby would be the stone rolled before her tomb. Life demanded love, lots of it in all kinds of ways. Damn if Irabelle wasn't giving all of hers to Plenty. Where was she all the times May-Belle talked about having some love to keep?

"You give him a baby, you're surely giving up your music then."

"I don't aim to forever, just while the baby needs me. Maybe then I won't be so lonely."

Ona sucked her teeth. "Ivoe, where did y'all get her from? Whose child is she? She didn't get no better sense than this foolishness she talking?"

"I didn't get nothing. Ivoe got all Momma's hopes. Seem like I got her regrets, or somebody's."

"Well, not Papa's."

"We was two peas in a pod, wasn't we?"

"And wasn't room enough in the pod for Timbo, Momma, and me. I never could figure out how you fit that big ole man around your pinky."

Over the years, Irabelle's pride from knowing Papa had loved her too much had turned to regret. Now, because Plenty had taught her, she knew that love was a balancing act. Too much of it was impossible to bear up under. If it was too heavy or too sweet or too anything, in the end love turned people in the wrong direction. It had turned her father and where had he winded up? She would try her best not to let it turn Plenty.

"How you so lonely when you got Plenty?"

Ona looked at Ivoe. Surely she knew her sister talked so much about Odell because she had so little of him.

"Y'all know how he is. He got some funny ways. Some people . . . some people don't want you too close. If you get close, they leave. And some just like leaving."

She was about to tell them the reasons didn't matter — a man left because he loved you or because he couldn't stand you. If not for her, maybe Plenty would stick around for the baby. But before she could speak Momma appeared on the landing, winded.

"Let Odell saddle you with children if you want to. Nothing's lonelier than being left with a child that can't understand your worry and needs, needs, needs."

"Y'all talking just like y'all ain't never loved and hated to lose."

"Father up in heaven. Honey, what exactly would you be losing? Long as I've known Odell he's never said nothing sweet about you. Don't wanna take you nowhere unless it's the bedroom. If you just wanna take care of somebody who'll tell you what you want to hear, the street is full of them. What's so special about him?"

Ivoe sat her glass down like a judge lands his gavel. "I would've got tired of Odell shitting on me — excuse me, Momma — then turning around saying I smell bad a long time ago. Listen, y'all, I got a train to catch." She threw a kiss to her mother and sister and squeezed Ona tightly.

"They must be fighting again," Lemon said. "I'm surprised to see you around here before the food ready."

"She might as well be with him — she

always waiting on him to come around," Ivoe hollered from downstairs before she closed the door behind her.

"What if I am waiting? Love's a train. It don't all the time run on smooth tracks either. Sometimes it travels through rough land. But it'll carry you long as you stay with it."

Lemon chuckled. "Then, too, Irabelle, every train's not Glory-bound. It's a lot of things to love in life but a lie ain't one of them. You don't love Odell. You love a lie. Now, your father . . . well, that kind of hurt don't go away. It just don't. But the kind of hurt you got — the Odell kind — it'll go away. Hot will cool if greedy will let it."

Late in the evening, after Lemon had gone home, Ennis read the window: JAM ON THE VINE, EST. 1918. Bulky iron equipment and shelves of things he had no names for made him think of Ivoe in his work shed as a little girl: the way she listened patiently, curious about what each tool did; how she poked her mouth out before he gave in to letting her do something he did. She wasn't happy until they went home covered in black dust from where she'd swept around the forge. At the sound of laughter round and loud like his boy's, his heart raced. What if they wanted no part of him? Too many years. How could they still need him? Tired like he was, holding on to courage didn't come easy as he reached out to knock on the door. After a few minutes he saw a woman through the window coming down the staircase.

Irabelle took her time to the door, hoping it was Plenty. Never mind she and everybody else had just put the badmouth on him, a walk home together would be romantic.

"Who are you?"

Even in daylight it would have taken a few seconds to recognize the man in front of her. His hair had turned a yellow gray and the sprouting tufts along the sides of his face were salt and pepper. Nearly all the light had gone out from his eyes. The picture of Papa in her mind put her off the heart's answer, until a low deep rumble called her name like a question, causing her to recoil as from a knife. Her body shook as the truth wound its way through her. Ennis took her in his arms. She felt lightheaded; everything in her seemed to pour out in a frail sound so strange it stopped the domino game between Timbo, Roena, and the twins. Ona paused from her knitting and ran to the landing to look.

"Father up in heaven."

For a long time the weight of caring for his mother, sisters, wife, and sons had scared Timothy. How did he shrink away from the things Papa could do effortlessly? You could hear it in his sobbing now, soft and high from the rough squeeze Ennis gave him: understanding and awe. Roena couldn't bear to watch it.

Junebug and Pinky took up the dominoes Ennis recognized as his own, letting them clink loudly into the small zinc bucket. Roena wiped down the table and Ona offered Ennis a seat. Before his behind met the chair Irabelle had poured him a glass of iced tea. Roena and Ona scurried around the kitchen, pulling together bits and nibbles of this and that for his plate: a couple barbecue ribs, a heaping tablespoon of potato salad, the syrupy pan drippings of baked beans, the last ear of corn. With the nervous joy surrounding him, Ennis could not have eaten more. Timbo watched him take the first bite of the rib. "Not too bad, huh? Your grandsons know a thing or two about barbecue." Ennis wiped his mouth and said, "They got it honest," which made everybody grin. Pinky and Junebug had never seen anyone eat corn on the cob like their grandfather, who pinched the butt of

469

the husk, gave it a strong twist, then pulled off the roasted leaves and every strand of silk in one fell swoop. He chewed slowly, listening as Ona explained why Ivoe had gone to Jefferson City. Timbo talked about the challenges of being a head foreman. Irabelle showed him the clarinet she played with the Three Deuces Trio, the piece of him she had refused to let go. It was after midnight when Ennis rose. They argued about where Papa would sleep that night until he said, "Surely y'all don't think I'm spending another night away from Lemon. I don't care how late it's getting to be."

Outside Lemon's bedroom window, the sky held a strange pewter cast and a full moon. She thought she saw a shadow fall on her tomatoes. Still getting used to the little house on Hickory Street. Three rooms sure made a lot of strange noises, but at least she had a garden. She climbed back into bed, muttering to herself, "For too many years you been seeing that man's ghost." Sleep had marched on when she heard rustling outside her window. She put on her robe and left the house. City raccoons loved to meddle with her tomatoes. *"Giiiiit,"* she hissed, rounding the corner of the house.

Something large and solid moved in the

blackness.

"Who there? Don't want no trouble."

"I don't mean you none," the voice said.

Ennis stepped into the moonlight, took her in his arms, and commenced a heavy cry. In her body was a longing she could not let out. She pushed against him, drumming her fist against his chest until she broke free. But he pulled her back, even closer. Her head fell against his chest. "Ennis. Ennis. Ennis. Where you been so long? Where you been?" She lifted her eyes, searching for what kind of hell had kept him away from her. His body felt different. Maybe it wasn't no kind of hell at all that kept him. Maybe somebody had loved him wherever he came from. Or pretended to. Any love that didn't come from her had to come up short.

". . . Go off and leave me . . . Leave us like that . . . for so long. So long . . . Ennis. Where you come from? Where you go?" She began a silent cry caught by her husband's chest.

In her garden he was surrounded by all the fragrances he had missed; scents he knew so well he learned to conjure them when the stench of his own urine and shit stayed too long in the corner of his cell and in his nostrils. In her garden surrounded by the fruits and vegetables he knew to be the spells of her magic, he wanted to tell her that he too had learned a thing about magic. Before, he believed God brought the seasons and the seasons brought the changes. Now he knew that a white man could take the seasons, roll them into one long dark hour just like you rolled a bale of hay, and make that hour stretch out into eight years. A white man could number your days so that must make him God. Powerful enough to put you before a jury in Neodesha, Kansas, where Ennis had nodded yes when asked whether he had taken water without any water rights. Sometimes you have to kill some of your dreams so the one that matters most can live. He wanted to tell Lemon that he stood at his sentencing less than half the man she knew him to be just so they could have this moment.

Lemon looked at Ennis hard. The lines of his face showed where hope had been torn out of him.

"You home now, Ennis. You home."

Ivoe followed the guard through the court-yard into a two-story gray stone building where he filled out the appropriate papers to gain them access to the administration office. She caught a glimpse of herself in the glass door. The shoes were the oldest pair she owned, a week away from the trash bin. She wore no lipstick or rouge and her hair was wrapped in the dowdiest scarf she and Ona owned. Luckily, the hem of her dress had come undone. She pulled a loose thread to make it worse. She hoped her costume of poverty impressed the warden, whom she was to meet ostensibly for an article on the necessity of incarceration to rehabilitate black criminals. White men, she had learned, found her easier to take when she was less put together and not so articulate.

Her questions began with the most basic of human concerns. Why was the nineteenth-century system of silence — absolutely no verbal communication between inmates — still enforced here when other penitentiaries had lifted the ban on conversation? What did inmates eat? Why were no provisions for educational or vocational training provided? For which she received prompt correction: white men were allowed to have one book a week from the library. With general human ailments, not to mention accidents, she wondered where the hospital facilities were located and raised a brow when the warden said there were none. Conversation eventually wound to the Knox men. With the aid of Ona's clubwoman friend, who worked for the court system, she had acquired the following:

Claude Knox — arrested June 6, 1920, sentenced from Jackson County to serve nine years for burglary in the second degree.

Charles Knox — arrested November 2, 1919, sentenced from Jackson County to serve eight years for obtaining property under false pretenses.

Frederick Knox — arrested September 23, 1919, sentenced from Jackson County to serve life for rape.

What her paper didn't say was that the three men were each gainfully employed and had known no trouble either in their native Jamaica or in Kansas City until their fateful encounters with the KCPD. In the case of Claude, the charge of burglary was fiercely contradicted by neighbors who claimed that he was hauled off after a police officer attempted to write a bogus summons for the improper parking of his vehicle, a brand-new sea-green Cadillac roadster. More perplexing was the case of Frederick, accused of raping an older white woman.

Folks along the Vine called Frederick "Freda." Clearly, these arrests weren't based on any real evidence. The warden responded that there were now twenty-four hundred men in his possession and that he could not be expected to know them by name. Only the most pathological could be identified by face and demeanor. When Ivoe asked about paperwork on the Knox men, whom she thought would be fine examples for her article, she was told no records were kept on Negro inmates. How then were Negro men ever brought before the parole board? The warden looked at his watch and said it would be a good time for her tour as he had work to attend to.

The tour began in the room inmates were "dressed in" — T-shirts made of rough brown muslin, gingham britches, and wooden shoes made by other convicts. The guard charged as her guide asked if she wanted to take lunch with the inmates. He had brought lunch from home and she was a poor sap for not having done so herself. The sunshiny day was betrayed by the dining hall's windows, full of dirt. Her tray of food contained one boiled egg, a slice of bread, and a bowl of cloudy soup. She skimmed the top of the gray water only to discover a cockroach doing the backstroke.

While her companion ate a hearty sandwich and drank a Thermos of coffee, a family of insects she could not name marched across the table. She looked away only to see a rat scurry along the windowpane. The rule forbidding conversation was harshly enforced twice during the half hour. One man was hit with a wooden paddle, starting a trail of blood from his ear. Another had an iron collar placed around his neck.

After lunch they entered a corridor filled with a frightful stench. The majority of the inmates were black. A light brown man with pumpkin-colored patches dotting his scalp where he had torn his hair out by the roots looked at her with scary, blank eyes. The inmate's feeble attempt to walk was complicated by pants so stiff with dried pus they made a crunching sound as he struggled toward them. At his cell the stench worsened, a fact she attributed to the open lesions covering his emaciated chest. "Last stages of syphilis," the guard reported. Where segregation might actually prove healthful it had no place. When she asked the guard if the pen took any measures to separate clean men from those with communicable disease he shrugged. "You think that's something, the crazy are mixed in with the sane." The stout convict before her had been sentenced to death until they learned of his mental illness, then his punishment was commuted to life imprisonment. From the look and smell of things, it would be a very short sentence. Cell after cell, forlorn faces looked out at her with livid hunger in the eyes. Some pleaded pitifully for help, others stood the distressing squalor with fortitude.

In brown overalls with a black stripe down the seam, Claude Knox stank when ushered into the small room, where she was allowed to speak with him in the presence of a guard. "No amount of soap and water can cut it," he said, embarrassed, soft. Claude had received two letters from Bunchee and was grateful to her for keeping an eye on him. "Coming from a house full of men, you'd think we would have that much covered." He was grateful for a bed inside of the prison, as he had heard "last year it was so crowded inmates slept in the garage and outbuildings." After three weeks inside, Claude knew some things: what not to eat no matter how hungry, which guards to obey at all costs (the guard in the room was not bloodthirsty). His oldest brother, Charles, kept his head low. His baby brother had died. At the morning call, two years ago, Frederick Knox had been slow to rise.

A guard swore at him and Frederick swore back. They put him in the black hole. From hearsay, Claude said of the black hole: "No light. Rations of a teacup of water and three squares of bread are provided once a day."

"The black hole killed your brother?" Ivoe asked, for clarity.

"No. Pity killed him."

For thirty-three days Frederick lived on the starvation diet. When he was released, people let him help himself to anything off their food trays. "Gorged himself for two days and died of a perforated colon."

Before leaving Ivoe handed the guard a package with stamps, paper, envelopes, and a little money. "For Mr. Knox and any man who wishes to write to me." More letters, more money, she promised.

On the train, Ivoe recalled the first year of *Jam.* How out of tune with the race her editorial voice had sounded. Basic civil rights were not contingent on excellence, nor integrity and moral virtue — with that logic thousands of whites were truly un-American. She felt ashamed. She brought her own brush to the picture America painted of her race, a picture that rendered her people a social problem even as they were chased down streets, hunted, and

jailed. Instead of red-inking crimes committed against them, she had nursed a bad case
of journalistic myopia.

Vexed by what she had witnessed and
agitated by an itch coursing down her spine,
Ivoe shimmied hard against the train seat
and broke into a silent cry. She unfolded
the *Weekly Clarion,* published by the inmates
and handed to her by a colored guard. The
thought of the prison's gloom, its sullen
harshness, seized her despite the almost
humorous tone of a poem by Convict
#25818:

Ten little convicts,
Marching in a line;
One failed to button his coat,
Then there were nine.
Nine little convicts,
Bemoaning their fate;
One spoke in the dining room,
Then there were eight.
Eight little convicts,
Gazing up at heaven;
One tried to scale the wall,
Then there were seven . . .

She gave up any effort at concentration at
the Columbia station stop.

Thoughts of Ona were derailed by an itch

that followed no logical sequence: behind the left ear, the side of her big toe, above her belly button, on the right buttock. Maddening! A strange shiver went through her body. An intense itch seized her left hand. Or was it a bite? Upon close inspection she detected nothing. Three hours later the train's engine died but her itching had new life. The sensation of pins pushing from beneath her skin racked her body. And still the occasional bite from an invisible foe. She followed the stream of passengers inside the station and stopped at the sound of her name. Irabelle threw a wave and called to her again, bouncing on tiptoe. Closer, she saw her sister had been crying.

And who was the man standing beside her?

19
HOLDING BACK THE RIVER
WITH A BROOM
OCTOBER 1921

The bell over the door of Muehlebach's
Apothecary chimed as Ivoe stepped into the
sharp scents of orange and vanilla. She
breathed in the heady combination and
started down the aisle of elaborate cabinetry
flanked with shelves of attractive bottles
holding herbs. "A teaspoon of the calomel
daily for a week and a few rubdowns with
neem oil should stop the itch." Ona had
made her promise that on future trips to
Jefferson City she would not visit inmate
quarters. She had escaped with only body
lice the first time but might not be so lucky
the next. Leaving the store, Ivoe glimpsed
the fanciful ironwork of the door and
thought of her father.

Papa's return still felt like a dream. At the
train station the man next to Irabelle was a
phantom, for just as he had disappeared ten
years ago there he stood — without rhyme
or reason. The arm holding her valise jerked

up and down like a nervous lever. Her voice made strange, guttural sounds as if she had forgotten how to talk; words crumbled like dry clay. Papa's face balled up and he grabbed her, his chest shaking with sobs and laughter. May-Belle used to say that to know where a man's been, all you had to do was pay attention to his walk. Papa wore a thousand miles: his shoulders sagged. The way he lumbered over Union Station's marble floor like some tired mule was enough to tell her he'd been in a place where promises weren't easily kept.

Ivoe understood the makings of her womanhood to be her family, the first trip out of Little Tunis, Willetson, printing with Ona, the church newsletter, the fire, *Jam.* But it was her father's return after her visit with Claude Knox, the horrid images of the Missouri State Penitentiary, a map of sewing pins, and the black box that brought her newspaper's purpose into sharp relief. Papa's return had given rise to important questions: What if the black man didn't abandon his family with the frequency some in Little Tunis had accepted as "rule"? What if he was stolen like her father, incarcerated or killed? For as long as she could remember, men like Papa and Claude Knox had been easy pickings. A decade ago she had charted the exponential growth of convict leasing programs, but the Texas Prison Board was not alone. Lord only knew what kind of work the Kansas prison had extorted from Papa — for "stealing water."

The clock read a quarter to ten. Ivoe gathered the copies of the *Eagle, Amsterdam News, Washingtonian,* and *La Dépêche Africaine* strewn across her bed. From Los Angeles to the East Coast to the Caribbean, the struggle continued. She glanced at the bedside clock, then at the photograph taken outside the newspaper's office the day they hung out the sign: Ona's arm was thrown over her shoulders, the other hand held on to the gray hat that had nearly blown off a second before Bunchee snapped the picture. The floorboards were cool to her feet as she patted around for her slippers, thinking of the morning ahead. First, the bank, then on to meet Junebug and Pinky before a meeting with the Kansas City Democratic Executive Committee. For the first time, *Jam* was endorsing a political candidate in that year's election, Thomas Smith for mayor. Smith was the only respondent to letters she sent to every candidate asking his opinions on extralegal punishment and policies he might implement to end it. She had convinced Smith that his road to city hall was paved by the black ballot. Today she was meeting with the committee to discuss a night primary mounted specifically for the Vine district at her newspaper office. In return for black support, Smith promised to prioritize an investigation into the city's police force and a pardon for Claude and Charles Knox, which she now planned to revise to a commutation of their sentences since a pardon implied guilt. She was eager to review this week's edition of *Jam,* which featured an article on the latest victory for Timbo's union (a nickel raise for every man in the packing houses), Irabelle and Plenty's wedding announcement, and, on the back page, an ad for the twins' barbecue franchise boasting the best sauce in the Midwest. First, she had letters to read.

"Better bring Bunchee or a wagon. You can't carry it all yourself," the postman had said the first week of October when a deluge of letters addressed to *Jam on the Vine* arrived from Jefferson City. Claude Knox's letter was the spark that resulted in hundreds of incendiary letters from inmates that told of unwritten but enforced labor contracts and torturous punishments for failing to meet unreasonable work quotas. The idea to print a convict letter on the front page of every future edition was Ona's. Still, disagreements over which prison news to share riled the two. Ona held that a column like "West Bottoms Black Man Sentenced for Trolley Robbery" ("David Green was sentenced to serve two to five years in the state penitentiary after he was found guilty of theft of goods from a streetcar. He will be incarcerated in the Jackson County jail until room is available at the penitentiary.") could be cited as evidence in arguments supporting black criminal pathology. Ivoe insisted that the purpose of all prison stories was twofold: an illustration of the white hunt on black men and a constant reminder of what punishment lay in wait for black lawbreakers. Every Negro wasn't a saint; if he contemplated wrongdoing, the prison column might change his mind.

Outside information on the Missouri State Penitentiary was scant, yet inmate letters began to tell a story about economics. Despite Missouri law prohibiting the sale of convict labor, the MSP was a great industrial plant that employed nearly twenty-four hundred inmates whose labor netted the penitentiary thousands of dollars. A singular case study: Claude Knox's eleven hours of husbandry a day was worth $22.40 a week, yet he had not seen one red cent. The twelve hours of piecework Convict #21981 provided for Wolverman Manufacturing Company should earn about $2,200 in ordinary salary, a living wage for a year, but he had received the derisory total of $24.00 for his labor since his sentence began two years ago. Calculations from convict letters were her only proof of the prison's violation, but they were the impetus for letters to the Missouri State Board of Managers, which oversaw the MSP, and to the Democratic Executive Committee calling for a review of the penitentiary's finances. By now she was no stranger to the DEC, which had received hundreds of her letters demanding the removal of certain police offers and an investigation of the police board, to which blacks couldn't testify to mistreatment and false accusations of crimes brought against them. Since the Red Summer of 1919, *Jam* had published more than forty articles in which she employed a tone of menace and the threat of violent resistance in response to the KCPD's malfeasance and nonfeasance. It was now the official task of *Jam* to document the unlawful incarceration of black men, exposing the corruption of Kansas City's police and the Missouri Corrections Department.

By the fall of 1924, Ivoe had found an ally in the prison chaplain John Hopkins. Hopkins's complaints of inmate treatment had led to his removal from the chaplaincy post, after which he sought out a reporter from the *St. Louis Post-Dispatch,* from whom he learned of the convict letter-writing campaign by Kansas City's firebrand journalist, Ivoe Williams. His letters to her detailed all he had gleaned during his religious counseling of white prisoners about MSP's contracts with the furniture factory, the license tag factory, and the three camps in Cole County where inmates quarried rock. Records of the inmate registry and any detail culled from memory he sent to Ivoe. Her editorials drew on this information.

The front page of *Jam* now posed the question: "Was your friend or loved one unjustly incarcerated? Call HW-2161." Inevitably, a little research here, fact-checking there, returned a sad verdict. More than half of the incarcerated black men had no criminal record, no evidence supporting conviction. As word of *Jam*'s cause spread, subscriptions reached new heights, from 2,161 in 1921 to more than 4,000 the summer of 1924. She kept her promise to the

Knox men, refusing to leave their fate to the printed page. Public addresses on their behalf were written about and included in her editorials. The week before Thanksgiving, her grief and ire appeared in *Jam*'s headline: "For Black Men America Is Land of the Unfree, Home of the Jailed! Missouri State Politicians Fiddle While Thousands of Black Men Rot in Prison." "Dear Reader, It is said that a still tongue makes a wise head, but if we continue to be mute we will be a nation without black men . . ."

The snow on the Vine was windswept, the buildings all looked so bleak. Even the sun refused to brighten the morning, deadened by a heavy, moist cold. A gust of wind howled down the block and through the skeleton maples shimmying off their snow. Careful to dodge heavy branches sagged by ice that crackled, Ivoe pried at the knot of her scarf, flung it over her head and around her neck, tucking the ends inside her coat collar. The clouds may have blotted out the sun, but she withdrew her key joyfully, the way she had every day since Christmas 1917, when Ona had joined her for good. After seven years together, her need for Ona was outsized. No other could help her sweep aside logic and manage her feelings in order to drag the facts out into a light that shone such ugly truth: her sister's face, the black box in Little Tunis, the black hole in Jefferson City, Papa disappeared from them for ten years — and those were just her experiences. Black America was running a race for justice it seemed hard-pressed to win. She hunkered into her coat, nearly bumping into a pair of men trudging out of the cigar shop next door to the newspaper's headquarters and home.

By some miracle the weather had not blown down the door, riddled with grooves and depressions as if it had been beaten by police clubs. What infraction had they devised against *Jam* this time? She tore away the paper pinned to the door:

"Chancellor John M. Elliot today issued an injunction restraining Ivoe L. Williams, Negro, and any other parties from circulating *Jam on the Vine,* a Negro publication, in Kansas City or Jackson County. The injunction was granted at the insistance of Mayor Tom Pendleton. It was sought following receipt here of copies of the paper containing an account of the Wolverman Manufacturing Company. *Jam*'s reports were held to be false in their entirety and thought to promote racial unrest by the Jackson County court."

Ivoe ran a gloved thumb over the filled keyhole and called out for Ona as she rapped on the door. She searched the ground for a rock to throw at the upstairs window just as a paddy wagon pulled along the curb and two officers jumped out and seized her.

"Gonna get your people in a world of trouble," the grim-faced guard said to Ivoe upon delivery of a sandwich and glass of water.

"We have always lived in a world of trouble. Kindly take back your tray. I do not wish to attract vermin."

Exhaustion took hold the way fear might as Ivoe settled uncomfortably on the hard bench, wriggling her wet feet from slosh-covered boots. Damp and cold, she wrapped the lone provision — a rough blanket — around her legs and drew up the collar of her coat. Denied a phone call to Ona, she tried to brace herself for the long night ahead. In a land where mob rule still had a firm hand, a race woman's position was precarious at best. Outside of the NAACP, to whom could she turn for help? Claude Barnett's Associated Negro Press, founded in 1919 to disseminate critical news features to all black newspapers, did not offer legal or pecuniary aid. And bail money had never been a *Jam* expenditure allocation. She realized the urgency of an emergency fund for such a crisis, maintained by an organization that aided all black journalists. Depending on how long they kept her, some of *Jam*'s tasks would have to be divided. She was no stranger to Jackson County's presiding judge, Harry S. Truman, but could not fathom what his ruling might be. No matter the outcome, Ona and Bunchee must keep the paper going.

The next morning she looked out her cell window and drew a shuddering breath, stunned by what she saw. Across the street, a quiet mob crowded the sidewalk. She craned her neck to see how far the human chain extended — beyond the end of this block into the next. In the blustering cold, shoulder to shoulder, they began to sway to a minor cadence as their voices swelled with song.

Heavy load, heavy load,
Don't you know God's gonna lighten up
    your heavy load.
Heavy load, heavy load,
God's gonna lighten up your heavy load.

491

The language of grieving never had words; the human heart does not speak but sings its sorrow. Ivoe heard theirs now, a plaintive refrain sifting through her soul. Somewhere in the crowd a baritone led them and made her think of her father. She could not catch the tears welling up at the gentle droning of what sounded like a multitude.

Some time ago the minister had asked why she'd stopped attending Stranger's Rest. Ivoe laid blame to the newspaper rather than her own shaky faith. She enjoyed her stay-at-home Sundays while Ona went to church. Ona had felt something that Ivoe didn't or couldn't until now: community. Everybody's little bit of goodness pooled together to lift someone higher.

Distracted by the clink of keys, she turned around as the cell door sprang open.

"They have a right to hold you for disrupting the peace in light of previous warnings," her attorney said. News of her arrest had made the morning papers: "Negro Woman Editor Arrested and Accused of Stirring Negroes into Frenzy." To escape jail sentencing she must promise to devote a column to the Liberty Loan program and encourage her readers to purchase liberty bonds in every edition of *Jam* for the next year. One document required her signature. The

Kansas City Commission on Race Relations Statement said that she would exercise more care and accuracy in handling racial subjects.

Ivoe could still hear the street singers when she wiped the cold cream from her face that evening and climbed into bed, where Ona held her tight and listened to the story. Ona was moved to tears hearing of the familiar and strange faces who had shown support through song. Now, she reached over to the little side table beside their bed for the subscription ledger, making little noises that revealed her pleasure.

"Ivoe, we're in the beans! We're in the beans, baby!"

Five thousand! The readership they once thought they'd achieve in six months had taken six years to win if you didn't count the "free readers." Passing the paper from person to person was an act so prevalent on the Vine, an accurate count of *Jam*'s readers would never be obtained. When she considered how the paper was recycled and its information passed by word of mouth, Ivoe knew they would never know the real number of lives *Jam* influenced.

BLACK PRISONER SHOT TO DEATH —
PENITENTIARY IS SCENE OF CONFUSION
by Ivoe Leila Williams

MISSOURI STATE PENITENTIARY, JEF-FERSON CITY, Mo. — A black convict's fear of another sentence to Missouri State Penitentiary's "black hole" of solitary confinement was believed responsible yesterday for a single-handed prison break in which the prisoner was shot to death and eight other persons wounded.

The dead man was Hughes Adams, 24, who was killed as he ran screaming across the big prison yard toward a row of cell-blocks. Seven of the wounded were fellow convicts and the other was a guard.

The prison was thrown into confusion by the outburst and for a time it was feared a wholesale break might ensue. Shouts of wall guards as they fired at Adams mingled with the cries of terrified prisoners running from the bullets that raked the yard.

Assistant Deputy Warden Charles Har-gus said Adams, serving a ten-year term from Kansas City for conviction of assault with intent to commit murder, had been released from solitary confinement only last Sunday. He had been found with a knife, the assistant warden claimed.

After breakfast yesterday morning, Adams broke prison rules by lighting a cigarette before the line of prisoners left the hall. A guard started him toward the captain of the guard's office, where punishment is meted out.

Adams broke from his unarmed keeper and raced across the yard. He had no chance to escape, and at first the gun guards on the wall fired around him. As he neared the cellblocks two bullets brought him down, killing him instantly. In prison argot, Adams "went bronco." Guards believed he broke away in a wild fit of terror over being returned to the solitude of the black hole. The wounded men all were struck by glancing shots and only slightly injured. The prisoners were Irvin Jones, Orville Brown, Joe Anderson, Harold Tuttle, Lee Cavanaugh, Roosevelt Williams, and Ben Wright.

A coroner's jury today exonerated the prison guards. The jury held the guards fired in performance of their duty. Guards Teddy Payne and Ronald Betts were named as the men who fired the shots that killed Adams.

20

Le Tumulte Noir

MAY 1925

For six days they had pitched about on the Atlantic in a small stodgy cabin fetid with the odor of stale booze and vomit. Now the vessel sailed calmly. Ivoe gazed out at endless loamy waves. Who would have ever thought a Negro girl from Texas could have sea legs? She pulled up her shawl against the spraying mist, sketches of Little Tunis on the canvas of her mind: newspapers, maps, climbing Momma's fig tree to think of a future she had no language to describe, a future like the present. Momma would come out of the house, look all around, before she thought to look up. "Come down from there, girl. Them figs don't need no company. Come down before you die your natural death." Always she detected some note of pleasure in the voice, for while Momma knew the view wasn't much, the vision was everything.

Since the maiden voyage of _Jam_ almost

seven years ago, their operation had grown from two to six. A deal secured by Ona with a black-owned printing shop, which printed the growing paper at an affordable price, freed up money for hiring three part-time journalists and Bunchee. As business manager, Ona oversaw circulation. Lily Turner — Ona's YWCA friend — contributed columns on homemaking. Celia Benton wrote about education, black literature, and music and maintained the back-page social column, The Vine in Bloom, highlighting the accomplishments of everyday people. In Celia's husband, Dr. Benton, who had opened the city's first colored sanatorium, they found the health and welfare editor. Ivoe's own column — Woman About Town — featured reports on her meetings with various factions from Kansas City's political machine. At age eighteen Bunchee, who had a flair for words and the moxie for finding the right story, often attended meetings with her, taking copious notes — like any good cub reporter in training. He fact-checked stories with the editor, sometimes compiling news from the wire service of the Associated Press.

Inside the *Jam* headquarters Ivoe was both at home with Ona and in the world, advocating for her people, the only worthwhile work she could think to do. Occasionally, at a late hour, Timbo dropped by, claiming the light from the window set off his concern. Accompanied by men from the packing plant, they retreated to the loft and sat down for union talk over fried fish or tomatoes, which Ona cooked up for them. The men's voices carried above Irabelle and other musicians, who often congregated after a gig to practice, jamming in the loft. This was the paper's greatest reward — family, community, including those far away whom she had never met. After two days on the train from Kansas City, their first stop in Manhattan before boarding the ship had been to the Seventh Avenue office of the *Amsterdam News* to finally meet one such ally.

The uptown train jostled through the subway tunnel from 34th Street to 125th, where they met *Amsterdam News* contributor T. Thomas Fortune. Their correspondence with Fortune had begun during the summer of 1919, following Ivoe's coverage of the Omaha race riot. It was Fortune's recommendation that she and Ona make the crossing for the Pan-African Congress in Paris. Urging them along Harlem's crowded streets, he was a gregarious guide.

For several hours they thrilled to sites they had only encountered in his paper: Garvey's Liberty Hall, Strivers' Row, Abyssinian Baptist Church. He pointed out the best nightclubs — the Sugar Cane, Connie's Inn, Cairo's — and the infamous Barron's Cabaret, where blacks worked but could not attend. At 140th Street, Fortune pulled them inside Tabb's Restaurant, where they peered out the window at the strangest scene.

"Mrs. Trace," Fortune said, and sighed. "Now there's a story for the ship. Welcome to New York City, ladies, where everybody's story is worthy of the front page."

Traffic halted. Horns honked. A man carrying a curious case — too small for a proper valise, too deep for a briefcase (Ivoe took him for a salesman) — pushed through a growing crowd to address the woman sitting in the middle of Lenox Avenue with a baby, or so Ivoe thought until the man twisted it away from the woman by the head and tucked it under his arm. Ivoe and her companions watched as the man helped the woman, engulfed in the loudness of an orange dress, rise to her feet. She looked to be about Ona's age — early fifties. She seemed confused and, despite the man's arm now snug around her waist to hold her steady, too alone.

After their feast of fried chicken and waffles, they rode the subway down to South Ferry and joined the squall of deafening chatter bustling up the gangplank at New York Harbor. Ivoe grabbed Ona around the waist, squeezed tight, laughing as the ship hove past the Statue of Liberty. Sailing to France where the dollar was strong and there was no Jim Crow. Aboard the RMS *Mauretania,* Ivoe had strolled the decks, socialized with passengers until the sunless opal sky turned dusky pink while Ona remained below, filling the bedside basins with vomit, her only reprieve the salty breeze through the crack of their tiny cabin window. Still, at night before the slap of waves against the ship lulled Ivoe into perfect sleep, Ona assured her that the congress would be worth more than a hundred difficult crossings.

"Father up in heaven."

Jammed against the rails of the RMS *Mauretania,* they waved at everyone and no one in particular as the ship moored alongside the wharf. Ivoe bounced in her shoes as a giddy Ona pounded her fist excitedly on the wooden banister from which sprang a rusty nail.

They spent the first hour in France stanching the blood flow from the gash in Ona's hand, soaking several towels before the ship doctor could bandage it. From Le Havre a train took them to the north of Paris, where upon exiting Gare Saint-Lazare a majestic, white-domed basilica caught Ivoe's eye. Here the city's black people lived in grand stone buildings — like those she had imagined while reading European novels in her youth — as well kept as any in Paris. In America one hotel in a hundred would put up two race women; in France they had their pick of first-class lodging. In the shadow of la Basilique du Sacré Coeur, along the steep, cobbled rue de Steinkerque, they secured a charming fourth-floor apartment without incident or the slightest inconvenience owing to pigmentation.

The Vine in Montmartre was no fringe at the bottom, no slum or ghetto of dilapidated tenements, but was nestled at the city's highest summit amid small theaters, quaint bistros, and nightclubs, which were full of that wonderful black noise: jazz. The French called the quarter la Butte — a colony of streets teeming with artists, itinerant musicians, black soldiers who had remained in France after discharge, and their lovers. Ivoe and Ona wandered to the open-air market at the edge of the village. They lost count of brown faces in restaurants side by side with whites or in the finest shops exchanging money for quality wares (fifty francs to the dollar!). A pair of prattling men parted the bustling crowd for them at the entrance to Pigalle. Rows of pushcarts overflowed with brass trays and candle holders from Algeria, Turkish carpets, potted herbs and spices, linens, chinaware, silver samovars, bargain wristwatches for gentlemen, ladies' parasols, and a bed of scarves. Ona reached for a gray silk twill scarf. A few steps farther along, a fine pair of shoes beckoned from a store window. Ivoe parted with two hundred francs (four dollars — for what would have surely cost ten in America) for the oxblood leather Mary Jane pumps with ribbon at the ankle in place of a strap. Thank you, Mr. Ferragamo.

"Why carry the old ones?" Ona said, prompting her to leave them behind. In the middle of rue Blanche, a few meters from the stunning Moulin Rouge, Ivoe and Ona stole a kiss.

Misinterpreted directions, wrong directions, slightly off directions, finally landed them at Le Grand Duc. The night air in the Pigalle was cool and balmy when they entered the raffish room no bigger than a telephone booth in Kansas City's Washington Hotel. During their crossing, Fortune had told them about the hub where they could meet other blacks newly arrived in Paris. They settled at a bare wood table, at once seduced by the small cavern of rough stucco walls and wrought-iron fixtures. A gentleman dining alone recommended the bouillabaisse. The soup — a greige broth with clams, cockles, and cuttlefish — arrived in chipped bowls, completely unappetizing in appearance, utterly delicious to the taste. As they huddled over a shared dessert neither could pronounce — a gratin of buttered apricots in pecan meal — a jazz quartet played "Somebody Loves Me." In Kansas City, a black person could not piss in the same toilet or spit in the same sink as a white person. Here, no separate stand-up counter, no invisible color line down the café's middle to segregate patrons. Ivoe sipped from her kir. Ona leaned forward and touched Ivoe's face in impulsive tenderness, flashing her a bold look of intimacy. After dinner they strolled boulevard de Clichy — Ona cloaked in a knockout gray scarf, Ivoe's new shoes bending to the humps of cobblestone. Taking in women in widow's weeds still mourning the millions taken by the guns at Verdun, the squeak of carriage wheels, the joyous reunions between friends, the noise of a city bursting at the seams, they returned to rue de Steinkerque late, appetites sated, black currant lips sticky and sweet. The only thing to do was make love and sleep without dreaming.

The cheerful sounds of chaffinches outside their window awakened Ivoe. For hours it had lain dormant, but now quiet joy, roused by the beat of wings and singing, gave way to a sigh. She felt her way back to the final moments of last night and a smile of reminiscence spread over her face. She turned on her side to watch Ona blissfully asleep, reflecting on the perfection of the last few days, then rose to dress — to make it begin all over again.

Looking down on the blooming courtyard, Ona complained of a stiff neck "and hunger!" For twenty minutes Ivoe had prepared to go out and retrieve breakfast, yet happiness guided her aimlessly around the apartment. Ona had cheated her out of the pleasure of seeing her in a different light; she moved as gracefully about as though they had lived there ten years, and had the uncanny knack for carrying home with her, unpacking and rearranging the rooms' furnishing so that the flat reflected the rhythm of their lives.

Ivoe stepped out into the sweet-scented morning air, greeted by hyacinth, thirty or forty blossoms on a stem. A few paces more, the fragrance faded into a delectable aroma — bread baking around the corner. Across the street, poodles and small hounds relieved themselves against a stone building while a street sweeper worked nearby. Clearly, the logic behind French municipal services was to serve the environment, regardless of who lived where.

Ivoe tossed copies of *Le Petit Parisien, Le Matin,* and *Le Journal* on the table. Ona eyed the weeklies greedily. Two out of every six words she understood, yet observations were noted. The French press used smaller font, more words per line, and half the space American papers gave to advertisements. Even the ads were fact-based, less enticing. Ivoe laid out a breakfast of coffee, bread, goat's cheese, and honey, relaying a scene she witnessed at the boulangerie. She put on a husky voice to enact the American black man cutting down the Frenchman who tried to cheat him. " 'Not another franc,' he said. 'Now politely give me all the bread I have paid for.' " Back home, any black man audacious enough to count his change in front of a white shop owner, let alone question him without fear of reprisal — especially in the South — was as rare as hen's teeth.

Ona wanted to spend the beautiful spring day in a twelfth-century crypt.

"My Methuselah, all of the fashion houses of Paris and you want to visit some old bones."

Ona rolled her eyes. Earlier that year when she turned fifty her name was lost and replaced by Ivoe with any epithet marking age: "Granny-O," "Biddy-O," "Dame Durden," "Blue-Hair" — pleasant reminders. What discouraged other women who had crossed the fifty threshold had brought Ona unexpected peace. It seemed to her that the appearance of an aging woman either opened the onlooker's eye or shut it. In the absence of ambivalence she took great comfort. On the street she appreciated people who changed their tempo for her — stepped aside on a bustling sidewalk, relinquished a trolley seat, or held a door open — so she understood how being ignored by masses of people might be upsetting. But how much time had been taken from her during her youth? How often had she been put out by casual nothingness? She liked that the swing of her hips no longer invited stares, or, worse yet, uninvited conversation. At fifty, her understanding of life was flowering in a secret garden no one, other than Ivoe, dared enter. How she had looked forward to this special peace that came with being disappeared by age.

Ivoe devised that Ona visit the catacombs without her and that they rendezvous in the afternoon for sightseeing. Until then, she had a difficult task: how to put on paper the spell Paris had them under.

LE TUMULTE NOIR, MY TRIP ABROAD

PARIS, France — To try to set down what two race women can do in Paris in three days, or even the main threads of the pleasures of Paris, would be like trying to catch the sun's rays in a bottle. The attractions are too numerous and too varied. Everyone who has visited Paris nurses a secret desire to return again soon. The city cannot be abandoned, for nowhere else in the world can one find a semblance of her charming and intoxicating atmosphere. All temperaments, tastes and aspirations find their satisfaction here. The words "Liberté, Égalité and Fraternité" carved on many of her public buildings proclaim to the world that she is free.

A day in Paris unfolds magically: A walk by the admirable Champs-Élysées to the avenue du Bois de Boulogne. There in that noble scenery of trees, flower beds and sumptuous residences one could watch passing by from 11 o'clock until 1 the smartest of the Parisiennes. Some walking, others in luxurious cars, not to mention elegant horsemen and horsewomen in the special "allée" reserved for them. Deciding on a restaurant is an impossible task. They are all so splendid, each with a celebrated cuisine and welcoming of blacks. Lunch over, you would linger for a while then take a taxi to the Louvre, eventually ambling about the Place de la Concorde. Finally, around 6 o'clock in rue de la Paix, you take note of shop windows sparkling with riches. All those who have breathed this rare atmosphere of elegance and civilization will understand what is called up throughout the world by the words "rue de la Paix."

Paris is full of strangers the year around, with Americans in full force. The sidewalks in front of various banks and tourist offices are piled high with American newspapers. Boys imported with the papers display the usual American hustle and are busy selling them to Kentucky colonels and others from down south, out west and New England.

What looks like indignation meetings on the pavement are simply crowds waiting for seats in the multicolored cars that make the "sightseeing around Paris" excursions. If your bus is going into the vicinity of the Louvre and the Palais Royal, you will see two remarkable churches: the Oratoire and the ancient Saint-Germain l'Auxerrois. The former was the chapel royal of the Louvre from Louis XIII to Louis XV. A bell from one of its towers pealed out the signal for the massacre on the night of St. Bartholomew in August 1572.

To get a full sense of the poetry and mystery of Paris after dark you would do well to take a trip on the river Seine around the city and let your imagination roam. As the vessel glides under the white lights of the bridges you can see a hundred thousand bulbs outline the World's Fair's pavilion and many buildings on either bank of the Seine, turning night into day again. In this setting you are likely to find Paris in its true self, shorn of confusion and trappings. Likewise, you might board an autocar at Place de l'Opéra about 9 P.M., take a whizz by the Bastille, Notre Dame and

Étoile and land yourself anywhere in the neighborhood of Montmartre.

Montmartre is the center of Parisian nightlife, attracting tourists from the four corners of the world. Here you find on Place Pigalle the famous Café du Rat Mort (or the Café of the Dead Rat), which a famous artist has described as the light-house of Montmartre. All assemble here: musicians, artists, stars of the literary and theatrical world, including our very own sable queen from down-the-road St. Louis, who opened *La Revue Nègre* at the Théâtre des Champs-Élysées to rave reviews. (Nothing my companion and I have experienced has met with equal rapture.) There is nothing slow about a cabaret in Montmartre. Everything is up-to-date. The songs are full of allusions to the most recent political events, scandals and risqué catchwords. Finally, around midnight, after the actors "take off" on a politician and imitate a jockey who has just won the grand prix, our very own home-grown bands start to jam. Any homesickness would be feigned when such sweet black noise ends the day.

À bientôt,
Ivoe Leila Williams

■ ■ ■ ■

Only in Paris could the wrong train deliver you to the right place. They had traveled too easterly before looking up from the map to see the Bois de Vincennes. Ivoe sighed at the sprawling, romantic park like those she had read about in English novels, replete with gazebos and hilly picnic areas. On their day in Manhattan, plans to visit Central Park's Ladies Pond and Ladies Pavilion were dashed by segregation. Here she and Ona could rent bicycles or a boat but settled for holding hands as they ambled among the trees. Late in the afternoon at Maison Prunier, their knees touched under a small corner table. Since the moment they arrived, Paris had taken their hearts; now, evidently, she had come back for their minds — a grown pair of women, swirling spoons through a creamy pink-and-yellow foam, giggling. They interrupted each other or sat in silence, beaming. A single crossing had made them different because time was different; a French hour differed from an American one in all the ways they were free to spend it. Hobbled by language and a poor sense of direction, before the congress she and Ona intended to drink in Paris until

511

drunk, starting with the modern industrial and decorative arts exhibit at the World's Fair. They hammered out more plans; Ona hummed a little under her breath the way she did whenever she felt delighted. The days before them flung wide open to strolling the royal gardens at Tuileries, spraying Babani perfume and feeling fine couture in shops along the discreetly elegant boulevard Haussmann, climbing to the top of that lattice iron tower on Champ de Mars, and more peach clafouti. For all these decadences they needed not bend themselves to accommodate the most inconvenient hours, or wait for the day when the colored ban was lifted. Just as the Associated Press had greeted them with calm affection and in little time sent cables to *Jam on the Vine,* their plans would run smoothly. Free to go and do as they pleased.

"Mesdames et messieurs. Nous sommes arrivés à la Porte d'Orsay. S'il vous plaît sortez." An open-air tram let them off before an intricately designed steel canopy. The path to the L'Exposition Internationale des Arts Décoratifs et Industriels Modernes had the usual concessions: a Ferris wheel, a merry-go-round, boats, and a skating rink. Umbrellas of every color on the banks of the Seine

gave swimmers respite in shade while band concerts drew crowds. Music from the left bank's band pavilion floated across the water, jazzing Ivoe and Ona along the esplanade of Les Invalides, Louis XIV's playground. A loud pop that sounded like a gunshot made Ona jump. Bursting showers of liquid silver nails and aerial bombshells of red, white, and blue shot high above the Seine. Peace and progress, the exposition's themes, hardly applied to life back home, Ivoe thought. No matter the game blacks always played to the white man's hand because of America's reluctance to turn her gaze away from slavery. In 1925 her government still clung to backward thinking with appalling tenacity. She recalled her family's first Independence Day in Kansas City. She was twenty-eight years old, Timbo thirty-four, the twins about ten. In 1917, Fairmount Park fairgrounds lifted the ban on blacks for July 4. Roena had fussed about Timbo working at the white fairgrounds instead of Swope Park, where blacks could enter year-round. She hated that in seeing their father work, the twins would also see how much better everything was at a fairground they couldn't attend any other month. At the Parker Brothers' invention, the Little Darky Shooting Gallery, where

Junebug and Pinky tossed watermelon-shaped discs into the open red mouth of an ebony face, Ivoe had tried to explain to Roena advice she had received from Ona: "Sometimes you have to bend low to follow through." Timbo was unwilling to scab. The fairground work wasn't *really* him. After the Game of Sambo the twins grew anxious for their daddy's game, pulling their mother and aunt along. A smack landed on Ivoe's arm. Roena had stopped dead in her tracks. "Well, ain't that a pretty howdy-do." At that moment Ivoe recalled the various images of a boo-hag that sprang to her childhood mind during story time. None of the boo-hags she conjured ever looked as frightening as what she and Roena saw: caricatured Negro faces with bulging eyes, large, twisted mouths, and startling hair painted on a large canvas scene of a cotton field. Dressed in silly clothing, contorted limbs frozen in a dance or on the run, the painted Negro bodies made the twins laugh. Ivoe stared at the three faces until Junebug pulled on her skirt, finally shifting her gaze to the hole where a face she knew peeked through. Timbo's eyes grew big; the red paint around his mouth drew his grin from ear to ear. He ran out barefoot from behind the canvas in torn britches and a dirty shirtwaist with a bright red kerchief tied around his neck. But it was the large yellow bonnet bedizened with broken flowers that made Ivoe bite her lip. In mock fear Timbo ran in circles, just missing the grasp of the white man standing before the canvas with a long whip, speaking in a boisterous voice. "Step right up and teach this darky a lesson about not doing his work." He lashed the whip. "Teach him well and win a prize." He waved a small bucket with three balls at the audience. The aim of the African Dodger was clear. Timbo returned to his place behind the canvas as Junebug and Pinky begged for change. Disgusted, Roena grabbed their hands and walked away.

Ivoe and Ona moved with the crowd jamming the banks of the Seine to enjoy the spectacle. As if by magic, at eight o'clock six beautiful women emerged from makeshift fountains in the river. The crowd watched, spellbound by the living statuary. When the lights changed color over their graceful tableaux, Ivoe saw that three of the women were colored. Paris had her ear tuned to jazz, the future, while white America still sang Mammy songs and longed for minstrel shows.

Ivoe ducked out of the rain, pulling Ona

beneath a canopied stall in the open-air market in rue Mabillon, Saint-Germain-des-Prés. An old woman beckoned from the rear of her cart. She spoke as Ona tapped Ivoe on the arm. Ivoe translated: "Sour cherries from Montmorency Valley just north of the city . . . cheap." The woman lifted the tarp covering small baskets of cherries, their scarlet skins split by the rain. Ona's mouth watered as she dug around for the fifty-centime bronze coin displaying Apollo seated on a throne with his lyre and serpent-entwined staff. At a cheese stall they had their fill of nutty, bland, and too strong. A freckled man with bright green eyes insisted they try the fresh chicken. While waiting for the rotisserie to stop, he entertained them, whisking off Ona's hat, putting it on, and juggling three pieces of fruit. An honest-to-God Frenchman — playful, silly, charming, all of that. Ona was certain she would remember the scene for the rest of her life. Finally, they descended underground for the metro.

They had planned to return to Le Grand Duc for dinner but were now too full, so they fell into Ciro's for *deux pastis* and dancing. The last notes of a slow drag played; the floor trickled down to a few be-guine dancers. A group from Martinique raised a raucous as the bands changed. Black American sound was contagious but they hated those dances — no gyrating; one must roll the hips modestly — and sulked against the wall. Ivoe grabbed Ona's hand, joining the others eager to claim a spot. On the downbeat, Ona raised her right foot then tapped the floor. Ivoe imitated. Tap, tap the heels of the right foot in front and slide. Here was the part in the music Ivoe loved best. A glorious sight. The merry dancers jamming to the music when all of a sudden, a caesura, a break from the rhythm of hurt, loss, a moment of freedom un-chained from someone else's rhythm — and the music starts again. Fingers snap, hips swivel, moans swell in the chest, the wood of the floor bulges: kick left with your right foot, kick right with your left. They all jumped up and landed, facing the center of the room, continuing the steps from the beginning. Ecstasy is the pitch of undulat-ing hips, eyes rolling to one side then the other.

Ivoe could dance all night. A big-bottomed woman stomping in place bumped into Ona, who laughed at first, then grimaced, plucking her skirt. She reached for Ivoe and headed for their table.

"I thought we were gonna hucklebuck

until the rising sun," Ivoe teased as they sat down. They were doing too much in Paris, it couldn't be helped. After daylong meetings at the Hotel de Malte, the city beckoned. Exiting the metro station, blocks from their flat, Ivoe would run into a journalist. There was some singer to hear, a theater troupe acting original works in a centuries-old church, or some debate on the political climate back home in full swing at a small café. More than a few of those evenings Ona had left her alone with *les bohémiens,* stating the hills and cobblestones were too much for fifty-year-old Methuselah. The last few evenings full of good entertainment and great conversations kept Ivoe away from their apartment until two in the morning. Ona twisted in her seat a little, yawned, then pulled Ivoe up to join the other patrons jamming to the center and all along the margin. The wooden floor shook beneath them as people danced everything from the black bottom to the beguine. Ona drew Ivoe close, singing along with Isabelle Patricola, a record they had worn out last year:

You were meant to be my loving baby,
Somebody loves me
I wonder who,
Maybe it's you.

Home sweet Paris on rue de Steinkerque, Ivoe leaned across the bed in her slip to reach the unfinished basket of cherries. Alternating between Ona's mouth and her own, she rolled cherry after cherry, ignoring the juice trickling down their chins. They talked about the club, complained about the work that awaited them in Kansas City, remarked for the eleventh or twelfth time on the splendor of Paris.

"Everything is perfect. Can't think of a thing we're missing," Ivoe said.

Ona rose from the bed. She threw open her valise, pulled out a box. She sat down next to Ivoe, giddy as a schoolgirl on graduation, and withdrew a purple velvet drawstring bag. Before opening it, she relayed news of her journey to rue Saint-Denis earlier that day.

Ivoe listened to the story of Ona's encounter at the curious shop. What she described could not exist. Such things lived solely in the imagination of European writers — Mr. Shakespeare toyed with the thought in her favorite play, *Measure for Measure.* The Marquis de Sade's Justine knew of them in the eighteenth century — but surely a woman could not walk in off the street and simply purchase one. Paris is not a city for nonbelievers. Ivoe's cheeks grew warm, staring at the maroon leather phallus on display across Ona's lap. Quickly, she reached out to cover it. Ona pulled the apparatus from beneath Ivoe's hand and stood with her back turned. She removed her skirt and made the final adjustment before turning around. *"Une consoler."* Ivoe fell against the bed laughing. Here was Miss Durden — eclipsed by none in intelligence and grace — with an alarming erection.

"You've been wearing those — those special underpants all evening, Ona?" She could barely catch her breath.

"Had them fit me in the store. Had to — if I wanted to wear Monsieur Consoler." Peals of laughter erupted from Ivoe.

"Hush, girl, before you start the people to thinking we're drunk and crazy." Ona crawled across the bed, kissed Ivoe until the waves in her belly stopped. All the play was gone from her voice: "You tried to dance the loving right out of me. But there's still some left."

Ivoe's legs trembled and buckled against Ona's shoulders. "Is it all right?" Ona whispered sweet, her hips rocking, the gleam in her eye pleasant lightning. A look from Ona and she was found out, every hope, every doubt. It frightened her, how much Ona knew, could see, and want her still.

"Um-hmm — you feel anything?"

Husky breathing was answer enough.

"You got me tingling all over. Make me melt, baby." She kissed Ivoe's forehead, feathered her tongue across the soft plump lips.

Sometimes their lives were too much. The heavy cost paid left Ivoe light as a leaf. More than anything she wanted not to be tossed about — the way life did them. She searched every crease, every line of Ona's face for the heart's memory. Rose to lick and suckle the dangling nipples. Ona rocked into her, left her filled, whispered into her ear: "Baby." The wet of her eyes, the quiver of her lips, was almost too much to take.

Sleeping Angelica had stepped off Rubens's canvas. She loved Ona this way — sprawled out and nude. Fresh as April, warm as May. After telling her what colors she saw this time, Ona had fallen asleep. Ivoe rolled over and grabbed paper and pencil. Questions and ideas flitted about like fireflies, refusing to land for very long. At a quarter to three in the morning, she curled into Ona, grateful for their time in Paris, a moment that would buoy her soul in life's most turbulent waters.

■ ■ ■ ■

Early in the morning of May 25, a phalanx
of black journalists strutted along the
fashionable rue de Richelieu. Fire for justice
had called together citizens of the Americas,
Ethiopia, Haiti, Liberia, Martinique; a
hundred or more representatives from the
newspapers of sixteen nations and colonies
converged on the right bank at the Hotel de
Malte. The mass meetings for the Pan-
African Congress convened in a large room
off the hotel lobby in which several tele-
graphs were furnished for journalists. Ivoe
skimmed the program. Now was the Greeting Hour when editors and journalists gave
introductions and remarks on their interest
in the meeting, what issues their papers
grappled with, the collective direction they
wished for the black press. Ona and Ivoe
took their seats, eager for the opening address by editor Paul Kellogg of *Survey
Graphic* magazine, the national periodical
devoted to sociology and social work. Kellogg's trenchant address implored his audience to protect the rights of people of
African descent and to be less concerned
with Negro history but fanatical about the
future. "If we keep looking back, that bear

is going to get us. We must forge ahead in the names of our ancestors who lost their lives so that we might have a stake in freedom. Lest we forget, there are places where we are yet found swinging in the wind." Delegates, politicians, newspaper people, and representatives from clubs convened in each room of the hotel reporting their findings on the health and welfare of black communities, unemployment, hiring practices and economics, black disfranchisement, and violence. Inflammatory speeches by several editors condemned social conditions in the United States, inveighing against President Coolidge and the government. One editor stood in a frightful rage, calling for a movement against the mendacity of white politicians. His speech erupted like the pent-up fires of a volcano: "Ink for blood! We must write to incite our readers to action. It is the only way the government's indifference and apathy can be dealt with." Ivoe recognized the man at once, for his paper was the only one she knew to include a large photograph of the editor on the front page. She had been reading the *Boston Guardian* since she removed a copy from the wastebasket in Lois Humphrey's office. The editor's gaze fell over everyone in the room. "After all, the thrust of the preamble is action . . . 'We the people' includes us." Without identifying anyone by name, the *Guardian* lambasted editors for not rattling more cages. "For those of you writing for the timid, I can assure you, you do them no favor. America will not give equality just because we behave and wait for it patiently."

"— After all, the words 'liberty and justice for all' have no meaning for us." Sometimes thoughts escape without aid of intention to speak. Ivoe cut the *Guardian* off. "We pledge allegiance to a nation that does not return the favor. The root of this problem is the ballot-less Negro's level of citizenship renders him ineligible for democracy. The government bills our nation as democratic but that is a claim we must refute. Far beyond rule by the people through election, a democratic government promised equal treatment for all. Where is the equality in underpaid labor, poor education and housing, substandard health facilities, lynching, police harassment and murder, wrongful convictions, and disproportionate incarceration? For the average Negro, how is living in American democracy much different from peasantry under monarch rule?" And she was not yet speaking on the prison system.

What she'd witnessed at the Missouri State Penitentiary was far worse than any feudal system's penal colony. "La belle France has shown us to what extent we do not live in a democracy and we must remind politicians of this lie at every turn. There will be no freedom, no justice unless every journalist is willing to press America to the mark of a true democracy, where even the Negro holds equal rights."

Charllota Spears, editor of the *California Eagle,* wanted to know what she and Ona did to mobilize black Kansas City women so that they might keep in step with their white sisters, able voters for the last six years. The door was opened by the *Indianapolis Recorder* to speak positively about *Jam.* Did Spears realize that blacks in the Vine district felt a greater sense of freedom and justice because of her paper?

Neither the women's rights movement, nor freedom or justice — interpreting law and punishing criminals — occupied her littlest mind, as Momma would say. Her thoughts circled prey she had eyed for attack since Austin's 1906 boycott, the lie all black people in America were expected to live under, the end result of America's war for independence against her mother country: democracy. Several years ago, answers to her deepest questions about society and citizenship awaited her discovery in the meager holdings of the colored library branch. Between dipping bonbons and writing the church newsletter she found Rousseau's ideas on reforming eighteenth-century France applicable to America's struggle for democracy. Nearly every hand scribbled down her reading recommendation, Rousseau's novel *Émile,* which she described as "a lyrical indoctrination on education of the whole person for citizenship."

His notions of egalitarianism, balanced with Tocqueville's *Democracy in America,* had eradicated such thoughts that dress code, proper speech, manners, would ever bring black people closer to their democratic fate.

"How, then, do we achieve this democracy?" someone asked her.

"First, we must exhibit an understanding of it in our own papers. Each and every one. Second, we must demand it. Of course, with our demands goes the understanding that the nation must learn how to listen to the portion of its society it has silenced for centuries, and continues to silence — with brute force."

Any foreigner who spent five minutes in a

black community and five among whites would note grave injustice, violations of the basic principles of American democracy. But so what? Claims, despite their truth, would do nothing to lessen the burden of injustice. It was like Ona told her twenty years ago in the printing shed, the newspaper was the voice of the people. "It is up to every journalist here and everywhere to spell out equal rights — to trumpet political and economic autonomy. It may take years before we are heard. No matter. The question remains: How high can you raise the voice of *your* paper?"

A clatter rang from the front of the room. In his haste to rise, a journalist from the *Philadelphia Tribune* had knocked over a glass of water. He took the *Boston Guardian* to task for impugning the constructive approaches of editors who addressed the ills of black communities before taking on the other race. As the meeting progressed two sides emerged, one accommodationist — those papers whose most critical eye was on blacks themselves — and the other militant — editorial slants that indicted white institutions, especially the government.

In the jumble of streets south of boulevard du Montparnasse, they stumbled across rue du Cherche-Midi and fell into a small café.

Ona had given a cheerful but tired "no thank you" when the Ardlan sisters, who published Martinique's *La Dépêche Africaine,* invited her to lunch, stating her wish to answer the call of that small bed in Montmartre with her name on it. To Ivoe's surprise and discomfort, the editor of the *Washington Afro-American* joined them. He was a crotchety fellow, short and stocky with fine white hair parted and combed to the side and light brown eyes. At the start of the conference he had snarled at her, "Who are you?" Proudly she replied, "Founder and editor of Kansas City's *Jam on the Vine.*" He waved his hand, speaking with an orotund voice. "No, no. When someone asks you who you are they mean to know what kind of journalist you are." For his condescension Ivoe gave an impatient glare, utterly ignored by the man. "Ask yourself this: What is the work of a black journalist? What is at stake for *Jam on the Vine*? Answer this and you will know exactly what kind of journalist you are."

It was the wrong question to Ivoe's mind. Who is the black press as a whole? There would always be disagreements on how to deliver the news, but could they agree on what to prioritize? "The better question is: What are we addressing collectively? What cause can we agree to fight for together?"

She paused. "Mr. James Weldon Johnson was inspired and guided by his enslaved ancestors when he wrote 'Lift Every Voice and Sing.' But what exactly do we have to sing about now when the present includes so much incarceration — slavery by another name. Many editors lack information. How many of our elected officials look into arrest rates? Understand the practice of sentencing black people?" She had visited prisons, observed their conditions. Researched labor exploitation and the health and death of inmates. Policing, sentencing, incarceration — her paper raised hell in Missouri. But *Jam* was only one voice. If every black paper in the nation devoted a column or two to the false criminalization of blacks . . . if every editor wrote with constancy to his congressman, his senator, requesting information, demanding results, they would be exercising the press in the ways in which it was meant to be exercised, as a tool for democracy.

Over a lunch of chicken fricassee, the Ardlan sisters had spoken of how *La Dépêche Africaine* had recently published stories refuting France as a paradise of tolerance. Jim Crow, it turned out, had a passport and a trunk of souvenirs. He had visited Martinique and Paris, where women still fought for the ballot. She was grateful to the Ardlan sisters for shattering the illusion that true justice lived an ocean away. For the visitor, life in France was kinder, but no matter where she was in the world, her race and her gender would work against her.

A clatter rang from the front of the room. In his haste to rise, a journalist from the *Philadelphia Tribune* had knocked over a glass of water. He took the *Boston Guardian* to task for impugning the constructive approaches of editors who addressed the ills of black communities before taking on the other race. As the meeting progressed two sides emerged, one accommodationist — those papers whose most critical eye was on blacks themselves — and the other militant — editorial slants that indicted white institutions, especially the government.

Ivoe massaged her temples to alleviate a throbbing headache. All morning the table had overflowed with the voices of zealous race women and men. Now, a man seated across from her began in a quiet, angry voice. "The time has come to set the record straight . . . to redress prejudiced coverage and to stop soft-pedaling the news to our people. There's blood on the land! Write about that!"

Once again, the *Defender*'s comment hurled them into dissension. The *Washington Afro-American* returned the putdown: "We should not all pander to the lowest form — sensationalistic photographs. The fact is, lynching numbers have declined. There is now a visible middle class among the increasing numbers of educated blacks in worthwhile positions. Some of us have seats in Congress."

"Whose very asses are glued to them! I'd rather be an outspoken foe of lynching than pander to the white race, including the president!"

"Reading your paper is like walking through a chamber of horrors. Mind women's and children's sensibilities. Give the people something they can use," vituperated the *Washington Afro-American*.

Ivoe listened to the debate with mixed emotions. The *Defender*'s point was valid — lynching was still unchecked in every corner of the United States. By now the images were almost commonplace, the public desensitized. Other issues begged for their attention — those country folks migrating to cities as if transition alone might solve the problem of black life. In her editorial, she had in mind the southern relatives of her readers when she encouraged them to fight the good fight where they stood, cultivate a leader from their own ranks. Build infrastructure, rather than fool themselves into believing northern whites were itching to give them a leg up. The Ardlan sisters spoke to each other in French before turning their gaze to her, encouraging her to speak her mind.

Finally, Ivoe stood, adjusting the collar of her dress. Whether in the Starkville Lyceum, a classroom in Austin, or a hotel in France, when she addressed a crowd she was still as nervous as a turkey in November. "They say justice is blind. In my opinion, she is color-struck, since it is a foregone conclusion in America that the Negro by virtue of his ethnicity is guilty. The black press must do everything it can to end judicial tyranny." She drew on her own experiences, starting with Omaha, detailing the events of how coverage of Willie Baker's lynching brought her the attention of city hall, whose letter had accused her of engendering bad feelings and an evil spirit in the hearts and minds of Kansas City's blacks toward their white neighbors. Before embarking for Paris, she had received a second letter immediately following her publication of a list showing the number of people killed by lynch mobs the following year and the reasons for their death.

Her voice rose as she spoke with the courage of conviction and urgency. "The press must nudge black congressmen to take greater interest in their state's incarceration rates. Do they even know how many inmates are black? What are they doing about policing in their state? Unheard, unseen, the fight for justice is simply struggle. At the very least we can elevate the struggle . . . print the story . . . a step toward democracy. France has shown me that our government has a long row to hoe on its promise of a democratic republic. Consider the judicial system, the trouble with racist juries, and our prison system, the unjust manner in which African American men are jailed without due process. As some of you may know, over the last several years I have dedicated *Jam on the Vine* to highlighting this travesty of democracy. While my methods are different, I agree with the *Boston Guardian* and the *Chicago Defender:* we mustn't back down."

"Be careful. They got their eyes on you now. They'll keep watching until they have enough to haul you to court under the Espionage Act," the *Philadelphia Inquirer* warned.

"Happened in Alabama," North Carolina's *Star of Zion* said. "Confiscated their mail before they revoked postal privileges. Tried the paper for sedition. Charged the editor with treason."

The *Arizona Black Bugle* made an impassioned speech on expanding the editorial gaze to include other groups of color. His state treated the Mexican and Negro "about equal — to that of a fly on a white man's swatter."

During lunch four delegates discussed the formation of a professional group. In closing remarks, they galvanized the room with speeches about further commitment to social justice, encouraging every newspaper to raise its ambition; complacency, after all, was some holdover from slavery.

"What gift was abolition if living is not safe," Ivoe said. "I have run from the South, from dogs, from a white boy barely old enough to chew tobacco. Are we to be the race that runs from the country, from the city, or will we stand for justice? It seems the greatest crutch will not be our government — not for some time — but the press. As such, there are some things we should agree on."

They convened to ratify the constitution for the Association of Journalists Representing the African Diaspora. The group's mission: to provide professional support, legal services, and emergency funds for all black newspapers, domestic and abroad. A committee was formed and a governing board was elected, including Ivoe Williams in the office of secretary.

Their farewell promenade in the City of Light followed boulevard de Clichy, where spring flowers paid their gratitude for the light rain by perfuming the air. The music of an accordion and one too many aniseed drinks encouraged a weary but happy Ona, who tugged at her skirt as though it fit too tight before breaking into her best Tin Pan Alley voice with a revised lyric — *I'm just wild about Ivoe.* At Cligancourt they ran up the steps. A black man raised his accordion a little then bowed in their direction. He put all he had into the tune, which made it sound churchy, jazzy, Frenchy too. All week Ivoe had seen black men leaning out of apartment windows, whistling at women, careening through crowds, and nobody ever accused them of wrongdoing. Before her now was something more spectacular. She grabbed Ona's arm, pointing to the men just a few paces ahead.

She'd seen black men prance up and

down the Vine and around Little Tunis all her life, but the air in the swing of those gaits was somehow different. It was one thing to jut your chest forward a few proud inches, step with the favored foot in exaggerated measure among your own people. But to walk like this where the whole world could see you? The men were nearly out of sight when she thought of Timbo, the way he pitched forward in his shoes as though he might need to run at a moment's notice. And Papa. She drew in a deep, shuddering breath.

"What's got your face so long?"

"Papa used to walk different from the way he does now."

On the boulevard de Rochechouart, Ivoe raised her shoulders, straightened her back, shook each leg to loosen her knees a little — her childhood routine before imitating Papa's gait. He looked so serious up top but down below, when you looked at his legs, you knew he was a man who could dance.

As though last night's red moon cast a spell on Ona, she had sailed all day without dizziness. Ivoe glanced at her watch — four P.M. French time and nine A.M. on the Vine. "The streets are still quiet," Ona said, inspiring a hook for Ivoe's next editorial. Quietude was the problem. *Jam* and its readers must speak louder and insistently. Call on government officials the nation over to respond to what she saw as a mounting crisis — incarceration — especially in the cities. She would call for black noise against secondhand citizenship; they must turn their backs on polite manners, which had taken precedence over common sense. What other group of people was taxed but sent their children to failing schools, received poor health services, and still couldn't vote in every state? Ivoe took out her notebook and began to draft:

LE PATRIOTISME:
ON THE DAWN OF TRUE DEMOCRACY

PARIS, France — The question "What is Freedom?" has been perched in my mind squawking for answers all of my life. For the past two weeks with the aid of French hospitality — which suggests President Coolidge and his administration study the *Déclaration des droits de l'homme et du citoyen* as a guide for treating people of color well — I have come to understand that Freedom is not just a word; it is a way of life. And the way is democracy.

In eagerness to get out of the storm-so-long and in an effort to make the government include the black American under the umbrella of justice, your editor chastised members of her own race. In ignorance I joined the ranks of many who would deny us the endeared name "American," a distinction more our own than five-sixths of this nation. For in culture, in blood, in nativity, we are decidedly more exclusively "American" than our white brethren who would rob us of our nationality and reproach us as exotics.

In the early years of this publication, I was under the impression that the black American needed conservation of his moral life; that self-elevation and social responsibility were the panaceas for the advancement of our resilient community. I am now convinced that neither self-help nor upright behavior alone can advance the race without federal or even state legislation.

The reason our nation snapped asunder in 1861 was because it lacked the cohesion of justice. Men poured out their blood like water, scattered their wealth like chaff, summoned to the field the largest armies the nation had ever seen; yet they did not get their final victories that closed the rebellion till they clasped hands with the Negro and marched with him abreast to freedom and to victory. The strongest nation on earth cannot afford to deal unjustly toward its weakest members and victims. A man might just as well attempt to play with the thunderbolts of heaven and expect to escape unscathed, as for a nation to trample on justice and evade divine penalty.

Ardent lovers of the American soil, it is my duty and yours to prod America to live up to her ideals and to not lose hope that someday she will. We must hold fast to America's founding principles and institutions. As your editor, I claim for the black American protection in every right with which the government has invested him. The rule of justice must be held high. If it is dropped it will be the duty of *Jam on the Vine* to pick it up and hold it higher.

Ona closed her book and rose to watch the breaking waves roll and recede past the ship's hull. The handwriting was on the sea: Bunchee's cable wire, received that morning, reported yesterday's headline of the *Kansas City Star Ledger:* "Federal Agents in Kansas City Target *Jam* as Source of Racial Enmity." According to the article, Ivoe was a persistent source of radical opposition to the government's established rule of law, wielding her newspaper as the most destructive weapon in Kansas City's political life. That *Jam* was the most constructive tool in black Kansas City was cause for further celebration. They were sailing home with invitations for Ivoe to lecture in Atlanta, Dallas, New York City, Washington, D.C., and London. They would arrive in New York Harbor without incident, spend the day and a half on the train devising how to expand the paper through staff-purchased stocks that would finance a twelve-page spread. At Union Station, she expected the KCPD, maybe even the mayor himself. Now with the newly formed AJRAD and black newspapers across the country committed to publicizing the legal embroilments of fellow editors, white authority posed a mere inconvenience.

"I've caught a chill, you coming?" Ona said.

Silence came down between them like a curtain on a stage. Ivoe's mind raced. She'd retire Woman About Town. On Democracy — a more apt title — lent focus to her weekly column, anchored the paper in its true purpose. She closed her notebook to think some more. The first order of business when they arrived home was to compile a list. *Jam*'s assailment of the mayor and his police commissioner would draw a federal investigation. She needed all the support she could get — names and addresses for every black politician in the country, from alderman to senator, on a clipboard within reach. They were up against a mighty bear, but each cell door flung open in the name of justice was an arrow in his tough skin.

"Oh, I'm just getting started good — be down shortly."

"Well then, carry on. Carry on."

AUTHOR'S NOTES

- Unusual for Texas, the extraordinary cold of the winter of 1898 refers to the Great Texas Blizzard of 1899.
- From March to June 1906, black Austinites launched a boycott to protest segregated public streetcars.
- Ivoe's *Willetson Herald* article "Walk a Little Longer" appeared as a newspaper article under the same title in the *Nashville Clarion,* September 23, 1905.
- Born and raised in Oak Park, Illinois, Ernest Hemingway wrote for the Oak Park and River Forest High School newspaper, the *Trapeze*. After graduating, he was a journalist for the *Kansas City Star* for six months in 1918, after which he joined the Red Cross as an ambulance driver. (I could not resist his path crossing Ivoe's, so moved his tenure at the *Star* up by one year.)
- Ivoe's *Jam on the Vine* article "The Col-

ored Soldier's Problem" appeared as a newspaper column under the same title in the October 6, 1917, issue of the *Kansas City Sun.*

- I moved the release of Sophie Tucker's "Mammy's Chocolate Soldier" (1918) and Oscar Micheaux's *The Homesteader* (1919) up one year. The fictional lynching of Willie Baker is based on the factual public lynching of Will Brown, which occurred September 28, 1919, on the south side of the Douglas County Courthouse in Omaha, Nebraska. (Actor Henry Fonda witnessed the lynching from the window of his father's printing shop across the street.)

- In 1919 more than thirty race riots broke out in U.S. cities. This nadir in our nation's history was dubbed Red Summer by writer-scholar James Weldon Johnson.

- The poem "Peaceful Village" was printed in the convict newspaper *Weekly Clarion,* published by the Missouri State Penitentiary in 1922.

- Ivoe's article "Black Prisoner Shot to Death — Penitentiary Is Scene of Confusion" was taken from "Felon Is Slain, Eight Wounded in Prison Break," which appeared in the *Modesto Bee and News-Herald* on December 29, 1931.

- W. E. B. DuBois spearheaded four Pan-African Congresses in Paris (1919); London, Paris, and Brussels (1921); London and Lisbon (1923); and New York City (1927). Although there was no Pan-African Congress in Paris during 1925, the International Exposition of Modern Industrial and Decorative Arts, which spawned the term *art deco,* was the World's Fair Ivoe and Ona thrilled to.
- Portions of Ivoe's editorial "*Le Tumulte Noir,* My Trip Abroad" were taken from "Ten Weeks in Europe" by Willis N. Huggins, which appeared in the *Chicago Defender* on January 17, 1925.
- Four sentences in Ivoe's "*Le Patriotisme: On the Dawn of True Democracy*" are excerpted verbatim from Frances Ellen Watkins Harper's "Duty to Dependent Races," in Rachel Foster Avery, ed., *Transactions of the National Council of Women of the United States* (Philadelphia: J. B. Lippincott, 1891), pp. 86–91. Another passage follows nearly verbatim the quote excerpted below, taken from Samuel Cornish's *Colored American* (March 1837): "Many would gladly rob us of the endeared name 'Americans,' a distinction more emphatically belonging to us than five-sixths of this nation and one that we

will never yield. In complexion, in blood and in nativity, we are decidedly more exclusively 'American' than our White brethren . . . who would rob us of our nationality and reproach us as exotics."

ACKNOWLEDGMENTS

Now then . . .

Art, for some, is much more than an object of comsumption, the latest fad, or a once-in-a-blue-moon experience; it is mother, father, sibling, best friend. I owe considerable debt to African American art, my greatest source of inspiration. From the unsigned spiritual and Joplin's rags to Mingus's bass, Battle's coloratura, and that honey-voiced one who sings of pipers, broken drums, and red guitars; from Dunbar's *Lyrics of Lowly Life* and Fauset's *Plum Bun* to Baldwin's *If Beale Street Could Talk* and Morrison's *Jazz;* from the cakewalk to the moonwalk, the Nicholas Brothers' tap routines and hip-hop's break-dancing crews; from the paintings of Lawrence and Motley to the sculpture of Lewis and Catlett to Saar's dioramas and Walker's silhouettes; from the comedy of Mabley, Pryor, Chappelle, and Epps to all that drama for the stage and screen: Hansberry, Kennedy, Burnett, and Lee; it is black art that demonstrates with heart, verve, and no shortage of courage exactly what it means to jam!

Firsthand research is always a worthy endeavor. This story benefited immensely from black newspaper archives at the Library of Congress and the Chicago Public Library. The following works were inspiring and useful: *Ida: A Sword among Lions* and *To Keep the Waters Troubled,* biographies of Ida B. Wells-Barnett by Paula Giddings and Linda McMurry Edwards, respectively; William G. Jordan's *Black Newspapers and America's War for Democracy, 1914–1920;* Charles A. Simmons's *The African American Press: A History of News Coverage during National Crises, with Special Reference to Four Black Newspapers, 1827–1965;* Stephanie J. Shaw's *What a Woman Ought to Be and to Do: Black Professional Women Workers during the Jim Crow Era;* Farah Jasmine Griffin's *Beloved Sisters and Loving Friends: Letters from Rebecca Primus of Royal Oak, Maryland and Addie Brown of Hartford, Connecticut, 1854–1868;* William A. Shack's *Harlem in Montmartre: A Paris Jazz Story between the Great Wars;* Charles E. Coulter's *Take Up the Black Man's Burden: Kansas*

548

*City's African American Communities, 1865–
1939;* and "The Boycott Movement against
Jim Crow Street Cars in the South, 1900–
1906" by August Meier and Elliot Rudwick
(*Journal of American History* 55, no. 4
[March 1969]).

Ida B. Wells-Barnett said, "The people
must know before they can act, and there is
no educator to compare with the press." To
the spirit and legacy of Ida; Charlotta Bass,
the first African American woman to found
and operate a newspaper (the *California
Eagle*); the *Kansas City Call* (going strong
since 1919); and the black press then and
now: thank you.

Leery of institutional praise (for some it
can send the wrong message — *this is the
way to go* — when the path must be organic
and individual, if the work is to be), I must
express great gratitude for Sarah Lawrence
College's graduate program in women's history, where many moons ago I learned the
benefit of marriage between historical
inquiry and imagination and how to use the
historian's tools, and the Sewanee Writers'
Conference, where I met Gail Hochman,
who like any stellar agent taught me about
the publishing world with patience, wisdom,
and generosity of time. Extraordinarily, Gail
adds to this mix boundless energy and

insight born of head and heart. Few others have so quickly won my respect and complete admiration like her.

Director Justin Ahern and the Noepe Center for Literary Arts provided ideal surroundings for the completion of this book (and a future book). Thank you so much, Justin, for your vision and commitment to artists, regardless of accolades.

Morgan Entrekin and Grove Atlantic don't merely publish books; they welcome writers and their manuscripts home. I count it among my life's big blessings that this story landed where passion for literature and true care for writers lives. Executive editor Elisabeth Schmitz believed in this story and so has my eternal gratitude. Assistant editor Katie Raissian showered the Williamses with deep thought and care, posed the smartest questions, cheered Ivoe and me along nonstop. She also guided me with stealth and grace through eleventh-hour revisions. Charles Rue Woods, a brilliant designer of books, graciously allowed my input and encouraged me with southern charm.

Here, finally, is the space to express long-held gratitude. I am especially blessed to have known and loved Abbey Lincoln — friend, sage, artist extraordinaire, who taught me how to live as an artist — *figure out what is worth saying, then put your shoulder to the wheel and say it.*

In her weeklong advanced fiction course in Provincetown (summer 2008), Amy Bloom provided critical, invaluable observation that pushed me beyond my perceived limitations and helped to change the course of my writing at a crucial moment. Thank you, Amy Beth.

I am most grateful for my unusual family — a lifetime in the making — including former elementary school teachers Blanche White and Victoria Zeritis. It was Blanche who first told me I could write a good story — in her third-grade classroom at Beacon Hill (District 163, Chicago Heights). For thirty years, she has persisted with the sometimes painful, always precious question: "Are you writing?" Beyond fourth and fifth grades at Algonquin Middle School (District 163, Park Forest), Vicki lent a hand in raising me, instilling a fierce independence and strong sense of self and indulging me with music, theater, and art. Blanche and Vicki, for propping me up all these years with expectation, faith, and the only thing better than love — devotion — you have my loving gratitude.

To my mother and sister, Brenda Jean

Long and Lisa Wilette Perry — my "first and forever" readers — the Williams clan and all the family: thank you for unconditional acceptance, support, and encouragment through the years.

Friends who brightened this journey, offered more gifts in the ways of friendship than I could ever put into words, and sustained me more than they know are owed much more than this roll call acknowledgment, and have my dearest appreciation: Malinda Walford, Rachelle Sussman-Rumph, April Mosolino, Cassandra Wilson, Suzanne Gardinier, Darrell Ann McCalla, Kamilah Moon, Rachel Eliza Griffiths, Nyala Wright, Isobel Floyd, Tiphanie Yanique, Karma Johnson, Hermine Pinson, Ellen Eisenman, Jacklyn Bookshester, Johari Shuck, Felicia Gray, Dana Boswell Williams, Jennifer Williams, Lisa C. Moore, Jason Perry, Lonnie Plaxico, Charlie Lott, Claire Andrade, Joe and Sheila Heit and the Heit family, and my sorors of Alpha Kappa Alpha. Tonya Engel possesses a mighty fine paintbrush, a palette of spirit and extraordinary color, and she is also my dear friend. The inspired cover art is hers and it makes my heart sing. A special thank you to John Richard Davis, who models with joy, discipline, and grace what an artist can be; and he also provides encouragement and a port in a storm. There are many others who aren't mentioned here by name, for I have always been blessed with an embarrassing number of the right friends and opportunities; I hope you know how much your support means to me.

In giving thanks, we reserve the best for last as some measure of the great extent to which the recipient has influenced our life. Ruth Goldie Heit, great giver of laughter, adventure, encouragement, and love, believed in this story from word one and blesses my life with unstinting support. She was the unequivocal champion of this book and remains the greatest friend I have ever known. Golden one, *you* are my profound gift. Ivoe and Ona thank you; their love will live forever, as will mine for you.

I am told my grandmother Helen Jean Williams "hoped on" me fervently when I was in my mother's womb. When I arrived, she instilled in me — in the *most special* ways — a work ethic, determination, pride. Big Mama's unconditional love sprang effortlessly but it is the gift of her unending inspiration that makes me marvel still. It has taken more than years, tears, music, art, and romance to heal all that broke after her passing. The truth is, the cost of great grief

is paid by fragments of the soul, yet in writing this novel I have learned what worthwhile things can be made of fragments.
— LaShonda Katrice Barnett,
Martha's Vineyard

Ki Olodumare gba a o.
Olodumare a ran rere si o.

ABOUT THE AUTHOR

Kansas City native **LaShonda Katrice Barnett** grew up in Park Forest, Illinois. Editor of *I Got Thunder: Black Women Songwriters on Their Craft* and *Off the Record: Conversations with African American and Brazilian Women Musicians* and a story collection, she has received a NEH grant and awards for short fiction, including the College Language Association Award and the Barbara Deming Memorial Grant. She has taught history and literature at Sarah Lawrence College, Hunter College, and Brown University, and holds a PhD in American Studies from the College of William and Mary. She lives in Manhattan. *Jam on the Vine* is her first novel.

The employees of Thorndike Press hope you have enjoyed this Large Print book. All our Thorndike, Wheeler, and Kennebec Large Print titles are designed for easy reading, and all our books are made to last. Other Thorndike Press Large Print books are available at your library, through selected bookstores, or directly from us.

For information about titles, please call:
(800) 223-1244

or visit our Web site at:
http://gale.cengage.com/thorndike

To share your comments, please write:
Publisher
Thorndike Press
10 Water St., Suite 310
Waterville, ME 04901